The Eden Prophecy

by Gerald Mills

Twilight Times Books
Kingsport Tennessee

The Eden Prophecy

Paladin Timeless Books, an imprint of
Twilight Times Books
POB 3340
Kingsport TN 37664
http://twilighttimesbooks.com/

First Edition: November 2009

Library of Congress Cataloging-in-Publication Data

Mills, Gerald W., 1935-
  The Eden prophecy / by Gerald Mills. -- 1st ed.
      p. cm.
  ISBN-13: 978-1-60619-187-3 (trade pbk. : alk. paper)
  ISBN-10: 1-60619-187-X (trade pbk. : alk. paper)
  1. Climatic changes--Fiction. I. Title.
PS3613.I5684E34 2009
813'.6--dc22
                                                    2009046069

Cover artwork ~ Kurt Ozinga

Printed in the United States of America.

Chapter 1

Spaceship Grellen-6. | Earth date February 26.

The decision was Char-el's to make. His sudden transition to audible speech signaled the end of mental discussion among the remaining five who made up his staff. They closed their mental channels and waited, each wishing there were some other solution, yet sharing their mission commander's mood of urgency. Previous leaders had faced difficult choices for Earth, but none so heartbreaking or inescapable.

He met each expectant gaze, then drew a long breath. "There is no reason to further delay our warning. I'll return to Earth tonight and set things in motion."

Second in command Taryn shook her head sadly. "So much death, Char-el...."

"But unavoidable. We dare not accelerate our long-term solution... not yet. In the short term we are counting on unpredictable factors and may already be too late. This is the humane way."

"You will use James Foster for the warning?" she asked.

"*If* there is time and if he manages to stay alive. The United Nations action we've all monitored prior to this meeting has unfortunately put him in the gravest of danger, yet he is still the best of all our choices at this moment."

Five heads nodded.

"Our alternative," Char-el continued, "is to move this ship into their skies and hope that our predictions of human mass psychological responses are wrong. We have, of course, seen exactly the opposite during the Venus crisis, and mankind has not changed that much in the three millennia I've been in command. Merely showing our ship could result in several hundred million panic deaths and trigger global conflicts that will certainly include atomic and biological retaliations everywhere. That part is most predictable. Of what consequence would our warning be then? I will make myself and our mission known to Foster as quickly as practical. He has the required character traits many times over, and of course he is known to billions by his pseudonym, Mudslinger. Notoriety is essential in this case."

"Where will you meet?"

"He will develop a sudden urge to visit Finland with wife Tricia. I will make first contact there. My goal will be to move him to one of our sites where my message will impress him the most."

"Giza?"

"No, not Giza. Manus. Its secrets will appeal to his engineering mind."

"What if he is wrong for the purpose, Char-el?" The question came from another of the five. "What if he balks for any number of reasons?"

"Then we know what we must do, regardless of the risk for humanity."

Quaker Hill, New York. | February 26.

NPA Special Projects director Howard Greenward was alone in his library when the story broke on the nightly news, something about the U.N. and a pair of "shocking new resolutions" passed that very afternoon. Half listening, he twisted his mouth with the adjective. Shocking? Was that what the man said? When had the U.N. General Assembly ever passed anything shocking? Yet CNN had assembled a panel of experts, led by Dr. Shelby Warren, to discuss the development.

CNN's Alex Travis had just asked Warren to explain whatever it was that was so shocking, and Warren seemed delighted with the question.

"The first resolution is more of a declaration than any call to action, Alex," he explained, chopping the air with both hands as if to emphasize every word he said. "It declares all terrorists and their supporters to be predators on the Society of Man, threats to the peace that are to be removed by any means possible. What it does is take away everything criminals have enjoyed up to now in the way of rights, things like lawyers, doctors, clerics, comfortable jails, decent food, visitors, fair trials, public advocacy... that type of thing. People who support terrorists in any way can lose their rights as well."

"Can you give us a few examples of support, Dr. Warren?"

"Sure. Comfort or concealment, food, shelter... withholding of information, just about anything that could help the terrorist. This can be taken to extremes, but whether it will remains to be seen. Now the phrase *'removal of threats to the peace'* appears in the opening paragraph of the original U.N. Charter, so that part isn't new. The difference, Alex, is that any member country can now remove *individual* threats to the peace without regard to due process, existing laws or the nationality of predators. No statutes of any kind, in any member country, can be used to provide haven or help the captive. Death or life in prison are the only two possibilities. Again, this redefines terrorists in new terms. It really doesn't change anything until they're caught, but then it removes all civility toward them."

"And the second resolution?"

"Ah, that's the real shocker. Returning to the original charter's opening paragraph, we run into the words *'suppression of acts of aggression or other breaches of the peace.'* Fancy language, but no teeth. The words apply to nations, not individuals or political movements, and we all know that terrorism has become a decentralized thing. Very hard to identify individual acts as being state sponsored. It would appear U.N. members were out for blood this afternoon, and the British came through with a proposal that would turn the original dishwater into acid. The idea is to name the terrorists, confirm their acts of aggression, put a bounty on their heads and pay off the executioners when bodies are produced."

"Murder them?"

"That is correct."

"The U. N. is sanctioning murder?"

"Right. The British used our American frontier days as the model. Gunslingers were our home-grown terrorists in those times. They murdered and robbed while helpless citizens wrung their hands and prayed. Decent men did their best to bring outlaws to justice back then, but were mostly losers until decency was put aside. Once the words DEAD OR ALIVE appeared on posters, our gunslinger era was soon over."

"Bounty hunters finished them?"

"Correct again. Bandits were tracked down, finished off and the reward claimed. End of story. The single bounty hunter was usually more effective than any posse. Now compare that to what is happening today, with political correctness and this pervasive concern about offending one person while trying to save thousands or even millions. The bounty solution will work, in my opinion. The list of terrorists grows longer each day despite ever-increasing rewards for information leading to capture, so the reward thing hasn't worked at all. Part of the problem is the reward itself. How big is ten million of anything to some tribesman, for example? Where can it be hidden? How long can the informer expect to remain alive? Thousands have already lost their lives, their families and friends killed, towns and all those in them destroyed in reprisals. As long as decent people persist in behaving decently, terrorism thrives, you see. So, yes, the bounty approach will indeed be sanctioning murder, but I think it will work."

Another of the panelists, Sidney Colson, raised a hand. "Dr. Warren, how will all the religions react to this?"

"There will a tremendous backlash from that quarter, possibly violent backlash. And there are the activists, and of *course* there can be errors—the occasional wrong person may be blown away and the bounty hunter made to suffer for his mistake—but infinitely more probable are mass deaths from one suicide bomber blowing himself up on a crowded train, or from bio-weapons or even the nuclear horror. The proposed solution may even spawn a new breed of suicide terrorists, working to earn recognition so the bounty applies to them, then offering themselves up for slaughter by their *own* people. The U. N. might actually end up funding terrorist causes, but remember that this is an assembly of nations, and *they* passed this resolution. It has teeth."

He paused only long enough to draw a fresh breath and reseat his glasses.

"On the flip side, since the time of huge rewards being offered for the capture of international criminals, nearly a thousand informants are known to have lost their lives through reprisals. An estimated ten times that number might be closer to the real thing." He glanced up as if looking at a teleprompter. "Ah... twenty-six were killed while under government-witness protection, and in one absurd case the informer and his family were all murdered while guards watched television across the hall. So that part is not working at all."

"But," Colson interrupted, "surely there have been beneficial results. You're only telling us about the negatives."

"Frankly, I wish there *had* been positives, and everyone seems to think there have been, but in truth there have been none worth mentioning. Not one single terrorist has been captured or killed as a direct result of information garnered this way. We've gotten a few bad guys using other methods over the years, yes, but not this way. In the same time span, terrorism has cost the free world nearly half a million lives and several trillion dollars."

Greenward poured himself three fingers of scotch and sat down to listen in earnest. The Brits were already calling it the Tombstone Resolution, named for the Arizona town. It stipulated a standard bounty for *dead* terrorists only, one million pounds Sterling in whatever currency the bounty hunter wished. It could be paid off in reindeer, if a Lapp turned in the body. Proof of the kill was still a challenge for the hunter, as a corpse had to be produced one way or another, and he was responsible for killing the wrong person. Yet the bounty was large enough to be shared, small enough to be real, and reprisals would be greatly lessened if the terrorist were dead instead of simply hiding.

Live terrorists were of no value whatsoever. If individual member countries wanted to continue their rewards for information, let them. They could jail or free their quarry as they saw fit, but if a bounty hunter got to the predator first, so be it. Further, sanctioned murder was not all that strange a concept, Warren explained. Advertisement of the fact was the only thing new. The scheme could fare no worse than previous methods, but here again, Warren stressed his opinion that it would work better.

"We have to ask ourselves what we want most. Terrorism is a disease like cancer that will kill us in the end if we don't cure it. We've always had the means to effect a cure, but not the will. This action by the U.N. corrects that."

Colson again. "By putting willful acts into the hands of individual… ah… murderers?"

"Exactly. Buy a gun, find someone on this new list of names, shoot him in the back or head and become an overnight millionaire as well as a hero. That's it in the most brutal terms. So, we end up as bad as the bad guys while we try to rid ourselves of them."

The Tombstone List of international terrorists would be updated weekly, published by the media in every member country, broadcast on the Internet in various ways and displayed in all police stations, post offices, libraries and other public buildings as chosen by each member country. Photos were encouraged.

Atrocities committed against *any three* sovereign countries, whether U.N. member nations or not, gained the perpetrators an automatic listing—their death sentence—if nominated. Once a name was on the list, any two countries could maintain the status. The nature of atrocities was of little significance, nor did the affected country or countries have an exclusive voice in listing a name. *Any* member nation or group of members could request a name be added to the list, once the atrocities and their perpetrators were identified, studied and detailed *beyond all question*, as long as the three-country rule was met. The nominating country had the right to remain anonymous. This aspect of the resolution assured that no single nation could be threatened with reprisals. "Beyond all question" was a burden to be satisfied by the nominating country.

The rest of CNN's panel got into it, with Travis playing moderator.

Atrocity was further defined as a "deliberate, destructive, wicked, cruel or brutal act resulting in loss of *any* kind, endangerment, disruption, injury, ruin, illness or death." The country so affected could be an incidental victim to an atrocity against some other country. A radioactive bomb or a bio-weapon, for example, might contaminate great areas. In such a case, all countries affected would count toward the minimum of three.

Finally, terrorists would be considered equally dangerous to society irrespective of religion, gender, age or mental state. An atrocity was just that. Accomplices? They were eligible for The List if their complicity was voluntary. In that event, they'd earned their death sentences, too.

The resolution had passed with almost the same majority as its predecessor.

Former Marine Lt. Colonel Howard Greenward clicked off the TV, saluted the blank screen and let out a whoop that would have made any Comanche envious. He then stood, executed a smart right-face, selected a metal dart from the half dozen standing in his pencil cup and hurled it at a life-sized photo on the wall. *Thock!* The dart hit James Foster's image smack between the eyes, adding another hole to the hundreds already there. A small piece of the target fluttered to the floor.

"You heard the man, Foster. The new game is called Name That Terrorist. I'm gonna show the world your picture and tell them who the Mudslinger really is." *Thock!* "You think not? You've already attacked two countries, sucker, so one more and you're history. Got a couple photos of you I couldn't use until now. Couldn't advertise your real name, either, but your Top Secret days are over. I'm a National Protection Agency bigshot these days, 'case you haven't been keeping up, and I'm about to make you a walking bull's eye, front and back."

Thock!

Tricia's hole-ridden picture hung a few inches away from Foster's. The third dart added yet another puncture to one of the sapphire-blue eyes. "You, too, slut. I may not have many pics of your lover man, but I have a fistful of yours. You'll be right next to your lover."

Greenward's mouth curled a bit at one corner. Just one more country besides Russia and the U.S. Which one would it be? He picked up a final dart.

Thock!

Lahti, Finland. | February 28, 10:06 P.M.

Landings on Earth were simpler than elementary quantum mechanics—a child could handle them. The only real-time challenge was collision avoidance with Earth aircraft when a landing was to be made close to civilization, as all other aspects of the landers and those aboard were invisible. This would not have been the case had Earth's technology been a whit more advanced, as there was always a detectable magnetic anomaly involved, but that technology was non-existent. As for radar, spotting a lander was like trying to see a needle by looking straight into its point at a distance of one Earth mile. Even then, the needle point would appear only as the tiniest of speckles, a hazy cloud.

The chosen landing spot was a schoolyard. British astronomer and lecturer Roland Storm stepped from the craft, suitably dressed for Finland's winter temperatures. He was quite invisible while in the lander's cloaking field, but once it returned to the mother ship he'd be on his own. That was the easy part, as he'd been Rolly Storm for more than forty Earth years, boasting a degree from Oxford. He picked up his modest suitcase and headed for the hotel hosting the famous Lahti 52-kilometer cross country race, less than a kilometer away. From here on, everything would depend on Foster's acceptance of the truth.

Or not.

March 2.

How many ski outfits might there be, Tricia wondered, before patterns repeated? She'd been watching thousands of skiers from the restaurant's raised deck, all waiting to race the "big one," and thousands more in line to run a shorter course. Spectators crowded rope barricades; kids played behind them. In all, twenty thousand Finns and no two outfits the same. Jim found the question intriguing as well.

They'd arrived from Greece the day before as Emilio and Maria Cruz, using expertly forged documents and posing as Spanish nationals for whom the Finnish language was a real challenge. Emilio laced his Finnish with Spanish inflections and little "mistakes," though in truth he was quite fluent. Languages had always been easy for him—he now claimed nine including his native Quechua—but the Finnish language was giving Maria trouble. Even so, Lahti was a first for her and she wanted to make the most of it. Once they'd seen the racers off, they'd visit the skiing museum where she'd try the ski jump simulator. It involved a large movie screen and a platform where the jumper stood. The trick was to jump off the platform just as if taking off from a real jump, at precisely the right split second. A jump too early or late meant a crash. It sounded like fun.

She felt a nudge at her shoulder. Emilio, eyebrow raised, waggled the thermos of hot port wine. She held out her cup for a refill and had almost turned back to the skiers when a Finn in a red-tasseled cap marched up to their table, presenting an envelope with almost military precision. The man's English and diction were flawless.

"Mr. Foster, this envelope is for you and Tricia." He turned to leave.

Foster? Tricia? No way! They'd never used the name Foster. No one could possibly know him by that name, or hers either. Her heart screeched to a halt as Jim snagged the man's sleeve.

"Kuka sinä olet?" he demanded, his tone commanding enough, but the startled messenger jerked the sleeve away, drooling like someone horribly afflicted. He shuffled quickly away.

"Jim, what on earth?..."

"SHHH! We're being watched. Keep your voice down and act natural. Don't...." His knee pressed against hers. "Do *not* twist around. Look at me. Smile... that's it. Act normal. Look at the skiers. Good. You can talk, but keep looking out there."

"But... how could he speak so perfectly one moment and slush his words the next? He sounded like someone with M.S. He even looked like it, the way he—"

"Good question, but how about the rest of it? You're not smiling... that's better. Look at the skiers. Okay, now did you get any of what he said?"

"He called you Mr. Foster and said the envelope was for you and me. He used our *names.*"

"Interesting you should say that, because there's no individual Quechua word for envelope. It takes a whole phrase to describe one, and you've never heard me use such a phrase, so how did you arrive at that translation? And how does a Finn learn Quechua in the first place, forget the M.S. part?"

"Wait a minute... *Quechua?*" She risked a peek.

"Perfect Quechua, every syllable, and I do mean every one. I couldn't have said it better. He even had the inner mouth sounds perfect."

"Jim, that was *English.* His exact words were. 'Mr. Foster, this envelope is for you and Tricia.' So how could he be?—"

She stopped. Jim's finger had gone to his lips and his head was tilted, eyes half closed. "Something fishy's going on here. You heard it in English, I heard the same thing in Quechua, and something tells me he couldn't speak either one. Maybe he slobbered something in Finnish or maybe he never said a word." He squinted at the envelope.

"What are you saying?"

"That man was a messenger, controlled by someone who may be watching us right now. He didn't actually say what we think we heard." After a hard swallow, he lowered his voice even further. "There is *no* way anyone could know us by our real names, here or anywhere we've been in the past four months, unless he had a talent something like mine. You know it as well as I do."

"But we've been so careful... how can anyone... I mean, here in *Lahti?* He'd have to have known we were coming here, right?"

"Let's say you're right. Then what? What does your logic tell you?"

"It tells me he was... in Greece, watching us. Well, doesn't it?"

"You forgot that the range of mental energy is mental. This person could have been anywhere when he learned where we were heading."

"So how did the envelope get here, fly?"

"Oh, he's here now all right, watching to see if we'll read whatever's inside. He isn't on the U.S. or Russian payroll, or I'd most likely be dead right now. Maybe both of us. Beyond that, he's a total mystery. He's either tracked us here or was here before we arrived."

"How?"

"When did we decide to come here?"

"Just two days ago. We were planning to ski in Italy, and you said... you said—"

"I changed my mind, right? I got this flash... let's go to Lahti. I even remember specifically thinking Lahti, not just Finland. That's when I got on the phone and found they were having the big race today."

"You're saying... but Jim, who can read minds? You said there were only a few in the world who could do it even the slightest bit."

"Nothing like this. Most fake it. I never heard of anyone who could *bend* minds this way, and that's what it is, not just mind reading. You were right about the messenger sounding like someone with a speech difficulty, but his mission was over by then, you see. We heard the way he normally speaks... sounds... I think. When he came up to us, how did he walk? Did you notice?"

"Like a toy soldier."

"Right. And when he ran away, he was more like half of a three-legged sack race. Maybe he did have M.S. *Our* minds were the ones being bent, not his. We were pointed out to him, he was handed the envelope and told to give it to me. Someone knew we were here or coming here, and knew exactly where to find us. We've used every trick I know to keep our identities secret, but it looks like the whole thing has been a huge joke. If he has a gun, we're in his crosshairs right now."

She frowned. "Why would this... person choose someone so afflicted to deliver the envelope?"

"Good question."

"Are you going to read whatever it is? Maybe it will clear up the mystery."

"Don't bet on it, and don't look around. Keep your eye on the skiers." He tore open the envelope, removed a small square of paper and studied it for a moment before showing her. It was one typed line: [-14,41.282, -75, 06.4286]

"Just numbers?"

"And brackets and minus signs. Makes no sense."

"It must mean *something*. If he didn't come here to kill us...."

"Take away Russia and the U.S. and that leaves only... *only*... three or four dozen terrorist factions around the globe who might be interested in my power, but how could any of them know... aw, Trish, the best mind readers known aren't that good. If they guess better than 50-50, they're called fabulous. It's smoke and mirrors. No one can bend minds."

"Just a minute, Mr. Forgetful. You put out all those wildfires with *your* mind and saved all those people in Yellowstone Park and whole lot more there in Ecuador. If it hadn't been for the tornados you created with your mind, America and Russia might have gone to war. You've spent your whole life using your special talent to help people, not to mention thirty million dollars you've already sent to your foster father for his work with street people. Why couldn't someone else have a talent like yours? You've always said you felt you were being controlled by some force on the other side. You hated not knowing why, and yet this envelope thing did happen just now. *Somebody* out there knows how to do it. Maybe the Russians or Americans found someone who—"

"No!"

"No? Why no?"

"This is definitely something else."

"All right, let's say… this *person* is being cagey because you have to believe in him first. If he just appeared, wouldn't you reject whatever he said he was? Until he proved himself?" She risked another peek, remembering to smile.

"You have a point, up to a point, but who knows about me other than the few we both know about, Greenward and his goons being at the top of the list? And if *they* can't find me, I mean us, how can they tell anyone else where we are?"

"So… the message sender maybe wants you to wonder about him, come to some positive conclusion before he takes a chance on a face to face. Maybe he's really someone like you. Maybe someone's controlling him, too."

"Just finding me would have been enough to make me believe, without this Dick Tracy code stuff. I sense something more sinister. Right now I *think* I'm speaking my real thoughts, but are they mine? What you just said makes sense, but were they your words or someone else's? We both just heard the same phrase in two different languages, spoken by someone who probably didn't speak at all. How can we tell our thoughts from someone else's? Or our observations?"

"What could we do even if we could tell?"

"Maybe we should get out of here right now… make a few quick moves. Our intruder may spend his time keeping up with us instead of working his tricks. We'll fly to Copenhagen, grab a car and move on the ground for awhile. If I can get in touch with Gordy Whittier, he might be able to set me up with some sort of mental block."

"Was that your thought or Charlie's?"

"Charlie?"

"We have to call the intruder *something*. Why not Charlie?"

"Did the name just pop into your head, Trish?"

"Yes."

"So was it your thought or his?"

"Mine… well… I don't know."

"See what I mean?"

"Well, then, how about this thought? We came here to go skiing. Unless Charlie has skis, he can't very well deliver any more cryptic notes out there, and you already said he couldn't be here to kill us. Maybe he *expects* us to panic and go running, and when we don't it will mess up his plans. He'll have to make contact again… maybe deliver the next envelope in person. We could make it a test, and besides, I want to ski before we leave. Don't you?"

"Trish, don't you see? He could send anyone he wants out to wherever we go. A kid, for example. Maybe even a dog."

"So we'll watch for kids and dogs."

London. | March 2.

The envelope's address was clipped from various printed pages and pasted down. For that reason it never went to MI6, its destination, but was diverted to New Scotland Yard's anti-terrorism group, where it was x-rayed, sniffed and submitted to chemical analysis. When it was finally opened, police immediately shut down the London tube system from Paddington to Liverpool Street, King's Cross to Waterloo. For the umpteenth time, Londoners were warned to avoid all transit systems, especially the Tube in its entirety, until further notice.

One hundred forty assorted detectives and tube system experts wearing hazmat protective clothing swarmed stations within that area for the next six hours, looking for a black plastic cylinder the size of a flashlight. Pedestrians were moved back from tube station entrances a minimum of thirty meters, and sixty buildings were evacuated. The evening rush stretched to night-long.

The cylinder with its ominous external antenna was discovered at Oxford Circus. It was immediately whisked to the Yard where it was gingerly taken inside a de-fusing chamber and placed over a downdraft exhaust grating that would take any fumes or powders directly to a decontamination room. Hopefully. VX was the greatest fear among those who'd found the cylinder, transported it from the tube station to a waiting van and then into the chamber. The thing was large enough to contain a small explosive charge, strongly suggested by the antenna. If it were to detonate, anything inside would be spread far beyond the few dozen meters of setback for those behind police barricades. Sarin was one thing, VX was ten times deadlier. Instantaneous death followed the slightest contact with the most minute amount of VX liquid, whether by inhalation or contact with the skin or eyes. Even with full protective clothing, including boots and triple-layer gloves, the smallest of explosions could tear away protective gear, exposing the wearer. He'd die in seconds. As an added precaution, all but the unlucky man inside the thick-walled chamber retreated to an outside room, where they watched via closed-circuit TV.

It was all for nothing. The cylinder was filled with ordinary baking soda—and a small, rolled-up note that might have come from any kind of printer.

If this had been VX, the message read, *you'd be counting your dead in the millions. Mudslinger.*

ဆလဗ

The visitor from Athens caught the Eurostar from London to Paris, then a taxi to the airport. The BBC was giving full coverage to the hoax as he boarded his return flight. Media spinmeisters fluffed the story thereafter, trotting out the Mudslinger's past atrocities—scenes from the Las Vegas disaster, burned-out hulks of aircraft and the subsequent trashing of the White House and surroundings, all interspersed with wildfire clips. Expert testimony on VX, Sarin and anthrax used up scads of air time. Although the wording of the note was never disclosed to the public, conjecture made it a detailed warning of future catastrophes.

By the time the Athens traveler de-planed, video screens everywhere were screaming "details" of a major new terrorist plot masterminded by The Mudslinger. The mystery figure had long been a folk hero to those hating Washington and all it stood for, but Europeans were suddenly aware that they could be targets as well, fears made the worse because no one knew what The Mudslinger looked like. London's counterterrorism vigilance ratcheted to the top, even though only three major powers admitted to owning VX. That left Sarin and biochemical agents for experts to worry about. Or tornados, or arson, or even a repeat of Las Vegas. Who was this Mudslinger? If he was real, his name belonged on that new Tombstone List.

One day after returning to Athens, the traveler boarded a jumbo jet to Dulles International. His diplomatic pouch contained notes, name tag and his official copy of the proceedings of a three-day symposium on advances in biochemical countermeasures.

Even though he'd only attended the opening session of the conference, his absence thereafter had likely gone unnoticed. He'd taken a flight from Athens to Orly that first afternoon and, after reaching London many hours later, took the Tube to Oxford Circus. The station was nearly deserted at that late hour.

Later still, he'd posted a letter addressed to MI6.

Chapter 2

Gunnison, Colorado. | March 3.

NPA Marshal Ollie Robinson clicked off the evening news and stared at his blank TV screen. There was more to the London bomb prank than what was being said, not that it wasn't typical of acts already assigned to the folk hero. Someone in London was setting Jim Foster up. It was this new Tombstone thing. Endangerment and disruption were atrocities, according to U.N., and the sharks were having a feeding frenzy over a typed name on a note.

Put Mudslinger on that Tombstone List? Why not the Penguin and Joker for Batman fans? *Someone* was fanning the flames. Someone who knew Mudslinger was a real person was pushing to have his name put on that list, along with any existing photos, but Jim had lived in obscurity until the Russian showdown. Other than the one or two in Washington who'd been involved with….

Greenward!

According to FBI Special Agent Harry Archer, the man's nephew, Howard Greenward was a psycho. "Uncle's hatred is a fixation," Harry warned. "In the few hours I spent with him trying to dope out Howland's owls, all I heard was how Foster was the most dangerous man alive and how important it was to kill him any way possible. I had to force myself to stay focused. Made no difference what I thought, or my position in the FBI, or what anyone else thought for that matter. Ollie, if you ever suspect he's going after Foster again in any official way, call me."

Greenward had clout these days, thanks to the NPA's top man, Clarence Towers, who'd appointed his long-time friend as overseer on all special projects. Unfortunately, those included the Yellowstone indictments, meaning Greenward controlled prosecution of the two men behind bars. He'd immediately made public his personal theories about the Yellowstone crimes, accusing The Mudslinger of being the ultimate arsonist and mass murderer without divulging Jim's name. According to "unnamed sources," Howland and Sleck were no more than unwitting pawns in a gigantic international terrorist plot financed by the comic-book villain himself. The public ate it up.

Time to call Harry, indeed, but not as an NPA employee.

When the resignation letter was on its way, Ollie dialed boss Walter McAllister's private number. "Walter, I just faxed you my resignation. Sorry for the short notice." The phone line dripped with silence. "Walter, are you listenin'? I'm not kiddin'. I'm hangin' them up."

"Why, Ollie?"

"Can't say right now. Maybe someday."

"Let me guess."

"You don't wanna know. Those were my terms when I came aboard, remember?"

"Ollie, you're the best marshal we've got. I can't accept your resignation. Let's talk it over."

"Sorry, can't back down on this one. I made the decision awhile back."

"You always were bullheaded. Can I ask you something, since you've made your mind up? I've been holding back on this one."

"No answer promised, but go ahead."

"Those good friends of yours who bought that plane from what's his name, that Morgan guy in Canada?"

"Tom Morgan, yeah."

"Who'd you say they were again?"

"Chris and Jenny. Christopher Perkins and Jennifer Drake if you mean formal. He's a history teacher, like I was, an adjunct professor these days. Why?"

"You always amaze me with your answers, Ollie. You *knew* who was piloting that plane in Yellowstone, didn't you? Where'd you meet them? Where do they live?"

"Okay, Walter, I smell a rat. What gives?"

"Just that I contacted Morgan not too long back. According to him, you met Perkins for the *first time* on the plane from Mexico only a couple days earlier, and you even played a trick on him... handcuffed him and told him you thought he was the Mudslinger. You didn't know about the girl until way later. *You* thought they might have been hiding from someone. That's what you told Morgan. That doesn't sound like they were your good friends."

"Shoot, Walter, you sure don't know Tommy Morgan. He's as gullible as they come. I go nuts trying to think up new ways to put one over on him, but he bites every time. Call it my hobby. Did you ever meet Morgan in person?"

"No."

"Do it. Feed him a line or two and watch those gears turn in his head. Then you'll appreciate what I'm telling you. I made the story up just to watch his eyes grow. Sorta sounds like I got him good this time. I owe you one for tellin' me."

"That's the best lie I've ever heard. Sure wish I had your knack, my friend, but off the record, I don't believe a word of it. Whatever you're up to, be careful. The weirdos are everywhere, not just over there in London. I'm going to sit on your resignation for a few days. Take some vacation. You've earned it. Couple weeks from now, if you still want to quit, we'll talk again."

That was McAllister to a tee. He'd guessed it had something to do with the London thing, but no sense letting him know he was right.

The second phone call was to an unlisted number in Washington, D.C., known to only a handful of trusted souls. Ollie gazed at his late wife's portrait on the opposite wall.

"This is what you'd tell me to do if you were here, Sandy. I sure hope you'll be proud of me."

Finland. | March 4.

A full day of heavy snow following the race forced Jim's decision—they'd leave on the next available flight for Copenhagen, where he was known as businessman Arthur Adams from London. Adams spoke excellent Danish, tipped well and had married "a real hot woman" in Danish terms, showing her off at favorite restaurants and hotels. Fru Adams had been accepted without question, but after the jarring incident with the note-carrying Finn, extra caution was mandatory. They'd leave Finland the way they came in, as Emilio and Maria Cruz. The decision almost backfired at Helsinki's airport.

As usual, he passed through customs first, one of half a dozen in a queue. When she followed minutes later, there happened to be no one in line. Unfortunately the customs agent, a language student who practiced at every opportunity, addressed Maria Cruz in Spanish. She knew exactly how to act, what to answer and how, but he seemed enchanted by her face, comparing her to someone or other he knew. After explaining that he was studying the language, he beamed a big smile and finally allowed her to pass.

The incident shifted Jim's already tense mood into high gear. What would await them in Copenhagen? Could they even exit the plane without another unpleasant surprise, or worse? Airports were dangerous places, terminal exits the most dangerous of all. Whoever this Charlie was, he'd known they would be in Lahti. What else did he know? Who would he have watching the exits?

Baggage claims were a second dangerous area, but retrieving their heavy luggage could wait. They left the plane separately, each with their carry-on bag. Emilio ducked into a men's room where he shaved his mustache while running the shaver over an already-smooth face. His small, oval glasses morphed into square tortoiseshells with heavy temples. He changed shirts inside a stall, added a tugged-askew knit tie and draped a long lock of hair across his forehead. Argyle socks replaced blacks, and a tweed cap finished the makeover. Arthur Adams left the men's room and browsed magazines in a nearby kiosk. He bought a booklet of Danish crossword puzzles and found a place to sit down.

Elsewhere in the terminal, Maria softened her taut hairstyle, changed black eye contacts to brown and deep red lipstick to soft pink. Her eye shadow disappeared altogether. A baggy sweater took the place of the satin blouse and ankle socks went over her nylons. Her black calf-length skirt, turned inside out, sported rows of daisies on a field of beige. Finally she popped a stick of bubble gum into her mouth, chewing it for several minutes before she left to rejoin husband Arthur. On the way, she popped a few bubbles. Anyone watching for Emilio and Maria Cruz at the airport exits would come up empty handed.

Their luggage problem was solved in the usual way. A skycap was happy to recover the items in the baggage claim area and find lockers for them. Lots of travelers did that, ditched their stuff while they shopped the airport kiosks between flights. Jim pretended to figure the exchange rate wrong and handed the man three times the usual tip when the keys were delivered.

An hour later they were safely away from the airport with just their carry-on bags. They'd return for the larger ones when some time had passed. Still, the Helsinki incident was unnerving enough to make them both jumpy, even though the flight itself was without incident. They'd requested separate seats and no one gave them a second glance. Jim's seatmate for the flight turned out to be a quiet British astronomer named Rolly Storm, who read all the way.

Psychologist Gordon Whittier didn't answer his Switzerland phone number. Jim shrugged it off, but once in the city proper he decided against using familiar settings and picked a much smaller hotel. Their rental car, four years old, came from an agency he'd never used before and instead of a restaurant where they were both known, he drove aimlessly for twenty minutes in less familiar parts of the city. When a car pulled away from the curb on a lonely street, he pulled abruptly into the open spot.

"Let's eat Chinese, babe." He pointed at a small sign half a block away. "I hadn't thought of it until that guy pulled out and left us a space, so if Charlie's been reading our memories of restaurants here, we've got a jump on him."

"We've had the jump on him ever since Lahti, Darling. No one could possibly have kept up with us. I think you've been worrying too much."

"He doesn't have to do it in a physical way. I'm hoping he can't zero in on quick thoughts."

The tiny restaurant had five booths down one wall, one booth unoccupied. A young Chinese girl, all of twelve, handed them menus and left them alone. When she returned, Jim pointed to each item and waited for her to jot down his choices. Then, in Danish, he said he wanted the order "to go."

"Let's eat in our hotel room, babe," he whispered, attempting a smile. "I've got an itch only you know how to scratch."

"Really? Well, I'm for that, stud. I never knew Chinese food did that to you."

"I'm full of secrets."

"I *knew* it. You've been holding out on me."

But his itch had nothing to do with sex. He was trying to outfox Charlie, and a hotel room seemed safer than anyplace public. The game was all about regaining control.

They stopped at a curbside newspaper kiosk for copies of the Copenhagen Post and Berlingske Tidende, already rubber-banded into rolls for handing through car windows. The Berlingske would be her next lesson in Danish once Jim was done with it. The other paper, in English, was mostly for tourists. He always bought it as a prop to bolster his Arthur Adams image, never bothering to read it.

Once back in their room, he picked at his food, then turned on TV, but immediately turned it back off. Unfocused thought—which TV produced—might leave a mind channel open for Charlie. They needed something beyond quick decisions and changes of direction if they were to dodge more mind bending. He tried phoning Whittier again. No dice.

She nosed into the remaining bag. "Would you believe there's another whole container of sesame chicken?"

"Everything was too salty. Bleahh! I need something sweet. Should've ordered some fruit."

"How about a fortune cookie?"

"I was thinking more like... okay, that'll have to do."

"I don't understand how they can put in enough food for six people, and only two cookies. This one's obviously yours. Catch."

"How'd you know this one was obviously mine?"

She displayed a dimple. "It was on top."

But instead of his usual grin, he suddenly paled. "Read your fortune, babe."

"I'm opening it now." She pulled out the paper strip and read it. "It says... oh, no!"

"Let me guess... a minus sign, followed by 75, 06.4286, then a bracket?"

"This is impossible. These were in sealed packages."

They locked eyes for what seemed like minutes, not speaking. Finally he stared again at the small strip of paper, suddenly twisting it this way and that, even looking at it edgewise.

"It's almost like a holograph. If I hold it so I can't really read anything, I can see the printed part change to something longer and lighter. The moment my brain can see any kind of real pattern, it shifts back to larger characters." He turned it over. "Both sides are the same. I'm supposed to see those numbers no matter what side I'm looking at."

"Same for mine."

"Charlie's in our heads again, overwriting what our eyes are reporting."

"We can't believe *anything* we see?"

"Or think. Some of our thoughts may be our own, but we won't know which ones." His shoulders slumped. "I'm whipped, babe."

"He never had to be in Finland, right?"

"Or here. He could be somewhere in outer space for all we know. There is no limit to the range of mental energy. This guy is like God. He's taken over our minds."

"Why is he playing games with me, too?"

"Because you must be included in whatever it's all about… something to do with my power." He paused. "This fortune cookie thing is an exclamation point, it's emphasis. Charlie repeated the same two number sequences even though he knows we didn't figure out what they meant, and this time used a trick we had to recognize as an impossibility. He wants us to know… *really* know… his power. He knows I'm stumped on the numbers. Even so, he repeated them so I'd know they were important. I'm to do something with them and he can easily give me some clue, but he doesn't. Why? Is it some kind of test?"

"You've asked the same question for the past two days."

"You were right about one thing, Trish. It means I'm to respect his abilities. I've got to recognize someone with infinitely more power than mine, even though I can't fathom the things *I've* been able to do all my life. He's as far beyond me as I am beyond a chimp. Now that I know the feeling I feel totally helpless."

"That's how ordinary people must feel about you. You don't even have to be in the same country to do what you do. Anyway, somebody's paying Charlie to do this. It can't be for fun."

"I don't know who or what he is… maybe someone right out of the Twilight Zone… but he's not human. Yes, it's the mental realm, but taking over someone's brain like that Finn, who slobbered so bad no one could—"

"Jim, wait. Was he *really* slobbering, or was that Charlie again? Couldn't he have made us think the man had M.S.?"

"It's…." He sank his face into his hands, talking to the floor. "It's possible. Every decision we've made might be coming from Charlie. How long we've been his puppets is anybody's guess, but right now this is all about these damn numbers. Look, we may be trying too hard. Charlie wants us to… wait a minute… what if they were some sort of coordinates? I never thought of that."

"Because Charlie didn't *want* you to think of it. Up to now you've been fighting him. Once you mentioned that chimp, you accepted his power. Maybe now he's letting you use your real mind."

"Yeah, but what's *wrong* with me, Trish? I should have suspected they were coordinates, even if they didn't look like anything familiar. Let's see… ignoring the brackets, we have two negative numbers except for the commas. The commas have been my problem all along. If they were periods… well, why not?"

A pad lay next to the room phone. He wrote the numbers on the back side of one page. "If the commas become periods, we have 14.41.282 and 75.06.4286, both negative. Fine, except that longitude and latitude always use letters 'N' and 'E' for north latitude and east longitude, so that won't…." He stopped. "Son of a gun."

"What?"

"Well, if north and east are the cardinal designations, the principal ones, they'd both be positive in a purely mathematical expression. That would make south and west negative. Let's say I'm right and see where it takes us, hopefully not some spot in the middle of the ocean. We rewrite the numbers as South 14.41.282, West 75.06.4286. Omigod… *that's* not in the ocean."

"You know where it is?"

"Yep."

Chapter 3

National Protection Agency. Washington, D.C. | March 4.

Kurt Stauf scanned the first four pages before closing the binder's cover in disgust. The Russian seal looked official enough, but the whole thing was a doomsday ultimatum nobody'd ever heard of, pure bullshit. The date put it just prior to President Winfield's nervous breakdown, following the destruction of Las Vegas. Whoever'd cobbled up the thing was missing a few marbles. China, Iran and North Korea were the big worries, yet here were the feckless Russians claiming they'd destroyed Vegas and Nellis Air Force Base with a weapon they'd taken out of mothballs. Had the weapon all the time. Yeah, right. Not only that, it was all woo-woo stuff. Only fools fell for that junk, but then Clarence Towers was no fool and Towers was the NPA's top boss. If *he'd* taken the thing seriously… well, maybe he wanted another opinion?

Towers' Special Pain-in-the-ass Projects Director was staring out the office window, waiting. He hadn't bothered with formalities, just dropped the binder on the desk. "This'll clear up a few things about the Mudslinger," he announced, taking up a parade-rest stance. "I'll wait while you read it."

"Sure, Howard. Come back a week from Thursday."

"Now," Greenward growled, not turning. "Clarence wants you to know what's in there, cover to cover."

"Look, this department has more than two hundred investigations ongoing. I've got serious work—"

"Clarence is in his office. Pick up your phone and tell him."

Stauf stifled words he might regret. Towers probably wanted confirmation it was a hoax, and just thirty-six pages? Ten minutes of scanning would do it. The quickest way would be to assume it was legit, then show why that was wrong.

No sense going back over the part just read. He skipped to page five. Okay, suppose the desperate Russians actually had something back then. They either hadn't pulled it off, or had lost their nerve, or

Winfield had foiled the attempt somehow—except that no president would sit on such an ultimatum without running over to The Hill with it. Winfield was no dummy; he knew how to handle such things. Then again, he made it into the looney bin not long after, and *somebody* had been behind the Las Vegas devastation. Could it have been the Russians? Aw, no use. The thing was riddled with impossibilities, and there was no mention of Greenward's favorite comic-book villain, Mudslinger.

"How long have you been holding this, Howard, why have you been holding it and how did you get it?"

Greenward turned, half smiling. "Did you read the whole thing?"

"My question first."

"Clarence thought Counterterrorism was the department best suited to run with this. By the way, what you just read is above Top Secret, your eyes only."

"*What?* This thing is a fake. What was Clarence smoking?"

"The contents of that folder were known to just four people in this country until now. Five, if you count John Hughes, Winfield's first chief of staff, but Hughes is dead, murdered by the man we're going to discuss. He's killed others."

"Who, this Mudslinger of yours? I've heard all that crap already."

"What you've *heard* was sterilized and planted in the right places. It mushroomed on its own after that. Winfield and Hughes actually met with the guy, hoping he had something our side could use to counter that document on your desk, which happens to be *very* real. Tell me you've heard *that* before. I haven't been at liberty to discuss it with anyone until now. The Russians wiped out Vegas to show us what they had. Mudslinger was *their* man the whole time, but we didn't know it. All we knew was that he had some kind of weird mental powers."

"Sitting presidents don't meet with weird unknowns."

"Winfield did, and there wasn't time to vet the guy. He wasn't in our system or on our radar screen, complete unknown. The main thing is we tried to get him to work with us and we were snookered. *He* was Russia's secret weapon. He did Las Vegas and then, after giving us the finger, he did the mud job on the White House. I was there with the president upstairs in the Yellow Room. We both saw him standing on the South Lawn with a white bicycle while that tornado he made was churning up trees a few dozen feet away. It came real close to him and he never budged. No sane person would have done that unless he was in control. Same with the Russian Chancery up the street. Slipped another twister right down the outside of the building like a sock and barely touched anything around it. A cop up there reported seeing him, same white bicycle. We found it later at the East Gate. Hundreds of people watching from doorways across the street, and not one saw him. Tell me that's not something out of the Twilight Zone."

"You haven't named this weirdo yet. What's the holdout?"

"How's James Foster grab you? It's an alias—his papers were faked by a pro. He was also behind those wildfires in Yellowstone Park and half a dozen others. His plan to bring down the government could have worked. Thousands of wildfires all at the same time? Hell, we couldn't even handle that New Orleans hurricane… and look what he just did in London. Paralyzed the whole city, and that was just him testing the waters. He's free-lancing for some terrorist group in my opinion, just getting warmed up for the big one."

"Give me a break, Howard. London was just some crackpot prank spun into something it wasn't by the media. Why didn't the Russians go through with their scheme if this Foster was everything you claim?"

"Say you're the president, Kurt. Vegas is history, over a thousand dead. Nellis Air Force Base is a few billion bucks' worth of junk. Your best scientists have just ridiculed the possibility of some new kind of energy field and everyone says there's no nation on earth capable of creating same, including us. Then the Russian ambassador slips this folder into your hands, says his people did it and tells you to get your act together for a friendly little takeover. They annex us without firing a shot and solve all their political and economic problems overnight. What grounds do you have to doubt it? If you send it to The Hill, will there be panic? Think before you answer."

"Okay, so it's the kind of thing people panic about, but the Russians have known for decades we'd wipe them off the face of the earth in a real confrontation. We've always been able to—"

"How exactly would we do that? According to that document on your desk, their weapon would disable everything we had, *including* our satellites. We can't fight a major war any longer without satellites.

Nellis was wiped clean, all the underground computers, planes, communications, everything. They couldn't even use bullhorns out there. We'd have lost everything with the push of a button. Forget Cheyenne Mountain, if it came to that." He started pacing. "Our scientists said the Vegas devastation was impossible, right? Scientifically out of the question."

"Why'd you bring this thing to me? What do you want me to do with it?"

"They said it was impossible, right?"

"Okay, so they said that. What do I do with this?"

"The Tombstone thing, Kurt, the *list*. Foster didn't qualify before the London subway bombing. Now he does, along with his slut girl-friend. Your old FBI files are filled with stuff on her—druggies, money laundering, tax evasion, guns, prostitution... it's all in there. Weapons, karate, you name it. She's a sky diver on top of it, and probably a pilot to boot. We know *he* is, since he was flying that plane over Yellowstone. So, put them both on the list. She's every bit as dangerous as he is, maybe even puts him up to things like the London bombing. Look, Foster's atrocities are self-evident. What if you were a Londoner in the subway and knew there was a Sarin gas canister about to go off in your face? Or VX? They thought it might be that, you know. Then *we* come along and identify the Mudslinger by name, along with his accomplice. What are you going to do, Mr. Brit, argue?"

He stopped long enough to pick up the binder.

"Finishing Foster will be a big feather in your cap, Kurt. This was the only way I had of convincing you and Clarence. It goes back into safekeeping and God help us all if it ever comes to the surface. You know, we almost had Foster back in July with those Yellowstone fires."

"Sorry to rain on your parade, but they've already indicted our il-lustrious past Secretary of the Interior Ben Howell for those fires and wholesale murder, along with slimy Marvin Sleck."

"Neither one has been tried yet. It was Foster's operation from the start, including the financing. Foster gave the orders and flew around in that silver plane, planting incendiaries and setting them off later. Howell thought the things were just surveillance devices aimed at improving the country's internal security. He swallowed the whole thing, believing he was doing the country a great service. He had no idea who he was dealing with because they all used code names... Helios for Foster, Icarus for Howell and Sleck was Daedalus. Look, I *proved* Foster was in Yellowstone at the precise time those fires were raging. I traced his plane all the way from Canada on down, first when he went through customs at the border, then over the fire in Montana and over another in Idaho just before Yellowstone. Why else would anyone be flying over the park before dawn on the fourth of July? He has unlimited funds and he's eluded us for two years, so he knows how to stay low. And I'll tell you something else, Kurt. He could blow this country wide open any time he wanted *if* he happened to have a copy of this binder. Just the first few pages would be enough to blackmail us to eternity. Imagine if this thing ended up in the wrong hands, for example, China. Speaking of which, my guess is he's setting up to take his talents over there when he's ready, there or Iran."

"Okay, Howard, you made your point one more time, but why's today different? He's probably smarter."

"These." Greenward shook several photographs from an envelope onto the desk blotter. "Foster and accomplice. She's a drop-dead knockout, as you can see by that bikini she's almost wearing there."

"I see. You're thinking Foster'll break cover if we publish these?"

"Guaranteed. The Tombstone Resolution applies to any terrorist who's attacked three sovereign countries. Add these pics to the names, and the Mudslinger is no longer fictitious."

"Well, I hate to say it, Howard, but you're one country short for your three atrocities. Besides us and Britain, who'd you have in mind?"

"The Russkies. He stiffed them, too. Trashed their chancery, remember? They were clever enough to lodge a formal complaint over it at the time. We use that and the London thing to formally put Foster and girlfriend on the hit list. Who's gonna turn us down?"

"Lousy picture of him. Grainy and overexposed."

"We never got a good one. Security camera took it as he came into the White House that one time, but he was being rushed right past the usual screens at the time, moving fast because Winfield was waiting. It's close enough."

"So... when do I learn *her* name?"

"Tricia O'Dell. Her old man's the publisher of The Beacon. Talk about rotten apples under the tree—"

"Hold on! Mike O'Dell is bad news, Howard, *really* bad news. You've got a highly-decorated war hero there with public support a mile thick. He'll come out with both guns blazing if we as much as whisper her name. When I was with the FBI, we had standing orders *not* to mess with the guy… from our legal department. They lost every time they took him on. We leave the daughter out of this."

"Overruled. Clarence thinks Foster will do something stupid because of her. He's already asked the president for an executive gag order that would make all information on both terrorists off limits to the media and anyone on The Hill. Congress holds back all questions, and the media all froth at the mouth. We present our case to the Tombstone Committee and speak to no one. As for O'Dell's guns blazing, where's the sonofabitch going to get his ammunition? He hasn't a clue to what you read just now, and anything else is all hearsay and baloney. I've dealt with the guy in the past, and he's no big deal. One wrong move, and he's supporting terrorists. Or how about influencing government policy by intimidation, et cetera, et cetera? The Patriot Act will shut him down, along with his newspaper. We could even add him to the goddamn terrorist list if he's not careful."

"I can't believe the boss would dismiss Michael O'Dell that easily."

"Call him. Ask him yourself if you doubt me."

"I'm not… I'm saying it doesn't sound like something Clarence would say. O'Dell has always seemed more of an irritant than anything else. Don't say I didn't warn you. I may just transfer all phone calls to your office. This your only copy of her?"

"We have a bunch, plus her college yearbook for a good face shot. I'll send over a nice, big glossy of that one. Maybe you can find a way to peel off that bikini. Enjoy your private moments with her, Mr. Stauf. Was that a 'yes' I just heard?"

"Where are they now? Do you know?"

"London as of two days ago, wouldn't you say? I'd guess Europe somewhere, but no matter where they go, there'll be someone with a gun."

Chapter 4

Copenhagen. | March 5.

"Cuzco is roughly thirteen degrees south latitude by seventy-two degrees west longitude," Jim explained, "and we're looking for minus fourteen by seventy-five. Every degree on the globe is about seventy miles in that region, so our mystery coordinates are about a hundred miles south and a couple hundred miles west. Give me a good map, and with three decimal places in the seconds' column I can figure it out to the nearest pebble. Except that... " He squinted, thinking. "Except that I already know where that would be."

"How long before you share your secret, Dr. Einstein?"

He added a dot to the sketch. "Nazca."

"Those desert pictures you can only see from the air?"

"That's the place. One's been called an alien landing strip by some. Abstract animals and geometric symbols, plus random, perfectly straight lines that cross over each other in a jumble. It's a mystery nobody's solved, but why would Charlie be pointing us there? It's barren. Nothing but locals and sightseers."

"What about the landing strip part, since you think Charlie's alien?"

"I said only that he wasn't human, and the landing strip theory is a washout anyway. If there were any early astronauts, they'd be so far beyond us... well, forget the alien part."

"No matter what he is, it seems like you're... *we're* connected in some way to that spot. We're supposed to go there?"

"He's... look, babe, we're guessing. I should get my mind off this and then come back to it. Toss me the Berlingske, will you?"

"Escapist!" She flipped him the rolled-up newspaper. "No matter, we're on our way to Peru again, right? That's what all this means?"

"No way. If Charlie wants to talk to me, he can damn well do it right here, and...."

"And what? You stopped. Jim? Hey, what's wrong? You're pale as a ghost."

"Shhh!" He waved her silent with one hand, dropping his voice. "Don't say anything more."

"But…."

He held up his newspaper. "We're both front page news. Trouble with a capital 'T', babe, big… big… really big trouble."

"Oh, Jim, no… NO! We thought they'd never dare. The consequences were too great politically, and Russia would expose the whole thing about Las Vegas, and that might set off a huge—"

"Your father's words, Kitten. I agreed with Mike at the time, but this is two years later with a different man in the White House and new faces in Moscow. Look here… 'Two More International Terrorists Identified.' Congratulations, Trish, you made it into the big leagues. Yummy photo, too. Mine's grainy and blurred. Wonder where they got it. I don't remember them taking pictures when I met with President Winfield."

"Must be from some security camera. You were moving. Mine is from my college yearbook." She ripped the rubber band from her copy of the Copenhagen Post and spread it out next to the Berlingske. "Same shots here. We're probably on TV and the Internet, too. Well, what's new? We've been fugitives seems like forever."

"What's new is this U.N. thing that puts a million-pound bounty on a list of terrorists, paid out only for corpses. We're on the Tombstone List. I'm blamed for Las Vegas and all those deaths, on top of trashing the White House and being the kingpin behind the Yellowstone fires, but here's the clincher… 'Foster tops the American NPA's own list of international terrorists.' So the National Protection Agency is behind this? What happened to our nemesis, Howard Greenward? Whittier diagnosed that creep as a full-blown psychotic. I figured if anyone ever came after us formally, he'd be the one."

"Ollie Robinson was an NPA marshal. Could it be him?"

"No, Ollie's solid as a rock. He thought it was Greenward who sent that warplane to shoot us down over Yellowstone. It happened so fast there wasn't time for anything official, and Greenward was the only one who…oh, oh… here's something else."

She was scanning as fast as he was. "The London Tube Bomber?"

"Three days ago, same day we got Charlie's note. Talk about your trumped-up story, some nut plays an obvious prank, signs it Mudslinger and I'm suddenly a deadly bomber. Look here, they're admitting it was all a hoax in one line, and in the next it was definite proof I'm planning to kill millions of innocent people before I make my demands known. What the hell is going on with this world?"

She lowered her paper. "Here they're saying the handwriting definitely matches that seen on other threats from James Foster, the famed Mudslinger just named to the Tombstone List. They're making it sound like they've been getting threats all this time, and supposedly the London caper did it for both of us. I'm your wicked accomplice, helping you plan and execute your attacks on society. I'm into money launderers and druggies. I'm a crack shot with guns of all types, karate expert, tax evasion... and a prostitute on top of it. They didn't even bother saying 'alleged' anything. It's a wonder they didn't add bank robbery and extortion while they were at it. Well, does it change anything? I mean, they were sending killers after us from the beginning. Van Oot and his team were after us, until he had his change of heart, and the Bolverk gang that almost killed Gordy were butchers paid to kill us. The FBI sent their hit men to El Hierro to wipe us out. We've been targets all along."

"*I've* been the target, Kitten, not you, and not with our pictures pasted all over the world. We've gone anywhere we wanted to in Europe with practically no worry about being recognized, but no longer. This is a vendetta."

"How does Charlie fit into all this?"

"Forget Charlie. Thousands of trigger-happy idiots will be matching these photos with everyone from midget wrestlers to circus clowns. Just listen to this... 'described as possibly European, or maybe from Cuba or South America, or even Russia.' They missed Madagascar and Tasmania. You're Irish, of course. They've got all your stats here... height, weight, eye color. They're either guessing about me or I've let us down somehow. We're going to have to disappear, and fast."

"*Forget* Charlie? A few minutes ago he was tearing up your insides. He's got to be connected to this in some way. Maybe he's the one telling them about us. I don't buy coincidences. Besides, Charlie knew we were here in Europe. How?"

"The London Tube thing. He can read, I'm sure."

"Not! We got the envelope *before* that happened. I'll bet Charlie was there in Lahti even before we arrived."

"One of those coincidences you say you don't buy? They've closed our doors with this U.N. resolution, Trish. We can't trust anyone, even if our name is Adams, because even though I don't look like the typical Peruvian I have this tan that won't rub off. Put us in Australia or South America right now and we'd be safe, but not Europe. We can't pass as Muslims, either, or Greeks, or any of the Mediterranean nationals. These papers were on the streets here before we registered, yet nobody gave me a second glance. Apparently there wasn't time for the story to take hold, but it will. Your picture is sharp, it looks like you and you're already a standout no matter what you wear. Gotta change that. What do we have in your luggage?"

"Just the big glasses. We'll have to buy something. Some flat brown shoes—wide toes, size seven—and black ankle socks and a long dress two sizes too big. I'll need a wide belt, but make sure the colors don't go with the dress."

"What else?"

"Epsom salts."

"*What?*"

"Shhh! It's to harden the water here. Soap suds and hard water, no rinse, and my hair will look like a witch's mop. I make it into a bun, add the rest of what you find, and violà… instant spinster with a touch of hag."

"Okay, but that's as far as we go. Disguises will land us in trouble. You can't be too spinstery or someone out there will wonder about my sanity in hanging out with you. We keep you out of sight as much as possible until we're out of Europe altogether. The question is how to do that? We can't use airports or trains any longer. Driving is just as risky, and the more times we appear in public, the thinner the ice gets. Trust me, we can't stay in *this* city no matter what. It's too international and has a history of terrorist attacks. Half the population here is foreign and the cops all have six pairs of eyes." He pointed to the small strip of paper from the fortune cookie. "And we can't be totally sure about Charlie. He must know exactly where we are."

"You just said there was no connection. Forget Charlie…that's what you said."

"Trish, was it me saying it?"

"Okay, so we sort of forget him, but just how *do* we get out of here? Walk?"

"My guess is they're trying to flush us out, make us do something foolish. That's why they've included you. They expect us to panic, hunker down wherever we are, which could mean they'll check all the hotels first thing. Every European country will be crawling with whatever agents the Americans have over here. They don't have a clue where in Europe we might be… yet. At any rate, we *have* to move. We can't stay in any one place."

"So?"

"There's the way I'd have chosen if I were doing it solo."

"Which is?"

"Open water… the ocean… in a small boat. You can fit twenty thousand small boats into one square mile of ocean. Reduce that to a single boat, and it's practically impossible to spot from the air. Once south of Gibraltar we'll be out of immediate danger, but it'll be roughly a thousand miles of hell getting there, considering it's March. Not to mention the water cops and sharp eyes wherever we duck into a port. They could be looking for us that way, although they'd assume some big power boat or a tramp freighter. On second thought, forget it. Too dangerous."

"More dangerous than sky-diving onto that Ekofisk platform in the North Sea? That was the middle of winter, too, Mr. Foster. Last winter, to be exact."

"Well, not quite *that* bad. Think you can stand a real ocean passage? It'll be no picnic."

"How real is real?"

"Well… Brazil? The Amazon River, to be exact. Once we reach the mouth, Peru is only a hop, skip and jump inland. A little different climate than Lahti, but interesting. Unfortunately, we stored our plane on the western side of the continent."

"Oh, *fabulous!* I've—"

"Shhh!" He gestured toward the ceiling. "From here on we can't ever be sure someone isn't listening through walls. Now what were you saying?"

"Only that I've *always* dreamt of steaming up the Amazon in hundred twenty degree temperatures," she whispered, "admiring those cuddly boa constrictors and crocodiles and cannibals with bones through their noses. And just think, we can be there in a day or two, right?" She made a moue, dropping her voice even further. "Just how far is that hop, skip and jump to Peru?"

"Two thousand miles on the river, give or take. We can treat it like an adventure, rent our own snakes and maybe a monkey or two. The riskiest part is getting out of here, plus being on the wrong side of Denmark. Esbjerg's a big port on the western side, with plenty of marinas and boatyards to cough up something seaworthy. I've been there a few times. How much cash do you have in your money belt?"

"The whole sixty thousand."

"Fifty-five in mine, and another forty in our big valise. Not enough. We'll have to tap the Swiss account when I find something."

"What kind of boat? And what do we do with it when we get to Peru?"

"Catamaran. We'll need at least the equivalent of a hundred grand in U.S. dollars. Wiring money is still totally safe. Our real problem will be storms and big winds and fog you can cut with a knife. March can be really nasty. We have to have all the coastal charts as far south as Portugal, places we can duck into if things get too bad to handle."

"Oh, I'm *really* going to enjoy this. So romantic, so safe, so comfortable. Oh… oh, my God, Jim… what will we eat? Beans? You know I can't cook."

"Don't worry about that, sweetie. McDonald's is everywhere… owwww!"

"So is my McFist… buster!"

NPA, *Counterterrorism Division, Washington, D.C.* | March 6.

"Howard, your Bonnie and Clyde duo might have been spotted in Helsinki."

"*Might* have?" Greenward's irritation showed. "All right, all right, fill me in."

"Close my office door and have a seat. You wanted to hear anything we found, your words, so here's our first lead. An airport agent in Helsinki remembered trying to get a tallish brunette to break a smile while she was being processed through just a couple days back. She was light-skinned, dark eyes, maybe black, exceptional facial features, approximately the right age. If she'd just given him a smile... well, anyway, she struck him as fairly close to our picture except for the eye color. He came up with a possible name. The flight was to Copenhagen."

Greenward examined the yellow pad. "Cruz? That's Spanish. The target is *Irish*, remember? Blue eyes."

"Eye colors are easily changed, as you ought to know. This woman spoke fluent Spanish and we did say Foster might be Spanish. An Emilio Cruz went through ten minutes earlier. We checked, and they came into Finland from Greece. Athens records show they used the same technique there... split up going through customs. We have their check-through times. Ten minutes again. People traveling together don't do that, Howard, but the ones we often look for do."

"Her dossier doesn't include any languages, and why would a Finnish customs agent speak Spanish in the first place? Okay, so call it a vague possibility. Maybe she learned Spanish somewhere. Did they fly *out* of Copenhagen?"

"Not on anything commercial. We're checking private flights. Both had Spanish passports, but no confirmation on that part yet."

"Mr. Stauf, it takes mere minutes to confirm passports, you have the numbers and your office has the horsepower, so what's the holdup?"

"The wheels turn only so fast with the Spanish bureaucracy, *Mr.* Greenward, and we had to reconfirm the numbers on the Athens end. Excuse me... this phone's been blinking for the past twenty seconds. Stauf here."

Three "mm-hmms" later he thanked the caller and hung up.

"Spain can't find any records. Not expired, just no records, nada. So much for your holdup problem, but I wouldn't rely on the answer being correct. There could be thousands of passports nobody can find over there. You were saying?"

"You may have something, Kurt. What were they doing in Greece? What name were they going under there? We need someone on the ground in Copenhagen. Who do we have to check the area? CIA?"

"A few, but I will not waste our time chasing ghosts. You think it's a bum lead, so be it. Just wanted you to know, since this is your baby."

"Too much about it is right to be a bum lead. Europe, a couple on the move, suspicious passports, suspicious activity, and she looks like the picture. If either of this pair turns up in Denmark, advertise it in the Danish media. Put on the pressure. Once we flush them out of the bush, let the bounty hunters finish them off for us."

"Without making sure they're the ones we're after?"

"Look, just find them and let me know. We'll discuss it then."

"And if they turn up in the city, in Copenhagen?"

"Birds have to nest somewhere. Check the hotels, especially the small ones. If we find them registered anywhere, advertise that, too, along with a reminder that the reward is waiting for anyone with enough nerve to pull a trigger. They can double their money if they get both targets."

"You don't want us to bring them in? Arrest them?"

"Did you forget what Foster can do to us if he starts singing? Let someone finish them off right there, unless *your* department wants to do a little free wet work. That way we close the final chapter on the Russian ultimatum, no public circus, no expense, no repercussions. No matter then if dribs and drabs come bubbling to the surface, or O'Dell comes charging into the scene. We can deal with that."

"The NPA doesn't do wet work, Howard, or even condone it."

"Of course not. What *could* I have been thinking?"

"And O'Dell hasn't raised his head. Maybe you were right about him. He knows his gorgeous daughter's a criminal, and nothing will change that. I'd bet you a week's pay he knows exactly where she is. He may even sneak off to help the two of them. We ought to be watching him very carefully, don't you think?"

"We've already bugged his house, cars, phones and some phones at his newspaper office. He can't brush his teeth without our knowing it, and we're not the only ones. He's got a list of enemies long as your arm."

"Howard, speaking of phones, your White House gag order doesn't stop ours from ringing. Right now we're holding off an army of reporters. Shouldn't we make some sort of statement?"

"Absolutely not. When nothing official came out after Vegas, the media made up their own stories. That's what we want here. It'll put even more heat on Foster to do something foolish. Give it a few more days and the phones'll quiet down. I couldn't care less about pundits and TV analysts. Also, I've taken care of the folks who live on The Hill. House and Senate both know we'll deliver a full report once one or both targets have been eliminated."

"You seem to have thought of everything, but one thing intrigues me."

"That being?"

"Mike O'Dell. Has he fallen off the face of the earth?"

"Possibly. He's keeping a low profile, not answering any of his phones and apparently staying at some cheap motel. I would, too, if I were him. Wouldn't you?"

Florence, Maryland. | March 6.

Ollie reached the rendezvous early, parked at the end of a long dirt patch used by truckers, then turned off the car lights and checked to make sure he hadn't inadvertently locked the doors. Dome and courtesy lights had already been taped, as Mike directed. He'd probably play it safe, checking from a distance, but the only way another car could approach was down the one-way exit ramp. Nothing to do now but adjust the rear view mirror and wait. Aside from sleet pellets slowly inching down the rear window, there wasn't much to see. Headlights shone once briefly about where the ramp left the main road, but they veered back and continued on. Couldn't have been him.

Back to waiting.

The rider's side door suddenly whipped open and a dark blue form slammed into the seat, launched from what seemed like a hole in the ground. One hand was thrust out in greeting as the door clicked shut with almost no sound. It all took place within a heartbeat.

"Sorry for the surprise, Ollie, but they've been watching me. Phones all tapped and my cars bugged as of two days ago. If I removed the bugs, they'd know I was onto them. I borrowed a car and got past them… one less trick I can use next time. Your Colorado call was to a number listed in someone else's name even though I'm the only one who uses it. Hopefully it's untraceable. How about you? Followed at any time? Anything suspicious?"

"Shoot, I sure hope not. Flew my own plane into Pittsburgh and drove down."

"File a flight plan?"

"Always do, but gosh golly gee, I changed my mind once I was airborne. No cars I worried about for miles, and we can forget aerial surveillance on a night like this. You surprised me. Never saw or heard you coming."

"That's what stealth is all about. You must have earned my daughter's trust. There aren't half a dozen people who know that phone number... it's the only one the spooks haven't discovered, far as I know. So bring me up to date. When did you last see her and Jim? Let's drive while we talk."

"It was back last July." He eased the car onto the macadam. "They showed up at my front door in Gunnison, brought me breakfast and spent most of the day. They knew I was an NPA marshal, but it didn't matter to Jim. His trust changed me... I hope you believe that. He told me the whole story, starting in Bermuda, everything. I thought they'd both hate me for what had already happened in Yellowstone, but I guess he felt I was in the wrong business. I used to be a preacher, you know, before my wife died in the 9/11... the... anyway I was to call you if I my group ever came after him in any kind of big way. Shoot, I'd call this Tombstone thing big."

"*Why* did he trust you? Something you said or did?"

"It's a real mystery. I just happened to sit next to him on a plane out of Mexico City. Later I caught up with the two of them in Yellowstone during the emergency... I was sent up there when the fires first broke out. We walked right into each other in the west entrance, which surprised me more than it did him. Two coincidences in a row. Thought sure I'd snagged the Mudslinger both times, until he set me straight about a lot of things. Here I'd just cuffed him and he was more concerned about Ollie Robinson than himself. Said I was a decent man trying to do decent things in spite of the Patriot Act. It shamed me. I took the cuffs off and we all took a walk. That's when I realized how terribly wrong everyone was about him."

"He's the noblest man I know, Ollie. Treasures all living things, including the people who'd love to see him dead. Takes bugs and spiders outside and lets them go. This is all about people hating what they don't understand. They'd rather kill him than deal with the ways he's different. He'd spent his whole life secretly helping people until he got dragged into this Russian mess. You know about all that, I suppose."

"He told me plenty. I quit the NPA just before I called you, so I'd be free to help in whatever way I could help."

"I admire you for that. Very few would do such a thing. Who's behind all this… do you know?"

"My guess is Howard Greenward. He's Clarence Towers' new assistant at NPA, which makes him the number two man. You knew that, I suppose."

"Anyone else?"

"He's my choice. I was with his nephew, FBI Special Agent Harry Archer, the day I arrested Ben Howland for arson… another coincidence in case you're keeping track. Harry'd already figured out the owls were being used to plant firebombs, but he didn't trust his own people or the NPA or anyone in Washington, because the owls might have been tied into any of those groups the way things are going these days. He thought he could trust Uncle Greenward, but it was a bad move. Uncle went off the deep end. Everything was Mudslinger this and that. Jim was setting all those fires so he could blackmail our government first, and then the world. Jim drove a president out of office and into the looney bin. Jim destroyed Las Vegas, and so on. The man was obsessed. Harry calls him a psycho. I learned a lot from Harry."

"Interesting that you were the one who arrested Howland. Call that coincidence number four. How about Howland's partner in crime, Sleck?"

"They caught Sleck with two hundred eighty dead bodies, all people in Howland's organization. Sleck gassed them… confessed to it. You won't see him again. I sure hope you know where we're going. I'm lost."

"Keep driving, we're fine. Did Harry mention that Sleck was on Greenward's payroll?"

Copenhagen. | March 6.

Arthur Adams' knowledge of the city and fluency in Danish were both assets, but the situation had turned desperate. Everyone who'd come to know him, bellhops to waiters to maitre d's, might be struck by the resemblance between one grainy photo and the man they'd always assumed was an English businessman with a tan. Nobody'd ever questioned it, but they might do so now that his description included that attribute. He'd have to avoid familiar haunts at all cost, yet it was unsafe for tourists and businessmen to walk safely in less-trafficked areas of the city, especially at night. He ditched the newspaper he carried as a prop, stuffed the tweed cap into his pocket, changed his brisk walking style to a shuffle with a slight limp, and rumpled his hair. The changes made him twenty years older and remarkably Danish.

It didn't take long to locate a pharmacy where he bought a small canister of Epsom salts. Not much farther, a second-hand bazaar produced two size-twelve dresses fitting his own definition of formless. The problem was that anything Tricia wore suddenly grew curves. Wide belts and black socks were easy—the store sold ankle socks in original packages—but shoes in size seven were a real challenge. The store had hundreds piled on a single table, some tied together, most not. He finally found a brown matching pair with run-down heels. They were eights, slightly square-toed. Oh, well, a wad of toilet paper in the toes, and they'd do. Hopefully she wouldn't have to wear them more than minutes at a time. He twisted his mouth with the thought. Men were just not equipped to buy for women, not even spinster types, but the mission was accomplished and not even nine P.M. Trish could do her hair in the morning, throw on a head scarf and they'd be on their way. It might even be possible to get some semblance of decent sleep.

Back at the hotel, Adams ignored the elevator for a second time. Such moves were now mandatory, even to the way he and Fru Adams crossed streets or boarded trolleys. Trish had often remarked at how he could wear a tuxedo in a room full of farmers and still be hard to spot. It was all in knowing what not to do, he'd told her, such as taking elevators. Stairways were always safer.

He paused at the third floor landing before easing the door open a crack, an ingrained habit affording him at least a glimpse of the hallway inside even if only in one direction. He could see their door that way, but no sooner had he glanced through the narrow opening than he froze, silently returning the landing door to its original position.

Someone was standing outside their room, leaning forward with his head cocked to one side! How long had he been there? Who'd sent him? There was only one way to find out, even if it meant a risky face to face. The man could well be moments from knocking on the door, pretending to have mistaken their room for another. And even though Tricia knew better than to answer it, he might already know she was in there. Arthur Adams could have been seen leaving earlier alone, so silence from within would indicate something furtive. That couldn't be allowed to happen.

When Herre Adams re-opened the door with a flourish, the eavesdropper was gone. Ten seconds of delay while considering options, and he'd disappeared, but to where? Into another room, maybe the one opposite theirs? There'd been no sound, which meant the man had been poised to disappear at an instant's notice. There was no safe place in the city anymore, not even a third-rate hotel now that the Tombstone List was being trumpeted in every imaginable way. Would there always be someone listening at their door from now on, or worse? So much for decent sleep.

Once back in the room, he warned her against anything louder than a whisper, then told her what had just happened. She paled. "What now?"

"Something tipped him off. If he heard me in the stairwell, he may believe he's been seen and won't risk anything more tonight, but we're out of here before he changes his mind. The problem is that he may have seen you when we arrived, so you can't change the way you look until we're somewhere safer. I'll collect our passports and check us out tonight, then we head back to the airport to pick up our big bags before heading west. My guess is they're checking anyone who comes here, and even though we don't look anything like the pictures, we *are* traveling together. The same thing will be happening all over Europe. Get yourself ready. I'll be back in a few minutes."

"Jim... we just got here. Won't they be suspicious?"

"Yes. I'll give them an excuse. We'll have to move fast."

But where could they go, he wondered? How could they be sure of anything now? Showing up at any inn or hotel on the way to Esbjerg in the middle of the night would be suicide, and it was too cold and cramped to sleep in their rented car.

He could think of just one possibility, something he hadn't done in two dozen years. Even that wasn't a sure thing.

Florence, Maryland.

Ollie's hesitation testified to his surprise. "Are you sure... about Sleck and Greenward? I don't think Harry knew it."

"Probably didn't. From time to time I have my people check on shady guys like Sleck, where they go and who they see. Sleck made several visits to Greenward's Quaker Hill estate in the months leading up to Yellowstone. The place is guarded by electronic surveillance a mile thick, plus dogs inside the fence. Nobody gets inside unless they're invited. Conclusion... business of some kind was transacted. The Howland-Sleck development and Greenward-Sleck visits were going on simultaneously."

"So *Greenward* is tied into those fires and murders? Why wouldn't Harry have tumbled to that?"

"No, I'm saying only that Sleck was there for some nefarious purpose over a period of many months while the Yellowstone thing was developing. When nephew Harry came along with the owl story it should have clicked into whatever dark stuff Greenward and Sleck were up to, but did it? Wish I'd paid closer attention. Did Jim fill you in on the Russian ultimatum that started all this? Did he mention Gordy Whittier, the psychologist who worked with him?"

"Everything he knew, and yes about Whittier, but Jim said he never actually saw the document."

"Right, because Winfield and cronies hid the thing. Its secrecy has kept Jim's name and picture out of the public eye until now. Whittier read the original document while the president and John Hughes looked on, and then they all discussed it at length. Later Gordy was able to quote the important parts almost verbatim, including the thirty locations the Russians chose for destruction—he'd written those down and committed them to memory—and he shared all that with my group of guys. At that point Greenward was the key player calling all the shots, and that's why I feel certain he's behind all this now. Something in the picture has changed." Mike pointed to a sign ahead. "Turn into that Wendy's."

It was sleeting heavily. Ollie parked and turned off the headlights. "Shoot, Mike, I'm really sorry to say this, but Towers was probably behind the Tombstone listing."

"How well do you know him? Would he insist on *seeing* the document?"

"He's a stickler, yes, but at the same time Greenward can make you think ice cream's hot. He and Towers are old buddies."

"We need to get this out in the open, make it into a public fight. They're wondering why I haven't exploded in their faces over Trish being called out as a terrorist, but *they* have to attack *me*, otherwise I'm just another father sounding off. When they do, I'll offer them a deal."

"You mean create a firestorm?"

"Exactly. I want you to write down everything you can remember about that document, anything Jim or Tricia might have mentioned like dates, names, places and such. I'll add what I know, but the one with the best info would be Whittier. We've got to try reaching him without compromising our side or his. He's succeeded so far in staying out of sight, thereby staying alive somewhere in Europe."

"And then?"

"We expose the ultimatum and its provisions, tie it to Las Vegas, and we have a major political scandal. The pols will take it from there, with a little help from my media friends. Why are you shaking your head?"

"The Patriot Act will shut you down, Mike. Harboring and concealing, material support to terrorists, intending to influence the policy of a government by intimidation, et cetera, et cetera. They'll tear your house apart looking for evidence, jail you and throw away the key."

"This thing will explode in their faces before they have a chance."

"The NPA is worse than the FBI ever was, Mike. You'll be fighting them from behind bars *after* they indict you a year or so later. Take it from Ollie Robinson, who's been involved in such jailings. What they'll say right off is that Jim's already proved he's a terrorist by trashing the White House. There were witnesses to that. Nothing further's needed."

"The first day of any exposé is always the deciding factor, the big one. Take it from Mike O'Dell, who's been involved in such exposés. Wham, a few million readers get the story before anyone knows it's coming, including all Congress, and the questions start flying. If they put me in jail after that, it'll be called a government cover-up and make things worse for them. If they shut down my paper, I'll already have the follow-up ready for release to all media through my attorneys. And as far as ripping my house apart, the boys at NPA and the FBI have already run their Sneak and Peek a few times, *without* the required notice. I always leave a few little juicy tidbits around in plain sight so they know I intended they see the stuff... my way of challenging them."

"That may be, but—"

"This is war, my friend. They've convicted two innocent people in the public forum and sentenced them to death. Our strength lies in a strong surprise attack. Our weakness lies in not having the ultimatum in hand. Whittier's recollections would be priceless, but only Jim knows how to contact him. They might trace any call I'd make to Jim's sat phone, so that's out."

"Jim gave me a couple other phone numbers along with yours. He figured they might come in handy some day. One was Whittier's, but I wouldn't call it from this side of the ocean."

Mike paused. "Think you can get over there without advertising the trip or leaving any traces?"

"NPA marshals never appear on airline manifests, did'ja know that? We're John Doe, and even though I sent in my resignation, my boss hasn't accepted it yet. I've still got all my IDs. That's the thing about my kind of work... nobody knows where I am at any given time except for my immediate boss, and even he doesn't know half the time."

"Ollie, tell me something... did you *really* think Jim was the Mudslinger that first time on the plane?"

"Shoot, no. Even when I snapped the cuffs on him, he never reacted."

"So why did you do it? Why the cuffs?"

"He asked me what I did when my suspicions about someone were borne out. I was just showing him how it's done."

Mike smiled for the first time.

Chapter 5

Denmark. | March 7.

Jim took them north out of Velje, picking successively smaller roads until they were in farm land. At three A.M. he stopped, backed up and turned down a gravel road. Moonlight had shown him what he was looking for: a low shed without any nearby farmhouse.

"This could be it, babe," he announced. "That's a hay storage shed, not the kind they use for pigs, and there's no farmhouse anywhere nearby. I'll go see." He was back in five minutes with a thumbs-up. They could get out their ski gear and climb into the same jumpsuits they'd worn in Lahti, then use the rest of their winter clothing as blankets. It was March. Nobody would be out checking on a hay shed. Better yet, nobody would be listening at the door, but they'd need to be up and away by seven. By the time they reached Esbjerg, Tricia's makeover would have to be complete. That Adams woman in the skirt with daisies would be no more than someone's faulty memory.

෨෬

While frumpy Fru Adams nosed about Esbjerg on foot, Arthur Adams worked the shoreline in their car. Danish frostbiters sailed all winter so "cats" were prevalent, but finding the right one was another matter, and discovering it was for sale seemed as improbable as winning the lottery. However, anything could be bought for a price.

He'd almost passed a junky commercial boatyard later that afternoon, but on impulse turned in anyway. The sign read *MADSEN BOATS* and the yard was squeezed between two larger ones showing forests of masts. The Madsen boatyard didn't show any masts from the road, but he'd vowed to poke into every boatyard, not only those catering to sailboats. This one seemed to draw him for reasons unknown. No one was inside the small office building, but a light truck was parked alongside.

He ambled into the yard, hands in pockets, surprised to see a single mast over close to the water. It was a ten-meter catamaran with a dark blue hull, quite out of place in the dirty slip. Someone had used it recently so it probably wouldn't be for sale, but it was the first decent cat he'd seen. Might as well look at the rest of her.

Fresh bottom paint? Damn! The first decent candidate in four hours of searching, and all the signs were wrong. The owner was probably a frostbiter. Still, it was intriguing. The tunnel between the hulls was high above the waterline, no bulges or compromises, and the outboard motor's knee-action mount raised it totally out of the tunnel when retracted. Clean design. Winches were Murrays in a land where Andersen, Harken and Barient winches ruled. Maybe the boat had been built in Australia? An inflatable dinghy was tied in place on the trampoline.

"She's for sale." The man shambling across the yard was elderly, with a full, white beard and a meerschaum pipe. Surprised, Jim quickly slid into his "Englishman trying to speak Danish" character. Before he'd finished his halting request to inspect the interior, the man had waved him aboard, gesturing three times with the pipe stem. He appraised Jim's clothes and sneakers, then waved one more time. "Take a look."

Ten minutes later, the pipe smoker was still waiting. There'd be no sense searching further, unless there was a glitch somewhere.

"Who owns the boat, sir?"

"My son... did." The answer was delivered with difficulty. "Died a month ago. I'm Karl Madsen. You're a sailor, I can tell."

"Sometimes, yes. Sorry about your son. My name is Adams. I apologize for my terrible Danish."

"It's pretty good. Most folks don't try. Saw you sighting the tunnel. Most never do that."

"I wasn't really looking for anything bigger than six or at the most eight meters, but... well, what's your price?"

He puffed on the pipe for a bit. "A ten's better than any eight, lots more room. Got new bottom paint. Sails are real good. Everything works and she's set to go. A hundred thousand if you want her now. My son would've asked a hundred fifty in the spring."

"She's sixteen years old, sir. Without a survey of the hulls and standing rigging, my risk is considerable. Seventy thousand as she stands, cash, wired to your bank tomorrow morning. I'll hand you the tax separately, also in cash. You can handle that part as you see fit."

"My son bought her new and kept her up. New outboard last year, all new sails the year before. Might come down a bit if you can move her right off."

He wants to haggle. Ninety's a decent price, even if his bill of sale shows half that to the tax folks. "I might cough up another ten, Mr. Madsen, but I want to take her out first. I'll leave you five thousand as a deposit and be back in an hour. If I decide to take her, you can fill in the paperwork any way you wish."

Madsen jabbed the pipe back in his mouth and talked past the stem, making it bobble. "You saying eighty? Well, if you're willing to go to eighty-five, you just leave some identification and you can take her out. If you're not back in an hour...."

"I'll be on time. You can watch me from here." He handed over his Adams passport and the man no more than glanced inside.

"Good breeze out there today. She'll go. My son had her all the way up to eighteen knots one time... that's what he told anyone who'd listen."

"Really? He must have been an excellent sailor." *On a flat sea, she should do at least thirty. Hope he isn't testing me.*

NPA, *Counterterrorism Division, Washington, D.C.* | March 7.

"No dice, Howard. No Cruz registrations at any of the hotels, no car rentals, no flights out under the name, commercial or private. The lead's dead. I'll have to pull off the field agents."

"It's *not* dead and there will be no backing down. Check the ferries out of Denmark. If Foster's on the run, he'll avoid airports and may not even drive. He and the chick might also split up and travel separately. They may be disguised in some way. This guy's slimy, Kurt, a real snake."

"Calm down. We could be chasing the wrong pair. They may not be running. Maybe they're house guests with someone in Denmark. And *you* called it a bum lead, not me."

"Those passports were bogus, and good bogus passports are beyond the reach of ordinary people. One of ours good enough to pass muster would cost twenty-five grand on the street, meaning twice that for the pair, but it does tell us we're looking for Spanish types. Two gets you five he's got a little mustache and her hair's drawn back hard. Black eyes could mean she's wearing contacts."

"Howard, how I managed to do my job up to now without your personal lectures is beyond me. Anyway, according to my understanding of the Tombstone rules we can update 'whereabouts' and 'last seen' at any time, so we'll post a possible sighting in Copenhagen and alert the Danish Police Service along with Interpol. Then we sit back and wait. You would not believe the sudden quantity of crappy info we're getting for names on that list. My department is running down hundreds of leads we didn't have two days ago, and I'm putting in twelve-hour days myself. Problem is, it's all garbage."

"When you start getting bodies instead of information, it'll be a different story. Let me know if anything changes. If our birds are in Copenhagen, they might be using another alias."

"If they're using another alias, they've already flown. Birds do that, Howard. They do not sit in their nest waiting to be picked off."

"Well, my gut tells me he's still in Denmark. I've tracked this guy before. I can almost smell him. In bridge, you play the hand to make it, Kurt. The cards have to be there, but if you don't play as though they were you might as well knit for a hobby. Our photos hit the newsstands, and what does Foster do? He panics, he ducks, stays off the streets. She does, too, especially with that face and figure, so there they are, holed up and trying to figure out what to do. They can't go out to eat, can't use planes or trains. What other avenues are there, besides the ferries? We close those off and we have them trapped. They sure can't walk their way out of it."

"You're stretching things, Mr. Bridgeplayer. They flew to Denmark two days ago, plenty of time to slip through. Another alias means they'd need *another* whole set of papers with differences in the photos. How do they change appearance overnight?"

"They'll be in a *panic* state for two days, Kurt. They won't go anywhere until they figure out how, and anything they can think of will require identification every time a border's crossed. Foster won't risk driving or renting a plane or hiring a private pilot. What does that leave him, bicycles? How does he move without crossing borders? You see, he can't."

"Howard, you don't *know* Cruz is Foster. Second, you don't know if they'll split—"

"A boat! Damn, why didn't I think of that sooner? Cruz... cruise."

"What? Aw—" *What did I do to deserve this?*

"Foster's a sailor. He'll know his way around waterfronts and use dockspeak. His type would line up *some* sort of boat, maybe a tramp freighter. He might even buy a little sailboat and slip off into the night. He'd know that game like the back of his hand. Jesus, why didn't I think of that before now?"

"You're nuts. It's March, you're talking the North Sea and he'd still have to show papers wherever he put into port. Maybe the tramp freighter idea is reasonable, but you're assuming he's running scared and I say he's not. He could be in South Africa by now. You also seem to think this is my only project—"

"Waterfronts aren't known for refusing bribes, and Foster's got money. Tell your people to add boats to the list. Any boat purchases, any commercial craft out of Denmark the past two days, tramp steamers under foreign flags, cruise ships, the works. He can go any direction, but my hunch is he'll try to get as far away from Denmark as he can, as fast as possible, once he decides to move. He'll most likely head east into the Baltic, but he can't travel fast enough to escape us if we stay on his tail. Tramp steamers aren't known for speed, and small boats are even slower. We'll just draw a circle based on his projected best speed, and he'll be in it."

"That circle won't be very big if it's a sailboat."

Greenward's grin was sardonic. "About the size of a noose."

Chapter 6

Esbjerg, Denmark. | March 7.

With typical Swiss efficiency, the wire transfer was completed by ten the next morning. Jim moved the boat to a temporary tie-up at a fuel dock while they shopped for provisions. A sporting goods store supplied backpack rations, a propane camp stove with a two-quart clamp-on pot, blankets and bedding and a tarp they could rig over the boat's cuddy. The boat had blankets, but not enough. Tricia put four more aboard, plus sleeping bags and a carton of chemical hand warmers. Any kind of real cold front sweeping down from the Arctic could force them into port if they weren't prepared to tough it out.

Once all that was on the boat, they headed for the city marina where Jim picked out a canister life raft, two pairs of binoculars and batteries for everything on board. Their last series of stops was for food. Surrounded by their purchases, they sat at the small dinette and rechecked their lists, totaling receipts and looking for items they might have missed.

"Well, Mr. Adams, our food bill came to a neat €1441.28. What did the rest cost?" She looked up. He was staring at her in the oddest way. "Something wrong? Oh, oh… why do those numbers sound familiar?"

"My total for the rest comes to €7506.43, Trish. I couldn't believe it, so I just rechecked."

"The coordinates! 14.41.282 and 75.06.4286!"

"Charlie's still with us."

Geneva, Switzerland. | March 10.

Ollie's park bench was tucked behind a rock outcropping, allowing him to watch the rendezvous without being seen. Three hardy patrons ignored an icy wind to sit at the coffee shop's outdoor tables, but everyone else was inside. Was Whittier one of them? Would he be watching the park, waiting to see someone approach before he showed himself? In that case, it could be wiser to just stroll about.

Other benches in the small park offered little in the way of concealment. An elderly blind man sat on the nearest one with a disc player cupped in his gloved hands, listening to music through earphones barely visible under his floppy hat. He'd been there for some time. At his feet, a golden retriever wearing a guide harness lay quietly on a small piece of carpet. Most other benches were unoccupied.

One of the coffee shop patrons left and a woman took his place. Of the remaining two men, one had been reading a newspaper the whole time. He suddenly folded his paper, got up and left. Definitely not Whittier, and now only five minutes to go. It was time to follow instructions, wander over and take a table. The rest would now be up to Whittier. How awful it would be if the meeting proved to be a trap, set up by those who knew Whittier's affection for Jim.

"Good morning, Mr. Robinson. I'm Gordon Whittier. I see you're as careful as I'd hoped you'd be."

The voice from behind was more embarrassing than startling. How could anyone have snuck up on him that way? The fact that no one had made it even worse. The blind man's dark glasses were off and his hand was out in greeting.

"Sorry for the cloak and dagger stuff, but anyone after Jim will try to find me. Why did Jim give you my phone number? Can you tell me that?"

Whittier listened, finally pulling a thick envelope from his greatcoat. "This may be the antidote to Greenward's poison. I started a personal notebook the day I was added to the *ad hoc* committee delving into Las Vegas, just days before I was called into President Winfield's private quarters and shown that Russian ultimatum. Everything about that document is in here, along with names, dates, places, things that were said and my personal observations. The battle behind Grace Botanical is all there, too, my side of it. Mike can fill in much more than I can about that part, but remember that Jim and I could have been gunned down without ever knowing what hit us. I intended to publish the whole story if Jim was ever killed or captured. How is he? Have you heard from him?"

"Nothing. Shoot, I hope they're both safe."

"It's Tricia I worry about. Jim's something of a tinamou, that game bird you can be looking right at and never see. Maybe Mike is right…

the best defense *is* a strong offense…but beg him not to stake too much on what I've written. At best it covers things he couldn't know or might have forgotten. I talked with him after the Grace Botanical attack, but there wasn't time to cover everything. You might also make contact with that FBI agent you mentioned. I sense something of an ally there, a decent type."

"What would you do, Dr. Whittier, to keep yourself safe if you were Jim… speaking as a psychologist?"

"Avoid even the people I knew or trusted and speak to no one beyond the barest necessities. I'd buy nothing more significant than food I could take with me, in small amounts and probably at busy supermarkets, using only small denominations in cash of the country I was in at the time. It's the Euro everywhere over here. No big purchases and no unusual mode of travel. I'm afraid, in this age of computers, that anything beyond walking would be a flare on a dark night."

"Do you think they're doing things that way? Your way?"

"Not a chance."

Esbjerg, Denmark. | March 10.

Jim pushed away from the dock just before dawn. With luck they'd reach the Cape Verdes in eight days, then restock before the two thousand mile stretch to Brazil. A dozen days for that leg if all went well, but making it through the English Channel was the trickiest part. It was busy around the clock, with unpredictable winds and dense fog. Weather advisories were usually wrong, especially when reporting on winds and wave heights. March weather made everything twice as dangerous.

Their plan was to be viewed as typical cold weather sailing nuts until well out of sight of land, but a west wind was hard in their faces. Nobody would deliberately sail directly *into* a thirty-knot wind, not even a Norwegian, so they clawed their way toward Britain at a snail's pace with the temperature hovering at twenty-five degrees Fahrenheit. The wind chill factor brought that down to eight degrees. Jim's dry suit and goggles were put to the test from the beginning, while Tricia huddled under the cuddy. Making things even dicier, no other nuts were out there.

Holland's port of Ijmuiden, two days and three hundred miles southwest, was where they planned to rest a full day before tackling the channel's four hundred miles of hell. They'd never get there this way, but conditions improved a bit by noon. The boat's responses were more familiar, they were well away from land and no other sails or ships were seen anywhere. It was time for magic.

With Tricia at the helm, Jim dropped sail.

A small, dark blue boat with sails furled would be invisible to anyone five miles away, especially on a choppy sea. A steady mental push from behind, another under the twin hulls, and they were up to fifteen knots—sort of. The extra lift from below kept all but a few inches of each hull out of the water, but waves were spaced only a little more than the boat's length. As soon as they increased speed, they plowed into the next wave front and were showered with buckets of ice cold seawater. Managing two forces was a snap for a man who could create tornadoes, but things were still not going well. When conditions finally eased at two P.M., they'd already been pounded for eight hours. Cold, wet and tired, Jim's mood was still upbeat. Conditions had started out bad; they would improve. The next challenge was to avoid being seen skimming along "bare poles" into the wind.

Twice they spotted a large ship on the horizon and were forced to hold up until it passed. After dark they could run with navigation lights off at whatever speed he could manage, but darkness was hours away. In the meantime, Frustration was their unwelcome companion. They'd make back part of the time if they got a further break in the weather, but that was not to be either. Rain joined Frustration just after midnight, beginning as drizzle, then becoming a frigid downpour mixed with sleet.

Tricia had her first taste of playing galley cook in a seaway, not that different from turning out a seven-course meal while galloping on horseback. Even with Jim steadying the boat, she managed only to boil water by sitting on the cabin sole with the camp stove braced between her knees. With safety tethers snapped onto the stern lifelines, they huddled under the cuddy, wrapped in blankets while nibbling raisin biscuits through their balaclavas and imagining the instant coffee was hot.

Jim was working on a mental solution to the weather problem. His imagery involved a monorail of solid air in the tunnel between the hulls. If he could get it right, the boat could bridge spaces between wave crests by "riding" on the beam. Fatigue was already gnawing at his concentration, but Tricia caught on to his mental picture.

"Something like a square telephone pole stretching from the top of one wave to the top of the next," she said. "Is that it?"

"In a nutshell, but we have to keep the rudder and daggerboards in the water in seas like this, or lose control."

"Why not make the beam like cooked spaghetti? Let it float."

"A flexible monorail? Why didn't I think of that?"

"Maybe have it floppy up and down-wise, but stiff the other way. Wouldn't it follow the waves and still boost us up enough to just touch?"

He tossed away what was left of his ice-cold coffee. "I don't believe it. I'm the engineer in this family, yet my non-sailing wife comes along with a perfect answer."

She wriggled under her blanket. "I did a good thing?"

"It's perfect. When daylight comes we can't be seen out of the water while going against the wind, but your way keeps us rising and falling with the waves. Someone has to be very close to notice anything different, and I don't see anyone like that out here. Do you see anyone?"

"Duh! Two in the morning, raining and sleeting, and he asks if I can see anyone. I can't see a *thing*, buster, not even one tiny distant light. I can barely see the front of the boat. Aren't you scared? Look... this is ice on my blanket."

"First, we're only out twenty miles. Second, that's why we paid so much for these dry suits. Now let's see what I can do with your idea." He momentarily closed his eyes, then stared straight ahead. "I'm doing this gradually. Can you feel anything?" He was suddenly grinning.

"Sure can. Wow, feels like a roller coaster. Less noise, too."

"We're six inches higher in the water." He closed his eyes again, and ten seconds later she felt a greater change. "The hulls should be just touching now, Trish. We're water skiing, literally. Must be doing twenty knots."

"How do you keep track of so many things at one time? You're pushing us with your mind, you're thinking of the monorail and steering the boat and watching the waves, and—"

"And loving you to pieces. Think you can take a bit more speed? I figure the wave crests are about a hundred feet apart. Thirty knots is fifty feet per second, so we'll be cresting every two seconds, about the same as standing up, then sitting down, then standing up, et cetera. The old German Oktoberfest thing. Could make you seasick unless you keep your eyes on the horizon."

"What horizon?"

NPA, Washington, D.C. | March 10.

Kurt made certain he shut Greenward's office door before sitting down, not that it would make any difference in the man's arrogance.

"My hat's off to you, Howard. Your favorite terrorist might have bought a sailboat, just like you said he would."

"Bingo! Do I know this pigeon or not?" Greenward's grin turned serious. "Okay, fill me in."

"A ten-meter cat was sold in Esbjerg on the west side of Denmark two days ago. Buyer was Arthur Adams, British passport. The seller, name of Madsen, reported the tax. He described Adams, but not the girl. He heard about her later on. Seems Adams and girl reportedly spent all day stocking the boat at a marina a few miles away, and were gone this morning. Madsen couldn't say where they were heading, but the weather was stinko, freezing *and* with a front moving in. Reports suggest they headed north. Maybe they were taking the boat to the eastern shore, where things are less stormy. That would tie in with your theory of a run into the Baltic."

"How good was the description of Adams?"

"On the money, but here's the interesting part. Adams spoke almost perfect Danish, very little accent according to this Madsen. The money came by way of bank transfer from a numbered Swiss account. Like you said, Foster has lots of money. He must have it all banked with the Swiss. So far, all your inputs on Foster are proving out. I might even start listening to you now."

"The girl?"

"No information."

"So the guy speaks good Danish. What's that tell you, Kurt?"

"That he must have lived there awhile."

"Right. Here's a guy with lots of money, spends time in Denmark, speaks the language. We have his name and he's with a girl. Now... does he stay in a back-alley flop house, a walk-up cold-water flat or a pricey hotel?"

"I say the hotel, but he also might own something there, let's say a flat. Could also be anywhere in Denmark, not just Copenhagen. Maybe Esbjerg. Maybe out in the country."

"Remember our bridge hand? Forget private property. Canvass the better hotels in the city for Arthur Adams any time in the past five years. He must have used restaurants where he's known, and he tips well if he's got money. Find those. Meanwhile... how fast can sailboats sail?"

"Depends. If he went north, he was making no more than eight knots, given the conditions over there now. Big waves on the North Sea side, way too big for a ten-meter boat. Our experts say if he goes west he can't average better than two or three knots into those same waves, if even that. He'll spend most of his time tacking and getting nowhere. Conclusion? Chances of his going west are nil, so it's north or south. They think it was north. Looks like you were also right about him being panicked. He never got a survey on the boat, just bought it cash on the barrelhead. I like your Baltic Sea theory. Also, he's single-handing the boat, no crew other than the girl if she's with him, so he can take only so much pounding before he collapses. He won't stay out there long before he's pooped or frozen solid. Then he'll have to put in somewhere, definitely in Denmark."

Greenward scratched his chin, concentrating. "Something doesn't compute. Anyway, it's good news. It's fantastic. Pick a point a hundred miles north, another a hundred south and a third going west maybe thirty, just in case he's insane. Connect the dots, and he's inside there somewhere. Post a description of the boat with every port inside a five-hundred-mile circle. Damn, we've got him!"

Chapter 7

Ijmuiden, Holland. | March 11.

Sail reefed and outboard idling for effect, they pitched and rolled their way through the breakwater entrance to the marina after dark. Ice hung thick on the rigging and lifelines, thanks to ever-present rain, and the deck was a crunchy skating rink. Breaking waves pounded along the shoreline outside the triangle-shaped marina and winds were forecast to average at least thirty knots, with gusts to sixty. Anyone out there would have a handkerchief hoisted in place of a mainsail, but then nobody'd be out there. They'd left Esbjerg thirty-eight hours earlier, covering 325 miles and averaging nearly nine knots in terrible weather, with punishing seas and the frigid wind constantly in their faces. There was no telling what they might achieve when conditions were right.

The surprised dockmaster tore himself away from the TV set, took one look and dutifully copied the names to his clipboard with no more than a brief glance at their papers. After selling Adams a London Times, he assigned them transient dock space at the end of the finger pier closest to the entrance, tucked behind three ocean-going yachts moored there.

Tricia stayed below. Some hot food and twenty-four hours of solid shut-eye and she'd be ready for whatever lay ahead—maybe. She was already getting the hang of operating in a galley while totally asleep, whipping up a scrumptious meal the way nature intended—unopened cans of beef and macaroni heated in boiling water, with the labels still on. Outside, dense fog rolled in, obliterating everything in a matter of a few minutes and creating ghostly halos around the marina lights. Fog horns came alive like a lake full of bullfrogs. Jim called it a good omen. Fog could mean the wind was easing, but the sounds of crashing waves only a few hundred feet away ruined the illusion. He fought to stay awake for his "steak and macaroni dinner," but something in the newspaper caught his eye. He struggled groggily back to his feet.

"Trish, forget the food. We have to leave now. Right now!"

"What? Oh, Jim, you *can't* mean—"

"Shhh! They *know* about the boat. They know we're using the name Adams, and all the ports have been alerted. We're sitting ducks here. The marina guy may already have reported us."

"My God, what'll we do? You can't see a thing outside."

"Anything except sit tied to a pier while our names are there in someone's roster."

"You're exhausted. So am I."

"Better exhausted than dead. If we can't see those moored yachts, nobody will see us sneak around them and out, but we can't afford to make a single sound. We've got to get back out into the channel. We can't stay in any port."

"What if they notice our spot is empty?"

"Good point. You stay on the boat. I'll move it away a bit, move the sailboat next to us into our spot and tie it up, then nudge you back and hop aboard. If the fog lifts a bit, maybe all they'll see is the other guy's mast where ours should be, and nobody will check any further. We've got all night before anyone's likely to see we're gone, providing the fog stays and we can get out undetected, but we have to do it now."

"What if we can't? Get out undetected, I mean."

"Then I may have to do something I don't want to do… to anyone." His gaunt look underscored the words.

ॐ

Jan Kuiper stood in the marina shack doorway, staring out. Channel foghorns made everything eerie and nothing was visible beyond a few dozen feet, not even the red and green lights on the breakwater entrance. He shut the door, then noticed that a fax was arriving. He'd dropped it into the wire basket on his service counter when the heading caught his eye. Arthur Adams, unnamed woman, blue-hulled catamaran? Why, they were no more than a few hundred feet away, at the end of the first finger pier. He'd signed them in just two hours earlier.

His pulse was racing by the time he'd finished reading. These two people were on that new Tombstone thing. Anyone spotting them had a choice: either report the sighting or kill them both for a huge reward. That's what it said, right there. Wow! He'd never killed anything, not even a chicken, but he'd been reading the papers and watching TV, and that list of terrorists was the same as a hunting license. He could be a hero and a millionaire. He wouldn't have to work any more.

His gun was home, but even if it wasn't he'd probably shake too much to use it. He'd be murdering those people, that's what it would be, just like shooting a goose or something. But... Hendrick Closson had a gun and he'd shot people before, lots of them... women, too... back in Serbia. *He* could shoot these terrorists while they were sleeping. He'd know exactly how to do it, and half a fortune was better than none, but Hendrick worked as a watchman, too. He wouldn't be off until midnight, three hours away.

It was one A.M. before Hendrick finally answered his phone. He was adamant.

"Stay put, Jan, and I will be there in an hour, no more. Tell no one. You just pretend nothing is wrong and don't lose your nerve and we'll be rich men in the morning, ja?"

"You're sure this is the right thing to do?"

"They blew up the London subway, Jan. Do you want them to blow us up, too? Remember, tell no one."

෨෬

Hendrick held his pistol at the ready in case they were surprised in any way, and together they inched carefully down the long finger pier, wincing with every squeak and groan of the wet wood. They were almost to the end before Jan realized something was wrong. He grabbed the other man's arm and whispered. "Wait, Hendrick... that's not the boat. Theirs was a catamaran."

"Someone else parked here first, then? Maybe they went to another pier? Were you watching them tie up?"

"This was the only spot I had left for a cat, because cats are really wide. Anyway, why would I have watched them?"

"Then did they maybe leave?"

"In this fog? They must be in the marina somewhere, maybe way down in the corner by Kennemerboulevard. Maybe they anchored there."

"Nah. We go up and down all the piers and check."

"I tell you they have to be anchored, Hendrick, or at the end of a pier because they can't fit their wide boat into a slip unless no other boat is there. All the slips were taken up. We won't be able to see them in this fog if they are near the rocks down there. We will have to go out in a rowboat, but—"

"Arghh, you are too impatient. We wait until daylight or until the fog lifts. You told no one?"

"Of course not. Who would I tell?"

"Okay, then we play cribbage and wait. If I stand on the rocks by the red light I can shoot this Adams when he tries to go through the opening. Maybe I can get them both if she is on deck. I am a real good shot with this thing." He stuffed the gun into his belt. "Then we are both rich men, Jan. What do you think? Do you want to bet me I'll get a twenty-nine point cribbage hand tonight? Ja? I think I like that as much as being rich."

෨෬

The channel was eerie, worse than any nightmare, without lights or shapes. Jim decided against using radar, since its signal could be picked up by anyone looking for them. The GPS was good enough to let them know where they were even if it couldn't tell them what was directly ahead—such as dozens of offshore gas rigs all over the channel, lit up like Christmas trees. Those lights would be almost useless in pea soup fog because various types of watercraft were often anchored near the rigs, usually with barely legal anchor lights. Any kind of collision at the speed Jim was pushing them spelled disaster, yet caution was to be abandoned. The alert could go out at any minute, and when it did the channel would seethe with pursuers.

They'd head straight out fifteen miles, following the charts. No gas rigs were shown in that zone, but rigs weren't the only problems. Fog never stopped or even slowed freighters. They churned along at a clip that made stopping or turning quickly almost impossible. "Get out of the way" was their message, even though maritime rules urged immense caution when conditions were extreme. Freighter fog horns were often indistinguishable from those on buoys or ashore, and fog muffled sound from engines or screws. A small boat directly in the path of these behemoths was doomed.

Nothing worked to calm Tricia's racing pulse, but in spite of all the fright and nail-biting she was awake at least. She'd taken two caffeine tablets, but still felt sick with fatigue. Jim was operating on three tablets. How did he do it? He'd been going for almost forty hours without even so much as a nap, yet there he was, creating his floating monorail and moving them as though there could be nothing at all ahead but smooth water.

Off to the north, the rumble of an unusually low foghorn joined others that made up the chorus. Half a minute later, the same rumble seemed closer. She was about to remark about it, when the cat's hulls plunged into the water, lurching them sideways. They were coming hard about. Jim shouted for her to hang on tight as the boat became airborne for seconds. A great whooshing sound bloomed louder behind them. The hulls barely touched water before they were airborne a second time. The next horn blast seemed directly over her head!

"JIM!"

"FREIGHTER!" The blue cat jumped a third time, landing askew. "Should have turned the other way. Hang tight, we're in for a rough ride."

His words were scarcely out before a huge bow wave, capped with fluorescent green-white foam, lifted and snapped them around at the same time. Then, like some dark, rust-stained wall, the ship passed them a boat's length distant, swirling away the fog just enough so they could see what had just missed them.

"JIM, IT'S COMING CLOSER!"

"SHE'S TURNING TO STARBOARD. HANG ON." The cat leapt a full boat's length, then skipped from wave to wave like a flat stone. The freighter's stern passed just as another foghorn blast rattled their teeth, coupled with the pounding of bass drums: *boom boom boom boom boom boom boom boom boom.*

Jim calmly turned them about and immediately started back toward the behemoth.

"Jim, what are you *doing?*"

"She's our ticket to ride, Kitten. Get ready, we're going to cross the stern waves."

"*What?*"

"We'll ride the wake. I can use the monorail trick far better on flat water, even if it's churning like a Jacuzzi, and a freighter can *see* where it's going. We can't. She's doing twenty knots at least. All we do is make sure she's not heading for a port, and she'll get us through until the fog lifts."

"Won't someone look down and see us? Oh… forget I said that."

"The crew would be inside even on a clear night. The best part is we won't show up on anyone else's radar either. All they'll see is that monster. Come daylight, we could be more than two hundred miles south of here, more if she picks up speed."

"*If* you last that long. How are you holding up?"

"I'm okay. My eyes are open at least. Here goes…."

The freighter's roiling wake was silvery with fluorescence that would last for minutes. Small craft could be swamped by the swirling undercurrents, but the most dangerous part was cutting into it from either side. Jim kept the cat parallel to the freighter's track and skittered over the series of stern waves like a water skier. Within five minutes they were a hundred yards astern of the beast.

"Piece o'cake, babe," he grinned. "Look, no hands."

"Oh, how can you joke? We almost were caught back there in that marina and we just about got run down."

"That's *why* I can joke. Get some sleep. Captain's orders."

"Nothing doing, Queeg."

"*Captain* Queeg. Do it, Trish. One of us has to be half human when the fog lifts, and I taught you to sail the standard way. We may have a lot more waiting for us down the line, assuming we get that far."

"Like what?"

"Don't ask."

☯

Ten minutes from landing at JFK, Ollie slipped Whittier's three-hundred page manuscript back into the envelope. It was beyond anything Mike expected. Not only had Gordy detailed all the events following Las Vegas, including everything that took place in the ad hoc committee on which he'd served, but he'd literally reproduced the original Russian ultimatum—all thirty-six pages worth—plus conversations in President Winfield's private quarters, Winfield's challenge to find a human antidote for the Russian secret weapon, all the impossibilities involved, even the use of psychometry. Whittier had brought forth a complete profile of James Foster, the man, trying as he was to understand his superhuman powers and use them for beneficial purposes. The world didn't offer many possibilities for that, as it had turned out.

When he and Tricia came to call in Gunnison, Jim reluctantly allowed glimpses of his life here and there, but here was the full story, delivered by a psychologist whose life work had been aberrant functions of the brain. He'd spent hundreds of hours with Jim, and in the process Jim's life became an open book.

Mike wanted names? There they were, along with times and dates. Details of the Bermuda assassination attempt and all those involved. More details of the attack behind Grace Botanical Labs, a supposed safe house. Exchanges with Winfield, and examples of how the president's mood turned so suddenly sour once Howard Greenward dominated the scene. Winfield's characterization of Jim as something expendable, not a human being.

Nowhere did Whittier mention his own personal losses or suffering as directed from 1600 Pennsylvania Avenue, the attempts to bring his successful clinic to financial ruin or his brutal treatment as a hostage kidnapped by those hunting Jim. Not a word about FBI agents shadowing his every move, nor a comment on how the danger behind Grace Botanical affected him. This was all about Jim Foster, born Luis in Cuzco, Peru, without any remembered last name or father. It spoke of a boy of six or seven and an unbelievable toy sailboat race on a windless summer day in a city thousands of miles from there. Between the lines was an essay on honor and faith and moral upbringings that would put most Christians to shame. Overriding all was a tale of deceit and manipulation, of two nations locking horns in a secret confrontation that spelled doom for the stronger of the two—unless the boy from Cuzco could in some way alter the course of history. And when he did, when the adversaries were given something greater than either of them could comprehend or control, he became an anathema to both.

Whittier's manuscript was akin to a bomb in a pillow factory. It could blow Washington wide open, and if it did two names would come off that Tombstone List. Mike would see to it. His exposés had made his newspaper, The Washington Beacon, what it was, one of the few majors left and widely hailed as the most accurate and well-balanced.

If only Jim and Tricia could stay alive long enough for any of it to happen.

Chapter 8

Spaceship Grellen-6. | Earth date March 11.

The Earth projection occupied a volume of forty thousand cubits in the ship's chamber used for such analyses. Since a cubit was exactly one ten-millionth of the distance from Earth's north pole to its center, forty thousand cubits rounded out to roughly 84,000 cubic feet. Fairly small, yet adequate for the purpose. The 80-foot diameter, three-dimensional image rotated slowly there, its orientation dependent on what was being studied. Any portion of its surface could be rotated to face the observation room and then zoomed to whatever size was relevant. One could almost reach out and touch it, so realistic and faithful was its reproduction. The image could be reproduced within reason for any time period in Earth's history within the past three million years.

The ship's computer had been requested to turn off the oceans, allowing study of the eastern edge of the Caribbean plate. First Scientist Lemkala-su then zoomed in until the total West Indies chain of now-dry islands filled the chamber. He spoke aloud to his two co-scientists and Second Commander Taryn, so the history log would record all comments.

"In this area alone, three new fissures since the previous Earth revolution. The net heat gain per revolution has been two billion Earth Thermal Units." He then rotated the globe to a point farther east, centering it on the North American and African plate seam. "Here again, significant ETU increases since yesterday. Earth has not adjusted internal pressures at this rate in the past sixty thousand years, according to our records, but more core heat must still be given off before equilibrium is achieved. What is so interesting about this is the rate of correction. Their sun has stayed at its present higher energy level longer than usual, indicating a possible third-order cycle with a fundamental in terms of millions of years rather than one tenth of that."

Taryn frowned. "Yes, but I still can't understand why our original estimate predicted a far more gradual correction. We are usually so accurate in these things."

"We are deriving the sun's energy cycle from three million years of record keeping, Commander. There may be missing elements. Allow me to put up the magnetic projection."

He addressed the computer with another mental command and the projection was replaced with one of the total solar system, brought closer until only Mars occupied the chamber. It appeared to float in a silvery lake. Further zooming disclosed small ripples on the side closest to Earth.

Taryn's reaction was immediate. "Anomalies? Already?"

"Yes. Not only products of masses, but interactive magnetics as well. We cannot monitor both Earth and Mars to track both ends correctly if repositioning distorts their magnetic fields. Their fields in turn affect others, even the sun. As you know, we need to be fairly close to each planet when measuring, and even then we must distill one field from many. I suggest we request two more ships. As long as anomalies are understood, we can deal with them, but they must first be monitored."

"Two ships may not be ready on such short notice."

Lemkala-su shrugged. "If anything of Earth is to be saved, we must exercise extreme caution while moving the project ahead at what amounts to breakneck speed."

"Then I must inform Char-el," Taryn decided. "He alone has authority to request more ships." She paused, thoughtful. "He originally wanted to confront Foster at Nazca. Now we may not have that much time."

The English Channel. | Late March 11.

The freighter's course took it straight down the channel at twenty-two knots for the next three hours, while Jim coaxed the cat to within two hundred feet of the unseen hull. Tricia finally curled up under the cuddy, tethered to a lifeline, and slept for two hours. She woke to the sound of a different foghorn.

"Jim?"

"Our freighter's slowing, Kitten. There might be another ship out there in front."

"Are you all right?" *He sounds so tired.*

"I think I... I'm a lot better now that you're awake. While you were sleeping I discovered something... oh, oh... he's making a hard turn to starboard."

"You can tell that from here? I don't see a thing."

"The fluorescent wake's veering to port. That's what—"

An ear-splitting, prolongued blast from their freighter drowned him out. Somewhere distant a second horn echoed through the dense fog. Three shorter blasts from their "escort" were followed by five quick ones.

"Amazing," Jim said. "This dope goes way too fast for fog, sees something on radar, turns hard to starboard, signals his engines are running in reverse—which they're not—and tells the world he's unsure of what the *other* guy is doing. That's what those horn blasts mean if he's using COLREGS signals. The other guy... oh, oh, now he really *is* reversing. Let's get out of here or we're chop suey."

She grabbed a handhold. "Won't the other one steer out of the way?"

"Hang on!" He swung the boat hard to port, plunging through the freighter's stern wave. The cat careened onto one hull and buckets of ice cold water drenched them both, but they were out of danger for the moment. Another five horn blasts from the freighter was followed by one longer blast. There was no answer from the approaching ship. Had it veered off? The answer arrived in a series of whoops and bells, then several reddish-orange glows that lit the fog ahead. Sounds of an explosion arrived a second later, followed by Jim's moan.

"I don't believe this. Now the whole world'll come racing out here." He brought the boat about and started them toward the spot.

Tricia grabbed his arm. "Jim, what are you *doing?*"

"There could be men in the water. We're only a thousand feet away."

"But we're targets, and... Jim, stop! You've *got* to close your eyes and your mind and let things take their own course for once. That whole world coming out here is also looking for us. Please?"

"If I was one of the men in the water, babe, survival time fifteen minutes or less in this water temperature, would you come after me? We're in the middle of the channel and it's two A.M. Shore boats can't get here in time to save lives."

"But what can we do even if we... find someone?"

"We're only a few hundred feet away from where they hit. If we're not needed, we can still... oh, my God."

A muffled *whump* heralded a much brighter reddish glow above their heads in the fog dead ahead, then visible flames and the groans of a ship breaking apart.

And from the water beneath the red inferno came cries for help— directly ahead.

Hastings Coastguard. Hastings, East Sussex.

Geoff Simms had been watch officer that August night the cruise liner Norwegian Dream collided with the Ever Decent, north of Margate. The winds were light then, with good visibility, and only a few of the cruise ship passengers were shaken up. It fell to Simms to coordinate helicopter rescue of the injured, then manage everything to follow, taking statements from both skippers and filing final reports. He'd testified at the inquiry and received a commendation for his performance, even though he'd considered it his job.

This collision was different—and a mystery to boot. Pea soup fog, air temperature just above freezing, rough seas, men in the water and one of the ships exploding and splitting in two. The casualty ship was a Panamanian-registered rust bucket with a Filipino crew who'd all jumped into the drink just before the collision. They must have known their ship was doomed, which meant they also knew what it was carrying. Short of salvaging the wreck from the bottom, no one else would ever know now for sure. At least there wasn't any oil slick—yet.

The bigger ship drifted nearby with its crew still figuring out how to lower their lifeboats, not that it mattered any longer. Their damage was minimal, so they'd be on their way once the paperwork was finished. According to the captain of the larger ship, the rust bucket was doing nearly twenty knots, which in his opinion was sheer lunacy. Shore radar confirmed *he* was doing twenty-two. They were both going too fast.

Simms puffed out his cheeks. This one was the full monty. His teams reached the collision site twenty-five minutes after the first call, expecting the worst. Survival time in the water was less than half an hour even for men in top physical condition—half that if they thrashed about—yet all six of the stricken crew were found sitting huddled under a pair of dry blankets in an inflatable dinghy a hundred meters from the larger vessel. They shot off flares when they heard rescuers coming, and waved a flashlight through the fog. Other than fright and exposure, they were fine. No injuries.

Their skipper told the story on the way back to base. Three of his crew couldn't swim at all. They were clinging to one life ring, the only one they'd had time to grab, when a dark-hulled catamaran appeared out of the fog, silent as a ghost. Two guys on board wearing dark foul weather gear with hoods. They weren't even sailing... the sails were all furled. And they weren't using their outboard, either. The boat just moved around like someone was pulling it.

Anyway, one of them threw a line and two more life rings to the non-swimmers. Guy never said a word, just tossed the stuff from maybe ten feet away. Then he dumped the inflatable off the trampoline into the water and tossed its line to the skipper, like he knew who was who without asking. The dinghy had a flare gun and a packet of flares taped to it, sealed inside a plastic pouch, plus two dry blankets and a flashlight, but that wasn't all.

Anyone who'd ever tried to pull himself into an empty inflatable wearing half a ton of soaked clothes and boots would know it was damn near impossible. With muscles weak from the cold, it was *really* impossible... unless someone was in the thing first to add some counterweight on the far side. Well, that dinghy might as well have been a slab of concrete. It never tipped, never flopped, never once skittered away. Something had it pinned in place. The skipper got himself in first, then hauled in all his crew. Same thing... the dinghy never moved, not even an inch. He even stood up to do it, that's how solid it was. Once they were all in and sitting on the bottom, whatever was holding it let go. From then on, it was like any other rubber dinghy.

When the skipper looked around, the sailboat was gone.

Convinced that God had saved him and the crew—the skipper'd crossed himself when he said it—he confessed to running "stuff." The cargo hold had been rigged to explode if any of the forward hatches were forced, and the collision did exactly that. Although the ship's log went down with the stern portion, he claimed his last port was Algiers. Well, he'd supply details in due time. Not going anywhere real soon, he wasn't.

One mystery down, one to go—a sailboat where there shouldn't have been one.

Simms checked his stack of bulletins for the third time. Nah! No way could any sailboat have made it all the way from Denmark in that short a time, not that size boat. Not even half that distance. Blimey, not even a quarter! Those two terrorists couldn't be much closer than western Germany, maybe just into the Netherlands.

The Filipino skipper said the boat had a dark hull, but it could have been black or green. As for size, an inflated dinghy on the trampoline said the boat had to be at least five meters, but the skipper didn't know that either. Wouldn't even guess.

The terrorist boat was described as ten meters.

Then there was the matter of the thing moving around with sails furled and no outboard going. Absurd. Maybe the skipper had been hallucinating, or maybe the boat had an inboard... no, that wasn't possible, either. Cats that small didn't have inboard engines, and yet the boat was moving like someone was pulling it with a rope, all different directions. And that part about the dinghy being a slab of concrete, well....

The pencil Simms was tapping on the desktop sounded different. Its point had broken. He tossed it and grabbed another, resuming his nervous rhythm. It helped him think.

The boat came out of the fog within a minute or two, so it had been right there when the collision happened. Coincidence? Maybe, but why would it have been there at all? The Filipino skipper was right about that part. And the pair on board was dressed for foul weather, yes, but....

The pencil point broke again.

Ah, what was the use? If it walked like a duck and quacked like a duck, it was a bloomin' duck. It had to be those two terrorists, even if it would have taken a miracle to jump a few hundred miles of nasty ocean without a soul noticing. The distance was three hundred fifty miles, and the earliest bulletin was dated the tenth, not even two full days ago. Even if both of them spelled each other at the helm, it would mean an average speed of—he calculated it—why, seven knots for two days and nights straight, into headwinds and bone-jarring chop in the worst kind of weather. Who'd believe that? There hadn't been one sailboat of any size out in the channel at night for the past three months. And even if there was some explanation, who'd believe a pair of fugitive terrorists would follow the unwritten law of the sea to help others in distress? That only happened in books and movies, not in the real world.

There was only one way to find out. Shouldn't be that hard to pick them up. The first distress call had come in at 0205, four hours back. If they ducked back into the fog… say a quarter hour later before the SAR boats got there… it would put them about twenty miles south, maximum, *if* they stayed in the channel and didn't duck into some port along the way. With every harbor from Denmark to Gibraltar getting the same bulletins, that seemed pretty unlikely. Winds were blowing from the south at ten knots, so that would slow them down, and….

Suddenly he threw the pencil across the room and sank his face into his palms. No, there was something desperately wrong with the whole thing, tragically wrong. Those two on the sailboat were genuine folks, not terrorists. His report would show a *black*-hulled cat, length as estimated by the Filipino skipper as five or six meters. The men in the water were unable to describe their rescuers due to fog and darkness. The recovered dinghy was an Avon, used, no boat's name on it. Flashlight, flares and flare gun questionable, except the flashlight showed signs of use. Blankets—used, one binding frayed. Lines and life rings thrown to the men in the water—none of them new. Nothing was fresh from any store; nothing traceable. No lives lost, thanks to the unselfish acts of unidentified passers-by.

He read his words over twice, made a typo correction, then printed the file out and signed it. Six A.M. *Let's see, now… if this Foster's as good a sailor as I now think he is, he'll be able to move that ten meter cat at twenty knots in any reasonable seas. If he's continuing south, he'll have to tack a lot with the winds the way they are, so bring that down to fifteen knots made good. He could be past Guernsey and out into the Atlantic by… maybe nightfall. That should get him out of trouble. Nobody will look for him out there, but how the hell did he ever make it this far? The guy must be some sort of superman, the kind who never sleeps.*

᭑ᦉᦉᬒ

"You're getting the hang of it now, Wonder Woman. Turn the radar on for only one or two sweeps every ten minutes and wake me if you see any blips inside this circle here. The center of the screen is us. Otherwise, just run for the same ten minutes on one tack and ten on the other as long as the wind holds. Get me up if it changes any. Remember to turn off the radar each time after two sweeps. Every so often check GPS position against the course we set in. There are currents that could push us too close to France." He slumped onto the cushion under the cuddy, half mumbling. "If the waves get any bigger, do what I showed you and keep her in irons. We'll be safe just sitting out here as long as nothing comes inside that radar circle, or until the fog lifts. They won't send out aircraft until then. Remember, the center of the circle is us."

"You already said that. Go to sleep."

"Sure you can handle it?"

"Jim, I raced stock cars, remember? They're a little faster than this boat."

"Just the same, whenever anything goes wrong out here it's never just one thing. No pits or pit crews, no tow trucks, no spares or ambulances. We're totally on our own. No mistakes allowed. Can't let your guard down for a minute."

"We're also without our dinghy, Mr. Good Samaritan. How exactly are we going to sneak ashore now? With the life raft?"

"We won't go ashore, not until we get to the Cape Verdes. I'm afraid you'll have to...."

His voice trailed off; asleep. Now all she had to do was watch the compass and sail the boat, remember to duck the swinging boom when she changed tacks, adjust the mainsail sheet each time, but only if it was needed; check the reflecting telltales with a brief flash from her red-filtered flashlight after every tack, watch the wind direction, check on the wave heights, monitor the GPS track, turn on the radar every ten minutes and wait for one sweep, turn it back off... oh, wait, first check for any bright blips inside the innermost circle on the screen, *then* turn it off. Watch for any moving lights among the stationary ones on the distant shorelines—they might be small boats that wouldn't show up on radar. Listen for any aircraft sounds overhead—there could be helicopters out looking as soon as the fog thinned—watch the clock and wake him up when two hours had passed. Do all that in the dark, while staying awake herself. She'd had two whole hours of sleep in the past forty-eight, so keeping her eyes open seemed more of a challenge than any of the other tasks. As for something going wrong, Jim's warning words were based on his dozens of years of blue water sailing. *Whenever anything goes wrong out here, it's never just one thing.*

But he meant things like storms or engines quitting or leaks or things just breaking at the wrong times, or even getting hurt. None of that was likely. The boat was performing nicely, sailing had turned out to be easy and the waves had lost much of their punch. Everything was working just fine, so what could go wrong? And even if it did, what could possibly make it more than one thing at a time?

Chapter 9

NPA, Counterterrorism Division. Washington, D.C. | March 12.

Greenward was livid. "Whaddya mean you *had* him? Son of a bitch, Kurt, I don't want to hear you *had* him. That's not encouraging news."

"Are you done spuming all over my desk?"

"Oh. Sorry. All right." He slumped into the visitor's chair. "What's it all about?"

"They got to Ijmuiden, in Holland, and—"

"What? Stop right there. That's three times as far as they could get in the time since they left Denmark. They couldn't make a hundred miles a day if the boat had wings. I've done some of my own checking the weather conditions over there, and they're bad, my friend, extreme-*e-lee* bad. Sleet and rain, heavy seas, freezing temperatures and a ten meter cat has no cozy cabin. The North Sea's been running minimum four-foot wave heights for days now, murder for a boat that size. The channel's been fogged in for the past three days. Wind's from the south and west, shooting right in their faces if they went that way. They couldn't possibly make more than a few miles an hour heading toward the channel. You supposedly know all these things, being a sailor."

"*You* had them panicked and cowering in Copenhagen for two days at least, Howard. Then you had them heading north."

"Or west. I did mention west. You agreed he wouldn't get far that direction."

"Yeah, *thirty* miles west or a hundred miles south or north... your words. Now listen... a cat pulled into Ijmuiden last night in that same dense fog you just mentioned. The man and woman on it went by the name of Adams. That's A-D-A-M-S, Adams. Why, that's almost identical to the Adams we're looking for, right? Same spelling, same sound? This couple looked totally whipped, like they might have had a really bad time out there. The dockmaster took their names and assigned them a space *before* he got the bulletin that told him who they were, okay? Rather than alert anyone, he decided to share the bounty with a friend who'd bring a gun. They went to where the cat was tied up, only another boat was tied up in that spot, so they figured the Adams boat had gone to the marina's anchorage area. The fog was so dense you couldn't see diddly squat, anyone leaving had to go right past them, so they decided to wait until this morning. These yokels were sitting in the marina shack waiting for daybreak, a hundred feet from the exit, and never saw a thing. No idea when it happened."

"Shit!"

"Still want to insist on that thirty-mile limit, Howard?"

"How far was it?"

"Over three hundred miles."

"It had to be someone else."

"The Ijmuiden dockmaster was convinced otherwise."

"Did he get the hull color? Any of the rest of it? Boat number? Did the boat have an inflatable on it? Did he even get the hull length?"

"Nope. They don't normally look at the boat for casual overnighters, and it was pea soup fog. But look… if it *was* Foster, he's not only a magician but an exhausted one. Somehow he kept the boat moving really fast, and—"

"That's *it!* Why didn't I think of that before? That thing he used to trash the White House was a wind storm. The guy knows how to make his own wind… don't ask me how. I *told* you he was a freak. What he did was…."

"Your logic leaves me breathless with admiration, bridgeplayer."

"I was *going* to say he made his own wind, but that still wouldn't get him past the wave heights. All he'd have done was plow into them faster and harder. He still couldn't make any time. Call it a hundred miles in twenty-four hours, except he'd never last that long. When did they pull into the marina?"

"Night of the eleventh."

"And they left Denmark around daybreak on the tenth. Almost forty hours? No man can take that kind of punishment that long. They holed up somewhere after they left Denmark. Look, if I had to do that same run under those conditions in an open *speedboat* ten meters long, it would take me probably fifteen hours at least, and then I'd need a week with a chiropractor to recover. There is no way any sailboat can do what you're telling me, not even in the best of conditions. Waves are the problem. Our birds are still in Denmark."

"Thanks for the lesson. So it wasn't Foster."

"Foster was nowhere near that port. He's got to be somewhere inside a circle a hundred miles from... where'd they start from?"

"Esbjerg. Denmark, case you forgot."

"From Esbjerg, then, any direction. Draw that circle on the map and he'll be in it. Keep looking, and make it count next time." On his way out, Greenward tossed a final insult over his shoulder. "No more of this impossible dream stuff. Don Quioxote you're not."

Kurt stared after the departing figure. *Oh, I'll certainly call you, Mr. Greenward, sir, providing my information is one hundred percent proven, but now that your expert opinion on sailing catamarans has been put forth you certainly wouldn't want to hear about two freighters colliding in the English Channel last night, not that far from Ijmuiden. The details wouldn't fit your contrived bridge hand.*

Contrived was the word for it. Nobody in the Winfield camp thought Foster operated out of Russia, because they'd found him in Bermuda, racing sailboats days *after* Las Vegas. In that case, who found him? Who knew he was there? If he'd been working with the Russians long before that, how and when did Greenward learn it? Was that contrived?

How about Ben Howland, who supposedly fingered Foster as the mastermind behind Yellowstone? That was according to Greenward, yet Howland wasn't allowed visitors other than family. How did that information get transmitted? More bridge hand stuff? Maybe it was time for a little research on Clarence Towers' Special Projects director, starting with Howland.

A few minutes of computer time produced a different picture. Ben Howland had indeed been under intense guard since his incarceration. Those having access to Howland did not include Greenward, or even Clarence Towers. Code names Icarus and Daedalus became household words *after* Howland was caught, but Helios, Foster's alleged code name, was never mentioned once. Greenward implied that the Helios codename was common knowledge to all those "in the loop." Not according to Google.

Catch me in one lie, catch me in another.

A check on Howard Greenward's itinerary for the past month placed him in Athens on the first through the third of March, attending a convention on—what the hell?—biochemical countermeasures? Greenward had no expertise in that field, so how was he vetted, and by whom? There'd been a similar gathering in Chicago three months earlier, and Towers had sent two specialists to that one. Why send anyone to Athens at all? There'd be nothing gained.

What about Howard's trip report? The routine paper form was filed under the general heading "Countermeasures." Conference proceedings were attached with a lazy paper clip. Who'd have thought to look there instead of under chemical or biochemical, or even WMD? And how long was the paper clip intended to hold the two together? Was Howard hoping they'd become separated? The trip's purpose was left blank, but under NOTES, Greenward commented on the keynote speaker's presentation and the value of the conference. No conclusions or recommendations.

The whole trip had been a yawner, yet the day following his return he was up on his Mudslinger soap box, pitching reasons for naming Foster and girl to the Tombstone List. Not one mention of his Athens trip during that tirade. The London subway bombing happened on the second of March, so maybe that eclipsed the conference and motivated him to risk bringing out the Russian thing, but it couldn't have been the original reason for his trip. The Athens conference began a day before the subway attack.

Why wasn't Greenward's itinerary sent down to Counterintelligence prior to the trip, and why was his trip report filed in such an oblique manner? Something about the Athens conference was all wrong. It was that old axiom again: *nothing could be assumed true until exhaustive efforts to prove it false failed.* So… go ahead and prove it false.

Iason Georgios was the conference organizer. Ten minutes after a call to the Greek embassy, Georgios was on the phone.

"By any chance, sir, did you meet with our Howard Greenward during the conference? One of his expressed hopes was to talk with you, I believe."

Georgios took a long time answering. He spoke haltingly, although in excellent English. "I believe I did *see* Mr. Greenward… once or twice during the early sessions, yes... but we did not speak. Not at all. As I recall, Mr. Greenward's chair was empty for most of the proceedings."

Empty? "Perhaps he was standing somewhere?"

"Not possible. Everyone was seated. He did not attend the keynote dinner either. I thought perhaps he was ill."

"Would you happen to remember in which sessions his chair was empty?"

There was another long pause. "After the middle of the first day, I did not see Mr. Greenward at all."

Kurt drummed his fingers on the desk blotter. Greenward had been there for half the first day and absent all the rest. His trip report commented on the keynote address, but that was given at the dinner he didn't attend.

Catch me in one lie, catch me in another.

Clarence Towers' weekly tirades were often about failing to share information, yet the Greenward trip seemed to be a secret. Was it secret to Towers as well? Trip reports were to be disseminated to all department heads, not filed away. Who'd even know about the report, filed as it was? And what about the Russian document itself? What about Clarence dismissing O'Dell as no big deal? *Clarence is in his office. Call him. Ask him yourself if you doubt me.*

How different things looked once the seeds of doubt were sown. Greenward was hiding something, *or* Greenward and Towers together. Time for another computer search. Mr. Greenward traveled on a diplomatic passport. It was a long shot, but if he'd left Athens any time during those three days there'd be a trail of some sort. First, a check with the U.S. embassy in Athens to see if he'd made the required check-in there. He hadn't? Not even by phone? Okay, then how about the airlines?

The English Channel. | March 13, 5:00 A.M.

The wind tip-toed around to blow from the north, sneaking up on her. She'd eased the mainsheet every few minutes until the boom was all the way to port, only to have it come slamming across to starboard with a tremendous *bang* when the wind gusted. The accidental gybe wrecked her confidence even as it woke her up. However, the fog was thinning out with the shift and the distant horizon was beginning to show tiny lights here and there. Time to drop sail, check the GPS and compass, then record their location with a circled dot on the channel chart. They'd gone only twenty miles in nearly three hours, but at least Jim was getting some rest. He'd never stirred, despite the tremendous noise. She could hold out for awhile longer.

They were mid-channel south of Hastings on the English side, and it was sleeting again. She was adjusting her goggles when she noticed a white light moving across the distant shore. Another boat? She watched for a moment, then decided to turn on the radar. The first sweep showed a small blip where she thought it would. One more sweep would show the blip's heading and speed. Oh, no! She switched the radar off.

"Jim, wake up!" She shook him. "Someone's coming at us really fast."

He was on his feet immediately, clutching the cuddy for support and shaking away the brain cobwebs. "What's the situation? How many?"

"One, coming fast and straight at us from almost west. Wind has clocked to the north, seas two feet, skies overcast, it's sleeting, and the time is five-twenty A.M. I dropped sail twenty minutes ago."

"Good girl. I see their lights now. Probably one of their big search and rescue types." He flicked the radar on. "I knew it would be the Brits when it happened, not the French. Hmm... ten miles. Plenty of time." He switched the set off again.

"How'd you know it wouldn't be from the French side? It's closer."

"They're on vacation. Okay, take the helm. That boat is coming for us."

She traded places while he began lashing the main. "Jim, how can the French be on vacation? It's the middle of winter."

"They're always on vacation. It's the only thing they do well."

"I see a searchlight. What are we going to do?"

"Reason with them."

"What?"

He braced himself against the cuddy and faced the oncoming lights. In a moment they'd disappeared, including the searchlight. She strained to see anything at all, then realized that all the shore lights on the British side were blotted out as well. Someone had painted a swath of black across everything. She stifled her surprise while Jim continued to stare at the blank space. Finally he nodded, reaching over to turn on the radar once more. He watched for two sweeps and switched it off a second time.

"They decided we weren't worth the risk. Remember the wind I made at Grace Botanical? That's what just happened to them, except they were whacked all the harder because they weren't prepared. Whoever was on deck manning that searchlight got a real lesson in why it pays to keep one hand on the boat at all times. They're probably fishing him out of the water right now. I'll keep everything churned up between us and them, and that'll keep them occupied."

"Won't they use their radar?"

He stared at the dark slice of shoreline. "It won't work while they're bouncing around. When they finally do take another look, I have another bit of magic in store for them. We have another hour of darkness before we have to be really careful of who else sees us. This is the Strait of Dover. It's narrow, dangerous and we don't want to be caught here."

"They'll radio to someone, won't they?"

"Maybe, but we were just a weak radar blip. They may have thought we were a small boat in trouble, but not for us to wait around and find out. I'll keep a storm raging between us and the English coastline, changing the wind every few minutes so it comes at them from another direction. In the meantime, with these wave heights and no headwind, we can fly. I'll take over and you watch that area."

He turned his focus on the water ahead and the wind increased until it was whistling in the rigging. The only other sounds were those of a drummer using steel brushes on the drumhead. *Sh… sh… sh shhh… sh… sh.*

"What's that sound?"

"Dagger boards and rudders slicing through the wave tops. She's really stable. The tunnel between these two hulls must be almost perfect. I wonder if?... Damn, it works!"

"What?"

"I'm using the trampoline like a wing to keep the prow from rising or dipping." He squinted into the space ahead, and the drum whisk sounds stopped. "We're completely out of the water on my monorail, and she's still stable. Blow me down, let's try that again." He eased the speed down, and the drum whisk sounds returned. "I know what's happening now. I'm pushing on all the stern surfaces and mast with the same force everywhere. All I really need to do is keep us from taking off... or taking a dive. Understand what I'm saying?"

"Don't forget the storm you're making behind us."

"That part'll run by itself. We need to be ten miles farther away before they take another look. At that range a fiberglass boat with one skinny mast is as good as any stealth aircraft, especially on a choppy sea."

🙰

"Bloody hell!"

Willy Lang's one-handed snatch at the lifeline was too late. The initial blast tossed the 28-foot rigid inflatable like a balsawood toy in a bathtub. Lang was in the drink before he had time to draw a breath, and the boat's hull came crashing down on him.

Inside the craft, Tim Dowling was slammed against the port side framing with so much force he dislocated a shoulder. Dowling was the senior man, but he could do no more than grab on with his good arm. Andy Cooper was the luckiest of the three. His glasses broke in half and he banged a knee, but he could still function and was now in command. This time it was real, not some training session. He had one man in the water, another incapacitated and a gale-force wind blowing foam and lather all over the windscreens and into the cabin. No way to see out.

Tim rolled over on the cabin sole. "Shut down the outboards, Coop, and radio in. Willy's out there in the drink."

Cooper was surprised when base reported no more than a few knots of wind. "We got a bloomin' 'urricane out here," he barked. "Tim's hurt and Willy's in the soup, can't see 'im. Can't maneuver until I do. Send out the big boat. Watch for Willy. Over."

"On our way. We can't see a thing on radar. Must be a patch of unstable air, so watch out for waterspouts. Over."

"Roger that." Andy was about to hook the mike back in place when the boat lurched again. Tim was on his feet by then. He almost went down a second time, but had his hand in a strap.

"I see Willy's strobe," he shouted above the din outside. "Starboard."

"Good Lord, he's 'alf a kick distant."

"Friggin' storm's pushin' us away. I can handle the boat once I get me shoulder back in." Tim braced himself against the cabin frame and gave his torso a violent twist, whacking against the metal. It didn't work. He braced once again, pulling his bad arm across his chest with the good one, and laid into the frame with a vengeance. The surge of new pain brought a howl, but it worked. He was able to move the arm a bit without help, and took over command. "Where's Willy now?"

"Off over there. I'll fetch a ring. You sure you can—"

"Get on with it and start the outboards. I'm okay."

When the second boat got there, Willy was shivering on the cabin sole, wrapped in a blanket and Tim's arm was tucked inside the black triangle sling that was part of the emergency first aid gear. He was still the senior man, so he ordered both boats rafted. The storm died just as they finished that task, but off to their east it raged on. The big boat had a more sophisticated weather radar, so they watched it on that. The freak storm had enough rain in it to be seen, but the shape was weird: a column roughly five miles across and stretching way up. Then something really bright appeared just about in the middle.

"That's a bloomin' waterspout," Tim groaned. "And look... there's another, a big one right where we had that little blip pegged. There'll be nothing but tiny scraps left of the thing if one of those twisters 'its it."

"What was it? Did you ever find out?"

"Nope. It was moving real slow when we were watching it on base radar, then it stopped. No radio contact, nothing at all. No lights we could see with the big telescope. We got that container ship and a pair of tankers heading down-channel. It was right in their path."

Cooper pointed at the screen. "The storm's moving south, Tim, and it's wider than before. I don't get it. I thought spouts only happened in hot weather."

"Well, don't think that way no more." He checked his watch—half past six. "We'd best separate and head over that way… mindful of the 'spouts, of course… and look for bodies in the water. Don't expect to find anything until full daylight." He twisted his mouth. "Don't expect to find anything at all."

Chapter 10

Cumberland, Maryland. | 5:30 A.M., March 13.

Cavanaugh's Bed and Breakfast was dark except for a small upstairs window toward the back, maybe a bathroom or hallway. Mike's instructions were to ring the doorbell, that someone would be there, but surely there'd be more lights than just that one. Could something have gone wrong, Ollie wondered? An elderly man with a quavering voice opened the door, introduced himself as Arthur Beale and pointed toward a front room where Mike, looking haggard, sat at a long table.

"How'd it go?" he asked. "Any problems?"

"None, except for jet lag. Whittier was relieved we're going to do something. He admires your courage and sends his best."

"Sit down, sit down. We don't have much time before I have to get out of here. Rumor has it I was spotted last night in a suburb of Waukegan, but it won't take them long to discover it's a ruse. I've got my lawyer, Manny Friedman, running interference on the phone and my double hopping around the country posing as me, sometimes using my credentials, sometimes his. He's an old army buddy. Media hounds are tripping over each other trying to catch up."

"Sounds like you've done this before."

"Right, except someone is feeding information to the papparazi within minutes of Manny's phone calls. They're out to trap me. How much do you know about Kurt Stauf? He wants to talk to me in private. Coffee?" He gestured toward a pot.

"I'm okay. He's counterterrorism, of course. Handles maybe two hundred in his department. I don't know him beyond his name and a few things I've heard."

"Would he be the one who put Jim and Tricia on the list?"

"Probably his department, yes, but I'd be surprised if he was the one behind it. He'd probably demand a ton of proof first. Why does he want to talk to you?"

"Exactly. Why?"

"Shoot, *nothing* happens at the NPA without Towers' blessing, so it's possible he directed Stauf to contact you."

"They expected the worst from me, it's been a week and I haven't peeped. Did *anyone* tumble to your trip? See anyone you recognized, anyone suspicious?"

"Not one. I kept checking."

"The NPA avoids me like the plague unless they're harassing me or my staff. Suddenly this guy wants to meet me—off the record—at a place of *my* choosing. He leaves a cryptic message at The Beacon, sealed in a double envelope that reaches my lawyer. That kind of thing always goes to Manny, but why the subterfuge?" He exhaled through puffed cheeks. "What did Whittier send back? Anything we can use?"

"This." The manuscript landed with a thud. "Three hundred pages, single spaced. He wrote it right after his showdown with President Winfield and Greenward. Said he kept records from the moment he went on that Las Vegas committee. Every name we could want is in there."

Mike closed the manuscript twenty minutes later, almost smiling. "It's good, Ollie. It's dynamite, the kind of stuff governments don't want known. Everything in here tells me Greenward's sitting on the original document. Maybe he shows it to Towers or maybe he just talks about it, but secrecy is suddenly out the window. Why? What's different now? A mysterious tornado nearly wrecks the White House and makes the Mudslinger famous, but nobody knows exactly what happened or even if there was some alien entity in the picture. Winfield's White House kinda sorta goes along with the UFO theory back then, but Brewster is at the helm these days. The alien personality is now called out as James Foster. It should have caused an small eruption over on The Hill, but nothing happens. Why again? A gag order from the Oval Office? It would fit Brewster's management style, but he knows only what he's told by the last one who whispered in his ear. He was never in the original picture. I think I just might dangle a few of Whittier's choicest items under Towers' nose and threaten to disclose the rest to Congress."

"What about your side of the picture, Mike? Does what you know jibe with what Whittier wrote?"

"Except for one thing. Those army commandos entering the Grace property did so expecting to engage Russian special forces called *spetsnaz*, That implies high-level G-2, since spetsnaz do not announce themselves. Someone in the Winfield party knew all about everything going on, and I say it was Greenward. We need to know a lot more about this link between him and the Howland arson-murder case. Any ideas?"

"How about Harry Archer, Greenward's nephew?"

"He's FBI. They haven't been particularly friendly to me over the years."

"You might change your mind about him. I sure did. I can be in Salt Lake City this afternoon." He picked up the manuscript. "Do you have a copier here? Once he reads this he'll know where we are and where we're going."

The English Channel. | Afternoon, March 13.

Tricia came awake with a start. "Where are we?"

"Ten miles off the southern end of Guernsey. The fog is back big time, but we're sailing west the normal way. While you were sleeping I tuned in some marine radio bands, and guess what? A small craft was reported destroyed by a huge waterspout right where we were a few hours ago. No debris or survivors. Isn't that the strangest thing? A waterspout in the middle of winter? Lucky it wasn't us. Mother Nature is not something to fool with when you're in open water, Trish. Remember that."

She managed a half-way grin. "We're finally out of danger?"

"Just leveled the playing field for awhile. I also tuned into the BBC's Top Ten Terrorist daily update, and we were the first names read. We're supposedly trapped inside a circle a hundred fifty miles from Esbjerg."

"They think we're way back there and still you say we're in danger?"

"We need to be five hundred miles away from land before we're relatively safe. We can hope to pull in behind another freighter when it's dark." He leaned back and put a foot up on the wheel. "Trish, I've been doing some thinking… about what Charlie did to us."

"You said forget Charlie. And you also said we had to be in South America or Australia before we were relatively safe. That just came down to five hundred miles. Is this Charlie changing your mind?"

"Charlie has nothing to do with my perception of our safety. No, these are my thoughts this time. I've spent a lot of time on the ocean."

"Have you forgotten those fortune cookies and the way our purchases totaled out? Do you realize how many impulsive last-minute items we both bought? I even put some things back and took others in their place without knowing why. It was all so the numbers would come out, meaning that he was making us buy exactly the right things in the right quantities. Are you sure he's not working your mind right now? You've gone full circle. How many caffeine pills have you taken since Esbjerg?"

"Can't tell about the mind part, but I'm thinking we need a new game plan. What do we know about the enemy, as your father would say? Help me put the picture together. For openers, let's assume we've been missing something and try to figure out what it is."

"Well, they know we're in Europe because of that London thing."

"They *think* they know. The London bombing happened March third, and we flew to Copenhagen on the fourth. Could that ridiculous customs agent in Helsinki have reported us?"

"Wouldn't they'd have intercepted us in Denmark if he had?"

"We got there ahead of the news releases, Trish, plus he could have reported us later, but that London Times described our boat and had us traveling under the Adams name, so Madsen must have reported the sales tax the very day he got our money. Damn! Why didn't he wait a few weeks? They probably knew exactly when we left the dock at Esbjerg, too. God, I'm tired. Can't even think. What day did we leave?"

"Tuesday, the tenth, but the BBC just said we were still *back* there close to where we started, and the other European stations are probably saying the same thing. Wouldn't that mean we weren't discovered in Ijmuiden after all? Except… except that we stopped to help those sailors last night, and I guess that ruined everything. Forget it."

"That collision was in the newscasts, too, but no mention of us. Not even about some sailboat happening by. If anyone suspected we were involved in that, they'd have come roaring after us. And whoever was on that patrol boat this morning couldn't have identified us either, not even as to what kind of boat was destroyed and sunk, so we've dodged the bullet for now. Thanks to the BBC, we're too far south for anyone to make the connection, but there's bad news, too. Two terrorists on the Tombstone List were murdered by their old German landlady. It's all over the news, including her new status as a millionaire, and that'll encourage others to be bolder. We'll have to watch for all sorts of possibilities now."

"She *shot* them?"

"Baked them cookies with something in them, they didn't say what. Maybe rat poison. Now she's a celebrity for the moment, but her story will inspire others and now we'll see a wave of murders that'll turn out wrong... mistaken identities or gun battles where the good guys finish six feet under. It's getting more serious by the hour, but I've been thinking... since we're out of danger, what say we head for the Mediterranean?"

"*Out* of danger? Jim, you just said we weren't, that we had to be five hundred miles from land. When they don't find us in northern Europe, who says they won't expand their search farther south? I won't feel safe until we're a *lot* farther away, like South Africa or Australia. Besides, there aren't any boa constrictors or crocodiles in the Mediterranean, and I had my heart set on that part."

"The key to safety is to act like we're someone else. If that Helsinki customs guy did report us they'll be looking for Emilio and Maria Cruz. If it was Madsen's doing, then Arthur Adams and unnamed boating companion. We just go back to being Luis and Maria Amaru. We've never used those names this side of the Atlantic. We'll speak in Quechua when anyone's around, maybe broken English, but never Spanish. In fact, I vote we work our way back to Greece again, by way of Italy... this time Genoa and that area. There's a fabulous restaurant in Boccadasse... Vittorio al Mare, tucked right underneath a church on a cliff that looks down on the Mediterranean. You're only fifty feet above the water. So many other places I haven't shown you. When we reach Greece, we'll cruise all the smaller islands we've never seen, plus hop over to Crete and Rhodes. They've always fascinated me. Then maybe we can make it to Cyprus and end up in Egypt. Have you ever seen the pyramids?"

"Darling—"

"If we act the part, we'll be seen that way. Look, we're not far now from Jersey. I know it's a stone's throw from there to France, but Jersey's protected by the U.K. and it's self-governing. I've been there. We can tie up at one of the private fishing quays, catch up on our sleep, then hop down to Portugal."

"This is really your idea, Jim? It's not Charlie doing this to your head?"

"Charlie's farthest from my mind. You just pointed out that they have us located way north, and here we'd be where they least expect us. They know we're on a sailboat and couldn't average more than eighty to a hundred miles a day in the very best of conditions. Slogging into head winds in the middle of winter with sleet, fog and rain and heavy seas is... what made you think it's Charlie?"

"The way you just rattled off those places, like that Italian restaurant, and Crete and Rhodes... well, it just didn't sound like you. You're usually much more deliberate. I'm suspicious, that's all."

He suddenly released the mainsheet, letting the sail flog.

"Hand me the binoculars, babe. There's something in the water ahead of us. It's... wait a minute... oh, oh...." He lowered the glasses. "It's another sailboat... I think. The fog's heavy, but it looks like just the hull. The rigging's all dragging in the water. She's been dismasted and she's directly in our path."

Tricia got to her feet. "I see it, too. This is unbelievable. There's not another thing out here, and it looks like someone just planted that mess directly in front of us. What are the chances of that happening?"

"Billions to one. Wait... oh, no. No! There's someone on it."

"*What?* Let me see."

"Incredible! First a tanker collision, now this? Here, have a look."

She focused the optics a bit. "It's a man, and he's waving." She heard a groan behind her.

"We're obligated to pick him up, Trish. If anyone was with him there may have to be a search, and that means calling for help. That wreck didn't just happen. It wasn't anything I did last night. If it had a wood mast, it's likely the hull was holed before he could cut the thing free, which means the whole mess could sink any moment. He could also be hurt."

"He doesn't seem hurt. Why would a wood mast make any difference?"

"Wood floats. The mast is still attached to the boat, but it becomes a spear when those shrouds go taut. Snap, back it comes like a battering ram, and *wham*, a big hole right at the waterline."

"Maybe we should change over to our Amaru names now, before we reach him? Call me Maria and I'll call you Luis."

His hand suddenly went to his forehead, and he closed his eyes. "I… guess so. Yes, you're right. Something doesn't feel… so woozy."

"You've had four hours of sleep in four days, and nothing but catnaps and caffeine the rest of the time. I can't understand why you're still on your feet."

"That's not it. Something else. I… I'll be all right. I think."

She kept the binoculars focused. The survivor looked to be in his mid-thirties, with a shock of black hair and teeth that must have made some orthodontist rich. "He doesn't seem hurt."

"Not hurt, and not a sailor either. No PFD, not even a life ring. Yep, it's a wood mast all right, sticking out of his starboard side. I'm coming alongside. Uncoil that half-inch Dacron line and toss it to him. Secure it first the way I showed you, rabbit down the hole."

She nodded. A quick bowline around the canopy support and she was ready at the starboard side of the cross deck. Minutes later the boat's sole occupant was aboard, looking a bit haggard and extremely red-faced, but otherwise okay. His first act was to shake Jim's gloved hand with his bare one. "Oh, my gracious, am I ever grateful you came along. I had the willies I'd be run down by some freighter or something."

Jim nodded. "Or sink, I'd say, from the looks. Anyone else with you? Anyone hurt?"

"All by meself. Headstay popped. Thought I was belly-up."

"When did it happen?"

"In the night. Oh, my…." He sagged against the cuddy, sliding down like a squirrel on a slippery pole. Tricia darted over, easing him down onto the pile of blankets and sleeping bags.

"He's ice cold, Jim. He's also *out* cold."

"Hypothermia. Roll him up in blankets and dig out some more hand warmers. Stuff them around him and close off everything except a breathing hole. And bring up two of those brandy nips from the medicine chest."

She disappeared below, returning half a minute later. "How many warmers should I use?"

"Five each side. Funny, while you were below my weird feeling disappeared. Maybe it's adrenaline. Not every day you pick up someone moments before his boat goes down, which that tub is going to do any moment now. And there it goes… gone."

She was on her knees, tearing open the packets and placing them next to the frigid body. "I was about to tell you the same thing, about feeling different. Something just washed over me, and now I feel almost rested."

"There's something very screwy about all this. That boat was a derelict that should never have been out here, a wood relic with rusty galvanized wire rigging. I got a look at its underside just now and it actually looked rotten. Hasn't seen paint in years. Our friend here is out in the channel without gloves or passable clothing in the worst kind of winter weather. One heavy sweater, and that's it. Furthermore, he's dry and the boat was full of water."

She looked up, palm against the man's forehead. "That's not all that's screwy. He's not cold any longer." She checked his hands and neck. "He was ice cold and now he's warm as toast, but the warmers aren't working yet. Everything else is cold except for him."

The toasty-warm creature suddenly stirred, then sat up and immediately clawed his coverings off. "Oh my, oh my, I'm so sorry. I must have winked out there, but there's nothing to be alarmed about. Not at all. I'm fine now." He was on his feet in a flash, smiling as if nothing at all had happened. "Much obliged for the rescue. My boat…." He glanced sideways, then at Jim. "She went down?"

"Seconds ago. Where were you heading?"

"Over to Jersey, to St. Helier, actually. Oh, thank you." He gratefully accepted both of the brandy nips Tricia offered, twisting off the cap on one and hoisting the small bottle for a obligatory moment, then downing the contents with a pair of gulps.

Jim, looking puzzled, waited until the man finished swallowing. "You were lucky, my friend. Did you set out from Guernsey?"

"England. Plymouth, actually. It didn't seem all that far, you see, and—"

"You were trying to sail from Plymouth to Jersey in *that*? In March? In the channel?"

"Yes, yes, she was a bit of a relic, I admit. Serves me right for being hasty, but I was doing just fine until that stay let go."

"What made you take such a chance?" Tricia asked. "What was so important in Jersey that you had to risk your life?"

"Well…" He paused long enough to toss away the cap on the second brandy nip and down the contents. "Ahhh. That warms me insides. Well, truth be known, I planned to just stop there just briefly, you see. Then on to Portugal and into the Mediterranean and Greece by way of Italy… Genoa, all that area. There's this fabulous restaurant in Boccadasse, Vittorio al Mare, tucked underneath a church, you know, built right into a cliff. You can look right down on the Mediterranean from just fifty feet above the water. So many other places I wanted to see. I was going to cruise all the smaller islands after that. Crete and Rhodes have always fascinated me, and then my plan was to cross over to Cyprus and end up in Egypt. How about you, Mr. Amaru? Have you ever seen the pyramids?" He smiled, draining the last of the brandy. "Maria?"

Tricia turned with one eyebrow raised. She looked stunned.

"Yeah, babe, it's what you're thinking."

"Something I said?" the stranger asked, smiling like a cherub. He ran a hand through his jet black hair, showing the rows of perfect teeth.

"You could put it that way… Charlie."

Salt Lake City. Utah. | March 13.

Harry Archer closed the manuscript, shaking his head. "This is almost too hot to handle, Ollie. According to Whittier, we were literally facing extinction as a nation, yet nobody in government was told. What does that say?"

"That Winfield couldn't trust anyone."

"Or *thought* he couldn't, or was assured he couldn't by someone close to him."

"Uncle Greenward?"

"Howard was Winfield's personal advisor and lifelong friend up to that point. He had more influence with H.J. Winfield than anyone else. Knowing him as I do, he'd have spun this Russian ultimatum into the scariest scenario possible, every negative he could think up. The Yellowstone mess is a great example. Howland tries to turn the country into a raging inferno so he can destabilize government and take over as a dictator. He's a certifiable nut, but no sooner is he jailed—thanks to one Ollie Robinson—than *someone* in Washington works it so the blame falls on Jim Foster, a.k.a. Mudslinger, and the media runs with it. Why? Howland is guilty of treason and arson, but overnight he's turned into a pawn in a much larger international plot. A fictitious multi-billionaire with tentacles into every terrorist organization known is behind the whole shebang. Nobody cares that the whole Mudslinger concept is comic-book crazy. I thought at the time that it was just normal media hype, but Whittier's manuscript here has changed my view. Uncle turned on Foster same as he does all those he can't manipulate, his sister—my mother—being one. He maneuvered Winfield after Las Vegas as sure as you're sitting there, but my question is whether it was only his doing, or were others involved? Are they involved even now? Did Jim Foster unwittingly appear in time to spoil someone's ambitions last July, and where in fact does Howland really fit? Why is his high crime being watered down until it seems he's the victim? Why is no one talking about Sleck, caught sitting in a truck with two hundred eighty bodies?"

"You're describing a conspiracy."

"Right. Howland was the darling of his party though he'd never declared himself a candidate. What if some covert group behind Howland was carving a clear path to the White House by removing political obstacles? What if the owls were part of a mass destabilization program aimed at destroying confidence in the administration? The problem with conspiracies, Ollie, is that if they're successful at all, they're also invisible. Back when I was doping out the real purpose of the owls, I wondered who I could trust with what I knew was a major terrorist threat. I might be blundering into the very group behind the thing, including my own organization, and I certainly couldn't take my message to the White House or anyone associated with the president."

"You really thought it could have been any of *them?*"

"Ollie, you would not believe the things we know about people who run this country. Secret organizations, billionaires, mega-corporations, foreign interests, all dictating how things are to be done. What congressional bills are to pass, what foreign policy we follow, secrets to hand over to our enemies in return for political favors and support, even which people to murder when the stakes are high enough. Our visible government is nothing more than the tip of a decidedly rotten iceberg. This manuscript of Whittier's hints at some of it, but the scary part is that Jim actually saved our asses—more than once—and certain powers wanted him dead almost immediately, back then and now. What secret group is behind it? Is my uncle a member? Is he a leader?"

"Shoot, now I—"

"Are we *sure* the assassination attempt on Jim and Whittier in Bermuda wasn't our own people, directed by such a group? Are we certain those attackers behind Grace Botanical were really Russian spetsnaz? That information came from the Oval Office. Who checked it? How would *you* check it? The thing had Top Secret all over it. Who really sent in Woody's Warriors at exactly the right time to thwart the Grace attack, and why?"

"Someone knew there'd be an attack, and knew precisely when, down to the minute."

"That's right, *someone* knew, but it was a Winfield-Greenward show at that point. Maybe the plan was to eliminate Whittier and Foster right then, but something went wrong and the original raiders had to be taken out instead. What about Gene Pelletier, the spy? Who planted him at Stanford Research, and when? Was he really an agent for the Russians… or might it have been for some secret group like the one I'm describing? That seems to point to collusion with the Russians prior to Las Vegas, doesn't it? How many more like Pelletier are there right now? The owls were a highly developed weapon system, but *whose* weapon system? What if the destruction of Las Vegas had been financed by the same group backing Howland, with the same purpose in mind… namely to drive the country into a panic so certain parties could take over? How does Sleck fit into all this?"

Ollie sighed. "Sleck worked both sides of the street, did'ja know that? I guess you did, but Mike O'Dell says your uncle was talking to Sleck several times in the months leading up to the Yellowstone fires."

Harry stared into his coffee for a long moment. "Howard claimed nobody ever came to the estate any longer, yet there were three ash-trays on stands in his library, all smelling of recent cigar and cigarette ash. He doesn't smoke, Ollie. He also had a giant, pull-down projec-tion screen recessed into the ceiling plus an elaborate projection sys-tem, installed recently. I know because the ceiling plaster hadn't been repainted. Poked around a bit and found twenty brand new folding chairs inside a closet. He already had half a dozen stuffed chairs in the room, enough for casual visitors. Who were these others for? How about a twenty-four cubic foot fridge in the same room, part of what I'd call a well-equipped bar. Two rooms away is his kitchen, with an-other huge fridge in it. Why the first one and not something smaller? How about a newly paved parking area laid out to handle eight cars side by side? Or six fully equipped guest rooms, each with a well-stocked fridge? All six fridges were cold and running."

"But no one ever goes there."

"Access to his property is totally controlled, fifteen TV monitors, each focused on part of a fence that's totally electrified, with barbed wire along the top. One entrance to the property, fully automated and controlled from the house. What's he hiding? Who's been there be-sides Marvin Sleck? Conclusion—members of some secret group with an agenda. Sleck's visits there seem to tie that agenda into Howland and his owls."

Ollie toyed with his spoon. "You think these people were backing Howland's insane plan to take over the country?"

"It's a real possibility, but with no way to prove it."

"Shoot, Harry, this implicates your uncle as a mass murderer."

"Why doesn't that surprise me? Getting back to Mike, what's he going to do with this manuscript?"

"He plans to confront President Brewster, Clarence Towers, Kurt Stauf and Greenward in a private, closed session. Failing that, he'll send copies to a couple dozen congressmen, maybe a few in the media."

"Stop him! Get to him and tell him to hold up on any meeting. We need to—"

"I can't. He's meeting Stauf tonight after midnight in a cemetery."

"Who asked for the meeting?"

"Stauf. He set the time, no reason given. Mike picked the place. His wife is buried there."

Harry paled. "My God. Mike could be walking into an ambush!"

Chapter 11

English Channel. | March 13.

As soon the rescued man heard "Charlie," he smiled.

"Tricia gave me that name not many days ago. 'We have to call the intruder something. Why not Charlie?' I'd planned a different kind of meeting, but the London subway bombing has changed everyth—"

"If you had anything to do with that subway thing, spit it out," Jim growled.

"Yes, well, the perpetrator was your nemesis, Howard Greenward, who contrived the hoax to put you on the Tombstone List. When he succeeded, I was forced to restructure our meeting this way."

"How did you come to know that? Who told you?"

"Well, how did I know you and Tricia were in Lahti? Or precisely where to meet you out here in the channel? You see—"

"Answer the question," Jim snapped. "You were never in danger of sinking, right?"

"Correct."

"And your hypothermia was faked," Tricia added.

"On the money as well. You may have noticed the sea calming just before you spotted me. That was so you'd not wonder why I hadn't sunk. The fog's return was mine as well, so that I could steer you to me without being seen from a distance. And as long as I'm confessing, I should say that I gave you both an energy boost just minutes ago, enough to hold you for another six hours. That's why you both felt suddenly different. In Jim's case, he said he felt woozy."

Tricia swallowed hard. "You did all that... with your *mind?*"

"I'll explain everything because I want you both to know. However, it would be best that we head immediately for St. Helier. No one is out here to see you skimming along on your monorail, and it will be quite dark when we get there. We'll get better acquainted over dinner at the Moorings, there at the foot of Mont Orgueil Castle, and after that you must both catch up on much-needed sleep."

"Let's get something straight," Jim snapped. "Anything beyond my booting you onto the St. Helier dock depends on what this is all about, so start talking right now. You damn well know we're not about to risk a restaurant or show our faces in public, so forget the baloney."

"Yet you were all for heading straight into the Mediterranean, remember? Visiting restaurants like Vittorio al Mare?"

"Your words. You were bending our minds."

"You found the thought acceptable, Jim, even pleasant. See here, we can all be dining together at the Moorings in an hour, also pleasant and much needed in your case. I can get us there in a fraction of that time, but you're doing well with your monorail. Take a moment to consider what you already know about me, starting with Lahti."

The answer was a long time in coming. Jim finally nodded. "Point made. So I take it we'd have met you no matter where we sailed. What's your real name, anyway?"

"Charlie's fine. Back in Copenhagen, you said I couldn't be human. For all you knew I could be somewhere in outer space, so you'd already made me an alien at that time. Aliens should be allowed a few liberties, don't you think?" He smiled again, but Jim's voice was suddenly husky.

"*Are* you an alien?"

"A visitor here, yes. My home planet, as yet undiscovered by your astronomers, exists in the Rigel Kentaurius system, but I've spent most of my life here on Earth. I must—"

Tricia cut him off. "All right, I've heard enough. Where are you *really* from and why were you sending us to Peru?" She got to her feet. "No one can calm the ocean, buster, alien or not, and while you're explaining just how you're messing with our minds, how'd you do that fortune cookie trick? How'd you make our purchase tallies come out to the nearest tad?"

"I must warn you that my answers may be extremely unsettling."

Jim rolled his eyes. "We'll decide that." He turned the boat about, heading due east. "You arranged this meeting. You have about an hour before I pitch you face first onto the St. Helier dock."

"Your reaction is quite understandable. First I shall address Tricia's reference to calming the ocean." He turned to her. "You were thinking of the famous miracle performed by Jesus of Nazareth, of course, but miracles are no more than manifestations of the mental realm. As you can imagine, Biblical stories do depart a bit from the facts."

"Oh, sure. You were there, naturally, and—"

A deep rumble from astern jerked her gaze that direction. Not two boat lengths behind their transom, a gigantic cleft in the ocean stretched into the fog. It seemed bottomless, wide enough to swallow a huge freighter while growing wider still. The effect created instant vertigo, like teetering on the lip of the Grand Canyon.

She screamed while Jim lurched for the boat's stern rail even though the boat itself showed no signs of sliding into the chasm.

"It's a *miracle*," Charlie cried, showing banjo eyes and spreading his palms toward the heavens. His capricious moment turned instantly serious. "Calming the ocean, parting the Red Sea or creating a tornado in Moscow while sitting in a dark room in Culpeper, Virginia, is all the same to those who know the secrets. Jesus learned them as a young boy while in Egypt, a fact suppressed by most of those rewriting the records to suit themselves. No one ever seems to wonder who his teachers were or how they came to have their knowledge. Can you imagine how the people of those times would describe this canyon in the ocean to others who hadn't seen it?"

"There's no bottom," she gulped.

"Oh, it's down there somewhere. We'll now put things back as they were." With that, the canyon began to shrink, the whole noisy process all but completed in less than a minute. "As for the rest of your concerns, I'll no longer influence either of you unless I tell you I'm doing so. In fact, I'll be looking for your honest reactions to what we are about to—"

Jim whirled. "Just how long *have* you been influencing us?"

"For some months now. Sorry, but if I hadn't, you both would have been dead several times over. Even this boat and the way you found it was my doing. My reasons for all this will become apparent by the time we reach St. Helier." He paused. "Enough of miracles. I would very much like to begin my real story by explaining the *significance* of longitude 75.06.4286 west and latitude 14.41.2822 south. Once I've done that, you will begin to grasp the rest of my message."

"They're coordinates for Nazca," Jim stated, still gawking at the foam-covered eddies behind them.

"Not just Nazca," Charlie answered, "but the precise center of a unique figure there, the one with just a head and two strange arms with fingers spread. We need some graphic aids here. I'll create a projector screen in your minds without affecting any of your thoughts in other ways. Let's see... about here would be a good spot." Using his hands, he framed a rectangle against the cuddy, smiled, and a moment later they were staring at an aerial view of the Nazca figure he'd just mentioned, projected on a white background.

"We are looking down on Manos, and you see the crosshairs in the very center of the figure. Jim, when you stated there was nothing there at Nazca except for locals and occasional sight-seers, you missed a significant point. Decades of speculation and theorizing *should* have decoded the message we left there, both with Manos and the rest of the figures and lines. Sadly, it hasn't. Now... Manos looks slightly human, doesn't he? A head with two ears, two outstretched arms, one with five fingers and one with four? Of all these Nazca figures, only this one was designed in this special way, one symbol of many informing the people of future Earth about our visits. The symbols are our calling cards. Jim, I can tell without looking that you are nodding behind me."

"Like Kilroy was here? That old World War II message that showed up in the darndest of places?"

"Yes, and with a purpose of galactic proportions. Here, Tricia, you will be our mathematician using this pocket calculator." He seemed to produce it without searching his pockets. "You run the figures while Jim concentrates on his monorail imagery. Manos is going to tell us precisely where he is, as measured to the exact center of the Great Pyramid at Giza, accurate to the nearest pebble as Jim so wisely said not many days ago."

It was her turn to roll her eyes.

He turned back to the image. "First, what major features do we see? The neck has a distinct right angle to it, the only right angle in the figure. In fact, the only one in *all* the Nazca figures. Pretty obvious it's ninety degrees, so 90 is a number we will use. What other features are prominent? Well, there are nine fingers—five on one hand and four on the other. Not ten, but nine. *Very* significant, don't you agree? We now have four significant numbers—90, 4, 5 and 9. Multiply them all on your calculator, and what do you get?"

"Sixteen thousand two hundred."

"Correct. Now our fundamental latitude at that precise spot is fourteen degrees south. Remember 14.41.2822? That's degrees, minutes and seconds, so fourteen is the primary part. Divide 16200 by fourteen."

"I get... 1157.14286."

"Divide that by 41, the number of minutes in our position there."

"Okay... 2822. Oh, my God!"

"Yes, 2822 is the exact expression, seconds and fractions, of latitude to that very point. The exact number is 28.2229965156. If you reverse the procedure, you come out with 16,200, which is what we encoded in Manos—90 times 5 times 4 times 9. But we are not yet done. When we created these symbols, the Great Pyramid was our original prime meridian—the prime north-south line from which all else is measured—and it is precisely 31.08.008 east of the *modern* day prime meridian through Greenwich, England. Manos will now tell us the precise longitude to that original line, which we must increase by 31.08.008, from 75.06.4286 to 106.14.4366. I had to use 75.06.4286 because you wouldn't have guessed the part about the pyramid. Now, do you think it remotely possible that such a simple figure in Peru could encode that kind of precise information? How about it, Jim?"

"Okay, I agree. It seems impossible. You've already used up the main features."

"But remember, we *placed* Manos where he is. That means we first chose the exact position, then created the figure around it. Now look, we take the remaining *less* significant features, which are his two ears and two arms. Two times two is four. Multiply 16,200 by 4 and you will get 64,800. Correct?"

"Right."

"Now divide that number by 106, and then 14, and what do you get?"

"Forty-three sixty-six."

"We began with 106.14.4366, right? That's what the actual meridian should be? Now multiply 4366 by 14, and then by 106 and you get 64800, which is what you get by multiplying five fingers by four fingers by nine total fingers by ninety degrees by two ears by two arms. Manos is telling you precisely where his exact center is located *because* we first chose a location we could easily codify, then created his shape. There were other reasons for choosing the Nazca region, but within the plateau itself was this precise location."

Jim stared ahead. "It's incredible. That precision gets us down to a grain of sand, not just a pebble. Kilroy was there."

"We left many such Kilroys, each in its own specially chosen location. Each has its precise location codified in a similar way. The famous Kulkulkan pyramid in the Yucatan is another. Think of how many millions of people have seen it in person or in photographs, yet a mere few have tumbled to its true meaning and nobody listens to them."

He replaced the Manos figure with a down-looking view of the famous pyramid.

"Observe... there are 91 steps up the pyramid in four staircases, making 364 steps, plus one top platform for a total of 365. That this is the number of days in the year was so obvious that no one thought to ponder any other reasons, even though it's a well-known fact that Earth's year was at one time three hundred sixty days. There are also nine terraces built into four sides in that pyramid, and 9 times 365 times 4 staircases times 4 sides is 52,560, which happens to be the number 119 times 42 times 10.5152, and that is the precise longitude of the center of the top platform: 119.42.105152—also accurate to the nearest grain of sand. If there had been any other number of steps, sides, terraces or staircases, none of it would have any meaning at all. Now I ask you if you think the inhabitants of the Yucatan could possibly know the precise location of the Great Pyramid of Giza? The answer is no, even if they had the mathematic ability required. We designed and built that pyramid. Let me ask you, Jim... have you ever been sick?"

"No. At least, I don't remember anything serious."

"No colds? Flu? Measles? Chicken pox? Mumps? Never any of the common ailments?"

"I'd have to say... no. I don't remember even having a cold."

"Ever suffered a wound of any consequence? Broken bones?"

The answer was no again. Tricia stared. "Jim, you never told me any of this."

"I never gave it much thought."

"People around you were sick," Charlie continued, "but you didn't catch what they had."

"Right. Not even there on the *puña*, that slum city outside Cuzco, when I was freezing nights and starving days. I was all of two or three years old. Cholera was rampant there, and I didn't get it even though I was drinking the same water and eating the same garbage. There must have been a dozen different diseases there, most fatal, and no doctors or hospitals."

"Do you know why you've never been sick, Jim? Can you guess?"

"My life has been a mystery from day one. Not being sick is just a small part of it."

"Then let it be a mystery no longer."

Geneva, Switzerland. | March 13.

The manuscript would fill Mike O'Dell's quest for information, Whittier mused, but it was also a bomb that could explode in his face. Greenward was the most lethal of those Mike intended to confront, a self-centered psychopath, callous and manipulative without conscience, remorse or guilt. Greenward controlled the high ground just as he'd controlled it all through the ordeal following Las Vegas. Without someone to counter his lies, he'd deny most of what was in the manuscript and spin the rest as needed. Who'd be there to challenge him? He was now advising old crony Clarence Towers the same way he'd advised old crony H. J. Winfield. In fact, Towers had been Winfield's appointee to the NPA post, so that could have been the result of Greenward's sinister handiwork as well.

President *pro tem* Stanley Brewster was a loose cannon with a well-earned reputation for listening to the last person whispering in his ear. He'd be a pushover for spinmeister Greenward in anything like this. Any presentation Mike might make of information related to events in the past would be seen by Greenward, Towers and Brewster as support for "terrorist daughter Tricia" and, indirectly, for Jim. Mike could well be jailed without recourse, no matter how many lawyers he retained. A better move would be to zero in on one or two key congressmen, perhaps someone in the judiciary, even a notable radio or television personality, but there was no substitute for having the source of his bombshell information there at his side.

And yet, if Mike was in danger because of Tricia, how much greater the danger for anyone who'd worked closely with Jim Foster? Greenward had never gotten over his failure to ruin the Whittier Clinic and its founder. He'd seize upon any excuse to have the final say, yet this trip back into the lion's den had to be made, dangerous or not. It was the moral thing to do.

He looked around his apartment one last time. Bruno would be fine for a few days with neighbor Arnold, and everything of importance was secured in the bank vault. It was time to lock up and leave. His airline ticket took him to Toronto, stopping first in Montreal where he'd de-plane—Quebec was less likely to cooperate with American requests—and drive to D.C., leaving any possible Toronto reception committee empy-handed. In case anything went wrong, he'd already Telexed Dr. Elaine Jameson at the Whittier Clinic, using the code they'd worked out over the previous two years. Just being careful.

Still, he had a sense of foreboding.

English Channel. | March 13.

The mere mention of a real dinner ashore had gotten to Tricia, who was below rustling up snacks from her extensive collection. They were only granola bars, but her attack of the munchies could not be denied. Jim tore at his wrapper, trying to put a positive spin on an otherwise horrible development. Charlie's arrival had increased their danger in spite of all assurances otherwise, and his canyon "miracle" added another dimension to the already crazy sequence of events, but on the flip side the boat's crew was now three. The world searched for two fugitives, not three.

"Okay, Mr. Alien, your energy boost seems to have helped my tolerance the tiniest bit, so start explaining this whole mess. Who are you and why are you here?"

Charlie swallowed, then pocketed the remainder of his granola bar. "It's extremely important for you to understand everything, so stop me at any time. I shall begin three million years ago. Our society then was well beyond where yours is today. We overcame the limitations of physics as your science presently understands them, and were reaching out to other star systems. Earth numbered among our discoveries closer to home."

"Stop there," Jim interrupted. "Since when is four light years close? That's how far Rigel Kentaurius is from Earth, right?"

"Four light years in your terms, a few Earth days in ours. We don't travel *through* space exactly… ah… well, the explanation is quite beyond the time we have so it must wait. We were nevertheless impressed with Earth's beauty and began sending a mission roughly every fifty thousand of your years. We'd discovered other worlds, but Earth was rather unique among water planets, so we turned our attentions here more often. We modified your ancestors' DNA little by little, based on knowledge of our own evolution. You were identical to our early forms, simply many millions of years younger. Your features and intelligence began to converge on ours some three hundred thousand years ago, accelerated in this way. Intervals between our visits were periods when our modifications spread by natural means. All mankind was destined by the Creation Force to evolve into its higher and higher forms throughout the universe, but obviously at different times. We simply speeded things up a bit in your case." Tricia's questioning look stopped him. "Tricia? Your turn."

"You mated with… with our earliest humans?"

He grinned. "Not physically, but it's a valid question. There is actually no need to mate in order to alter DNA, or even for conception to occur. Your Christian religion merely *theorizes* on Mary's so-called immaculate conception, first because no one suspected there could be any other way possible, and second because the theory fit well into the rest of the invention at the time."

"Invention? Charlie, first you implied there were superior teachers of some sort teaching young Jesus all this mental stuff, and *now* you're implying that Mary's conception wasn't immaculate. What are you trying to tell us?"

"Oh, her conception was certainly immaculate in theory, just wrong in the assignment. We were very much involved, but always unnoticed as to our true identities. Remember, Tricia, we were three *million* years ahead of where you are today. When it came time for certain happenings here on Earth, we helped them along. We influenced the people of those times as I have influenced you and Jim in these past months, but always, always unseen. Jesus was one of many we assisted in this way. If this all seems blasphemous, consider how we'd have been viewed back then if we allowed our true nature to show. Would we not have been considered gods in a time when gods were the order of the day? And would not that have diminished everything we were trying to accomplish?"

"You're saying there is no true God?" she pressed. "In your view?"

"Oh, quite the opposite. We simply don't personify the Creation Force by giving it human form as depicted on the ceiling of the Sistine Chapel. It is simply the Creation Force, without human attributes. All religions of Earth are inventions. I don't mean the term to be derogative in the least, only descriptive and honest. That's what they are, regardless of what inspiration has spawned them.

"On another note, today's humans did not descend from Adam and Eve, nor did they evolve naturally from earlier, ape-like forms as your paleontologists believe. There is no missing link. The definitive, final changes that produced modern *homo sapiens* took no more than a single generation during one of our visits. We simply helped your natural inhabitants evolve more quickly along our own biological lines, which were identical to yours. If we hadn't happened along, your evolution would have progressed to an identical end, given another one or two million years or so. Incidentally, we gave Earth the name Gaia. Many Earth terms and names came originally from us." He dug out his granola bar and took another bite. "Am I going too fast?"

"No," Tricia answered, "but I'm sure glad you warned us. Keep going."

"All right, then. We concentrated first in what is now Africa, which stretched over much more of the globe at that time, fashioning your races and their subsets after our own and placing them in areas where some still dominate today. Your anthropologists have yet to discover that there are very few differences among humans worldwide. Oh, how they strain to prove otherwise, but your land masses had other shapes, you see, and their relationships to Earth's axis of spin were far different back then. Frigid zones of today were tropical in the past, with continents that no longer exist. Land bridges of those times have all but disappeared and everything was different. There were periods when your polar ice caps all but disappeared, other times when they grew to several times what they are today, all part of Earth's cyclic nature, in fact quite normal for water planets. Your scientists refute the cataclysmic history of Earth, when all about them are records of multiple upheavals of the type I just mentioned. We are convinced they'll forever refuse to see the remarkable truth before them."

Jim frowned. "You're saying everything we've learned is one big error?"

"Sad to say, that's quite close to the truth. A few courageous souls do see the correct picture, but the rest drown them out. The Flat Earth Society is alive and well in its many forms. Now... after your geographic poles last changed position, we again mapped Earth's new continental shapes, crustal distribution and core activity. It was then that we discovered the crust hadn't finished its most recent shift, that instability remained and does so to this day. Further, the new distribution of land masses and crust thicknesses spelled possible disaster for humankind in major ice episodes to follow. The imbalance was precarious and the prospects quite discouraging. Further, your system was moving into a particularly active portion of what you call the Milky Way and has penetrated a good distance since then. Even so, we felt there could still be time enough to finish your development. Those—"

"Charlie, wait," Jim said. "When you say the crust hadn't finished its shift, what do you mean?"

"Well, Earth is fatter at the equator than the poles, the result of centrifugal forces on the molten core. If the crust is to slide a significant amount over the molten core, as it does when the poles of rotation shift, it must stretch in places and contract in other places, rather like a tangerine peel twisted the wrong way about on the fruit underneath. Shifting requires force, the same as your hand twisting the tangerine rind, but if the force available is too weak to finish repositioning, the results will differ from theoretical predictions. The crust needs to slip further, but can't do so without some added external force.

"There was tremendous loss of life during the most recent pole shift because mankind had multiplied to thousands of times its numbers during earlier episodes. Your predecessors were quickly approaching our own early development, so we decided to stimulate the survivors with examples of what might be, glimpses of creation itself. We wanted you to reach beyond the finality of death, eventually mastering it as we had. Not a message easily conveyed, but one well worth planting, so we began adding many more examples ten thousand years before the present era. We believed that we would announce ourselves to you eventually in the proper way, once you were capable of grasping the truth."

Jim interrupted again. "I've never understood this whole UFO thing, which is what Trish and I are hearing, right? Why not just land your ships and announce who you were?"

"I know it seems odd, but we've done that many times. Thanks to the absence of today's instant worldwide communication, our ships were simple hearsay beyond those who actually saw them. Hearsay turns sour when it involves something unbelievable. Even today you have us as little green men with huge heads and big eyes, abducting our victims and all that. May I defer the answer until later as well? It will make more sense then. What we did instead of showing our ships was to walk among you in more recent times. We've been among you for many thousands of years now." He paused to take another bite of granola bar.

"You're right," Jim stated. "I guess even today, any ship from deep space would cause mass hysteria. People think they'd be calm and collected, but look how they react to me? So... instead, you left examples like Manos?"

"Precisely. The physical ones remained in place even as more were added, but many were keyed to our system of coordinates and encrypted with information that would someday be mute testimony to our visits. Most still mystify your best thinkers, but you see, they were only examples, not tests as they are purported to be. Your scientists constantly ridicule the obvious in favor of their theories."

"Why the Great Pyramid for the prime meridian?" Tricia asked. "What's the significance?"

"Simply that the pyramid in Giza is one of our examples, meant to be exactly what it is, a puzzle of such intricacy and challenge that none of your ablest people of that time, given full understanding, could have built it. We located it at the precise center of Earth's geographical land mass, as measured at that time, a feat possible only from space. There was as much land north as there was south, east as west, when measured to a point exactly opposite the pyramid on the other side of the globe. It's almost true even today. That alone should have screamed our message, since there was no way any being on Earth could have known that fact. Your engineers today can't build the pyramid in its original form, even though they've deciphered many of its more obvious mysteries.

"The sad fact is that, were I to state the design requirements today in your age of computers and moon walks, the first arguments I'd hear would be that no structure can take into account so many requirements at one time, that desert sands can't support such a colossal weight, and so on. The pyramid is undeniably there, complete with all its intricacies, but your historians and others are blind to the fact that there were but rudimentary tools and means available to the Egyptians to create such a work even if they were competent in other ways. It testifies to far more than just the knowledge needed to create it. We did incorporate many of the ideas and beliefs of the Egyptians at that time, but your version of the Creative Force, which you call God, does not erect monuments.

"We did it. The Egyptians constructed it, yes, but *we* were the architects, not Hemiunu, the pharaoh's spiteful little vizier. We conveyed instructions through him because he was useful to us, but he had nowhere near the required capability on his own. It did not take one hundred thousand imported slaves, as your historians theorize, but roughly four thousand normal Egyptians eager to work on such a prestigious project. They were paid workers, not slaves. Nor was it built using some far-fetched inside-out method or huge corkscrew ramp system. The project was completed in a tiny fraction of the thirty years estimated by Herodotus and others like him. Most of the stones were *created* at the site, not quarried as supposed, using *our* power sources and technology. Granite blocks, where we used them, were quarried using our power sources and then transported by means unknown to your scientists today. The distance was five hundred miles, or twelve seconds on the clock, depending on how you wish to express it. Finally, cement used for the casing and elsewhere can't be duplicated, as it contains a material not found on Earth. Finished stones were levitated and placed predominantly by women we trained, and—"

"Women?" Tricia leaned forward with her question. "Why women?"

"Because they resonate at higher frequencies, you see. Well, I guess you wouldn't see, but take my word for it. Mental energy has its favorites. Women, it seems, find its mastery a bit easier than men."

"Well, that's *so* true!" she sighed, fluttering her eyelashes. "Did you hear that, Mr. Sourpuss?"

"Just ignore her, Charlie. What about getting the stones *up* the pyramid?"

"Yes, yes. As I said, no monstrous ramps of dirt or beasts of burden dragging the stones on sledges and rollers from their original quarries, as your artists imagine. No ingenious methods of hoisting stones up the structure as it grew. Levitation is no more than control and positioning, as there is no weight involved. Women again. Of course, since levitation is impossible in your modern world, it's never considered. And as for the casing, no thousands of workers laboriously polishing limestone flat to within fifty thousandths of an inch or using bronze saws to cut stones with such accuracy that they could be stacked with precision equal to five sheets of typing paper squeezed together. Where were such unique events recorded, considering the Egyptians were excellent record keepers? The events have been replaced by suppositions, childish to the extent of being laughable, yet also tragic because they deny the obvious. That's why your experts can't agree on how it was done or how long it took. What a shame."

He sighed, shaking his head.

"Estimates of the laborers needed to complete the pyramid range all over the map. Herodotus failed to comment on the additional eight hundred thousand Egyptians needed to support, feed, house and care for his imagined hundred thousand slaves, nor did he bother describing the logistics involved, or comment on how an agrarian society so dependent on the Nile could literally abandon all normal livelihoods for thirty years. Where are the records of those serious new burdens on the native population? Scarcely a million adults occupied all of northern Africa then, forget the Nile delta. To cover that minor problem, it was proclaimed that all those slaves were brought in from surrounding lands. Still no explanation of how all those people were supported. The population of those times had no modern devices to make such support manageable, even more reason to label the reasoning as sheer ignorance.

"Rather than challenge Herodotus, succeeding historians lined up behind him. The Great Pyramid is a major example of human arrogance. Instead of accepting it as proof that Earth was not the central hub of the universe, all references to *our* presence here were erased save for the most abstract of hints. Earth people shun knowledge whenever it takes them where they are uncomfortable. How am I doing so far? Jim?"

"Quite interesting. Keep going."

"Finishing my pyramid story, then, we sent all but one of our ships back home upon its completion. Similar monuments were built by Earth people, copies erected more or less along the lines your historians imagine. Sadly, all our teachings and instructions were destroyed by the envious pharaohs, who had no such powers. The several hundred women whose mental abilities had been so exquisitely enhanced were stoned to death when they failed to perform equal feats in life-threatening situations. No records of their deaths were recorded.

"It's also worth mentioning that the pyramid cubit is precisely one ten-millionth of the straight line distance from the mean crustal surface at the North Pole—that is, absent any ice—to the center of Earth, accurate to six decimal places. How would any human living then have known such a number? Even today, your historians pretend it was simply a coincidence, a lucky guess. How big is a cubit? Let's see... the distance from my elbow to my third fingertip is... or is it the second fingertip? Where on the elbow? Or should it be a pharaoh's forearm we use? Which pharaoh? You see, there was no absolute definition, yet every measurement on the pyramid is based upon that precise number. Again, only possible if measured from space. It's totally absurd to think that, in an era where the cubit was a variable subject to whim, the rest of the mathematical genius found in the pyramid was attributed to the Egyptians, and yet it was. It is today.

"Now... as for Nazca... your people strive mightily to explain those markings, all theories wrong. Not one academician is willing to admit that Earth had been visited by an advanced race without first explaining the significance of those lines and figures. There is no real significance to *any* of the lines, other than our intent that they be symbolic of our higher intelligence and technology. A few of your archaeocryptologists recognize Manos for what it is, an encryption of its precise location relative to the Giza pyramid. We took the rest of the images from the minds of those who lived there and reproduced them for amusement, adding some geometric shapes and modifying a hillside to give the people of that region a glimpse of their own future. This was one of the few times when we risked bringing our landing ships into view. We found the locals extremely receptive and gave many of them rides above the symbols, so they could see their own thoughts created on the desert floor using natural elements. Stones were simply swept together to make lines. The random straight lines were created by those locals we treated to a trip aloft, playing with our controls. They were able to watch their handiwork as it unfolded beneath them. That was sufficient for their level of awareness, but their awe failed to last. As in all the other cases, the problem was rooted in a lack of communication. We were too early, too anxious to see you progress."

He finished his granola bar with a flourish, neatly folding the wrapper and sticking it in his pocket.

"Jim, you earned your degree in engineering. What's your opinion of the theory proposed by Earth scientists, that Peruvian natives laid out those lines of rocks over hill and dale with laser precision?"

"It's a stretch. Maybe it can be done today, but…."

"But if the lines were created from a stationary platform well above the plain?"

"That's different."

"Yes, yes. You see, that should be so obvious to your scientific community there can be no argument, and yet the idea is ridiculed. Some of the figures are imagined to be linked to religious ceremonies… not all, mind you, just some. No explanation for why they all aren't. Some of the straight lines have been described as appearing to be a landing strip for alien craft, but those who were merely describing an impression have been ridiculed for saying such was indeed the case, even though they never said so. Distortion and ignorance rule the day with loud voices.

"Moving further north, your best and greatest thinkers estimate it took 30,000 laborers seventy years to carve and fit those massive stones in the fortress found at Sacsahuaman. Where did natives learn to lift and position hundred ton shapes? How is it no knife blade can be slipped between the joints, even though *none* of the cuts are straight and many look like jigsaw puzzles? Such techniques were intended to preclude forever all arguments that indigenous people built the walls. Again, we see arrogance in place of simple logic, ignorance shouting louder than reason. Your experts today can't reproduce Sacsahuaman, yet common natives *must* have done the work with bare hands and flint. It could not have been visitors from another world, fashioning the fortress in the style of less complicated human works, so the totally absurd becomes accepted fact.

"Equally illogical is the proclamation by some that the Inca must have been space aliens because they were so different from the natives there. Could it not be equally possible that the Inca were *enhanced* by the very visitors who created the Nazca lines and Sacsahuaman and all the other examples? No, of course not. The Inca were therefore aliens from space, even though not one shred of evidence points in that direction. The truth is that they were actually indigenous people to whom we gave special insights and physical features. In order that they be treated with great respect, we changed their skin color and facial contours a bit, something you already knew, Jim. You mentioned it on that plane flight when you were sitting next to Ollie Robinson."

"How... how do you know what I said back... is there *anything* you don't know about me?"

"Oh, I didn't actually know it. You remembered the incident as I was making my remarks just now, and I simply tuned in. By the way, I see Jersey on our port side. We have no more than fifteen minutes before we must slow down, but with this natural wind and the ocean behaving we'll still make twenty knots."

"What makes you so sure we aren't in danger? Our pictures are everywhere."

"Neither of you will be recognized as long as I'm with you. See?" He was suddenly the Finn who'd handed Jim the envelope, with the same red-tasseled cap.

Tricia gasped. "*You* were that Finn in Lahti! You were right there all the time."

"Yes. Nothing about me has actually changed, you see. This is all taking place in your minds. However—and this is most important— *everyone* in Lahti saw me this way, not just the two of you. I can effect the same type of changes in you, but they must be subtle to be really effective. Since you were considering the use of your Amaru papers just before I came aboard, I suggest emphasizing typical Peruvian features and skin color on you both. I propose to teach you how to do this for yourselves, but for now I'll supply your camouflage, so to speak. I'm already known in St. Helier, so I'll just be me when we pull in."

"But how about cameras at customs check-in?" Jim asked.

Charlie's smile was mischievous. He tapped his forehead. "The illusion takes place up here regardless of who or how many may be looking at a video screen. In the event we ever do need to pass detailed scrutiny, however, we should alter you both a bit. A deeper tan for Tricia should work quite well. I'll set up a harmless melanin stimulation process that works as she sleeps." He paused, suddenly thoughtful. "Now... I did promise to clear up a mystery. Jim, you've just endured five days of physical demands in the worst of conditions with no more than a few snatches of sleep. You survived the *puña* as a young boy, while around you people young and old died of starvation and cholera, yet you never even got the sniffles. You were born with godlike mental powers. What does it all tell you?"

"Am I... was... all right, was it your people?"

"Yes, you are essentially one of us, Jim, although you are definitely of Earth's humanity. You've been chosen for a very special role here." He paused, letting his words sink in. For a moment no one made a sound.

Jim stared ahead. "Who was my father?" His voice was suddenly hoarse.

Charlie hesitated. "The answer may not be what you expect."

"As long as it's rational, I can handle it. Was it that priest from Lima?"

"No. You have *my* DNA, Jim, which makes me your biological father. I may look your age or even younger, but Manus was my creation along with a few dozen others. Earth has been my project since roughly seven hundred B.C., but I'm considerably older than that. We mastered the art of cell restoration five million years ago. I'll tell you more about that later on."

"You... and my mother... you...."

"Not what you're thinking, although she was quite the beautiful woman. As I said earlier, immaculate conception—your theologians' term—is *not* the divine mystery they'd like all to believe."

Jim sagged back onto the helmsman's bench. "Then..."

"Don't try to grasp it all at once. If I had not told you the truth, you would still be who you are. Soon you will understand far, far more."

"Charlie," Tricia interrupted, "the things you've already said... if you've been around that long, were you by some chance involved with an event in Bethlehem two millennia ago?"

He grinned. "Tricia, I will say only that we have indeed contributed to mankind's development in many ways. You'd best re-examine what you know of that period in light of what I've just told you."

"You're from... Rigel what?" she asked.

"Rigel Kentaurius, the name your astronomers gave the star system. Our sun is far smaller than monster Rigel, of course, closer in size to your own, with just four planets. We call ours Eden. Your Biblical reference to a garden by that same name makes it almost an imaginary place on Earth, eventually becoming Samaria and now Iraq, but that is not true. We referred to our planet by name when we announced ourselves to residents of that region during a visit some thirty thousand years ago. The name survived through many translations. Of course, your modern lexicographers discount all external sources, assigning a Sumarian origin meaning a plain. The term originally referred to one of our landing spots which, incidentally, was nowhere near modern Iraq."

"You're saying Earth *itself* was the garden of Eden"

"Allegorically speaking, yes, but not much longer. Sadly, we've concluded that most life will come to a tragic end in less than thirty years. The reason is rooted in something else I haven't told you."

Chapter 12

Salt Lake City.

Harry paced. "Las Vegas and Nellis airbase taken out with over a thousand dead, our secret ELF transmitter knocked out, yet not a peep from the White House. Winfield forms ad hoc committees when he already knows who did it. He takes a wild gamble to find someone with superhuman powers, taps Whittier to produce same, but Whittier's a complete unknown who just happens to be handy at the time. Does it mean that Winfield thinks nothing will come of it, or is he simply a developing lunatic? Whittier hasn't a clue as to where in the world the only such person he's ever seen could now be, forty-some years later, who he is or whether he's even alive. He produces Jim Foster in Bermuda by using psychometry... woo-woo stuff he personally despises. He and Foster are damn near assassinated before they even get out of Bermuda, but who knows about them being there aside from Winfield and cronies? How does any hit team get there so quickly otherwise?

"Whittier and Foster go to a safe house in Virginia, where Whittier is to dissect the goose and discover the secret of the golden eggs. Whittier has no reason to suspect the White House even if the Bermuda episode unnerved him, but while he and Jim are in this secret facility there's a second assassination attempt, and this one shows real planning. Who knows Whittier and Foster are there, Ollie, other than Winfield's group? An elite army commando team saves the day, but the White House knows nothing about it. Someone is lying, Jim wisely sees he can trust no one, begins to operate on his own, defuses the political time bomb his own way and then disappears. Instead of being hailed as a hero, he's suddenly a deadly terrorist, courtesy of Uncle Howard." Harry stopped pacing and turned. "It appears Jim gets into trouble every time he tries to use his special talent to help others."

"Shoot, Harry, he's now an arsonist and murderer on top of everything else, also courtesy of Mr. Greenward."

"The whole thing is sickening. I want to take a closer look at Uncle's recent visitors there at his estate. Getting hold of his phone records isn't a problem, long as I don't use them, except that he makes his most important outgoing calls through his computer. They're sanitized that way, since they go out through his ISP. We'd need a good hacker to track those, someone we can trust. The FBI has plenty, naturally, but this can't be official, not yet. You wouldn't just happen to know one would you?"

Ollie smiled. "So happens I do."

St. Helier, Jersey, English Channel. | March 13, late evening.

Charlie bounded onto the dock at Gorey Pier and immediately greeted the nearest man by his first name, like a cherished friend. No telling what mental image was being projected as they chatted, but no one mentioned customs. The dinner menu was everything Charlie'd promised, too, with roast duckling *à l'orange* the house specialty. Once their waiter departed, Charlie leaned forward. "Now, Jim, about your mission—"

"You said I've been chosen for some role. Why me?"

"Interfacing with Earth's people has never been as problematic as it is today. Hollywood and television, with few exceptions, have cast alien life as threatening. As a result we see irrational fears and suspicion intertwined with the political motivations, nuclear threats and various jihads of your real world. Nobody trusts anybody else, not even so-called allies, so any message we might try to convey would cause upheavals of its own. We're automatically an enemy or threat or something vile. The very few who'd ever view us correctly would be smothered by billions who'd attempt to nuke us at first contact. Even worse, you all look like us and vice versa. Who'd believe we were anything special?

"Many years ago our high council decided we'd need as our intermediary someone recognized by as many Earth people as possible, absent political or religious motives. Religions have become as divisive as anything political, you see. As unstable as Earth's situation is today, we can no longer wait. We must communicate a dire warning to all mankind, one we'd hoped we would never have to deliver.

"Your alter ego, Mudslinger, is known from jungles to polar caps in the same way Superman is. I propose to have you deliver our message. I will speak through you. That's as succinct and simple as I can make it."

"But how about SETI and other groups all looking for alien intelligence? Don't they count with your high council?"

"Not for this situation. Oh, yes, they're hoping that electromagnetic impulses will tell them intelligence exists out there, but the only rational means of communication through space has nothing to do with electromagnetics or the speed of light. If they'd focused their attention on mental communication, they might have discovered us hundreds of years ago, but that never happened and perhaps never will. Other than a few enlightened thinkers, the rest blindly accept whatever they hear. Your religions have devolved to little more than inventions without substance. Roughly five billion of your people categorically reject any possibility of superior beings or other civilizations of any kind simply on religious grounds, another instance of blind acceptance. Your age of information is being used to spread political and personal propaganda, driven by greed and various forms of lust instead of truth. The sad result is that mankind today is incapable of understanding its own planet, even though answers and examples have been available since the Middle Ages. Your people have simply refused to see them, and now it may well be too late."

"Too late for… what?"

Charlie took his time answering. "A major geophysical upheaval looms in Earth's immediate future, one that will claim virtually all life here. A solution of sorts *may* be possible, given more time, but recent developments show that we can't bring it about in time to avert the disaster. We have been witnesses to similar upheavals in Earth's past, so my words are backed by three million years' worth of data. *This* is the message we must put across, without delay."

Tricia's eyes widened. "You can't be… oh, you can't possibly mean the global warming scam. That is so—"

"No no, *not* that. You're absolutely right—it's a scam of the worst kind. The danger lies completely in the opposite direction."

"Then—"

"That unfortunate idiocy has masked this far more serious natural event having nothing to do with man, something that *should* have attracted major attention a hundred years ago. I'm speaking of undersea volcanic activity, of course, which all but a few thousand of your enlightened scientists have totally ignored. Not gigantic eruptions, you understand, but thousands of smaller fissures unnoticed on the ocean floor, mostly at great depths. Some are smaller than a city block, others the size of Rhode Island, new ones opening constantly as others disappear. In the past two months alone we've counted a net increase of nearly four hundred, adding to some thirty thousand already pumping heat into the waters. The net increase appears to be geometric, and there may even be a major crustal rupture in the making, though we can't predict any time frame for that kind of thing. We have seen these very precursors several times in Earth's past."

He paused as their waiter arrived and went through the customary wine-cork ritual before filling the wineglasses. After the obligatory toast, mostly for the benefit of the other two diners in the room, Charlie set his glass down and leaned forward on his elbows.

"The major difference between what I am about to tell you, versus what you will hear from any other source, is that our information is factual, stored in our data banks. None of it is guesswork."

"Okay, but how does this differ from the global warming stuff?" Jim asked. "You said the danger was in the opposite direction."

"It's simple physics. Steam created by each fissure is absorbed by sea water, along with immense quantities of heat, carbon dioxide, acids and elements such as sulfur, so there is nothing visible on the surface to indicate what's going on in the depths. Your people haven't developed ways of detecting these fissures from space, and you don't maintain tens of thousands of deep-sea stations as we do on Eden, so it all goes unnoticed except for an accidental discovery here and there. The net result is continual warming of the oceans, eventually leading to constant deluge—this is important—which in turn leads to an ice age and eventually another warming period. These cycles were normal until an event of some four thousand years ago disturbed forces beneath Earth's crust, forces we'd monitored for millennia, raising internal heat, and... well, all sorts of things changed.

"We immediately plotted the new sub-crustal conditions, and our predictions have held ever since. Have you noticed a recent surge in violent storms? Rainstorms measured in feet instead of inches? Floods where there have been none for centuries. Category five hurricanes in both hemispheres, plus massive typhoons in the Pacific and great, sweeping cold fronts bringing record-setting low temperatures to places like Florida and Mexico? La Ninã and El Ninõ have outstripped all adjectives for years now, and how about earthquakes and tsunamis?"

"Indonesia," Jim began, clicking off his fingers. "Turkey, Japan, central China, Iran, Iceland, Norway, Peru."

"Mount St. Helens," Tricia added, "and another big one in South America last month, this time Chile."

Charlie nodded. "Good. Now add Pakistan, Taiwan, the Kuril Islands, Alaska—they had a 9.2 magnitude there in 1964 and a 9.0 last year—Italy, Armenia, Tibet, Turkey, Pakistan, India and Montreal, Canada... just last week in the Indian ocean, plus one south of Jakarta. Volcanoes as well. There have been seven major new ones on land in the past five years plus several more so-called dormant ones such as Vesuvius, Mauna Kea, Soufrière and Mount St. Helens coming to life. Three to four times the average, all unusual, but not one peep from the Kyoto crowd. Geological events of this type are not part of any climate change, you see. Now, the *real* problem is the fault line made up of the North American/ Eurasian plates and further south the South American/African plates. This line passes up through Iceland and the Arctic Ocean, crossing above all of Siberia. On the southern end, it passes completely around Africa and meets with other faults in the Indian Ocean."

As he spoke, a simplified Mercator projection of the world formed on the white tablecloth. He traced the fault lines on the platter-sized creation with an index finger.

"We're the only ones who can see this projection, so don't be nervous. This part north of Iceland... from here to here... has recently opened an alarming number of fissures into the Arctic Ocean and along the Siberian coast. Our monitors predict that more and larger fissures will open all along the rest of the fault, almost to the Antarctic end, in just a few months. This same fault line has been fairly inactive for thousands of years, but when the rate of new fissure appearances grows exponentially in the way it has, ocean temperatures do jump quickly. The rate of rise has more than doubled in recent months, and now the oceans are as warm as we've ever seen them." He exhaled, looking thoughtful, and the map disappeared. "It means that Earth is roughly two decades from entering the most severe ice age since our first visits here three million years ago, far worse than the most recent one."

Tricia's hand went to her mouth. "Tw... twenty years?"

"I'm afraid so, Tricia, yes. Eight thousand years prior to Earth's most recent pole shift, the north pole was located in the Atlantic ocean, approximately on today's Tropic of Cancer. Land existed where today there is only water, and vice versa, and this major fault line I've just described was aligned more along the equator of that time. All forces along that line were directed differently, and the ice caps of that time covered two much smaller continents, neither of which is above water today. Equatorial South America was under ice then, whereas Nazca, in Peru, enjoyed a climate equivalent to that of the Canadian Rockies today. Northern Siberia was subtropical, even tropical in places.

"It was about that time when we recalculated the trajectory of a major comet that had been threatening your solar system for more than a million years, a practice we'd followed every few thousand years." He paused, thoughtful as he sipped his wine, then made a moue. "*Something* had changed since the previous observation."

Tricia wiggled on her chair. "What major comet?"

"You call it Venus and your scientific community would call my statement ludicrous, but it was indeed a comet, originally burped as a molten ball from your planet Jupiter, which itself is still exhibiting great core instabilities your scientists haven't discovered. To get some idea of relative sizes, picture this molten ball as a cranberry next to a fairly large beach ball, Earth being only a bit larger than the cranberry. The comet's elliptic orbit brought it back from the remote reaches of the solar system every 67.9 Earth years, passing obliquely through the ecliptic of your system's much older planets. Somewhere along its most recent travels it had shed roughly half a percent of its mass—perhaps by colliding with another object. That may not seem like much, but the planet had always passed between Mars and Jupiter. If we'd failed to intercede, it was destined to smash into Earth within five orbits, roughly 3700 years ago. Well, Earth had a close call instead."

"Why?" Jim asked. "How could you have done anything?"

"Actually, we did two things. We changed the comet's course and increased Earth's orbit over a period of eighty years."

"Wait a minute, Charlie. How do you—?"

"Quite an enormous task, but not in the moving so much as the precision required. It was our first challenge of that type, but with such a lengthy orbit we had to make thousands of corrections. The rest of your solar system could well have been affected by anything we did, you see. In the end, we had to let Venus pass quite close to Earth in order to get just the right slingshot effect, and even then we weren't perfect. The electromagnetic interchange between bodies was enough to throw off our calculations the tiniest bit, pulling Venus and Earth about two hundred miles closer than anticipated. As a result of that slight error, the orbit of Mars was changed in the centuries to follow, with disastrous results for life there. Earth survived, but with chaos and tremendous loss of life as well. Without our intervention, far more than Earth would have been doomed. History actually records this event in a way, since prior to this event there was no Pallas Athene for the Greeks or Venus for the Romans. Then, quite suddenly, both new names sprang into being as gods, or should I say goddesses, both referring to the same new luminary in the sky, Venus."

He paused for another sip of wine.

"Now... thousands of years earlier, Earth experienced a pole shift caused by ice, and this is where your scientists and their theory of uniformity are prime examples of *homo ignoramus*. Polar ice caps were twelve to twenty *miles* thick, much, *much* thicker than anything postulated today, and covered roughly four times the area your scientists imagine. One of the major problems with the classical theories is that they ignore the drastic effect of lowering of Earth's oceans in the process of building so much ice. Much more land is exposed, you see, but since experts do not allow the one, the other cannot follow."

Jim eyed the ceiling, thinking out loud. "More exposed land means even more ice, because ice forms on land long before it forms over water."

"Ah, you're getting the picture. As for the time it took for all that ice to form, the correct number is forty years—not thousands—with very little glacial movement prior to the shift. What is most important about all this is that in the period immediately before the *start* of those forty years, Earth's mean ocean temperatures were just one degree higher than they are today, using the Celsius scale."

Tricia gulped. "Just... *one?*"

"I'm afraid so, yes. Today's scientists have absolutely no idea how to measure mean global ocean temperatures, so they are just guessing. Fifteen years ago your oceans were four degrees from the all-time high. The increase has accelerated. Each time your oceans have reached the temperature they are now, Earth has quickly entered an ice age. Your next one is right around the corner. Unfortunately, it may be the last one for mankind."

Chapter 13

Toronto International Airport.

Montreal's airport was teeming with police and officials of all sorts, thanks to a terrorist scare the previous day, so the idea of driving from there was abandoned. It was on to Toronto, but things there were nearly as bad, with customs lines backed up and agents operating in pairs at most stations. Whittier studied the situation before choosing a single-agent line. There was no other course but to go through and hope for the best.

The agent was a jowly woman who beckoned him forward without looking up. He put down his passport, then unzipped and opened his briefcase. The passport went under a document reader while she began with the usual questions. Satisfied, she nodded at his opened briefcase, then withdrew the passport and riffled through the pages, stamping a blank spot before handing the booklet back. He drew a long breath. From here on he'd be relatively safe, except that she hadn't waved him forward. She was checking a video screen.

"Sir, let me have that passport again?"

Oh, no! He handed it back. She slid it into the reader a second time, gazing again into the hooded screen.

"Your profession?"

"Doctor of psychology and M.D. I've been directing a clinic in Europe for two years as well as one in Buffalo, each treating mental illnesses."

"We have a U.S. directive to arrest you, sir, for aiding and supporting terrorists."

Steady, Gordon. "Oh, there has to be a mistake, madam. I haven't been in the States for nearly two—"

The red light above her station flashed before he finished the sentence.

Two armed security guards—one with gun drawn—led him away in handcuffs after relieving him of everything on his person. Under the new U.N. rules, he'd be denied any contact with his choice of attorney, or anyone for that matter. A security van was on the way.

"Sure would hate to be you, asshole," one of the pair said, "but it serves you right. You should've stuck to doctoring instead of playing traitor to your country, eh?"

It was the last civil thing they said before leading him away.

St. Helier, Jersey.

Charlie's bombshell prophecy was put on hold once their food arrived, but Jim soon returned to the subject at hand. "Charlie, I thought the last ice age ended ten or fifteen thousand years ago."

"A rather inaccurate deduction by your scientists. Ice *ages* are actually strings of ice episodes separated by periods of glacial retreat that come and go with regularity. Your scientists track them by means of glacial deposits, et cetera, but without any real knowledge of shorter periods when ice fields melted. Yes, glacial flows leave evidence of ice extremes, but warmer periods do not. Your population was a tiny fraction of what it is today, and still it suffered great setbacks with every episode. I'd estimate that, in the time we have been witness, your polar caps have all but disappeared half a dozen times and then waxed to many times the area they cover today.

"At any rate, irregular distribution of surface mass due to the ice caps finally caused the pole shift that trapped those famed wooly mastodons with buttercups in their stomachs, there in Siberia. They certainly didn't start eating in that position on the globe, but that's where they ended up. The greatest portion of the shift took place in less than one day, with the crust sliding more than a thousand miles, and it was all over in a matter of one week filled with horrible upheavals, devastating earthquakes and tidal waves. Advocates of uniformity insist a shift would take many thousands of years in the absence of any outside cause, even to stating that it would be fairly gentle, but in this case the cause was centrifugal force and it was anything but gentle. Witness whole islands composed of mastodon tusks north of Siberia, for example. Mastodons do not congregate by the tens of thousands to die together, nor do wooly mammoths travel thousands of miles from their natural habitat seeking buttercups growing in arctic temperatures.

"Uniformity advocates also insist that Earth enters a severe cooling cycle and ice formation thereafter takes centuries before amounting to anything. Infantile thinking at best. First come heavy rains, then a perpetual deluge that floods the land everywhere, all continents, fed continuously by immense increases in evaporation from warmer oceans. In colder regions, rain becomes snowfall that *cannot* flow back to the ocean, so ice builds at the rate of one meter every three days at the start."

Charlie held his hand ten inches above the table top.

"From here to the floor twice in a week, then three times a week, then four. In one year, over one thousand meters and still building. Earth has already recorded four feet of plain old rain in a single day, in Nepal not so long ago. Texas recently recorded three feet. Imagine that happening as snow over more than half the world at the same time, both poles. Four feet becomes forty when rain falls as snow, all in a single day, and remember that both poles are refrigerators no matter how warm the rest becomes. They're always cold enough to turn precipitation into snow, then ice, but first there must be heat.

"Volcanos are the way hot planets maintain thermal equilibrium with their crusts. Since the near disaster with Venus, Earth's volcanic activity has been steadily increasing, a fact your scientists have missed because they don't include undersea events and they certainly did not have accurate records prior to 3700 years ago, but present acceleration shows us that a major correction is taking place. Our scientists estimate that within thirty years Earth's population will be all but eradicated by ice, floods, poisoned atmosphere, disease, earthquake or subsidence of the land, famine or another pole shift, putting the present poles as close to the equator as they were in the past. Tides thereafter will be hundreds of feet high, daily tsunamis if you will. When the pole shift occurs, stresses on Earth's crust will trigger hundreds of major new volcanoes on land and beneath the oceans, blocking the sun with ash, spewing poisons and creating perpetual darkness. Violent storms will sweep across the land and oceans will wash over mountain tops. Lowlands and plains will be lifted many miles high while other parts sink beneath the oceans as the crust convulses atop a molten core that is shifting shape from an egg on its side to one on its end. Earth's crust is actually thinner than the eggshell in relation to the mantle and core, which continue to rotate on the original axis as though nothing were happening on the surface. The crust slides to a new location to counteract centrifugal forces. No continents will be left untouched."

He mumbled a few private words, then dove into his duckling. "Hopefully I haven't spoiled dinner. Nothing is less appetizing than cold duck. More wine?" He proceeded to refill the glasses without waiting for an answer.

Toronto.

Whittier's mind raced. The guard sitting opposite him in the security truck hadn't said a word, but was watching him as though he thought any minute his captive would break the handcuffs and attack. The man didn't seem all that approachable, but the effort had to be made.

"May I speak?"

"Wasting your breath, meathead, but be my guest."

"I'm a doctor working with people who have serious brain disorders, and I've been able to rehabilitate or even cure a great many over the years, including those given up for lost. Someone has mistakenly connected me with this terrorist thing, probably because I've been in Switzerland for a few years now, but I have a clinic in Buffalo with my name on it. Do you know the Buffalo area by any chance?"

"Been there."

"Cheektowaga, then. It's the Whittier Clinic, in Cheektowaga. I'm scheduled to supervise several major operations there tomorrow. Someone there should be told what has happened, that there's been a mistake and I'm temporarily delayed."

"You should have thought of that earlier. No calls allowed."

"No calls by me, no, but you could do it for me. Where are they taking me?"

"Centre o' the Universe. That's downtown Toronto to you. Comfy cell waitin' there."

"Will you do it for me? Ask to speak to Dr. Elaine Jameson. She's the director. My wallet is there in that bag by your side, with what they took from my pockets. Take what money you need for the call.

Just tell her I've been delayed and she should cancel the operations."

"Nothing doing. Everything in there's been counted. You have no rights, bud, and that means no phone calls."

Good. He gave it a thought or else he wouldn't have mentioned the money being counted. "This isn't about my rights, sir. It's about others who'll be hurt or even jeopardized because of this foul-up. You'll be doing them a great service, maybe even saving a life. Think of them, not me."

The man flicked his gaze briefly, making eye contact for the first time. "What kind of brain stuff do you fix?"

"Usually it's what others in the medical profession can't fix. For example, we've pioneered methods for overcoming Asperger's Syndrome. That's where—"

"I know what it is; my sister has it. You can fix *that?*"

"Sometimes yes. It depends on the individual. If she's in the area, you should ask her doctor to send her to us for an evaluation." *What a break! Time to shut up and let him think. Elaine knows how to reach Mike O'Dell's lawyer.*

"So this woman who runs your place... what do I say to her?"

"Just tell her I can't be there for the scheduled appointments, and that she should inform my associates in Washington, D.C. They might as well save themselves a wasted trip.

St. Helier.

Dazed, Jim picked up his fork. "You've seen this kind of thing happen other times?" he asked, forcing himself to follow Charlie's example with his own duckling. Tricia hadn't moved. She simply sat there, mute.

"Previous missions to Earth have recorded precisely what I'm describing, yes," Charlie answered, "but your population was a tiny fraction of today's billions. By the time your people finally wake up, a hundred million will already be trying to escape the elements by moving toward the equator from both polar regions, but how will they survive while doing so? How will residents of those warmer areas cope with having their numbers doubled and tripled in a matter of months? Millions more won't be able to move quickly enough, crops will fail everywhere and famine will rule the day. Flooding and incessant downpour will add to the misery. There will be no place to go, you see, nowhere to settle and above all no food. Technology won't apply." He paused, letting his words sink in.

Tricia broke the long silence. "There's no way to reverse this?"

"We may be able to prevent the final polar shift, but I fear it will be too late for humanity. Jim, you look puzzled."

"It's the sliding crust bit. Why did your people wait so long on this? When did you know about the undersea fissures?"

"Oh, they've been ongoing for many millions of years, but only in the past fifty years have we seen unmistakable signs of this major correction. As to why we held back, tell me when in Earth's recent past there was a more appropriate time? Go back as far as you like."

Jim looked thoughtful. "You couldn't accomplish much of anything until our age of communication was in full bloom. That came after a string of wars, and now we're in the age of terrorism. Political bickering is at an all-time high. Everyone's a blogger, even little old Granny Frickett, yakking about every topic under the sun, so who'd listen? Who would believe you? I think you're right—there's never been a best time, and now you're saying there's no choice in the matter."

"Precisely. Sad to say, your people simply will not change their attitude about tigers until one is chasing them. Only the most sensible among you would consider our warnings fortunate, were we to offer them directly as outsiders. The rest would conclude we were creating panic so we could invade Earth, or some similar lunacy. Our biggest worry would be in Earth's most prestigious scientists ridiculing our warnings and turning all Earth in the wrong direction. They are already doing that with the Kyoto scam, protecting their financial grants and reputations by aligning themselves with a political movement. How do they sleep at night, I wonder.

"On to your crust shifting question. In relative terms, an eggshell is actually thicker than the earth's crust in many places, thinner in others. Crush that shell into dozens of pieces and cement them all together with rubber cement. Each piece is as strong as before, but not where it joins its neighbors. You now have what amounts to Earth's crust sitting atop a globe of mostly molten iron, about as fluid as pancake batter. That globe is eight thousand miles across, turning at the rate of a thousand miles per hour at the equator. Friction keeps core and crust moving together. If somehow you grabbed the crust with a giant hand and held it, the internal core would keep right on turning at the same speed."

Jim nodded. "That part's fine, but where does the force come from? What's the giant hand?"

"Consider how lopsided the land distribution is at present, compared to ages past. Well, you wouldn't know that part, but take my word for it. Ice will accumulate much faster in today's northern hemisphere this time because far more land exists there. Any new ice cap will cover Algeria, Libya and Egypt, all China and most of India, and all the way into Mexico in the western hemisphere. Picture it as a massive mountain three times higher than Everest, covering all the land I just mentioned. This added mass, making one pole area far heavier than the other, will unbalance the spinning top and the crust will slip until the greatest mass is aligned with the *core's* equator. The inside surface of the eggshell in my example is not at all smooth, and since Earth is oblate to start with, the adjustment can be as much as twenty miles up and down in places. Huge cracks between Earth's tectonic plates will spew poisonous gases into the atmosphere and lava across the land, killing what few may have survived until then. Life on Earth will have to start all over again. There are only two courses of action open, and we have very little time in which to achieve either. The better of the two will take too long, I fear, but here they are.

"First, we can design and help build a moon colony that will support some one million souls, using our ships for transports as well as many other functions such as excavation and power sources. This is no easy task, since any colony must be sequestered deep underground. Even then, we must stand guard out in space to protect against larger meteors. Your technology is inadequate for such a project, so we must educate all your scientists and engineers at the onset. The problem is that such a project will take thirty years even if it's started now, using any current paradigm. Your developed nations must work together toward that single goal, cooperating as never before. Every iota of human energy has to be poured into this task, and finally there is the problem of choosing those who are to survive. I fear it will never happen, even if the alternative is annihilation. Time will be frittered away bickering over profits and deciding how best to make fortunes. Then, too, there could be religious wars. We can only hope none of these things will happen."

Jim grimaced. "Your million souls would all be politicians, billionaires and lawyers. Okay, assuming all this going to happen the way you say, what am I supposed to do now that the whole world is out to kill me?"

"*Us*," Tricia corrected, finally starting to eat.

"I'll remedy that problem shortly," Charlie replied.

"Why me in the first place?" Jim continued.

"Because you are universally recognized no matter the language or country. A New Guinea aborigine knows the Mudslinger even if he can't name his own tribal leader. You've been credited with all sorts of powers, mostly untrue but at least complimentary. You're apolitical, with no allegiance to any nation. Devoted most of your adult life to helping others, cherish all forms of life and you've proven your integrity in hundreds of ways. The act that created your Mudslinger reputation spoke volumes about you as a person and said it in all languages. Finally, you possess powers you don't yet realize. The thing you've most wanted as Jim Foster, all through your life, is some way to use your gift to help others. Well, this is it, Jim, this is it. Together we can put on quite a show, but understand that the world will listen but briefly before political forces close the window of opportunity. Our message will survive, once delivered, so our challenge will be to create a true miracle, a blockbuster event that will set the whole world abuzz, something beyond all logic."

Tricia's eyes widened. "Miracle? Like the one you did behind the boat?"

"Does anything come to mind?"

"You mentioned parting of the Red Sea." she said. "The Israelites escaped the pharaoh's army when Moses parted it, and they all got across. That kind of miracle?"

Charlie's smile was cherubic. "I'm afraid my little demonstration behind your boat has overly influenced you. That's the Biblical story, yes, but hardly a factual one. In terms of impact, however, it's a wonderful example. Yes, our goal depends on something like that."

She frowned. "It was a fake?"

"The story has been embellished to such a degree that fact no longer applies. Were those Biblical reports of a 'strong east wind' really that believable? Supposedly it blew for a whole day from that quarter—which, by the way, was all wrong in terms of direction, as bodies of water in the region run generally north and south—and in the process of blowing it dried up the mucky bottom of a reed-filled lake—if the term was Reed Sea, as some scholars postulate—enough so an estimated two million Israelites could cross. Or, if you will, dried up the bottom of any body of water. That in itself would be a miracle by any stretch of the imagination.

"First, a wind strong enough to separate waters would also have swept away all humans and livestock, including the pharaoh's army hot on their heels with all those imagined chariots the Egyptians hadn't actually started using for such purposes at the time. Chariots came into use a hundred years later. Setting that little detail aside, those fantasy chariot drivers delayed long enough for the supposed two million Israelites to cross safely to the opposite side, then came charging after them at a gallop.

"Notwithstanding the fact that scholars can't even agree on where this body of water was, let's discuss two million. That's the number experts say is most probable, however flawed their logic may be. Putting fifty speedy runners shoulder to shoulder, you'd need forty *thousand* rows of runners to make two million, each row about two hundred feet wide. Picture that in your minds. It would take more than ten hours for all those rows of speedy runners to pass the starting line at full gallop, and far more time to cross whatever dry sea bed they supposedly crossed. My example uses runners, but what about women with babies, the elderly, feeble and sick? Did the slowest of them hold the others back? Did that mean it would take two or three or four times the ten hours for them all just to pass that starting point? Maybe half a dozen days? How much food do two million people need every day? How was all that carried, considering that their so-called manna from Heaven came later? Two million is very wrong, you see. Or the army at their heels is wrong. Or the wind that parted a sea is all wrong. The whole thing has been distorted beyond belief."

"So where did it happen?" Tricia pressed.

He chuckled. "The *Biblical* version of the actual event didn't happen at all. Once again, scholars and historians totally ignore the possibility of any outside cause. After all, it was a miracle, and common people can't create miracles, can they? Especially imaginary extraterrestrials."

She appeared stunned. "*You* did it? Your people? I mean, you made that canyon in the ocean a few hours ago."

"Let's just leave it said that the *incident* is there in people's minds, controversial and vivid thanks to DeMille's epic film. We can use something like that to draw attention to Jim's role as messenger. We *must* have the world listening when our message is delivered."

Jim held up an index finger. "Okay, but—"

"Please hear me out. The media is attracted to anything controversial, startling or political, as you both know. Put all three together and the world will know about it within minutes. It has to be colossal, to work. I have such an event in mind, but I promised not to influence you. Let's see if you can read *my* thoughts for a change, Jim. It's imperative we work on the Americans, I believe, since they are most influential, or perhaps the Chinese, since they are poised to dominate the political world as it exists now. Your incident should last long enough for the media to react, say at least half an hour. Any ideas?"

"The Americans suit me just fine, Charlie. I owe them."

"And?"

"Well, unless I have my dates wrong, there's an economic summit on the calendar in a few days, in Munich. Air Force One will be landing there."

"Yes, yes, the G-8 summit. Good. You're on track."

"What are you two talking about?" Tricia fumed. "I'm a part of this."

"Tricia, you are very much a part of it, so here's a question for you. How long will it take every TV station in the world to interrupt broadcasting for a startling event involving Air Force One, with President Brewster, his staff and a dozen reporters aboard, all in communication with their ground counterparts? Put on your journalistic thinking cap and take a guess."

"I would say... ten minutes, assuming it was something momentous like Kennedy's assassination."

"Right. No matter the time of day or night, or whatever the country, a truly startling event would be broadcast within minutes."

She put her fork down. "Something's going to happen to Air Force One? And the world is going to know about it immediately?"

"As it's happening."

"So when do I find out what *it* is?"

Jim drew a long breath. "It works like this, Trish. When the plane touches down...."

By the time he'd finished outlining his idea and answering questions, the rest of her dinner was cold. She glanced first at Charlie, then back at him.

"Why am I getting a creepy feeling about this?"

Chapter 14

Salt Lake City.

Nils Van Oot's number was to be used only in an emergency involving Jim or Tricia, but that didn't guarantee the man would be there. He might not answer at all, or the number might not work any longer. Ollie heard clicks at the distant end, but even they were ominous, suggesting the call was being traced.

He was about to close the channel when a metallic voice came on: "State your name and purpose."

He thought for a moment. Van Oot had been instrumental in coaching Jim during the Yellowstone crisis. In fact, he'd hacked into Greenward's computer enough to steer Jim away from capture. How could that be turned into name and purpose? Something about the Yellowstone incident?

"State your name and purpose."

"Beavers in Wyoming fly faster than warthogs from Idaho."

Another click, then a rather deep voice. "What color beavers?"

"Silver."

"How many warthogs?"

"One, from Boise."

"Were you sent to me, Mr. Robinson, or are you doing this on your own?"

"On my own. Shoot, how'd you know it was me?"

"Only you could know those details and also have this phone number. What can I do for you?"

"Is it possible to resurrect phone calls from a certain estate in Quaker Hill, New York, made within the past two weeks?"

"Mr. Robinson, I maintain more than four hundred tracking programs on persons of interest around the globe, including the weasel who lives there. My file contains *all* his calls, including those made from his computer, for the past nine months. I haven't reviewed it recently, but a copy can be forwarded to you. I'll need a safe destination address, so find a public terminal in Salt Lake City and send a wordless message to q2@nvab.dk. I will send you the file as soon as I receive your transmission. Prepare to record several megabytes. I think you and your FBI ally will find what you need."

"You know about him, too?"

"You met him in Colorado on the fifth of July last year, and he is related to the weasel. You are calling from his city of residence at the moment. The rest is simple logic for anyone with computer skills such as mine."

"Can you tell me anything about our mutual friends?"

"I've been waiting for contact, but there have been no calls."

Cumberland, Maryland. | March 13.

Mike shrugged into a black parka, checked his Glock 20 and slipped into the roadside brush a mile from the cemetery. The meeting was to be at two A.M., testifying to Stauf's naiveté. Darkness wouldn't stop anyone with infra-red equipment, in case the NPA man was worried about being seen.

A basic rule for any clandestine meeting was to arrive well ahead of the other party, and in this case the cemetery's hilltop setting provided a commanding view of all approaches while offering plenty of security. Massive oaks dotted the knoll, with a few crypts and sculptures thrown in. The cemetery's bottom edge on the back side bordered a golf course, separated by a high cyclone fence. Little to worry about from that direction, including someone with a silenced rifle and high-powered night vision scope. The area of interest would be all on the cemetery side of the hill.

His FLIR hand-held imaging camera/binocular combination showed hotter objects as jet black while their cooler surroundings were anything from greenish-gray to white. A reasonable range for any expert sniper in daylight would be three hundred yards. Cut that almost in half at night, say five hundred feet. With no leaves on any of the trees, and no evergreens, any sniper would have to find something else for his perch.

Now where would a sniper hide?

St. Helier.

Tricia's Peruvian passport photo showed her as too pale-skinned in light of Charlie's proposed deep-tan makeover, but they could remedy that with a counterfeiter Jim had used twice in the past, in Barcelona. Once that was done, they'd fly to Munich. As for the boat, it would be hauled and draped with canvas in the morning.

Tricia twirled her hair around a finger. "Jim, how do you know this Barcelona person's still in the counterfeiting business? You never mentioned him to me."

"He is a she, Trish, an allergy specialist with an established practice. You're looking darker already, by the way. Charlie, is that possible, or is it the lighting in here?"

"Oh, she started darkening once I'd mentioned it, yes. UV is the normal stimulant, but the chemical reaction it triggers can be stimulated mentally. Color is reflected light, so her skin is simply absorbing more of the light spectrum. Dark photos are the best for passports, by the way, assuming they match their owners. You should both have new photos, so Barcelona it will be, but it's time now to call it a night." He checked his watch. "My energy boost has been holding you up like amphetamines, but when I release it you'll both sleep through an earthquake. Meet me here tomorrow at three P.M. Any questions?" He started to rise, but Tricia was holding up a finger.

"One," she said. "I have to know this, or I won't sleep. You say you've been here for almost three thousand Earth years, so… since the Israelites *didn't* cross the Red Sea the way everyone thinks, is the rest of the Bible wrong, too?"

"Perhaps half is, shall we say, less than accurate. The original texts were fine, but not after the experts were done correcting them. Ezekiel is a perfect example. The poor soul tried to describe one of our landers, using his own terms for things he didn't understand. After religious scholars turned it all into allegory, the account was anything but. Couldn't be a spacecraft, because that would be ridiculous. Now I hope I haven't spoiled your sleep."

She smiled. "Oh, you haven't. That's what I've always thought."

Chapter 15

Cumberland. | 1:55 A.M., March 14.

The solitary figure paused every so often as he made his way up the cemetery hill. Was he checking instructions, or just making it look like he was? Mike lowered the FLIR. If anyone else was watching with infra-red optics, it would be Stauf's loss. *He* was the one who wanted secrecy for the meeting. He'd undoubtedly be wired, with a receiver behind his car's visor and a recorder under the seat.

"Over here, Mr. Stauf."

"Mike?"

Who else did you expect? "You're on time, I see. Now let's hear what's on your mind."

"I think you know." The other man extended his hand in the dark, finally withdrawing it.

"Not in the mood for handshakes. You people apparently expect me to save my daughter and in the process deliver Jim Foster. Don't you know me better than that?"

"That's not it at all. Let's say I'm being directed by… others. I'm beginning to doubt some of the inputs when it comes to your daughter, so are you willing to answer a few questions?"

"Your inputs are wrong."

"I can't discuss them… you know that."

"And this isn't high school. You've dragged me here so you *can't* discuss anything? Is that your message?"

"Foster's guilt is already established, but I'm not sure about Tricia. Perhaps she shouldn't be on the list as a *willing* accomplice, even though she's reportedly traveling with him. I want her to know she can give herself up, cooperate with us in bringing Foster to justice and in the process save her life. I need facts I can't seem to get from available sources. How much do you know about her relationship with Foster? I'm only trying to help here. Perhaps if you told me—"

"Born at night, but not last night, Mr. Stauf. One direct answer on my part to *any* question about my daughter makes me liable to charges of harboring and concealing terrorists, by *your* department's definition and rules. You can then throw me in jail for my refusal to answer further questions, and there I'll rot until I do comply. I can recite the whole Patriot Act in case you've forgotten to bring along your copy, but more significant is your own department's repeated violations of it. You've recently searched my house three times without the required notice. I've been one of your targets ever since the NPA was organized, and your FBI buddies used every trick in the books trying to get something on me, so no dice on Tricia or Jim. What's the real reason for this meeting? I hope that's not it."

"You could help your daughter if you'd just see things differently."

"We just covered that. Why a *secret* meeting, Stauf? Not for questions you know I won't answer about inputs you can't discuss."

"Let's say I wanted to explore certain avenues without others in my organization knowing."

"Howard Greenward?"

Stauf's long silence told its own story. After three false starts, he managed a reply. "Okay, we'll do this a different way. Tell me what you know about Greenward. You should be able to answer that without your imagined repercussions."

"No comment on Greenward until you strip buck naked, bend over and spread. I'll use your pencil flashlight with the red cap for my inspection. Even then, your shoes will make a journey of about fifty feet from here, with a little help from my arm. Otherwise I'll assume you're wired."

"Always the tough guy, Mike? Okay, you win on that point. Greenward's been put in charge of this… vendetta against Foster and your daughter. For the record, I'm not wearing a wire or recorder."

"Of course not. What could I have been thinking? There are a good dozen ways to conceal transmitters these days, starting with that flashlight and finishing with a belt buckle, so we'll call it a device and that'll do nicely. Now, do I detect a bit of resentment in the word vendetta? You're not suggesting Mr. Greenward is calling all the shots by any chance? That you're taking directions from him on this?"

"What I'm trying to do… the reason for this meeting, if you will… is verify something about your daughter. That ought to interest you."

"It doesn't. Did Greenward show you the Russian document?"

"The what?"

"Don't babble, Mr. Stauf. This is America. We're supposed to be on the same side. Did you *read* the Russian document Greenward showed you, the ultimatum?"

"I have no idea what you're talking about."

"He assured you, of course, that you were seeing the only copy… that it would go back to where he's been holding it these past two plus years. He'd have said that no one besides Towers, the late John Hughes and our past president had ever seen it. You chose to believe all that drivel without bothering to check for yourself, am I right?"

"You're talking in riddles, O'Dell."

"Mr. Stauf, you were hoodwinked, and you gave him permission to do it. It's the man's nature, but perhaps you can offset that nasty habit of his. I have—on paper, packaged and ready to distribute—a complete and detailed description of every item you read about, *plus* dozens of names, dates, precise times of day and incidents outside your investigative prowess that you did *not* read about. My collection extends beyond anything Greenward knew or pretends to know now, and assembles the remainder of the story in such a way that everything in the Russian document becomes crystal clear to anyone who might read it. Anyone at all, say anyone in Congress for openers. That ought to interest *you*."

"Where would you get such information? From your daughter?"

"Ask Greenward for the parts he left out."

"My question doesn't pertain to your imaginary Russian document. You just stepped in a big pile of your own shit, O'Dell. You admit to owning information that could greatly damage this country if revealed. That makes *you* a potential threat to the nation, doubly so since your newspaper gives you the means to spread that damage as few others can. If you don't immediately hand over all information in your possession, I can order you held for contempt. We will throw the key away if I do. Everything and anything you have in writing, O'Dell. All tapes, discs, recordings, memory chips and anything else you can produce. Your words are now on record as of this moment, this meeting."

Gotcha! That was easier than I figured. "Apparently you're the nervous sort, Mr. Stauf. When you're nervous you think too fast, and that makes you sloppy. Probably a holdover from your FBI days. The device you denied having on your person works both ways. In order for you to use the recording being created down there under the car seat, you'll be compelled to explain my reference to the very Russian document you deny having read, a black folder with the Russian coat of arms on the cover, containing thirty-six inside pages in case you forgot to notice the page numbers as you read. Now think back. Did I say anything about the *nature* of the information inside that folder? No? Tsk! What could possibly have you thinking it would have anything to do with damaging this country, since you've never seen what I'm talking about?"

"*Anything* to do with Russia is potentially damaging to this country, O'Dell."

"Russia's in no condition to damage *any* country, not even little Luxembourg. Could it be that you actually did read the contents of that folder and it's your knowledge of the contents that tripped you up. Hmmmm?"

"My department exists to neutralize threats like you, O'Dell. I'll give you twenty-four hours to produce what you have before our people come knocking on your door. We know every move you make, and precisely when you make it. You can't pee without our knowing."

"Hate to disappoint you, Mr. Stauf, but right now there are several dozen copies of the subject material all addressed, stamped and ready to mail to select congressmen and certain of the media. There'll be an explosion when they open their mail. What I *might* consider is a trade of sorts."

"You're threatening to undermine the government with your so-called information unless we take your daughter's name off that list?"

"I've had this information all this time and you've not heard a peep from me. That's about to change unless I get what I'm after. Don't you want to know what that is?"

"Blackmail in this context is another form of terrorism. I hope you have a good lawyer. You'll need him."

"Mr. Stauf, I've never formally accepted the Distinguished Service Cross awarded me by Congress, something even you might know. However, I can choose to accept it at any time and I suddenly have the urge to do just that. My request has been prepared, with instructions to present it to the appropriate parties if any of several scenarios play out as a result of this secret meeting of yours. Would it seem probable I'd request an audience with leaders of both houses, given the nature of the document you're denying? Do you think I'd be turned away? And are you also aware that my combat decorations entitle me to an audience with the president as well? Now… just how eager *are* you to have me locked up and charged with blackmailing the U.S. government? Does your sudden silence imply thinking, I hope?"

Stauf finally cleared his throat. "Okay, what do you want?"

"You, Clarence Towers, Greenward and President Brewster together… for one hour. Four of you, not three, not two… four. I don't care what's recorded or who else hears what I will say. I'll disclose everything in that hour, minus interruptions from any of you, and thereafter I'll answer questions. My purpose is information sharing for the *good* of the country. It will take a full hour just to deliver my part, but during that time I will detail all of James Foster's activities, from his previous life to the way in which he was tracked down at the request of President Winfield, to his magnificent sacrifice in giving up his private and very quiet life to try and help our country in a time of great need. I will cover his bravery while he faced a battery of experiments that could have killed him a dozen times over, plus actual assassination attempts by Russian spetsnaz and our own misdirected commandos, from the moment he appeared on our American scene until he disappeared, that day being June 25 almost three years ago. Tricia's involvement will be included, right down to her being drugged and raped by three of the FBI's finest. All factual. The records are still over there, file and folder. As for Jim's actions since that time, I'll share what I know. You'll have no say in what I choose to disclose, and my sources of information will remain my secret. As a final concession to me, you'll correct world opinion that Jim Foster and my daughter are terrorists… assuming I convince you collectively they are not. I expect you to vote on that upon the conclusion of my hour. I want this to happen immediately, not next week or next month."

"You're nuts, O'Dell. No way will I even suggest such a thing, not even to Towers."

"You're afraid of Greenward. If I were you, I'd be afraid of *me*, not him. I don't want to rip this country seam to seam, but I will definitely do that as an alternative to my more reasonable request. I'll leave it to you to think it over, but my alternate plan is already in place and it will launch in spite of whatever nastiness you decide you'll try. I'm quite accustomed to dealing with the enemy, as you well know. Don't be one."

"Your goddamn blackmail won't work on me, O'Dell. Twenty-four hours. Not one second more."

"You are not listening well at all. Play the tape several times. I want your answer in that same twenty-four hours, or I will lift the lid. You've heard of Pandora, I presume?"

Stauf turned off the recorder under the rider's seat, removed the tiny transmitter from his flashlight, then the receiver behind the visor. He sat in the dark car, thinking. O'Dell should have been on the defensive, but he'd attacked. Further, he knew far more than Greenward claimed. Described that Russian document right down to the number of pages in the thing, plus inferring there were dozens of other names, places, precise times of day and incidents, but how would he know any of it unless he'd been an accessory in the first place? That would make him as much a terrorist as Foster and the girl, unless... unless there were others in Washington who also knew about the document, contrary to every assurance Greenward had given. The prospect did *not* produce a warm fuzzy feeling. And what about O'Dell's face to face challenge? That said he held the high cards and it also made Howard Greenward a liar. Howard's trip to Greece and his statements about Howland... could they all be part of a personal vendetta? O'Dell might have been right about that, but how in hell could the guy recite things Greenward said and did, almost to the word? How could he possibly know Howard was calling the shots on the Foster case?

Perhaps Greenward deserved a closer look, and a good place to start was H. J. Winfield, the man who'd been president when it all took place. Soon to be released from the Lonsdale Rehab Center, Winfield received visitors these days, walked about the grounds, played chess and bridge and was back to doing tough crosswords in the Sunday Times. If questions were phrased right, his answers would shed plenty of light. For example, what happened following Las Vegas and when had Foster entered the picture? Who knew of Foster or even where to look? Ah, *there* was an interesting question. Someone knew who he was and where to find him, this at the very time the Oval Office was launching ad hoc committees and announcing that the nation's best scientists were confounded. Why would they have gone after Foster only then, not earlier?

Winfield's obsession with the Mudslinger cost him his sanity, but Greenward was his closest friend and personal advisor all through that period. Was Howard playing the role of master chess player, moving chess pieces to suit his own idea of how the war game should be played? It wouldn't be the first time an American president had been the pawn of his own advisor. The bigger question was whether Winfield had come to believe Foster was in fact working for the Russians *prior* to the Las Vegas attack, or later. When and how did he reach that conclusion? The answer to that question would determine, in a way, how much of Greenward's story was a lie and where the lie began.

As for any meeting between O'Dell and the others, out of the question. Brewster would be on his way to Munich in two days for the G-8, and Towers would turn thumbs down on any meeting with O'Dell in the first place. If Towers had *his* way, O'Dell's name would be on the Tombstone List right along with his daughter's.

The Lonsdale Rehab Center was on the route back to D.C. Time enough to catch a few hours of sleep. There was a motel back a few miles.

80CB

The man in black, sitting against an oak tree, lowered a pair of high-powered night vision binoculars. They'd been trained on the upper reaches of the cemetery throughout the meeting, registering both forms as black silhouettes against a much brighter background. The one Stauf had met was still up there, most likely hiding behind one of the tombstones. He'd been standing there one second, gone the next. No way in hell could he have known he was being observed, but in any case he hadn't moved far from the spot. Could've been a woman, of course, but the two forms were never within ten feet of each other. It would remain a mystery for the time being, but Mr. Kurt Stauf would bear closer watching from now on, much closer. This kind of meeting was typical of the new-age mole, and Stauf's position in the NPA made him an automatic suspect, what with the likes of Foster operating the way he did. Witness the way Foster'd already destroyed Ben Howland, one of the nation's greatest patriots. What if Stauf's contact had been Foster himself? The world's leading terrorist chatting with America's head of Counterterrorism? By no means out of the question. Stauf could have been doling out scraps of erroneous information on Foster being in Europe, when all the time the sicko was right here. Yes, time to do a little digging into Mr. Stauf's activities in the past few weeks.

On his way back to the car, half a mile away, Greenward made several more sweeps with the binoculars. Still nobody in sight up there, and Stauf's vehicle was long gone. Maybe the other party had gone down the backside of the hill, but even that was impossible without being seen while going over the top. Most likely he'd simply dropped down behind one of the stones and might not move for an hour.

After one final sweep with the glasses, Greenward pulled away the pair of saplings that all but covered his Mercedes, backed out of the little side road, then made a U-turn and drove a full mile before turning on his headlights. Just like old times back in the Marines.

Mike snapped the lens caps back onto his camera/binocular. He now had three sharp images of the Mercedes license plate, taken without the reversed imagery feature, plus a half dozen shots of the car's scowling driver from a distance of ten paces. Two were full-face and all were enhanced by the camera's infra-red illuminator.

Greenward was getting sloppy. He'd forgotten that stealth worked both ways, but then his military days had mostly been spent behind a desk. Stauf, on the other hand, was a total amateur. If he'd counted on keeping the thing a secret, he'd failed miserably in that respect. Greenward not only knew about the meeting, but knew when and where it would happen, or else he'd followed Stauf without being detected. Even so, he hadn't known who the second party was to be, otherwise why sit against a tree scanning the meeting place? Tsk!

Right equipment, wrong tactics. To see someone, you had to be looking where the person *was* at the moment, not where he'd been. Maybe
Stauf was already suspicious of Howard Greenward, maybe not, but
there was no guessing where Greenward's suspicions lay. He'd watch
Stauf like a hawk from now on.

Mike removed the miniature recorder tucked beneath his jacket
collar and returned to his own well-hidden car not fifty yards from
where the Mercedes had been parked. Things didn't look promising.

Chapter 16

St. Helier. | March 14, 3:00 P.M.

Charlie'd been busy while they slept.

"I arranged to have the boat hauled and painted ," he announced when they re-joined him, "and we have a private flight to Barcelona all set to go, soon as you're ready. Our pilot is waiting. Dr. Diaz expects us this evening."

"How? I never mentioned her name or how to reach her."

"You thought of her. Our mission together requires me to monitor your thoughts, but I promised not to influence you, and that still holds. As to anything truly private or personal, I'm three million years ahead of you both." His grin was impish.

"Charlie, Sylvia Diaz is on the other side of Spain and they have only light aircraft here in Jersey. How did you arrange—"

"It's a Lear, and the owner is someone I've used several times. He was happy to jump over from England, and he'll take us on to Munich as well, so no worries about booking a commercial flight. Now we *must* move quickly as the G-8 dignitaries will start arriving in Munich tomorrow and we must be in position before then. We will go first to the Besucherpark, where an artificial hill is topped with an observation deck. The entire airport can be seen from there, both runways."

Tricia looked puzzled. "Assuming we get there and Jim does his stuff with the plane, are you going to make some sort of speech then?"

"In a way, yes, but Jim will be delivering it. Isn't that right, Jim?"

"I'm a cackle in an elephant dungeon." The voice that came forth was totally foreign.

She wrinkled her nose. "What?"

"Blime zax fernmo appentish wacko lushford! Ha-ha-ha."

It was Jim's turn to look puzzled. "What did I just say? Charlie, what did you just make me say?"

"Just giving Tricia a little example. You won't be aware of what you're saying or about to say, nor will you need to concentrate in any way at all. We can work all these details out on our way. Ah, here come your breakfasts."

"But we didn't order anything...." She stopped. "I should have known. Will I get a fortune cookie with it?"

NPA Headquarters. | 3:15 A.M., March 14.

"What? You're crazy. This thing is pure fantasy, a hoax. What was Clarence smoking?"

Hardly the words of a man charged with eradicating terrorism, Greenward mused. Could it be Stauf had already crossed over to the terrorist side? That he was sympathetic not only to Foster, but a few others... like O'Dell? The way he'd defended the muckraker was sickening. O'Dell knew damn well where his daughter was hiding, which made him an accessory.

How did the cemetery man figure into the picture?

A really *clever* mole would hide his tracks, but Stauf was ex-FBI, which translated meant Fucked-up Bumbling Idiots. Where were all the honest people? Was there no one left who could be trusted? What did Stauf's secret meeting say about the rest of his activities to date? And what about those reports on the Foster sailboat sightings? What if he'd been planting false leads with the Europeans, confusing their search?

Stauf's computer was accessible to anyone in the NPA with access codes, but a thorough search for the keyword *cemetery* produced nothing. How about Cumberland? A quick search of NPA data banks turned up thousands of names, all business owners rated by levels of suspicion, social contacts, families, associations, internet practices and memberships, sexual preferences, newspapers and magazines, who they slept with and who their wives and sons and daughters slept with: old FBI files, useful at times, but not this time. Why that cemetery... unless some of Stauf's family members were interred there.

But cemetery records for Cumberland's slumberlands showed no Staufs.

Everything Stauf had recently created using his computer was business as usual. Travel records showed no previous trips to Cumberland,

and the appointment log showed a blank for everything after six P.M. Stauf left the office each day at that time, yet there he'd been at his computer the previous evening, a little past nine, staying until ten. Unaware he was being followed, he drove to the airport where he changed cars to a rental. From there he'd driven straight to Cumberland. What did he think the rental car would do, keep him from being seen?

Greenward paced. The mole *must* have left a trail of some sort. What if he'd been wired? That would be *de rigueur* for some clandestine meeting, but if he'd used NPA equipment it would be logged out in his name. Those logs were available to anyone in NPA. Bingo! He'd signed out a full complement—flashlight transmitter, car visor receiver and recorder. NPA regs required him to record the intended use in his activity log, but there was no such entry. Another infraction. *Catch me in one lie, catch me in another.*

So... he'd recorded the meeting, fair enough and in keeping with any typical mole, but who was the other party? What about Cumberland itself, aside from the federal penitentiary there? Wait! There *had* been something back when that FBI agent had been killed up north of there. That was when... shit, that was the time none other than Mike O'Dell had been booked on suspicion of murder. He'd been in Cumberland on some unspecified business he'd never described, and was known to have a revenge motive. He was caught trying to flee the country by private plane.

It was finally making sense. Stauf's defensiveness about O'Dell had to be a smoke screen, part of his strategy. The man had even bet a week's pay that O'Dell knew exactly where his daughter was. Interesting, but what if Kurt *wasn't* a mole after all, and had simply been trying to score a coup, corralling O'Dell and somehow getting information out of him? It would explain his caginess, unless... unless the meeting had an altogether different purpose. What if it was all O'Dell's doing? What if he was manipulating... damn, *that's* what it was, it had to be. O'Dell was worth millions compared to Stauf's five figure income. A little cash on the barrelhead? Who'd know?

The computer listing of Cumberland business owners showed Michael O'Dell as the owner of Cavanaugh's Bed & Breakfast and a second check on the cemetery brought up Carolyn O'Dell, Mike's wife of long ago. So the meeting was O'Dell's doing after all. He'd doped out who it was at NPA he could bribe. The idiot thought he wouldn't be seen in the dark, way up there on that hill, but he'd forgotten about infrared in the hands of an expert. At any rate, Kurt ought to have reported O'Dell's request to Towers, made the whole thing official, but there was still time to make things right if he divulged what he'd learned. If not... well, the next few days might bring things to a head. Foster and slut girlfriend were priority one and two. O'Dell would make it three. *You're playing in the big leagues, Kurt, me lad. Hope you have the good sense to come clean up front.*

Time to check his own email before grabbing a few winks and running a shaver over his stubble. There were twenty messages waiting, but the most recent was from Towers. The rest could wait.

Surprise, Howie. Brewster wants you in his party for the G-8 in Munich, maybe for added security. Call me as soon as you get this. AF-1 leaves morning of the 16th. Towers.

Of all the stupid... why? The O'Dell development could signal a breakthrough on the Foster case. It needed exposure and follow-through, someone who knew the facts and how to use them to counter O'Dell's lies. That couldn't be done camping out in Munich. Besides, Brewster was only using the G-8 for a photo op. He'd have his Secret Service boys on the plane, and once they'd landed at Munich he'd be safer than he was at home. The Germans were good at what they did. Short of terrorists blowing up the whole damn airport, there was no way any of them would get close enough to worry about. Strike added security as a reason.

But you didn't argue with an imbecile.

Salt Lake City. | Morning, March 14.

Van Oot's email produced twenty-six single-spaced pages listing every call to or from Greenward's Quaker Hill estate, plus calls made from three separate cell phones and his desk at the NPA. How had Van Oot achieved *that* piece of hacking, since NPA firewalls were inpenetrable? Ollie winced. No wonder the terrorists were gaining ground. Anyone with the right computer skills could turn the NPA and other organizations into an open book, long as he didn't get caught.

Nothing in the emails implicated Greenward in mass murder or arson, nor was there any reference to a secret group with an agenda, but phone records told a different story. There were several dozen recurring numbers, calls to and from Greenward's estate, fully half of them originating on his computer. Harry wasn't surprised.

"He uses his computer so he can scramble voice. Now we see who owns the destination numbers." He transferred the e-file to his computer and shortly the owners' names emerged. "Look at these, Ollie. Industrialists, bankers, one media giant, two from the oil cartels, pharmaceuticals, transportation… biggest in the nation… and shipping. It goes back to… why, to the point where Brewster assumed the presidency."

"There's our friend Sleck," Robinson pointed. "Look at all those calls to him in the period leading up to Yellowstone."

"I smell politics here, Ollie. Were they loading the dice for Brewster's replacement come election time?"

"Sleck's specialty was creating psychological profiles of criminals for government agencies and big city police forces, but he also worked the other side of the street, did'ja know that? Mike said he'd been following the guy for years."

"A conspiracy for sure, but also conjecture until we catch Uncle red-handed. With anything this big, a few more murders here and there are almost guaranteed. Mike had better watch his back, unless it's too late."

"I'd better warn him."

"I thought you couldn't reach him by phone."

"That was yesterday. I might be able to reach him now… if nothing bad has…." He whipped out his cell phone. "He warned me not to say anything in the clear. What kind of code can I use?"

"Alpha mike foxtrot if full bull finds you first. Full bull means bird colonel, which means Greenward. The rest translates to 'final bye bye.' He should get it."

"If I reach him, what's next?"

"Sleck might be open to singing a bit about certain meetings at the Greenward estate. Depends on his view of the justice system, his being a criminal expert and all that, but right now he's the fall guy for Howland, who was supposedly duped into thinking he was involved in a secret national security program. That's Uncle's doing and it makes me sick, but that's what everyone thinks. Sleck ought to be saying to himself, 'Hey, why am I in this alone?' It helps that we have a court order separating Sleck's legal team from Howland's, at Howland's request. Neither felon can communicate with the other, and that has Sleck in a wringer. He might just be approachable, perhaps for even the remotest chance to get his sentence commuted to life. My involvement with Uncle regarding the birds puts me in a legal position to know about Sleck's going there to his estate a few times. Sleck's lawyers will have to be in on this, but they won't argue."

"How about Howard? Will he raise a stink?"

"Ollie, how will he know?"

Lonsdale Rehab Center. | Morning, March 14.

"Mr. President?"

Winfield was practicing on a small putting green as Kurt approached. He looked up, straightened and smiled, then upended his putter and let it slide until it hit his closed hand.

"Hello, Kurt. The folks here told me you were coming over for a visit. Hear you're in charge of anti-terrorism these days. That's good, good. I've been keeping track these past few months, you know, getting back into the swing of things, so to speak."

"They say you're ready to walk out of here, sir."

"Two days from now I'm my own person again. Back to normal, at least in my own mind." Winfield smiled, gesturing at a nearby bench. "I'm just not sure where I want to go, now that I'm no longer president. Stanley Brewster's doing a fine job, a fine job… don't you think so?"

"He can't hold a candle to you, sir, if you want the truth. I'd like to see the day when you're a major voice in the scheme of things, the way you were before. Our problems seem to be growing by the minute."

"Those days are over for me, I'm afraid. Well, like the old song goes, I didn't slip, I wasn't pushed, I fell. That Vegas thing was the straw that broke the camel's back, or so they tell me here, but I've given up placing blame. No future in it."

"You brought up the one topic that's always interested me, Mr. President, the Vegas thing. I've been wondering about this James Foster who came into the picture...."

Winfield squinted. "What about him?"

"Well, how exactly did you discover he was a Russian agent? What gave him away? I've always been curious."

"Hell, *I* never thought he was anyone's agent, Kurt. That Russian business was all Howard's idea. Foster was a John Doe, just a nobody who had a special talent we needed. I never expected we'd find anyone like him, never knew anything about him when we did, and didn't much care. He was our best shot at... say, how'd *you* come to know so much about Foster? I don't remember ever mentioning the name to Clarence."

"Through Howard Greenward, sir. You probably know Clarence made Mr. Greenward his special assistant. You've also heard, I suppose, that Foster and his girlfriend are on the Tombstone List as international terrorists, shoot on sight, all that. That was Howard's doing. He has a real vendetta going for the Mudslinger, as he calls Foster. I have a few doubts, which is why I'm curious."

"Howard is Towers' right hand man? I didn't know. Well... I guess I thought Foster might be a terrorist just before my breakdown, but not any more. No way should he be on that list, or his girlfriend either. Who besides Howard was behind that move?"

"I have no idea. He hasn't really confided in me, other than in trying to get me to go along with it. He claimed Foster caused the Las Vegas disaster, all those deaths. Is that right?"

Winfield stared into the distance for several long moments. Then he turned and locked eyes. "*Who* besides Howard is saying Foster was in any way involved with Las Vegas, Kurt?"

"The story's run in all the papers and on the internet. Foster supposedly left clues that he was there... in Vegas... and Howard insisted that was true. Foster was also the mastermind behind all those wildfires in Yellowstone, all the murders, and Secretary Howland was just a scapegoat. Howard's personally talked to Howland since then, or so he says. There's no record of his ever visiting the man in prison, but I don't see how he could have gotten the information any other way."

"Has he said anything else that has you wondering?"

"Well, yes. He claimed to have attended that biomedical counter-measures conference in Athens, but—"

"Why on earth would he go to *that*? It's not his field."

"Well, sir, I'm wondering if he actually did go. His report included a summary of the keynote address at the conference main event, but the conference chairman said Howard never attended that dinner. I did a little further digging, and Howard was in or around Paris at precisely the time of the London subway bombing. When he returned stateside he was fuming about how the bombing ought to prove to the world what would happen unless Foster was stopped. He wanted me to put Foster and the girl on the Tombstone List immediately."

"Well, he's totally wrong about Foster, and you're correct in doubting him. In my judgment, Foster was a quiet man who didn't quite understand his talent. He seemed quite humble. We'd hoped he'd shed light on some sort of answer to the mystery forces behind the destruction of Las Vegas. That is, I hoped he would, prayed we could learn something about his special talents in time to do something with them, but I was alone in that. As it turned out he gave us an answer, a good one, but not the way we all thought. His move was a brilliant example of strategic thinking and possibly the only thing that saved this country. I didn't see it then, but I do now. He's no terrorist, no sir."

"You're saying he stymied the Russ... sorry, I didn't mean to lead you, sir."

"You were going to say Russians. At the time, yes, we suspected them, but none of us had a clue. During the time I've been in the looney bin I've done a lot of thinking. I had a nervous breakdown, Kurt—that's what it was, according to the docs. Too much stress all at once, can happen to anyone. Part of that stress came from thinking I'd helped create a monster in Foster, like some horror film character. We developed his talents, you know, brought them out. I had a psychological guy... Whittier. He was on one of my committees studying the Las Vegas thing. He found Foster for us, brought him back here, used drugs on him and increased the guy's natural abilities a hundred times over. Later I believed... I was *led* to believe that Foster would hire out to the highest bidder and take over the world. Name whatever organization you want, if they hired him they could rule. They'd take us over, all of us, this country, Britain, Russia, Germany, all Europe, the whole shebang, all through this one man. That's what I was led to believe."

"Foster really has that kind of power?"

"Power, yes, but he's not the kind who'd use it to hurt a soul. He risked his life trying to help us, risked his life, Kurt. He volunteered, mind you. Didn't have to do it. Wasn't even a U.S. citizen."

"How about the mud job on the White House?"

"Awesome. Perfect. Never harmed one soul doing it." Winfield chuckled. "The building needed roof repairs anyway."

"Who led you to believe he'd... you know... hire out to anyone? Who was saying that? Was it Greenward?"

"Let's... it was... it was him, yes. We tried to bring Foster in, give him protection and all that, but he flew the coop instead. Don't say I blame him. Your questions have helped me refocus, Kurt. Get back to your office and tell Clarence I want to talk one-on-one with Stanley Brewster immediately, today if possible. If Stanley can get over here in person, all the better. Then ask Clarence to clear you officially for whatever I have to tell you. I want you back here for another chat soon as you do that."

"He'll want to know what I was doing here talking to you in the first place."

"Tell him I sent for you. I'll back you on that. Tell him I said you were here doing your job, talking to me. Something you've said has me greatly bothered, and I want to get to the bottom of it." He suddenly smiled. "It's all coming back."

"Sir, there's something else. I think you should know."

"Yes?"

"I hadn't planned to mention this to you at all, but I think now that it could be important, especially if you're about to talk with President Brewster. Last night I met with Michael O'Dell. He—"

"Now there's a true patriot for you. Good man, O'Dell. We're still waiting to hand him that Distinguished Service Cross he earned a few dozen times. Back there when I was heading for the boys with the straightjackets, I thought the opposite about Mike. Thought he'd murdered an FBI agent; thought a lot of things, all wrong. Wrong! Well, what did he have to say?"

"Sir, it's not the best of news. He asked me to arrange a meeting between him, Howard, Clarence and President Brewster, lasting one hour. This has to do with Foster and O'Dell's daughter, who is Foster's girlfriend. O'Dell claims to be holding what he calls a complete compilation of all the events from Las Vegas forward, including all the details about Foster, you, Howard and others, and the fact that it was the Russians who were behind Las Vegas. He has what amounts to an ultimatum from the Russ—"

"Stop. Stop right there." Winfield stroked his chin, then drew a long breath. "It appears that my worst fears have come back to haunt me. So, O'Dell's coming in with guns blazing? Can't say I blame him."

"That's what it sounds like, sir, only he says he's just interested in setting the picture right among us. I'm supposed to be there, too. He mentioned thirty-six pages in the Russian document and hinted at a few things in it, things he says will rip the country open. It so happens I'd already seen the document, again thanks to Howard Greenward, so I assure you that everything O'Dell said was on the money, but he claims he's *also* compiled all sorts of other details, names, places, times. He's threatening to lift the lid if nobody will listen to the facts. Says he has dozens of copies ready to mail or hand to key congressional personnel and the press. If he doesn't get his interview, boom."

"We can't let him do it. Bad enough Howard showed you the thing, but if it ever gets out...."

"Wouldn't President Brewster know how to handle that, sir? Surely he was in on it."

Winfield's quick glance was remorseful. "I kept Stanley in the dark about this whole event, Kurt. He... Stanley is somewhat of a reactionary, you see, easily swayed. At least he was when he was my veep. He's been in the traces long enough now so maybe he's got a better grip, but at that time... well, let's just say I decided the best course for the nation was to include as few as possible. Howard was one. My chief of staff was another... John Hughes, you know, before he died. If Stanley had been in on it, we might have had our Armageddon. I never really liked Stanley all that much, and he never liked me, but sometimes political expediencies rule, you know. Look... you just get a move on and get back to Clarence with my request. We'll have to head this thing off at all costs. Have Clarence call me here if he has any doubts. Maybe he can spring me from this place today instead of two days from now. Damn, this is just like old times!"

"Sir, the G-8 summit is three days from now. Won't President Brewster be busy getting ready and all? He may not have time to—"

"Whatever Clarence says, Stanley does. If Mike O'Dell lets that thing loose, there may not even be a G-8 summit."

Chapter 17

Barcelona, Spain. | Evening, March 14th.

Sylvia Diaz was a high school dropout when Graham Foster's rehab team spotted her in Boston—broke, hungry and already well-entrenched in crime. He offered her a second chance. After three solid months of tutoring, she aced her GED. Six astonishing years later she emerged from Tufts with her M.D.—two years early—and earned certification as an allergist/immunologist.

Her parents and heritage were in Barcelona, so she set up practice there. Her new professional status made the earlier career choice easy to conceal. Who'd have thought anyone with her talents and credentials would deal in forgery by choice? Yet it remained a fun skill as well as a diversion from runny noses and chronic asthma. She enjoyed flirting with danger as much as outfoxing the authorities. A little bit of the street still ran in her blood.

She met them wearing a bulky sweater, jeans, sneakers and oversized glasses. After the brief reunion with Jim, they ate at a restaurant in a seedier part of the city—more than half of Barcelona qualified as slums—and an hour later walked several zig-zag blocks before stopping at a steel door badly in need of paint, nestled between a cobbler's shop and an empty storefront. The door's main features were several long dents, great flakes of peeling paint and twin deadbolt locks. A single flight of stairs led to a second door, also with double locks, opening into a dingy, cold-water flat with drab furnishings, a torn curtain on the only window and a pile of dirty dishes in the sink.

"It's been this way for years," she explained. "I keep the cobwebs off the dishes and dust things occasionally, but if anyone ever breaks in here they'll take one look and move to the next mark. As you can tell from the surroundings outside, this isn't an area known for break-ins." She smiled, then went to a side room door and flipped on the lights. "Ta da! My workshop."

The immaculate room was filled with equipment, file cabinets and optics being the most recognizable, but others with purposes not easy to guess. A boom microscope occupied part of a long table, along with a variety of lamps. Then came box-like items, an oven and refrigerator, plus several cabinets of drawers on each side. In another part of the room she had a photographic setup. A closet was her darkroom.

She looked closely at Jim, comparing him to the Spanish passport she'd done for him not over two years earlier. "You and Tricia have been spending far too much time at the beach, my friend. You're inviting skin cancer."

Jim chuckled. "It's reversible. Charlie did it."

"Of course he did. You said you both want your Peruvian papers redone, but I have another suggestion. Can Tricia speak any Greek or Italian? I know you can."

He nodded. "We recently spent some time in Greece, yes."

"Toasting in the sun the whole time, no doubt. Greek documents are best because the Greeks are terribly tough on counterfeiters, so their documents are rarely challenged." She grinned. "I have all the authentic stuff here. First we get your new photos." She posed Tricia first. "Tricia, I want you to look sober in this. Tight-lipped for the photo, but always smiling when you're in any face to face situation. Jim, you be thinking of some good Greek names to use."

"She's Helen, I'm Timothy. Our last name will be… how about Manos."

Charlie held up a hand. "Jim, we both know why you're suggesting that particular name, but you ought to know something about the name's background in case you're questioned. The Greek equivalent of Smith might be better, something like Pappas."

"Let's see… the name Manos is commonly found in the Epirus region, particularly the county of Ioannina and town of Aëtópetra? Probably half a hundred people there by that name. Is that what you meant, Charlie?"

They left just after midnight with new passports and a driver's license for Jim, dated two years earlier. It looked its age, thanks to a scuffing machine that simulated years of wear and tear in a matter of minutes. What had started out as a newly laminated card emerged looking quite authentic. Sylvia had hundreds of counterfeit customs stamps from places all over the world. Both passports were stamped to show Mr. and Mrs. Timothy Manos as having mostly traveled in the Mediterranean region. Actually, Jim had indeed been in every place selected at one time or another.

An arrival in Munich by mid-afternoon meant they could use the Besucherpark observation deck in daylight and still have time to check roads outside the airport. Charlie was certain Air Force One would use the south runway because that one was set up with freight buildings and hangars at the western end, far from the terminals. The largest hangar at the end would likely be set up for the media, but there was just one little problem: if Air Force One used the north runway, their plan was blown.

Sunset Motel. | late afternoon. March 14th.

Mike hesitated before punching the cell phone TALK button. The incoming call couldn't be coming from Manny Friedman, since they'd talked half an hour earlier, but there was always a chance the phone had been traced from that end. In any case, the motel parking lot was a safer place to talk, even if talking meant grunts and whistles. The wrong kind of grunt might dictate a hasty exit from the motel, but the caller in this case turned out to be known.

Alpha mike foxtrot if full bull finds you first. Ollie Robinson had never been in the military, yet he'd spouted military jargon and then hung up. His call was a warning. AMF could mean several things, but "full bull" could only mean Howard Greenward. The sanitized translation for *alpha mike foxtrot* was getting oneself killed by being careless, and the jargon had to belong to Harry Archer. "If full bull finds you first" implied that Greenward had turned predator, which in turn meant Stauf must have run straight to Greenward after the cemetery meeting.

Greenward was not above murder. Perhaps it was time for a change in strategy.

When the phone vibrated just minutes later, a successful trace was an even greater possibility. Ollie might have been careless, and computer phone tracing systems looked for voiceprints in any answer. Unless a bona fide caller said something without any prompt....

"It's Manny again. Safe?"

"Go ahead."

"Just got a call from a Dr. Elaine Jameson, who said she runs the Whittier Clinic in Cheektowaga, New York. Seems Whittier has been delayed and can't be on hand for the scheduled appointments, end of message. She had no idea where he was, but he'd previously faxed her from overseas and hinted he might drop in for a visit."

Whittier? "Something's fishy. I never expected he'd leave Europe."

"The message was delivered by a Toronto man in a Canadian Customs uniform. Had a daughter with Asperger's Syndrome and wanted to know about the clinic."

"It's the Tombstone thing, Manny. Gordy probably tried to come in through Canada, and they snagged him. Now they'll try to extract information out of him in exchange for letting him go."

"The Jameson woman had my number from back when 1600 Pennsy was trying to drive Whittier Clinic into the poorhouse. Here's her phone number. Am I to do anything?" He read off the number.

"Nothing for now. I'll be in touch."

Definitely time to change strategy, but running to Gordy's rescue would be too dangerous. The official view would be that he knew Jim, was in constant communication with him and even provided resources in one or another way. As for Greenward, the best defense was always a strong offense.

First order of business—a message delivered to the Oval Office, courtesy of the Secret Service.

Lonsdale Rehab Center. | Late afternoon, March 14.

The administrator came in person, flanked by a pair of attendants.

"Mr. President, we've been instructed to release you immediately. Your doctors have signed all the release forms and there's a government limousine waiting outside with two other cars. Our understanding is that you'll travel from here to the White House for an audience with President Brewster. We apologize if this sudden change in plans disturbs you in any way, but—"

"No, no, not at all. In fact, I'm looking forward to talking with Stanley. Anxious to get back into it, you might say."

"We were told there'd be no announcement," the administrator went on, "so you should have no press to worry about. We'll announce your departure tomorrow morning, sir, if that sits well with you."

"Do it. I'm out of here."

ᏇᏨᏋ

"Hello, Stanley."

The gray-haired man standing stoop-shouldered at the green-tinted Oval Office windows turned with a slight smile that broadened immediately. "Oh, good. I was worried there'd be trouble getting you out. The doctors, you know." He strode forward and their hands clasped. "You sent word you wanted to talk to me ASAP. Sit down, sit down. Did they tell you I'm getting ready to leave for Munich?"

"The G-8, yes. I wanted us to talk before you left."

"This must be really important then. So… what's it about?"

"Stan, there's something I should have told you back when it was all happening. I apologize, but at the time it seemed best to keep things under wraps and you were off there handling that crisis in the Philippines. It was the Las Vegas incident. Something horrible was handed me by Kuchomov, the Russian ambassador."

"So it *was* the Russians after all?"

"They had a new kind of power beyond anything known, but the bottom line was that they gave us… me… twenty days to inform Congress that it was all over for the U.S. They'd annex us without firing a shot, take us over. The thing they had… well, it would have taken out all our reactors, all our defenses, satellites, you name it. They had teams all over the country, waiting for the signal to send us back to the Stone Age. If I'd let out one peep, you know what would have happened on The Hill. The Russians held all the high cards and we had nothing. We needed some cards of our own, but our own scientists, the best we had… well, they essentially tried to say Las Vegas never happened. All we would have had going for us if war had been declared were our submarines, and even then I wasn't certain. Most of them need operating satellites for targeting. What kind of ending would that be? Howard Greenward told me that in three days we'd be nothing but roving gangs, three out of four of us dead from disease if not from everything else. Nonexistent society, a hundred nuclear reactors melting down… well, enough said. I took a big gamble, and it paid off. We found the one man who could give us an ace we didn't hold, and what an ace it was. Do you know who I'm talking about?"

"Not a clue."

"He's known today as the Mudslinger because of what he did to the White House. James Foster."

"The *terrorist?*"

"Not, Stanley, N-O-T. The guy risked his life for us, and he didn't have to. Now listen to me. What he did at the end was enough to make the Russians blink, and he did it skillfully enough so our own people, our citizenry, bought the UFO crap. We encouraged them to think it was UFOs, remember? The White House damage was a small price to pay. If they thought it was aliens did it, all the better, but listen… right there is where the trouble started getting worse. Howard, whom I trusted implicitly because of our long friendship, planted all sorts of nightmares in my head."

"About what? Foster?"

"About the possibility anyone with Foster's kind of power would sell out to the big terrorist groups. He kept at it until I couldn't sleep thinking about all the possibilities. I was up to three times my usual dose of sedatives—nobody but the doctor knew, of course—and then I had to take double uppers each new day. Foster was out there somewhere, we didn't know where, but he'd always impressed *me* as someone who wouldn't hurt a fly. I'd promised him he could return to his private life when the crisis was over, but Howard wouldn't stand for that. The way he put it, Foster was a doomsday machine with enough power to bring down any nation. We needed to hunt him down and kill him before he did the unthinkable. Well, *I* did the unthinkable, Stanley. I ordered that good man killed."

Brewster was silent a long time. "So Howard Greenward was your real problem."

"He's *our* problem now, Stan, yours and mine. He's got his hands on the Russian ultimatum I had locked in my personal safe, and he's shown it to at least one person, Kurt Stauf over at NPA. Probably others, too. In my opinion, Howard has a personal agenda of some sort, and if he erases Foster, well… who'd prove him wrong? I lost my grip over the Russian business, and I admit that, but Greenward appears normal and you know what they say about psychos appearing and acting normal... until one day—"

Brewster grimaced, cutting him short. "Wish I'd known this. I just asked Clarence Towers to assign Howard to Air Force One when I go to the G-8 a couple days from now. I remembered you saying how he was such a good observer at things like this, and since this conference is my first... well, now you're saying he's a psycho?"

"Might be, Stan, might be, but the clues are all there. He never let up on me for a moment, even when he *knew* what I was going through. He's pushed Stauf the same way to get Foster and girlfriend added to the Tombstone List, and I'm asking myself why. Howard is now Towers' right hand man, which means our top protection agency director is subject to the same kind of garbage, and Kurt claims he's caught Greenward in all sorts of lies. Whatever Howard is, he's no longer my friend. I wouldn't trust him at all if I were you, and that's not all."

"There's more? I should think that would be enough."

"Tricia O'Dell, Mike O'Dell's daughter, is Foster's girlfriend. Kurt Stauf arranged a face to face with Mike couple days ago, don't ask me why, but it seems Mike has a *copy* of what amounts to the same Russian ultimatum, plus all sorts of supporting data... names, places, dates and times. I have no idea where he got it, but he's threatening to blow the whole thing open if he doesn't have an audience with you, Greenward, Towers and Stauf. He's got dozens of copies of the thing, and if he doesn't get his interview yesterday, he'll drop the bomb."

"Where's O'Dell now?"

"Your guess is as good as mine. Why?"

"Because I intend to *give* him that interview on Air Force One. If what he has to say is contrary to Greenward's agenda, we ought to find out quickly enough, right? Let's dump them in the crucible together and see who survives. Do you feel up to the trip?"

"*Me?* I... well, you mean as a tag-along? I suppose I could. I feel as fit as ever."

"You'll have a window seat. Your old one, matter of fact."

"Hell, Stanley, why not? I'd enjoy watching those two face off. Frankly, I'd bet on O'Dell, but you'll have to isolate them from others, your staff and all that. Might be a good idea to keep them separated from each other, too, board them at different times, all that. We can learn a lot from initial reactions when they face each other."

"My suite is soundproof, as you well know, but first we have to find O'Dell."

"I wish I had a copy of the Russian thing in my hands right now, but I'm sure Howard lifted it from my safe once they'd hauled me off to the cuckoo's nest. Wonder how he got the combination, or how long he had it? I'm not sure what O'Dell might be holding."

"Or where he got it?"

"No. Except that... well, the only other living soul who knew what was going on was that psychologist, Whittier, the guy who found Foster for us. He once ran some sort of clinic in upstate New York, until we... that is, I... gave orders to ruin him, run him into the ground. Howard convinced me if we put the screws to Whittier, he'd tell us where Foster was. Could be O'Dell got his information from Whittier, but I thought the man was dead by now. That's another thing—"

A series of short beeps cut him off, followed by a pleasant female voice.

"Mr. President, sorry for the interruption, but the message center has received something they have labeled highly significant, from a private party. Shall we send it in?"

"Please do." Brewster shook his head, half smiling. "I got one of these just the other day. Sometimes I wonder about our message center guys."

"There are nuts out there, Stan, mostly Bible thumpers and bearded weirdos, but you never know. Maybe this one wore a clean turban when he called in."

A White House page knocked twice, stuck his head around the casing and extended a standard yellow message form, folded in half. Brewster beckoned. "Come on in, Jason. What do we have here?"

The lad seemed surprised to see a former president standing with the one he'd come to know. He held out the note, then spun about and left without a word. Brewster opened it, scanned it quickly, then handed it over. "Take a look."

Below all the Secret Service details, time of day, originating phone and history was a short transcript: *I have what amounts to the Russian*

ultimatum, dated June 4 of two years ago, and great amounts of sup-
porting information, courtesy of United States patriots Gordon Whittier,
my daughter and citizen of the world James Foster, the most sincere and
noble man I've ever known. I fought and bled for this country. I don't
wish to tear her open, but I will unless we talk now. I will approach the
east gate at 1900 hours. You can have me killed, lock me up or know
the truth. Either of your first two choices will cause the information to be
released. Your choice, Mr. President. Sincerely, Michael O'Dell, DSC.

"What's DSC?" Brewster asked.

"Distinguished Service Cross. He earned it five times over, never accepted it."

Brewster took a deep breath. "I don't know about you, H. J., but I like this guy already. His timing couldn't have been better. Let's bring him in."

"Come in, Michael, come in." Brewster charged across the famous carpet, offering his hand in greeting. "You know H. J. Winfield, of course. Everybody does. Have a seat, have a seat. We could have received you in my private quarters at this hour, but we were both here anyway on other business, and we're keenly interested in hearing what you have to say. Did you bring anything with you? Did they confiscate it?"

"Nothing this trip, Mr. President, because of that very possibility. I intend to present the information in my own fashion rather than handing it over beforehand. I hope you understand."

"Definitely. Couldn't have said it better. Here's what we have in mind, Mike. You've taken a *great* risk in this thing, and we recognize that. You're also one of our highest-decorated heroes from the Vietnam era. I've been told of your exploits. What we'd both like you to do is accompany us on Air Force One to Munich. I have to attend the G-8 summit there, but during the flight and perhaps on the way back I believe we can come to some sort of understanding about everything. I'll give you your interview hour and then some. President Winfield will be with me. What say you?"

Mike exhaled visibly. "There are three others I'd wanted present, Howard Greenward being the most controversial of the three, but former President Winfield will be an acceptable stand-in for his former advisor, yes."

"Good. You'd bring the document you profess to have, along with any proof of some things I'm sure you've heard or discovered from others?"

"What would constitute proof in your mind, sir?"

"Affidavits, signed and properly executed. Photographs. Recordings. That kind of thing."

"I'll go you one better. How about an eyewitness who's experienced nearly everything I can present?"

The only sound was a grandfather clock ticking in the corner. It was Winfield who finally broke the silence. "An *eyewitness?*" He turned to Brewster with a quizzical look.

"All right, who?" Brewster asked.

"Let me make something quite clear. I'm not intending to *defend* anything in the sense of some courtroom scene, so when I say eyewitness I mean the real thing, not some bystander picked off the street. I'm talking of someone who can name names, cite places and times, recite nearly verbatim things that were said in this office by President Winfield and others."

"Gordon Whittier!" Winfield's whisper might as well have been a shout.

"You know where he is?" Brewster asked.

"My question first, sir. Will Dr. Whittier fulfill your need for proof? I want you and President Winfield both to understand *exactly* what took place two years ago and since that time. I can produce Dr. Whittier. Will you guarantee me your fair and impartial audience?"

Brewster smiled. "Why wouldn't I, Mike?"

"Forgive my being blunt, sir, but that's an oblique reply. As of this moment, Dr. Whittier is being held behind bars. He's been labeled as aiding and abetting a terrorist—namely Jim Foster—and the order for his arrest may well have come from this office, therefore my question."

"Well, it hasn't, Mike, it hasn't. I swear I wasn't aware of any of this. Were you, H.J.?"

"Stanley, I've been in the damn *looney bin!* Did you forget? That order had to come from Towers and company. Kurt Stauf brought me up to date on what's been going on over there."

"Towers, eh?" The President turned back to Mike, though he was speaking to Winfield. "I may have a little talk with Towers and company. Meanwhile I'll have Dr. Whittier released and brought here, offer the man some form of reparation for all this, plus an apology. The more I hear, the angrier I get. Now look... there's something of a confrontation going to come about on that plane, Mike, and I'll be frank about it. Howard Greenward *will* be aboard. I'll insist on it, so your wish will be granted. Let me also be frank about the fact that we—H.J. and I—think it might have been Howard who engineered this whole terrorist bit, putting Foster and your daughter on that list. She's his girlfriend, yes, but—"

"She's his legal wife, Mr. President, and has been for some time."

"His *wife?*"

"Why should that puzzle you? I want them both exonerated, removed from the Tombstone List and honored for what they have been and are—patriots. Jim isn't even an American citizen and look what he gave of himself. He risked his life because he's selfless when it comes to the welfare of others. Give my medal to him. He deserves the highest honors this country can bestow."

Brewster held out his hand. "I do like your style, Michael O'Dell. I'd say we have a deal, then. Are you willing to shake on it?"

"Mr. President, we do have a deal. You will find Dr. Whittier in custody in Toronto, courtesy of their airport security. As for me, I look forward to a face to face with Mr. Greenward. I doubt the reverse is true. He most definitely is not a member of my fan club."

"Good. Excellent! I like the way this is all coming together. Mike, you're a seasoned traveler. Report to Andrews' main gate as yourself on the sixteenth at 0800 hours—did I say that right?—with whatever luggage you'll need for several days. You'll be cleared to enter the base. Someone will be there at the gate to escort you to my plane with instructions to... yes, I think to my private suite, in fact, my office. You'll be escorted there, with someone to protect the door. I'd like you to remain in there until I call for you shortly after we take off. Please bring several copies of whatever documentation you have. Will you do that? Security will supply you with a diplomatic pouch on the way out. Put the copies in that and apply the yellow bands around the outside. Can you be reached between now and departure time?"

"Not if keeping this off the radar screen is the concern, sir. My phones are tapped, my house is under round-the-clock surveillance and my employees are constantly being harassed. However, I will be there as you request, with the documentation. On the other hand, Dr. Whittier may need some help getting here before takeoff."

"He'll make it. President Winfield and some of my staff will arrive at Andrews separately while I'll be hopping over on Marine One along with Howard Greenward. It's important that Greenward *not* be aware you or Whittier are aboard, so you'll both be boarded first. In fact, you *and* Whittier will both stay in my office. The seats there are takeoff-equipped. Our people will have instructions for that part. They and the flight crew run the plane anyway... keep all those reporters in their places. Any questions?"

"No, sir. I'll be there."

"General O'Dell, when this is over to your satisfaction, I'd enjoy being the one to present you that Distinguished Service Cross awarded you by Congress. In fact, I'd be honored."

"I retired as a colonel, Mr. President, but thank you. I'll consider it."

"President Winfield and I agree that your rank in retirement should be elevated to Brigadier General, by my executive order, whether you decide to accept the medal or not. Consider it done. Good day, General. See you tomorrow morning."

Chapter 18

FBI Regional Headquarters, Salt Lake City. | 7:00 P.M. March 14.

Special Agent in Charge Francis "Jack" Daniels normally went by the book, but he made exceptions now and then. Harry prayed this would be such a time as he wrapped up his summary.

"Frank, I saw how Howard used access privileges he shouldn't have had to get into the NSA computers, the CIA's, ours, NSO, you name it. He made a private call or two to a Connecticut number that later turned out to belong to Marvin Sleck, Howland's mass murderer. I saw how he functioned and heard some obvious lies, but now comes the hard part for me. Howard is involved in some sort of political conspiracy involving heavy players. One's a multi-billionaire. I believe this group has been involved with political assassinations. There's a link between Howard and André Nicola, the pilot killed in that single-engine plane crash in Yellowstone last July. I checked out Nicola. He was jailed six times in four European countries for various misdemeanors and felonies before he was thirty. Greenward brought him over here to work as an estate gardener. Frank, the guy never gardened in his life. Furthermore, the plane he crashed had a Magnum 50-caliber gun set in it. Who flies a rental plane with that kind of weaponry?"

Daniels grunted, one eyebrow raised. "Any names in this conspiracy group?"

"You'd recognize most, if not all. We'll have to cover the ground one more time to make it legal, subpoenas for phone records and the like, but the names are all there. Don't ask me how I got them and I won't lie, okay? I was there on his property as his guest, so all this is confirmation of what I observed and suspected. In a way, I'm investigating suspicious activity involving U.S. security. That much is legit."

"We do what we have to do. What else?"

"I worked this investigation with a partner, Ollie Robinson, the NPA air marshal involved in Howland's arrest. We both believe Greenward was involved with Howland, that his organization was in some way connected. Ollie suggested they might have been paving the way for Howland to run for the presidency. At first I thought that was far-fetched, but I decided to think along those lines, and guess what I found? Paul Norton and Walter Farley were both renowned burrs under the Howland saddle. They were sure to make big trouble for him in the event he ever did decide to toss his hat in the ring. Both died mysteriously within a month of each other, both ruled accidents. Dwayne Denney and Bob Small died in that plane crash, also ruled accidental. They were also anti-Howland all the way. Senator Waycaster drowned while swimming alone. Frank, he was once on the Olympic swimming team. Also ruled an accident, no autopsy, and he was anti-Howland. All these deaths have occurred since Winfield left office."

"It's conjecture, Harry."

"Sure it is, but we do have a way to check it out, and his name is Sleck. He was there at the estate several times leading up to Howland's arrest."

"Got proof?"

"How's every phone call in and out of the Greenward estate for the past two years grab you? There are your names."

"Jeez! How'd you get this?"

"Ollie happens to know a good hacker. Point is, they can all be produced a second time legitimately. Those records can't *all* be erased, and in this case Uncle Howard hasn't a clue anyone suspects a thing."

Daniels fingered the printouts. "First, let's try your Sleck idea. If that produces anything at all, we can use it to subpoena the phone records."

"Sleck might try for a life sentence instead of the alternative."

Daniels scanned the phone list again. "I don't like this, Harry. We need to know a lot more about Howard Greenward, flag him before he does anything rash even if he is Towers' fair-haired boy. I don't trust Towers any farther than I can throw him."

"Open for a suggestion? Greenward doesn't know Ollie Robinson from Adam, and Ollie's skilled at sizing up people who aren't what they pretend to be. He's already volunteered to help any way he can, knows all the facts and he's *not* one of ours, so...."

"He's NPA. We can't use one of their men for this."

"Ollie sent in his resignation a few days back. He's a free agent."

"Okay, set it up, then. If your instincts are correct, the president could be a target, too. There are plenty of influential people who'd love to get him out of the way, put an end to this economic slide." Daniels flipped through the list a third time. "What time is it in D.C.? I'm going to circumvent all normal channels and put a call directly to the White House. In fact, I'm going to tell Brewster we've got a tail on Mr. Greenward, tell him who we have babysittin' the guy, and why. I'll back you, but Harry...."

"What?"

"If you do this kind of thing again, better have another job lined up."

Munich. | Late afternoon, March 15.

The airport's dual runways were laid out on an almost east-west line, with passenger terminals, cargo buildings and connecting roads in the space between. Just south of the perimeter fence was a public road, but it would likely be patrolled often. Across the road, another fence surrounded a conical hill with a VOR transmitter on top, located opposite the runway's midpoint. That would be an ideal spot, Jim mused, if only he could get inside the fence, past security cameras and the occasional helicopter. Bad deal there, too. At any rate, a row of low junipers west of the VOR hill would be an excellent place to hide.

He drove the public road twice without seeing airport security vehicles, then canvassed the farmland south of the airport, meandering along dirt roads and studying nondescript houses while Charlie and Tricia familiarized themselves with the terminal buildings. The airport had consumed a complete town when built, and these homesteads had probably belonged to that township. Apparently anything outside the airport's perimeter fence was considered low risk, but appearances could be deceiving. It would pay to be very cautious.

After dinner, they all found a shopping mall and sat in a busy coffee shop.

"Tricia," Charlie began, "when chaos erupts, reporters become lemmings following any stern voice giving direction. We want a crisp, professional woman, stunning in the eyes of males in the media group or among those guarding them, who can bully her way into a crowd of reporters and have them jumping through hoops. You have the face, body shape and personality. You also speak six languages, including excellent German. You also earned a degree in journalism and your father owns one of the most successful newspapers in the U.S., so you know what makes reporters and networks tick, especially reporting from the field. Five networks are covering VIP arrivals—Americans, British, Germans, French and Italians—four languages, all of which you speak well. We need only to dress you properly. You'll have a small megaphone. No one will question a knowledgeable, properly uniformed woman giving orders, not even airport security.

"Your objective will be to get the media vans out to the plane, keeping them at least two hundred feet away so as to be outside the cluster of emergency vehicles. You'll explain that their cameras are about to record one of the most astounding events on record: the President of the United States trapped, along with his staff in his personal plane, by some unknown alien force."

She looked surprised. "You want me to actually say it's an alien force?"

"Yes. Plant the idea as soon as possible. Tomorrow we'll study the terminals, all exit doors, stairways, balconies, restricted areas, administrative areas, security, parking layouts and as much of the terminal layout we can cram in. Dignitaries will all have landed by tomorrow evening, since the conference is the following day. Air Force One will leave the U.S. mainland sometime mid-morning, the flight will take not over six hours, add six hours of time zone and we'll be at nine or ten P.M., so we should be ready two hours before that. Japanese and Russian delegates arrived this morning, Canada's delegates arrived yesterday—they're always early—so that leaves only Italy, France and the U.K. They could arrive any time tomorrow, but I think only the U.S. plane will arrive after dark."

He turned to Jim.

"A visible surface can be imparted to any solid mass of air you create, so that you and anyone close to you can see the surface. I suspect you will need this. Create a block of air above us, there against the ceiling, and tell me when you have it."

"Okay, it's up there."

"Now watch." He smiled. "No, don't look at me, look at the block."

"Yes, it appears shiny."

"But *only* on the side facing you, and only when viewed at an angle. There's no reflection if you look at it squarely. Now it's your turn. Same routine as always. Visualize it, desire it and step out of the way. I'm taking my influence away now."

"I still see it," Tricia piped up. "It's like looking into a prism."

"It's reflecting the colors around us," Charlie explained, "but don't try to analyze it. That's the surest way to interfere with mental power. Simply let it happen. Now why are we doing this, Jim? Can you guess?"

"You want me to see something I'll create."

"But only when you want to. Here's what will take place." He spent the following twenty minutes detailing the event that would shock the world. When finished, he sat back. "Well, Jim, what do you think?"

"That it's highly probable I'll be dead before one word is spoken."

Toronto. | Noon, March 15.

"Dr. Whittier, you're free to go. We have a car waiting outside that will take you back to the airport, where we understand there is a plane waiting to take you directly to Andrews Air Force Base in Maryland."

"Who released me, do you know? Why Andrews?"

"Someone on your plane will be able to supply that information. Our orders are to get you to the plane immediately. Have a good day, sir."

The aircraft was a Falcon with a crew of three. A middle-aged hostess served him a white-tablecloth dinner and wine, saying that he'd be accommodated in VIP housing at Andrews. In the morning, unless he refused, he'd travel with the president on Air Force One, to Munich. He concealed his surprise.

His meal was barely finished when he was told to fasten his seat belt. Ten minutes later he was ushered off the Falcon by a man in a crisply ironed uniform with a bright red fox insignia on it, then to a car. "Dr. Whittier, we have quarters prepared for you, with all the amenities you'd expect in any top-rated hotel. Fridge in the room, fully equipped, plus a small bar. Room service for your meals—there's a menu on the dining room table for your convenience—clothes pressed, any personal needs, just ask. The schedule tomorrow morning is for you to be ready to travel at 0900 hours. We will ring your alarm at 0700 hours. Is that time enough?"

"More than enough, thank you."

"My name is Mark Matthews. I'll be available for anything you need. Just pick up the phone and dial 22." They pulled up to one in a row of identical houses. "There are no outside locks on the doors, since this is a secure base. However, you may use the deadbolts on the inside if you wish. Good day, sir. It's a pleasure serving you."

The White House, South Lawn. | March 16.

When Brewster didn't show by 0910 hours, Greenward cut across to Marine One from the eastern end of the White House. Grumpy, he gave the uniformed Marine guard no more than a nod.

"Good morning, Mr. Greenward," the Marine said without expression. "Are you carrying?"

"Yes, a P229. NPA directive."

"Yes, sir. I'll make a note of it. Your luggage is already aboard, sir."

The Helo was empty. He took one of four forward-facing seats nearest the starboard window, then stared out at the Washington Monument without seeing it. Clarence Towers had lied bigtime about getting the trip canceled. He'd originally said not to worry about the G-8, that Brewster had withdrawn his original request. Obviously, that wasn't the case.

"The Man is really antsy about having you on that plane, Howard, for reasons he didn't offer. He may have something in mind for you to do over there. At any rate, he's suddenly taken a liking to you after all these months, so you're going unless we haul you off for a quick lobotomy or something. You're due at the White House south lawn at 9:15. The chopper leaves for Andrews at half past nine sharp with you, Brewster and a pack of Secret Service suits on it. I'm sorry. You made your point to me and I made it to him, but he wasn't buying any excuse. As a matter

of fact, he seemed to shrug off the whole O'Dell topic as something he couldn't afford to think about right now. Your suspicions may not have set too well with him. Either that or something was bugging him."

Brewster wouldn't know a terrorist if he was sitting next to one. Suspicions, hell!

The object of his loathing suddenly appeared in the aft section doorway. Trailing Brewster were two Secret Service agents who took their seats without a word. Brewster slipped into the port side forward-looking seat and buckled himself in. The agent opposite him leaned forward, checked the buckle, then settled back.

"Morning, Howard." The greeting was delivered without eye contact. "I take it you've been on Marine One before."

He's not even sitting next to me! "Mr. President, I was surprised to—"

"My apologies for dragging you along on this jaunt, but I'll make my reasons clear as soon as we're airborne out of Andrews. Until then I'd like you to sit with the reporters on Air Force One. Keep your ears and eyes open for me during the flight. I'm learning there are many things to be gleaned from reporters, things they won't say in my presence. Sometimes they forget who's listening. Then you and I will talk later. Can you do that?"

He opened a folder and began reading without waiting for an answer.

Andrews Air Force Base, Camp Springs, Maryland. | Morning, March 16.

Mark Matthews showed up at 0730 hours, checking to make certain the guest from Canada was up, and returned half an hour later with boarding instructions and a diagram of the plane's interior.

"You'll be escorted to the president's private office aboard, sir, where you'll remain until called, sharing the space with another gentlemen, Mr. Michael O'Dell. Do you happen to know Mr. O'Dell?"

"The newspaperman? Yes, I met him a few years ago." *So Mike's behind all this? Guess I shouldn't have worried about his abilities after all.*

"The president's suite is fully equipped, sir. Someone aboard will see to it that you and the other gentleman are comfortable during and after takeoff. However, I caution you to avoid discussions with anyone other than President Brewster until you are called into the conference room or asked to remain there in his office, whichever he prefers. Those are my instructions."

Mark described the plane as a huge motel suite, including a conference room seating eight. The president's office seated five abreast and one alone in a high-backed chair. Journalists and guests entered the plane through a tail door, using a staircase to reach the middle deck. Their area in the plane resembled the first class section of an ordinary jetliner.

The starboard side of the middle deck included the president's executive quarters, with private dressing room, workout room, lavatory, shower and office. Whenever the plane rolled up to an event, it always came to a stop with the *port* side of the aircraft facing gathered onlookers as a security measure, to keep the president's side of the aircraft out of view.

The plane's upper deck was devoted to navigation, communications and the cockpit.

ജ ഐ

"Glad you made it, Gordy." Mike was grinning.

"Mike! They had me in a Toronto jail. I thought I was clever enough to sneak back into the country, but they'll get you on anything at all now. Is it safe to talk?"

"Looks like we'll get our chance. H.J. Winfield's going to be here along with Brewster and Howard Greenward. I've been assured that Greenward hasn't a clue he'll be confronting me. I'd wanted a couple others from NPA, Stauf and Towers, but I'll settle for what we have. Winfield's better than Towers any day. I understand he's stable again."

"Ollie Robinson mentioned this man Stauf. What's his role?"

"Heads up the NPA's anti-terrorism division. He and Greenward may have collaborated to get Jim and Tricia on the T-list. This guy's a nasty piece of work."

"Have you shown the manuscript to anyone?"

"That's what we're here to do. You're to corroborate everything except for the parts I added. I have four copies with me, but there are dozens more set to go if we fail. We can lose this battle and still win the war."

"Well, I'm ready. I have a few scores to settle with Homer J. Winfield and company."

"Take a hard look before you unload on him. I not only saw a changed man, but Brewster actually impressed me for the first time. He's a nitwit by media standards, but I think not. Something of a change is going on, but I can't put my finger on it... yet. Anyway, our main target is Greenward. Could be he's been the key player from the git-go."

"What about Stauf?"

"We talked two nights back. I think he's Greenward's puppet."

"So nothing much has changed."

"Except that Brewster's had nothing to do with Greenward until now. That *could* mean I somehow got through to Stauf, and all this is the result, but I don't think so."

"We'll find out soon enough. So... this is Air Force One? Pretty impressive."

"Cost us taxpayers roughly $400 million. Wonder what Wilbur and Orville would think."

෮෬

They'd been airborne ten minutes when Brewster strode through the doorway, all business, with H.J. Winfield on his heels. Expressionless, Winfield headed for the single chair without so much as a glance sideways at the two men who'd jumped to their feet. Whittier watched Brewster take his place behind the big desk. *His body language says he's not as far along as Mike thinks. I'd better watch my step until I see something different in his manner.*

"Relax, gentlemen," Brewster said, leaning forward on his elbows. "Please sit back down. Dr. Whittier, I understand you and H.J. Winfield know each other from more troubling times. And Mike, I also understood that you also wanted Kurt Stauf in on this interview. I've accommodated you. They're both on the plane, but neither knows you're here. In fact, neither knows the other is here as I have them separated. I have my reasons, but they'll both join us when it's time. First, we'll cover some ground. By chance does that pouch hold what I requested? May I see?"

Mike stood, came forward and placed the pouch on the desk. "Mr. President, this is just background for—"

"No formalities needed when we're in private, Mike. I'm just Stan and he's H.J. I know you intended to make a one-man presentation out of this thing, but I prefer to discuss whatever is in here as we go. What say you?" He withdrew four binders, handed one to Winfield and the remaining two back to Mike, who drew a long breath.

"In these circumstances, that should work, sir... Stan. This opus was mostly prepared by Gordy here, during and immediately following the episode that ended with Russia withdrawing their threatened takeover. I've added my sections where applicable, parts Gordy knew nothing about. The back pages support whatever footnotes you'll see."

Brewster hefted the binder's weight, arching an eyebrow, then riffled slowly through the pages at first, then quicker, turning a page every five seconds or so. He glanced at Winfield, who was flipping pages at almost the same rate. "H.J., anything you see that seems wrong, I want us all to hear it together."

"This is incredible," Winfield murmured. "Almost a perfect replica of the original document. How did you do this... Gordy?" The question was asked without eye contact.

Whittier cleared his throat. "I was totally focused the day you showed me the Russian document. I recorded everything I could recall about it, including everything you said in that interview."

"This smacks of total recall," Winfield mumbled, turning another page.

"That doesn't seem right," Brewster interjected. "I've never known anyone with total recall, unless it's staged or faked. Not to doubt you, Gordy, but what exactly did H.J. say that sent you off looking for this Foster person? Do you remember?"

"Whew! That's quite a challenge, but give me a moment." *Winfield may have put him up to this. He hasn't made eye contact yet, and that says he's uncomfortable.* "I'd just finished describing Jim Foster as a young boy I'd seen in a Boston park, but said I had no idea if he was alive, where he was or his real name. President Winfield's exact words to me were, 'Find him, Whittier. I don't know how, but do it. I want you to understand that John and I are not going to sit here doing nothing for the next twenty days, but if you can deliver enough of anything to use in a bluff, I'll take that chance. We can NOT take this problem outside this office, other than through you in this way. Do you understand?'"

"My God!" Winfield gasped, locking eyes briefly. "Stan, those were *precisely* my words, and that was… what, Whittier, almost three years ago? John Hughes and I had a recorder going, and I played that interview over many times."

Startled, Brewster began reading in earnest, finally holding up a hand. "Okay… okay, that's a plus. I begin to see what was happening here. You were handed this… this *thing* from the Russians, H.J. You realized it was beyond anything The Hill could handle rationally and decided to gamble, to bluff, as we just heard. I was in Manila when it all happened and you said there was no reason to rush back, that it was just some sort of atmospheric anomaly. Was that Howard's doing?"

"He… yes, Stan, it was. He said that if you came running back it would make the thing look political instead of natural."

"And it was *also* his idea to look for some antidote for what the Russians claimed they had, right? What kind of antidote could anyone find in twenty days, for God's sake? All our reactors? What did Howard have to say about them, about meltdowns?"

"That it would be the end of mankind. He said even if the Russians carried out half their threats, we'd revert to the Stone Age within three days, killing each other over cans of beans. He does a great job of painting doomsday pictures, I'll give him credit for that. That was early in the game and I was still functioning rationally then. It was my own idea to try and find a way out, not his. I turned to Dr. Whittier—Gordy, here. He was heading up my third ad hoc committee at the time, looking into the woo-woo stuff for us after the original committee chairman met with foul play. We weren't leaving a stone unturned, but I knew I was reaching for the impossible. It was either that or risk taking on something none of us understood. As far as we knew, the Russians could finish us whenever they felt like it. Las

Vegas was proof of that, along with our secret ELF transmitter. They took that out, too, as I told you."

Brewster's gaze swung back. "Gordy, how did *you* know the boy you'd seen would turn out to be Foster, and what the hell is psychometry, anyway?"

I knew this was coming. "It's esoteric art, sir, against every scientific principle I'd lived by until then, therefore abhorrent. Still, it was the only game in town. I happened to have among my possessions something the boy dropped that day, an amulet he wore around his neck. That, plus help from seven psychics, led me to him through a series of clues that, taken one at a time, meant nothing. I still don't believe it, but that's how it happened."

"According to your report here, he was in Bermuda racing sailboats, yet he had this awesome power. Why would any man with such power do nothing with it?"

"I asked myself the same question at first. What would I have done if it had been me? Join a carnival or rule the world? Jim was remarkable in realizing that if he showed his power to anyone at all, he'd be as good as dead, a modern witch in old Salem. In my professional opinion, he was right."

"But he came here..." Brewster paused, turning to Winfield again. "He came here in spite of us literally spitting on him his whole life, according to what I just read. I know what street people endure... worked with a bunch of them way back in my college days as a project. Foster had no obligation to us at all, so *why* did he do it? Why didn't he just say 'nuts' and go about his life? Could it be he really did have some ulterior motive?"

For a long moment the muted sound of the plane's engines was the only sound. It was Mike who broke the relative silence. "That's something only Jim can answer, but I can tell you this... in his view, the measure of man's nobility is the way he treats those less fortunate than him. Why couldn't it be that he truly wanted to use his power in some beneficial way?"

"If he was here, I'd ask him myself. Since it's out of the question, we'll pass on it. Mike, you wrote that you thought at some point that H.J. was being coached. Why'd you think that?"

"Because he changed his tune so suddenly. My team and I were working with Gordy and Jim by then. Gordy decided to meet with President Winfield, only to be told that Foster was a deformed freak, a major weapon that could not be allowed to fall into enemy hands. Also that he was too dangerous to remain free and that his death would be sanctioned if he didn't come in. This was completely the opposite of anything up to that point. Subsequently Gordy was held against his will, definitely Greenward's doing."

Winfield nodded, somewhat sadly. "Mike's right. Howard had already begun to turn my head around with things he'd never said earlier. He was convinced the Russians knew everything we were doing with Foster, and that Foster was some kind of illegal player, a mystery man who might in fact have been working for them from the start. The fact of Foster and Gordy throwing in with unknown people looked very suspicious at the time. Howard convinced me Foster was a megalomaniac, a psychotic."

"So," Mike continued, "we all concluded that Greenward was calling the shots. In truth the Russians tried to kill both Jim and Gordy in Bermuda and again at Grace Botanical Laboratories in Virginia, that time with five spetsnaz agents armed with Uzis and grenades. Implying in any way that Jim was a Russian agent was outrageous."

"So you say here, Mike. How exactly did you get those details, since I understand that we slammed the lid down on the whole mess out there at Grace? Birds weren't allowed to fly over that property. How'd you find out the guns were Uzis, for instance? Did you go up and inspect the weapons?"

"I was in there with a team of my own, yes, hoping to extricate Jim based on our belief he was being used as a human guinea pig. We knew nothing of what was really going on inside, only that his forcible removal from Bermuda—by Gordy here flanked by Secret Service men—was witnessed by my daughter, Tricia. My team wasn't alone. A U.S. Army commando team was inserted at the rear of the property at the optimum moment to take out the Russians to the last man. Someone had to send those guys in prepared to kill, ordering preparations for that skirmish well in advance. That same someone had to know exactly when the Russians were inserting *their* team, right down to the minute. The explanation we were given—coming from Mr. Greenward—was that the whole thing was just a coincidence." He twisted to confront Winfield. "What coincidence could have led chairman of the Joint Chiefs General Joe Dugan to suspect there was anything happening there? What might have led him to instruct General Woody Shaw to send in a fully prepared and briefed commando team whose men knew full well they were going against Russian spetsnaz and were in there using silenced automatic weapons for that specific purpose? Why did Shaw lead them himself? Was that coincidence, too?"

Winfield's mouth hung open. "Shaw was actually *there?*"

Brewster drowned him out. "DUGAN?" he boomed. "What the hell was *he* doing in all this?" He paged ahead, scanning for the name. "The chairman of the Joint Chiefs is not allowed to give military orders, H.J."

"He didn't, Stan, he didn't give any order. Shaw volunteered to send in a detail of his special Warriors based on Dugan's hunch that something important was going on in there. It was just a hunch. Nobody controlled Dugan, and you know that as well as I do." Winfield sighed. "Frankly, I can't believe Shaw was actually there either. Do you have proof, Mike?"

"Quite a bit. I had a little unscheduled talk there among the saplings with Sgt. First Class Manny Flores, service number 76803354, one of Woody's Warriors. He lost an argument with my elbow, and when he woke up I—"

"Hold on. You're how old... sixty? And *you* took on one of Shaw's commandos?"

"When the student is ready, the teacher will appear... sir. I identified myself when Flores woke up and learned that he and the others were *told* there'd be spetsnaz there, that Shaw and his team were to take them out. Yes, the Russians were armed with Uzis and grenades, easily recognizable from a distance of thirty feet. The remaining commandos were Robichaud and Pruitt. You can check the records, if you can find them. In my judgment the Russians went in there to destroy the buildings and everyone in them. At any rate, Gordy and Jim remained alive because of Shaw's team."

"I agree," Whittier said. *Good for you, Mike. That's as airtight as it gets.* "Nobody outside of a privileged few was to know Jim and I were in that place to work together, but we had a spy among us, someone I thought I'd chosen of my own free will. It turned out he was a Russian source agent, which meant I'd been set up well before Las Vegas. The Russians must have figured early on that I represented some sort of threat to whatever plans were unfolding, rather a strange conclusion since I'd been ignored in my profession on this side of the Atlantic. Seems I'd known this agent for at least a year, met him at a conference where I delivered a paper nobody listened to, but that doesn't explain how anyone other than his Russian masters knew what we did there at Grace Botanical, or knew times when Jim and I were outside the buildings. Supposedly our resident Secret Service guards had the place locked down tight. Their man in charge, name of Riordan, was extremely efficient in my view, so it wasn't a case of laxity out there. What we asked after the smoke cleared was exactly how Generals Dugan or Shaw could possibly have learned about the spetsnaz raid and its precise timing. The answer was unsatisfactory by any standards."

Mike took up the thread again. "One day prior to the raid behind Grace, *someone* flew an army surveillance chopper directly across the Grace property at 6:43 A.M. at an estimated six hundred feet—the correct altitude for close camera work—and returned on the reciprocal azimuth two minutes later."

Brewster raised an eyebrow. "And just how did you know *that*? My God, how did you know Foster was in there in the first place?"

"Skill or art, it's your choice, sir. One of my team was ninety feet up in a tree bordering the property at the time the chopper came over. I have several hours' worth of his observations on voice record. The events he recorded are summarized on page 56. We believed Jim was being held there against his will and that Gordy here was in fact some government kook drugging the hell out of him. Things get warped when all the facts aren't in, as we all know."

Brewster turned back to Winfield. "What about it, H.J.? Did Greenward know about this? Could it be that this spy was reporting to him as well as Moscow?"

"I never gave it a... this spy... um...."

"Pelletier," Whittier supplied.

"Yes, Pelletier. You chose him *before* you went to Bermuda looking for Foster, Gordon, which means you were definitely being watched by Moscow even if you say your peers on this side of the ocean ignored you. *Something* you were doing in your profession posed a threat, else they'd never have singled you out. Howard couldn't have known that. Truth be known, I personally never thought anything would come of your efforts. How could I? You saw this boy way back in the seventies, never knew who he was or anything about him, and then a bunch of psychics come along and tell you where he is? I should have stopped you right there, but I wanted to convince myself I was doing everything possible. Howard was painting his doomsday pictures in technicolor and surround-sound, and my only thoughts were to grab at anything that might throw the Russians off track. If nothing worked, then I'd have gone to Congress. Sorry, Gordon, but that's the way it was."

He's focusing attention on his predicament. Stay with the raid. "Still, we were never given a satisfactory answer about the raid at Grace. The timing was so perfect it looked rehearsed. Jim and I happened to be outside the buildings, as we always were at that hour of the morning. Fortunately we were out in the trees or we might have been caught in the crossfire or shot leaving the buildings."

"Where's the spy now?" Brewster asked. "Do you know?"

"We were told he was killed in the raid. That could have been planned, too, by either side."

"Okay, so that part remains unexplained," Brewster said. "Now when was it that Howard started saying Foster was a Russian agent? That's the key question here, H.J., don't you agree? Seems to me all this points to Greenward believing that about Foster. If he truly did believe it, perhaps it wasn't as malicious as it sounds. When did he first say it to you?"

Winfield stroked his jaw. "It was right after that Grace Botanical raid thing. He insisted we force Foster into protective custody, and when Gordy refused to deliver the man to us on a silver plate, Howard went ballistic. Foster was suddenly the greatest menace society had ever faced, too dangerous to remain alive or free, or words to that effect."

"So… as long as Foster is under Greenward's control, he's an okay guy, he's golden. Foster nearly gets himself assassinated for the second time, along with Gordy here, decides to play his own game—which is what I'd have done in his shoes—and Greenward goes bonkers because he loses control. Is that it? And then he convinces you that Foster's a madman ready to sell out to the highest bidder. How am I doing? Am I right?"

"That's it, yes. Then I signed an executive order setting Bob Allen and his FBI boys out to kill Foster on sight, something they do from time to time behind the curtain, as we both know. I'm appalled that I did it, looking back, but I was already a broken clock. Howard was running the show."

Brewster nodded. "And that's where I came into the picture. So, where are we now in this interview? Gordy?"

"We're where your executive order nearly got me killed. Greenward and Bob Allen of the FBI hired bounty hunter Nils Van Oot to hunt Jim down and kill him for a fee of fifty million dollars. Interesting to me that money like that can be flung around without leaving traces, but it's beside the point. Someone else hired a competing team for the same purpose, perhaps the Russian side."

Brewster's quick glance at Winfield indicated surprise. He turned back. "Any sense I ever had about secrecy in government is dissolving before my eyes. How'd *you* learn this, Gordy?"

"The Russian bastards used me as bait. Almost killed me. Van Oot stole me away from them, got me patched up by his own doctor and subsequently learned the man he was hunting was a totally decent human being whose only sin was in being endowed with a superhuman power he'd never once used against anyone. Van Oot eventually met Jim and became my friend in the process. A quite remarkable man, Van Oot."

"A killer nonetheless."

"Killing has been mankind's companion since Cain slew Abel. It matters little whether the jawbone involved is wielded by an individual or a nation."

"Amen," Mike muttered.

"Hmm. Can't argue that one. Now finally we come to Kurt Stauf, who claims Howard pushed him to have Foster and Mike's daughter added to the Tombstone List. Van Oot didn't finish the job, so in this way some other trigger-happy idiot would do it, and in the process Howard's great fear would be erased. I admire Foster's ability to stay alive this long."

"Stauf considers *me* as much a terrorist as Jim," Mike said. "If I failed to hand over that binder within a twenty-four hour window, he threatened to declare me a traitor and have me put away. Patriot Act, et cetera."

Brewster sighed. "Can you *prove* he said that?"

"We met two nights ago, in a cemetery in Cumberland where my wife is buried. He asked for the secret meeting, I chose the venue. Ask him to produce the recording he made at the time. If he denies making one, I'll provide my own."

Brewster touched something below the desk top. A female voice answered. "Yes, Mr. President?"

"Sue, please send Howard Greenward in here. He's sitting back with the media group. Upstairs you'll find Kurt Stauf in the communications room. Send him here as well, but only after Mr. Greenward is in here with us. Last, have one of the Secret Service agents posted just outside my office door once both men are inside. Thanks."

When the connection was closed, Brewster spread both hands on the desk top. His sweeping glance included Winfield. "Gentlemen, does the name Marvin Sleck mean anything to either of you?"

Chapter 19

Munich International Airport. | March 16.

Charlie stood unnoticed against a wall and read a German newspaper while he worked his magic on the stuffy information-desk girl. She was all smiles when Tricia approached.

Yes, incoming planes carrying heads of state used the south runway because the building at the extreme western end was set aside for television crews. There'd be TV vans there from several networks, and motorcades to München would leave from that end of the airport. Airport Security was fully in charge of handling all the VIPs and their entourages. However, German police always escorted motorcades away from the airport for destinations in München itself and had already done so for most of the arrivals. In fact, the south runway was closed to takeoffs at least half an hour before any incoming VIP plane was due to land.

The girl was noticeably proud when stating that the airport was more than capable of handling normal traffic on just one runway, but something wasn't right. Announcing a major landing event that way implied certainty that no terrorists with shoulder-fired weapons were anywhere within range of the airport or its approaches. How could the Germans be so sure? Anyone could use two-way radio, and the practice of emptying the taxi strip had to be well known. Were airport security teams scouring the countryside hour by hour, twenty kilometers in all directions? If so, that would complicate things greatly and there'd be no way to check.

Yet, awareness was better than ignorance.

Tricia's role in marshaling the media teams suggested she'd best belong to airport administration. Her uniform would be the official greenish-grey jacket-skirt combination, with white blouse, dark blue tie and a large, blue capital "M" on the jacket, identical to those seen outside the airport on huge signs. A double gold stripe on the cuffs would get her past almost anything not requiring a magnetic badge. Her engraved name tag would read Greta Wirth, Koordinatorin. It meant anchorwoman as far as media types were concerned.

A München store sold official uniforms to those with "proper airport credentials." While Charlie browsed nearby, she presented her new "Helen Manos" driver's license, remembering to be arrogant and brittle. Whatever the young store clerk *thought* she was looking at, the license turned out to be exactly right for the specified uniform. She sent the selection to the backroom tailor to get its gold stripes and insignia while a pair of gold name tags was prepared. Meanwhile, Tricia picked out two uniform blouses and some stockings she needed anyway. After thanking the clerk for being so patient, she moved on to her next stop—a shoe store. She'd need low-heeled black shoes and a black leather shoulderbag for the small megaphone.

While she was shoe-shopping, Charlie addressed his own uniform needs. He'd be recognized instantly as a high government advisor—oberregierungsrat—in this case, German customs. The insignia were gold leaves and floral buttons on a green field, with gold edging. It was bold enough to get him past any manned checkpoint in the airport, since only Berlin would send out such a person, and who'd dare question reasons as long as his identification was correct? He could hand them a bingo card and they'd imagine they were seeing an authentic ID. He added an official German Customs dark green parka with the same insignia. Since no one would think to order an oberregierungsrat from Berlin to do anything at all, he could remain as invisible as a football official in a sea of players at game time.

They bought three two-way radios before leaving the city. More reliable than phones, and faster.

Jim spent most of the afternoon at a public computer terminal, nervously studying the Boeing 747 still being used for Air Force One. The plane's tail was sixty-three feet high with an overall fuselage length of nearly two hundred fifty feet. A little pencil and paper work and the formula for his big stunt began taking shape. Next came a search of modern firefighting platforms, some of which could reach heights well over a hundred feet. Whoops! Leave it to the Germans to have something like *that* around the corner, even if such a truck wasn't in the airport's fire brigade. Recalculate! He'd use the plane's fuselage as a measure to assure it was at least two hundred feet up, assuming he could even see its shape with all the airport lights behind the plane as it landed… not good. Too easy to miss something critical.

He twiddled his pencil. The runway itself would be totally clear, and at a landing speed of 170 miles per hour that was about....

He sketched the final picture, then found a quiet place where he could take himself into self-hypnosis, away from the real world to a twilight state where nothing distracted, nothing cancelled, where he was receptive to information beyond all conscious awareness, where intuition and perception bloomed to giant proportions: the mental state called *theta*. Once there, he visualized the picture he'd just drawn, examining it from every angle.

When he emerged many minutes later, he was ready.

Air Force One.

"Come in, Howard. I'd like you to help us analyze something just handed to me not fifteen minutes ago. You know Mike O'Dell and Gordy Whittier, of course, and you definitely know the man on my left here."

Winfield smiled. "Hello, Howard. They booted me out early."

Greenward paused, one hand still on the door's handle as if deciding what to do. There was a distinct change in the set of his jaw. "I see you think these two represent something worth your time. I don't share that view, as you must know."

Brewster held out the binder. "I'm well aware of your views. You'll be given a chance to present them. Here, this won't bite. Have a seat there on the end. We'll be joined in a moment by Kurt Stauf. I've asked him along for his insights, as I've been told you two worked together recently on the subject of this meeting, and I wanted your combined opinions."

Stauf's surprise rivaled Greenward's anger. He accepted the fourth binder, originally Winfield's copy, stared briefly at Mike, then rather stiffly took the seat closest to Winfield's high-back chair, leaving a space.

Brewster once again spread his hands on the desk. "Gentlemen, I want both of you to read the contents and be prepared to tear them apart or accept them as they are, any portion. President Winfield and I have given the material a going over, and at this point I now believe a great injustice has been handed out to a man to whom our country owes a huge debt of gratitude. President Winfield has as much as stated that Jim Foster is a hero by all the accounts in this binder. He admits he did not formerly hold that view, so the contents of the binder have changed his mind. There are things in it he didn't know, couldn't know or had only fragmentary information for.

"We have five hours of flight time ahead of us. In the next half hour or so I want to know why I should not *immediately* call our U.N. ambassador and have Foster and wife removed from the Tombstone List. That's right, his wife. Furthermore, I want to know why we should not issue a statement to the effect that Mr. Foster has mistakenly been labeled a terrorist when in fact he is exactly the opposite. Howard... Kurt... both of you begin reading."

Greenward scowled. "Mr. President, this is nothing but a goddamned hanging committee. There are facts you can't possibly understand. You were in Manila, for crissakes, and President Winfield was under tremendous pressure. It was this very situation that *caused* his mental collapse. Isn't that right, H.J.?"

Brewster twisted his mouth. "You're saying right off that I'm mistaken, without reading a word."

"Look... sir... both these... O'Dell, there, and Whittier have ulterior motives behind everything they say, whereas I'm only interested in the truth. O'Dell twists words any way he chooses, always has, and Whittier refused a sitting president's direct order to deliver Foster. Refused! That's treason in my book. His exact words were 'Go to hell, Mr. President' even though Foster was one of the worst threats to this country either of us could imagine at the time. Go ahead, ask Whittier if I'm not right, since he's sitting here."

"That's all in the binder you're to read, Howard."

"Maybe so, but not in those words?"

"Yes, those very words, yes. Go to hell, Mr. President, yes. It's in there. I read it."

Greenward's scowl deepened. "Taken out of context, no doubt. How about the event of just two weeks ago? Foster signed his *name* on that London subway bomb note. Talk about your megalomaniac—"

"No, Howard, he didn't," Kurt objected. "*Nobody* signed it. Cut out letters were pasted on the envelope and the word Mudslinger was typed inside. I labeled it a prank. You insisted it wasn't, that it was exactly what Foster would do to prepare the world for a major blow, that you knew the man backward and forwards. Your conjecture doesn't make it fact."

Brewster leveled a finger at Stauf. "Kurt, you told President Winfield something about that very incident a day or so ago. Repeat your Athens findings for our benefit."

Stauf 's palms went to his ears as he collected his thoughts. Clearly the order made him uncomfortable. "All right... the London 'bomb that wasn't' happened during day two of the Athens conference on biochemical countermeasures. Mr. Greenward attended that conference, but was present only the first half day, according to the conference organizer and chairman, Iason Georgios. Mr. Greenward's trip report, which I finally found filed obliquely under countermeasures instead of several more appropriate headings, summarized the keynote address while omitting the trip's purpose. Penciled comments cited some of the high points given at the banquet that same first night and mentioned conversations with several of the delegates there, except that Mr. Greenward didn't attend that banquet. Further, my department received no notice of Mr. Greenward's trip to Athens, in violation of rules laid down by Director Towers. Shortly after his return from that trip, Mr. Greenward came to my office with what appeared to be an official Russian document dated June of two years ago, threatening our country with extinction unless we subjected ourselves to them. It had to do with the Las Vegas incident. In Mr. Greenward's view, Foster was responsible for the Las Vegas destruction and deaths and was working for the Russians at that point. Foster was also blamed for the murder of President Winfield's chief of staff, John Hughes, and others unnamed. The Yellowstone wildfires were also Foster's doing, according to Mr. Greenward. Foster financed Ben Howland's bid to bring down the U.S. government and acted as the brains of the organization."

Greenward, livid, shot to his feet. "Do I get to say anything here?"

"Shut up and sit down, Howard. You'll have your say. If any of these statements are wrong, I expect you to correct them. Go ahead, Kurt."

"Back to Howland, supposedly Jim Foster went by the code name Helios, a name I'd never heard. Howland himself allegedly supplied this information to Howard, person to person, but I subsequently learned Howland has received no visitors other than his lawyers since his incarceration. At this point Mr. Greenward insisted I move immediately to get Foster and Foster's girlfriend on the Tombstone List. He supplied photos of both so we could run those in the media releases. Not much later, the girl was supposedly sighted in the Helsinki airport and we learned that Foster, who was traveling under the name Adams, bought a sailboat in Denmark two days later. Mr. Greenward became fanatical, frantic in my opinion, about eradicating Foster before he'd left Danish waters. If he was placed on the Tombstone List, chances were he'd be blown away before he'd gone a hundred miles, according to Mr. Greenward, but in spite of that assurance I was asked to provide department manpower over there to try and flush him out."

Brewster nodded at Greenward. "Your floor, Howard. Is any of what we just heard true?"

"*Totally* distorted, every bit of it. Mr. Stauf has forgotten, if he ever understood, what the NPA is all about. Foster is a known criminal, a murderer as well as a terrorist. Mass murderer if you include Las Vegas. Double that if we want to discuss the Howland operation. Foster gave the order to murder all those people found in the mine shaft. They were gassed *en masse.*"

"Howard," Brewster sighed, "Director Towers briefed me daily on every aspect of our nation's then-current security issues when I took over the presidency. I don't recall Foster's name ever coming up. Doesn't it seem strange to you, in hindsight, that our nation's security chief would place Foster so low on his list of priorities? Let's back up a minute to that Athens thing. You're implying that you were in fact at that banquet, or did I miss something?"

"I certainly was. How Georgios could say what he said is beyond me, but the man does go about stroking his beard in a semi-fog. He and I had a long conversation prior to the dinner, and we spoke the following day on two occasions. I think he's senile."

"Kurt?"

"Mr. Georgios claims he saw Mr. Greenward only the first half day of the conference, then not at all. He seemed quite lucid to me, although hesitant to answer. I asked if it weren't possible that Mr. Greenward was indeed there, shmoozing and moving about. He said absolutely not. I got the impression he didn't want to rat on an American delegate of such high standing."

"All right, we'll come back to this question. Open the binders, both of you, and tell me if the first dozen or two pages are a complete fabrication, partly so, or do they in fact *essentially duplicate* what was in the actual Russian document, as far as content and the original Russian intent?"

There was a pause of several minutes as both men flipped pages. Finally Greenward looked up. "This is nothing but guesswork. The real thing was—"

Winfield's raised palm stopped him in mid-sentence. "Howard, this is on the money and you know it. It's almost word for word, right down to what the Russians said would happen if we didn't capitulate. All those thirty locations are listed there, and they're accurate. *You* supplied me with a lot of other scenarios the Russians didn't cover. Isn't that what you're remembering now? If I didn't know better, I'd have thought it might be an earlier Russian draft I was reading here. I even remarked about how Dr. Whittier managed to do it totally from memory. I'm envious."

"What I told you back then was accurate, damn it! This is *not* that document."

"We all know it isn't that document," Brewster snapped. "Does it essentially say things the way the original did. Yes or no?"

"If you don't care one whit about accuracy, it's approximately… who besides Whittier put this together anyway? He couldn't possibly have known some of this stuff." Greenward closed the binder without scanning further, then shot a hostile glance at Whittier, who simply smiled.

Brewster moved his gaze to Stauf. "How about you, Kurt? Do you think it's accurate?"

"This looks awfully close to the one Howard showed me, yes."

"Good. At least we have one agreement of sorts. Read the next thirty pages with care and indicate when you're done." He glanced at his watch. Ten minutes later both men had nodded and once again Brewster took over.

"Okay, now you've just reviewed a history of what happened in the three-week interval *immediately following* Las Vegas. Foster was in Bermuda, seen there by hundreds while he prepared for a sailboat race at the very time the Las Vegas attack occurred. His involvement with Howard and President Winfield began some days after the event, so—"

"Not in my book it doesn't," Greenward interrupted, glowering. "With his talents, he could have set the whole thing up in advance. Was he in Moscow when he made that tornado there, or in Buffalo when he made that vertical storm thing? He was sitting out in Virginia for the Moscow tornado. We had our ambassador in Moscow reporting on the whole thing, minute by minute. Foster doesn't have to be anywhere near the places he destroys. And the part about him putting out wildfires is pure bullshit. He *started* those fires in areas where his organization placed something beforehand that would put them out after some sort of radio signal was sent. I traced him all the way up from Ecuador, Brazil and places like that. Name a spot with a big fire, and he was there. I tracked his plane, damn it. Secretary Howland told me he'd been *hoodwinked* into that whole thing. He thought the damn things were *sensors*, a huge network of sensors. If the nation's security could be enhanced he was all for it because he's a true patriot, the complete opposite of Foster. Howland loves the country, and there he sits taking the rap for one of the worst arsonists in history. He was set up as Foster's fall guy in case the operation didn't work, never tumbling to who Foster really was. How would he know? Am I the only one who isn't blinded by all this bull? Foster was setting himself up to blackmail any nation he chose, can't any of you see it? First set the fires, thousands at a time, then put them out when paid enough. He was building his reputation. The man's a—"

"Enough, Howard. Any arsonist can *start* a fire. All it takes is a match. This guy can put them out with his mind. He's proven it. Further, you've forgotten that Ben Howland's voice is on tape ordering the murder and disposal of two hundred eighty people."

Greenward's face reddened further. "Tape recorded on a Wal-Mart special in the great outdoors. That tape was *faked!* It won't stand up in court. I can make you one just like it."

"Howard, in spite of your personal views, I believe this document clearly tells a different story," Brewster said. "It appears to me that your perceptions are based on a paranoid mistrust of this man."

"Mr. President, he's a friggin' alien and when *that* truth comes out, you'll be holding the bag, big time. What does it take to convince you that no one on earth can conjure up a tornado or blow away billions of transistors the way he did?" Greenward stood, spreading his hands. "Look, I tried to *save* this country from waking up some day and finding it was just someone's toy, but apparently my intentions are for nothing. Foster's an alien freak, I tell you. Argue all you want, but don't come running back to me when we go belly up. *Nobody* can handle absolute power like that without being totally corrupt. History's proven it over and over."

"Interesting philosophy. All right, in your judgment I'm hugely mistaken. How about you, Kurt?"

"I'm voting for Foster."

"Then we have a definite division here. On Howard's side, Foster's a criminal of the worst sort, an alien freak. On the other side, the man's a hero. Sit back down, Howard. I have one final item to bring up. This may or may not have anything to do with the binder you're holding, but I'd like your explanation of why, on several occasions, Mr. Howland's partner and alleged mass murderer, Marvin Sleck, was a guest at your estate in Quaker Hill, New York, specifically in the two-month period prior to those Yellowstone fires?"

Greenward paled for the first time.

"Also, Howard, I've been given a list of eight prominent names, powerful folks, wealthy folks with whom you have had many, *many* phone conversations over the same time period. They've *also* been guests at your estate, which is none of my business except that our Mr. Sleck happened to be there at the same times. Would you like me to name the seven men and one woman on my list here, or do we understand each other?"

"Some sonofabitch is setting me up. Who told you all that crap? O'Dell? It sounds like him."

"I confess having a hand in it," Mike smiled. "I've been keeping tabs on Mr. Sleck for several years now."

"There ya go, that says it all. Well, *I* scarcely know the man, other than what I've read in the papers. Whoever told you he came to my place was smoking something, and who the hell are you to spy on my private affairs, anyway, O'Dell?"

"You are welcome to examine my files on Sleck. He is well known for working both sides of the street as an expert on the criminal mind as well as one for the criminal mind, and I'm a newspaperman. It's the nature of my business to know about such people and their associates. Sorry, but I can name dates and times of day for his visits. I use professional detectives who change from time to time, and none of them smoke anything, thank you."

"Well, unless your gumshoes photographed Sleck going and coming, with my estate buildings in the background, there's not a chance you can—"

"They are taken in the vicinity of your main gate, with your estate name showing. There are multiple photos in my files along with quite a few other interesting tidbits."

"You're a liar. My estate is totally protected. The main gate is a quarter mile in from the public road. A cockroach couldn't get that far without someone in my house detecting it, so the only thing *anyone* could possibly photograph are trees at the distant end of my driveway. I don't believe you've been within fifty miles of my estate."

"You forget, Mr. Greenward, that my military specialty was enemy surveillance. When was the last time you thought of checking for cameras just *outside* your main gate? I personally installed four there more than a year ago, soon after I first learned of your associations with Sleck. I'm *not* a cockroach, you see, so your security system can obviously be compromised by anyone who knows his business, and Sleck was not the only visitor those cameras identified. You spent a small fortune keeping people out, but you forgot how the British were defeated at Singapore in 1942."

"Nice try, O'Dell. There are *no* cameras between the outside road and my main gate. I have infra-red beams all over the place out there. You'd have tripped half a dozen."

"Speaking of infra-red, did you know that a single helicopter flight over your property recently disclosed thirty-two trip beams? You really should shield those things from above, just a friendly word of advice. You should also know that I photographed *you* at the Cumberland cemetery two nights ago, face on at a distance of thirty feet. Four crisp, clear photos of you and a few of your car's license plates. You're what we call an open book, Mr. Greenward, desperately in need of some good psychiatric help along with a lesson or two in stealth electronics."

Brewster held up his hand. "Enough. I've been told there are twenty-six single spaced pages of computer printouts listing phone calls in and out of your estate over the past two years, Howard, and Mike here says he can produce his own records, including photos of people and their cars entering your estate as we just heard, along with dates and times of day. We have what amounts to proof, at least in my book, that you are a major player in whatever connects eight powerful people to alleged mass murderer Marvin Sleck and possibly Benjamin Howland—"

"Hold it right there—Mr. President." Greenward's expression was suddenly surly. "Sleck's expertise happened to be of interest to one or two of my guests, yes, because of his value to various law enforcement groups in the past. He was brought in as a lecturer, nothing more. As I said, I scarcely knew him. My denials should be understandable, considering the private and sensitive matters that have brought these so-called prominent people together. I offered to be their host, so it's only natural that I protect their privacy. Sleck never gave any of us reason to believe he was involved with Foster. Had we only known—"

Brewster again held up a hand. "Howard, one of the names on your telephone lists was Benjamin Howland. In the course of two years, you spoke with him more than forty times by phone. You conversed with Sleck sixteen times, ten of those in the two months prior to the Yellowstone incident. Sleck and Howland have been indicted for arson and murder. It's inconceivable that anyone as savvy as you would fail to detect their close association. Much as I hate to do this, I'm restraining you to this aircraft on your honor until we land back at Andrews—you may not de-plane in Germany—and I suggest you get yourself a good lawyer stateside. We've only scratched the surface here, and you may have some acceptable explanations for it all, but there's cause to doubt a great deal of what you say. You may know that I practiced law before I entered politics, and this alleged involvement of yours with Sleck and Howland makes me reasonably believe you've committed one or more felonies involving the security of the country. I'm sorry about all this. I believe you were at one time a great help to this nation, as well as a good advisor to H.J. here, but no longer."

Greenward's laugh was forced. "You're *arresting* me? On a bunch of hearsay and outright lies? Whatever happened to Miranda, or don't I qualify?"

"The office I hold is a civilian one, Howard. I'm restraining you, using the plane as the boundary, not arresting you. You're free to enjoy its amenities as long as you stay aboard. However, my Secret Service agents are fully qualified to turn my restraint into a true arrest, in which case one of them will read you your rights. You'll have to make the rest of the trip in handcuffs if it comes to that. Your choice, but I prefer to keep this as civil as possible until you have a fair hearing, with counsel. Do we understand each other?"

"What choice do I have, since you hold all the cards... at least for now. Just remember, I'm warning you... all of you... you're going to regret this. I happen to know what I'm talking about, in spite of all your hogwash and illegal snooping. I really hope Foster's waiting in Munich for us, the bastard! Then you'll come running back to tell me I was right."

"Fine. We'll do just that." Brewster shifted his gaze. "Gordy, we haven't heard much from you in all this. Do you have anything to add? Any comment Mr. Greenward should hear? You've suffered quite a bit of personal abuse in this whole affair, plus some severe financial losses I understand."

"What personal abuse?" Greenward demanded. "Is that going to be another lie I have to face?"

"I wasn't addressing you," Brewster snapped. "Gordy?"

"No comment. I'm just thankful I was able to set the record straight."

Brewster's smile turned sad. "I understand. Well, Howard, you're free to return to your seat aft. The rest of you, please stay. The sooner I reach U.N. Ambassador Connally, the better I'll feel, and then I'd like you all to help me draft a statement to the world. We are about to name a new American hero... even if he isn't American. But I'm sure he can pass the exam if he chooses."

He paused long enough for Greenward to do an about-face and leave. Then, smiling, he turned to Gordy.

"We have some time left in which I want to hear everything you know, in your professional capacity, about this man Foster and his paranormal gift. I'm sure I speak for H.J. here, and you, too, Kurt. To me, this situation has evolved from Mr. Greenward's neuroses to the point where he's created a monster of his own."

"What will happen to him now?" Gordy asked.

"Good question, but not ours to answer."

"Still, watch him closely, Mr. President. Speaking professionally, your description of him as psychotic is accurate. I'm not at all comfortable with his talents for twisting events to suit his needs. He *heard* you say Jim was a hero, that you'd have him removed from the Tombstone List along with Tricia, but I suspect Mr. Greenward will insist you had no concept of reality when you said it. Acting on that basis, he could well continue on his warped path. He is totally consumed by his views of Jim, and psychotics follow their own rules without regard to others or to the consequences of their acts."

"What do you recommend... as a psychologist?"

"That you make the arrest formal prior to our de-planing at Munich."

Brewster grunted. "Perhaps you're right. There's plenty of reason, and I'd almost decided to do that a few minutes ago. My sense of fairness probably overrode my good common sense. Very well, as soon as we land safely in Munich I'll order it done. He can't do much until then, except to sit and think about his defense. Besides, I arranged to have someone babysit him back there. The babysitter is a complete stranger, of course, but I thought it prudent under the circumstances."

"Stan, what's this about landing safely?" Winfield asked. "You never used to worry. I was always the one. What happened?"

"Call it awareness. Someone recently told me landing is the most dangerous part of any flight."

Munich International Airport.

Tricia's "German-only" debut had her nerves on edge, but they steadied once she was inside the main terminal. No one looked at her name tag, though a few glanced at the double gold stripes on her sleeves. She worked herself into character, bought a newspaper and waited for Charlie to show, suddenly realizing that the tall, blond man she'd been looking at for several minutes was him. Blond? Oh, well sure. If he could make himself into a Finn with a red tasseled cap, he could do "tall and blond."

He acknowledged her nod, then headed for the escalator to the observation deck, where he'd watch the south runway taxi strip. Meanwhile she'd use German TV to help keep her focused. She'd just begun thinking in that language when a chirp in her black bag startled her. The two-way radio! She almost answered "hello," catching herself at the last second. "Ja?"

"Taxi strip's already empty, don't know how long." The radio's *shhhp!* told her the channel had been closed.

Oh, no! Jim won't get the thirty minutes he needs. Heart pounding, she quickly headed for the nearest bank of arrival and departure monitors. If the taxi ramp was already empty, that meant... oh, no... *there it was!* "Amerikanische Delegation zu G-8" the line stated. No runway or gate supplied. How long had it been posted? She strode briskly toward the escalator, spotting Charlie on his way down. His brief nod told her he'd already gotten through to Jim, who'd now have to move out of hiding to a spot where he could watch for the incoming plane, submerge himself to that mental state he called theta, then launch the most astounding miracle of modern times.

She bit her lip. There wouldn't be enough time.

Chapter 20

Air Force One.

Sleck must have been singing from his prison cell, Greenward mused, trying to cut a deal and save his neck. What else could it be? Someone a lot smarter than O'Dell might well have tracked one or two in the Quaker Hill committee and produced names, but never all eight, so it had to be Marvin Sleck. Even so, how much could Brewster deduce about the committee just from knowing names, and where did he get those pages of phone calls in the first place? What snooping sonofabitch had been?...

He stopped his mental rant.

Since Brewster already *had* the names, what could possibly be wrong with telling the truth? None of the eight had the slightest inkling that Foster had pulled the old con game on Ben Howland, or that Sleck was already in cahoots with the terrorist. Come to think of it, Sleck might even have been *part* of Foster's original plan, before the two of them went to work on Howland's trusting nature. Foster was a real snake charmer when the situation called for it, and Sleck had hoodwinked legitimate law enforcement agencies more than once in his career, even when they knew he was shady.

The simplest truth would be that the eight prominent people wanted to promote Howland's run for the presidency, based on their respect for a true U.S. patriot. They'd formed a political action committee, a PAC, no different than dozens of others in the political arena. That would explain all the phone calls, and Howland himself could confirm the fact since he'd been urged on several occasions to throw his hat into the ring. He knew full well who his supporters were. Sleck's one or two visits were to... to... well, he was a psychologist, wasn't he, same as Whittier? He was there to help them convince Howand to run, to give them a profile on their man, learn what made him tick. That was it! Why couldn't a criminal psychologist work his skills the other way?

Put all that in your pipe and smoke it, O'Dell. Cameras, my foot! You don't even know where Quaker Hill is. Before I'm done with you, you'll be the one needing a lawyer.

A sardonic smile replaced the frown. Foster's implication in the Howland mess would be the icing on the cake. Some of those phone calls had been used to track Foster and his plane. All the pontificating in the world wouldn't erase that fact. They showed a record of Foster's arson trail, starting in Kalispell, then the Sawtooth range and finally the fires in Yellowstone, proof positive. In contrast, the so-called evidence planted on poor Ben Howland was a faked audiotape, made outdoors on a portable recorder. Ridiculous! In fact, the man who made the tape even admitted to stalking Howland. How much more loaded could a picture get?

As for certain political assassinations Sleck had recommended to the Quaker Hill committee, who'd believe anything he said about them? They were confirmed accidents, every one, and Sleck's part had never gone beyond profiling the victims.

Now that Brewster's mind had been poisoned by the Whittier-O'Dell connection, turning attention away from Howland-Sleck and redirecting it at the world's number one criminal would be more difficult, but not impossible if Brewster was willing to talk one-on-one. Winfield would be easier to sway—a few choice words and he'd be right back in the nuthouse where he belonged—but the best of *all* solutions would be having someone blow Foster away. Dead men made notoriously poor witnesses in their own defense.

Brewster's threatened arrest was highly unlikely if he wanted to keep the Russian ultimatum a secret. Unlike Whittier's stupid fake, the real document would blow the top right off the U.S. Capitol. *Boom!* Perhaps Brewster realized his mistake already. Dumb, yes, but not *that* dumb.

With that thought, Howard Greenward exhaled a long breath and opened the latest issue of *Newsweek*.

The south roadway.

Charlie's terse radio message came as a kick in the stomach, but something worse trumped it. *Three* airport security cars were suddenly cruising the south road, each half a mile from the next, sweeping brush and hedgerows with searchlights! All were focusing on the area south of the road, forcing him to hunker down in the shorter brush at a time when he needed to be standing at the fence, watching the eastern sky. The VOR hill kept him from seeing the end of the runway from his hiding place, yet his mental creation needed to be in place all during the aircraft's final approach. Tiny lights were already visible in the eastern sky, perhaps ten minutes out. He had no other options and no time. If he began too early, any TAW system aboard the aircraft would detect something under the plane or directly ahead, and....

The thought stopped him cold.

The plane's radar altimeter would detect *anything* solid beneath the glide path, long after normal terrain avoidance warning equipment ceased functioning. Even if they were twenty feet off the concrete their computer would take over, pulling them back up while they still had airspeed. *Why didn't you think of that until now, stupid? Where was your head?*

He crouched back down with mind racing. He'd have to resort to the backup plan. If air blanketing the runway were thickened, it would shut down the engines. He'd used that idea when first trying to quench fires, abandoning it for a better way, yet it might just work here. Jet engines would starve and quit in seconds. Without thrust reversers, the stunned cockpit crew would have to apply the brakes earlier and harder than usual *and* his own mental force would be slowing the plane as well. They'd be down to half their touchdown speed in half a dozen seconds. A rather severe landing for those aboard, but there wasn't time to dream up any gentler method and no time to practice.

One of the security cars had just passed. Now! He crashed out of hiding and through the low brush to the roadway, only to confront the following car a mere two hundred feet away. *You're out getting away from your wife. Just saunter along with your hands in your pockets. That nearest set of landing lights could be Air Force One. Three miles per minute at an approach speed of 170 knots... four minutes at the most to touchdown.*

Now there was a flashing red light behind him.

Focus on the imagery, keep track of the plane. You can manage two things at one time. It would be normal to look behind you, so do it. Look bored. Stay focused. You live only a couple of miles away. You can even describe one of those farmhouses you saw this afternoon. Stay focused. Three minutes to touchdown. Why are you out walking?

The car slowed, matching his easy stride, and the window rolled down. "Was machen's denn hier draussen?" A powerful flashlight was aimed directly into his eyes. Even so, he smiled broadly as if enjoying some huge joke.

"Ach... meine frau! Ich benötigte etwas frische luft." He made a choking gesture with both hands and put on a disgusted face. Wives were notorious reasons a man might be desperate for fresh air, so it was an answer many a married man would understand—hopefully.

The guard grinned as he flicked off the flashlight and raised the window.

Two minutes shot and his night vision ruined, but it could have been worse. The incoming plane was definitely heading for the south runway. No time to make it to the fence now... he'd have to manage the whole thing right there on the shoulder. He stopped walking and began breathing deeply. Everything around him receded within seconds and the imagery flooded in, so startling in its detail he forgot to breathe at all.

But something about it was different. He could sense it.

Air Force One.

It was co-pilot Frank Oddo's turn to land the bird. Aside from a bit of bumpiness an hour back, the flight had been CAVU in pilot jargon—ceiling and visibility unlimited—and still was. He set their rate of descent at the gentlest glide allowed: 500 feet per minute at 170 knots for the whole final approach, with the AOA up a degree or two.

The landing gear locked into place just after crossing the outer marker, seven miles from the runway, at which point he dropped the speed back to 160, increased flaps a notch and backed the engine power down a bit at a time, watching his airspeed and trimming the nose down slightly. A little more power and she was back to 170 knots again. As they approached the MM, or decision point beacon, he went to full flaps, spooled up the engines to keep her at the right glide slope and again trimmed the nose down. The huge flaps rumbled and shook the plane a bit, but the glide slope was just about perfect.

"Feeling fine," he told pilot John Summers as the plane passed the airport fence. Summers didn't acknowledge; he was busy with his own end of things. There never was that much conversation during a landing, arguably the most dangerous segment of any flight.

Oddo began his flare and held the pitch angle when the plane was thirty feet off the deck. The mains touched so gently the plane barely shuddered. When they were totally down, all that remained was to lower the nose gear and steer.

Summers shook his head. "I hate it when you do that. What grease are you using?"

Oddo grinned without turning. That kind of landing happened once in a hundred flights. The next one might be a nightmare, just to balance things off. He raised the spoilers, selected full reverse and waited for the reversers to kick in. Once the plane slowed to 80 knots, he'd hold the manual brakes in and kill the reversers as soon as speed slowed to sixty. No need to slow further until the last few hundred feet of runway, since they were heading for the far end at least a mile ahead. Sixty knots, for a plane almost a football field in length, was about the same as fast forward for a turtle.

But Oddo's grin vanished just as the nose wheel touched. All four engines labored down, groaned and quit in unison as if they'd run into pancake batter, while all hell broke loose in the cockpit. Computer whiz kids had never counted on all four engines quitting simultaneously during this phase of landing, with no other warning signs in advance. Things like that just didn't happen in the "war rooms" of places like Boeing. Even if there'd been some huge flock of birds suddenly blanketing the whole runway, engines would *never* quit simultaneously.

The plane suddenly put out its own hooks, acting as if it had just landed in a flooded rice paddy.

"Engines out!"

Frank barked the useless words, reaching for the manual brakes even as he realized their rate of slowing was greater than anything the reversers could have delivered. Summers was already on the pipe reporting an emergency situation to Munich's tower, while three audio and visual alarms heightened the shock of finding they were in trouble, big time. One of the flashing red visuals indicated that they'd lost engine power. Duh! Then, only a few seconds later, deceleration pressures eased and they both reeled back in their seats. The plane seemed to be rolling normally.

"Frank, what in *hell* did we hit?" Summers growled. "What could've killed the engines?" He quickly shot down two of the audio alarms.

"Brakes on. I'll drive." The words were more a gasp.

"Roger that. Brakes on hard, but I'm getting no response. We're not slowing." He pointed at the ground speed indicator in disbelief. It was holding at 70 knots.

"What the hell is—hey, we're coming off the ground." Oddo's voice rose in pitch. "We're *climbing!*" He watched the pointer on the back-up mechanical altimeter. One turn around the dial was a hundred feet in altitude, and the pointer was moving fast... up.

"No way." Summers reached over and tapped the dial face.

"It's barometric, John, it cannot lie. It's... look, up twenty feet since... jeez. Thirty! Now forty—"

"Where was it when it started?" Summers eyed the pitch indicator, squinting.

"Who watches? Munich's strip is flat, John. We've both been here before, and cripe, we're *still* doing 70 knots." The remaining audio alert kept right on sounding. *Beep... beep... beep... beep.* "Something has to be pushing us... pitch indicator shows a definite nose up, but all wheels are down and the radar altimeter's zeroed out."

"Look outside. We must be up a couple hundred feet, but radar alt still says we're at zero. That means there's something under us. We're up on it. We're slowing. Forty knots. Twenty."

"Get serious. The runway was clear all the way. What could be?..."

The plane shuddered to a halt. It had all taken place too quickly for reality to catch up, but at least they'd stopped a good half-mile short of the runway's end, so that danger was past.

"Well, whatever just happened, it... *yikes!*" Summers feet were suddenly bracing against the instrument panel as the plane tipped forward. They were both abruptly sitting the wrong way on the end of a see-saw, staring down at the concrete with oblivion a mere two hundred feet below. Someone had stopped the film right there.

Beep… beep… beep… beep.

Summers recovered his voice ahead of his partner. "My God, Frank, the president!"

℘℘

Mike had spent too many hours piloting shot-up aircraft and landing in muddy fields to miss nuances like the change in engine pitch two seconds before they all quit.

"Trouble!" he barked, just before being thrown hard against his seat belt by deceleration far too severe for brakes alone. His single-word reaction was involuntary. Nobody else uttered a word. There was nothing to do but ride out whatever it was.

He analyzed even as he braced for impact. *All engines quit together. Slowing too fast for brakes alone. Something else slowing us. Fifteen seconds since touchdown. Eighty knots when engines quit, severe deceleration for a dozen seconds, normal feel—until now. What's this? We're rotating? Impossible. There's no way to get this bird off the… oh, no. Something must be on the runway… they're trying to hop it. Wait a minute. We're stopping.*

But before he could give voice to his thoughts, the plane began to tilt forward. Was the nose gear buckling? There'd been no impact, nothing to damage the gear, so how could there be no noise or jarring, no metal against metal? The barely perceptible initial tilt became more severe by the second, as if the plane were rolling off a cliff. Screams echoed down the plane's long corridor—the tail was rising faster than the nose dropped—but then the tilt stopped. The angle had to be at least twenty degrees, judging by runway lights outside, and they were well off the ground. That sensation of climbing up on something had been valid after all, but what the hell could have been put in their path and why did the engines all quit? For a long minute there was no sound save for someone still screaming in the plane's stern area.

Gordy was the first to speak. "Mr. President, I remember hearing you say you'd enjoy meeting Jim Foster, or did I imagine you said that?"

Brewster was still pitched forward, with a hand clutching his fore-head. His head came up. "No, I said it. Why bring that up now?"

"I think you may get your wish. He's here."

಄ಃ಄

An eerie feeling of detachment swept over him when he ap-proached the fence. The blue and white plane resembled someone's desk-top model—except for the missing pedestal. It wasn't possible! He couldn't have done it—yet he had, and his conscious mind strug-gled with that fact—but something had seemed different, akin to be-ing pushed from behind while climbing a hill. Had Charlie's mental energy somehow boosted the process? Even if true, there was no time to waste. Emergency response teams would smash into the invisible pylon as it was now, a shadow shape two hundred feet thick and as wide as the plane's wingspan. Its vertical sides needed flaring at the bottom. The ramp stretching back to the plane's touchdown point had to be dissolved as well.

Desire brought forth the imagery; results followed automatically. Done! The changes were in place simply because he felt they were in place. That, too, was part of the mental realm.

Time now for the walkway to the plane. It would flare at the bot-tom as well, with sides and a top: a transparent tunnel stretching from fence to fuselage. Steps at his end would get him over the fence, and thereafter the slope would be up about one foot for every six feet forward.

He re-checked the road. It was empty, but inside the airport flash-ing red lights were streaking toward the plane with sirens blaring, some coming down the runway. He'd gotten rid of the ramp just in time, but some unpleasant surprises were in store now if any of the rescuers decided to drive beneath the plane. Would the Germans do so foolish a thing? It would be contrary to any human instinct—unless German emergency procedures required driving beneath suspended planes.

Slightly amused, he retreated into the brush. An hour was to pass before the next phase, time in which chaos would build to a fever pitch while TV viewers all over the world switched channels to the most fantastic live coverage ever. Charlie's statement about Germans not performing well when things didn't work as expected would now be put to the test. They'd see the Boeing jumbo-jet perched as high in space as the plane was long, realize there wasn't a thing they could do about it, but follow their training anyway. Fire apparatus of all kinds would scream to the site with no thought given to the impossibility of rescuing anyone with ladders—the highest rescue platforms would fall way short. Frenzied security personnel would run in circles shutting down the south runway, cutting off all access to and from the airport and so on. Others would scope out the pedestal, outlining its exact perimeter, maybe even painting it to make it visible. That effort would be well along, perhaps even finished, before the more observant among them pointed out that the pedestal faithfully followed the plane's contours overhead.

Several searchlights were already trained on the plane, and the airport's central portion was a mass of flashing red lights and shrieking sirens, yet Charlie's show was only just getting started. Charlie's show?

It had been his show from the beginning, starting back in Lahti, but what if he turned out to be something else? Was Earth really just a few years from entering an ice age, and would it really happen as quickly as he said? What if his real reason for being here is to?... *No! Stop that. You must not doubt him or this will all be for nothing.*

The first of several emergency vehicles had just collided with the flared pedestal. Two others followed in quick succession, resulting in a clutter of headlights all at crazy angles. They'd actually tried to drive beneath a three-hundred ton monster poised to come smashing down at any instant? Another of Charlie's predictions come true, and now there were but forty minutes left before James Foster would appear live on TV sets all over the world. Did it mean an end to his frustration? Were his powers now—finally—to be used beneficially, or would this be another terrible letdown?

Charlie's people had to be equally frustrated. Three million years waiting to embrace Earth's civilization, only to be denied in hundreds of ways once man and his technology reached the proper point. Now, with the age of information in full bloom, there were wars and religious jihads and atomic or bio-agent saber rattlings around the globe. Political expediency had replaced integrity, and the United Nations had become the dictator everyone had feared. Could the Eden visitors hope to do better now compared to centuries ago? It would indeed take a spectacle such as this to galvanize Earth's people, compelling naysayers to listen, even to think out of their box for a change. The warning had to reach Earth's citizenry without media bias, political slant or malice toward anyone. But it was still scary, and definitely dangerous.

If anything went wrong, it might not happen at all.

℘℘℘

The terminal complex was a cacophony of shrieking alarms and sharp, snappish announcements shouted over the public address system, while security personnel and airport employees raced past Tricia in all directions. In any emergency, it seemed, Munich International personnel were all to be in some stipulated place before doing anything else. Dogs suddenly appeared, some leashed, many others free. Were they to sniff out explosives? Their handlers ran along with them, shouting commands. Travelers scurried out of the way.

Oberregierungsrat M. Adler grabbed Greta Wirth's hand, pointed to an airport utility vehicle outside the building and darted toward an exit door with her in tow. The door's piercing alarm added to the din as they charged down a stairway. Three frantic men overtook them on the first landing. Charlie motioned them past, then raced after them, bursting through the ground-level door onto the tarmac. The utility vehicle was still there. They dashed to it, she vaulting into her seat while he reached for the key. Missing! She heard a sharp *crunch*, and then they were moving—without the engine.

"Had to smash the transmission," he growled, just as a fire truck shot by with siren blaring. Close behind it was a medical van. Somewhere east of the terminals a monster siren split the night air with enough power to reach the city of München, twenty or so miles away.

The three who'd charged past them in the stairwell sped by in a military-style van. Charlie stayed with them, veering away half a mile later. He threaded his way across a torrent of cars and trucks arriving from his right, then headed for the farthest of the buildings, a huge hangar. Two dozen gawkers were clustered outside the structure, all staring east at the spectacle. Koordinatorin G. Wirth leapt from the rider's side, megaphone in hand. She raced up to the immobile crowd, snapping at them in German.

"Why are you all *standing* there like startled sheep? There is some freak thing happening out there, some alien force. The American president is trapped up there with his staff. It's *news!* It's what you are best at. Get out there. Mein Gott, get those vans *out* there now, quickly."

She'd glanced around, expecting security types to converge on her, but the only uniforms in evidence were worn by hangar personnel, all standing outside and staring at the spectacle on the runway.

"Where are the security people?" she demanded, adding bite to her words.

"They left," someone said in German, "soon as the alarms went off."

She brought one hand to her forehead, withdrawing ir with a flourish. "Ah, who needs them? Take the trucks out to the airplane's *port* side, but stay well back, sixty meters at least. Maybe eighty. No matter what happens you will want to keep the cameras on that side, watching the door. The American president is *on that plane!* Something has got to happen."

"Will it crash down?" someone else called out, this time in English. "Will it explode?"

"Do you think I know zat? It has to be some alien force, but if down it comes you want to be out there with your cameras running, don't you? Nozzing will happen inside here, so pick your spots and don't get too close. Tell anyone who stops you we have permission from the top. Put up your masts and record everything. They will send out searchlights, so it soon will be like day out there. Move! Don't waste a second. The whole world will be watching. You will never have an audience like this again."

She strode among them, repeating the message in German, then Italian and finally French. The two German media vans were already on their way, with French and Italian teams close behind. The Americans had the most equipment to bundle back into their single-but-larger truck. They were still at it, sliding cases into one of the two large belly bays. She called to them in English, foregoing the megaphone. "Hey, can I cop a ride out there?"

One of the team grinned. "Hop in, baby."

The other five ran for a car parked well away from the hangar door. In less than a minute the truck was on its way, with the other car close behind. She sat stiffly, staying in character—using English, but with a little accent thrown in.

"Vot's your name?"

"Steve Bradley. I'm the reporter, they're my team." He sped toward the other media trucks, all of which had swung out onto the runway and headed for the area lit by the plane's landing lights, several hundred meters down the tarmac.

"Ze others are setting up too closse," she pointed out. "Better you stay back in case it comes down. If it doesn't, then maybe... mein Gott!"

The first of half a dozen converging emergency vehicles had just connected with the pedestal on the starboard side of the plane... flipping on its side although there was no other hint of a collision. The two following it corrected that impression when they piled into the wreck, streaking sparks. A headlight went out.

"Slow down. Those trucks just hit into sommezing."

"I see it," Bradley said. "Man, this is crazy. There's nothing there to hit."

"Well, *sommezing* is holding up the plane. I can't see anything, but zere has to be...." She let her voice taper off.

"Twilight Zone, right?"

"Vhat? Oh... I know, yes, like that. Sommezing alien." *You have no idea how accurate that is, buster. Now if only Jim can pull off his part. I wonder where Charlie is now? Probably out there where that accident just happened.* "How high up goes your mast?"

"Fifty-six feet. In meters, that's...." He squinted one eye, calculating.

"You should go out on the grass and... mein Gott... zere is *nozzing* holding the plane up!" Her hands went to her temples instinctively. "Stop here... here is good."

Bradley stood on the brakes. The car with his crew came alongside.

"Ja, zis is good," she said. "I must now go to ze others and make them move back." She forced a half-smile his direction, then flung her door open. "I vill check back up on you later." She was away before he had a chance to reply.

When the sound of helicopters rose above the growing din, she broke into a run.

Air Force One.

Whittier's calm announcement of Jim's possible presence was as startling as the landing itself, judging by the silence that followed. The first to react was Brewster, whose swivel chair remained locked in the forward-facing position. He struggled with his harness. "Foster's *here?* How can you possibly know that... unless you knew before you came aboard? Did you set something up just so we'd—"

"I'm guessing, sir, but knowing his capabilities... well, consider that we're now perched high on something that can't possibly be out here, yet a glance says we're still centered on the runway. What possible structure strong enough to support this plane could have been placed in the middle of a runway used around the clock? Yet, here we are. We also seem to have reached this height gradually, which makes the structure a ramp at least one mile long."

Mike continued the thread. "Gordy's right. All four engines quit together just as if someone had thrown a switch, this on a plane that's maintained to the max. No engine power, therefore no thrust reversers, yet we slowed as if we'd landed in six inches of thick mud. Something was at work beyond just brakes, and it was much more powerful than reversers."

"And we end up tilting down," Gordy finished, "even though we didn't run into anything. We stopped completely and *then* came the pitch forward several seconds later, almost as if a giant hand pulled up the tail and held it there. It's a statement of some kind, and I'm suggesting the giant hand may be just that, a giant hand created by a man I'm sure could do it. Now we look outside and what do we see but hysterical knee-jerk reaction on the part of the Germans, the Keystone Kops trying to carry a ladder sideways through a doorway. Whatever they're seeing out there, it's destroyed the discipline they're famous for. Ruling out some alien power, everything smacks of Jim since he's the only human I'm aware of with such capabilities. I submit to you that a man who can create and orchestrate a tornado starting with a clear sky can do just about anything. In that, I do agree with Mr. Greenward, unfortunately."

"Damn this seat... there." Brewster unsnapped his harness and slid forward onto his rump, propping his feet against the bulkhead before twisting about on his knees. "I'd vote for the alien power, Whittier. Your so-called friend may have done some of those other things I read about, but no way is he going to raise a plane like this, not even a little one. Air Force One is nearly three hundred tons."

I know, Mr. President, I know. "Mental force doesn't follow any of the physical laws we all accept as normal, according to Jim. Weight never enters the picture except to create a barrier to normal individuals. That makes his talents alien by their very nature, yes."

"Amen to that," Mike added. "That's what kept throwing me about him. I saw this normal-looking man, but accepting the things he could do evaded me for the longest time. He and my daughter jumped off a cliff down in Peru... without parachutes. It was a four thousand foot drop, about the same as the Half Dome out in Yosemite, but he just floated them down. They also jumped together at night from ten thousand feet, in freezing rain and strong winds over the North Sea. He landed them on a platform out there the size of your back yard. I've jumped in combat dozens of times. What they did is impossible. I've given up trying to understand."

"But," Brewster sputtered, "then... why *this*? It makes no sense unless he's trying to create some kind of international incident. I just can't buy into your theories, either of you. This has got to be something else. What about you, H.J.?"

Winfield was slow in answering. "I'm afraid I agree with Gordy and Mike. Absent any other reasonable explanation, it's either Foster or little green men from another planet. God help us if Howard was right after all. He warned us. Kurt? How about you? Does this change your views any?"

Stauf finally found his voice. "I... no, it doesn't, but what can we do if it really is Foster?"

"We wait," Brewster growled. "Given a choice between him and something alien, I'd rather deal with someone who at least *looks* human."

Chapter 21

Munich International runway.

Tricia suddenly realized she'd known exactly where Charlie would be even though the sea of flashing red, amber and blue lights below Air Force One created double images of the hundreds of would-be rescuers milling about. He'd never explained what his role would be, but she'd imagined he would rile up the rescuers, influencing what they reported back to airport officials. *Ja, I tell you the airplane is up on something very hard, but we can't see anything. What are our instructions? What should we do?* It wouldn't occur to any of them that maybe there'd be no instructions or orders.

She flicked on her megaphone and aimed it at the Italian media crew. "Hey," she cried in Italian, "you are way too close. Move the truck farther out. You will get a wider view so you can show all this going on under the plane."

"We know our business. We stay right here," one of the men shot back, almost snarling. He was short, wearing a red coat that reminded her of Napoleon. All he'd have to do would be to stick his hand between the gold coat buttons.

She strode over to him, remembering to be arrogant. "Are you saying you already *know* what's about to happen? Well... do you? Are you too dense to see that if the plane slides off whatever it's on, it'll come right down on you?"

He stared up at it. "It will come down straight if it comes down at all. We are in no danger here."

"Okay, *cacasenno*, if you're so sure of that, you just stay right here. We all know there's absolutely no danger of fire or explosion if it comes straight down, so you'll be totally safe here not even fifty meters from where it will go up in your face." She looked away, then back, arching one eyebrow. "Don't worry, we will mop up whatever is left of you and inform your families."

He scowled at the obscene insult, but before he could retort she moved toward the French crew, motioning them toward the grass as well. The area south of the runway was better anyway, since the cameras would be aimed right at the plane's door. Millions would see that Jim was standing on nothing when he got to that point.

ဆာလ

Considering Brewster's reputation for indecision and waffling, Ollie mused, the baby-sitting assignment had come as a real surprise. Daniels' phone call warning of a possible conspiracy was barely an hour old when a black two-seater jet with minimal markings landed at Salt Lake City. An hour later it was on its supersonic way to Andrews AFB with a passenger who'd thereafter be known only as "O. Robins, consultant." Other than the Secret Service detail, no one aboard Air Force One would know that Robins was on board to keep a watchful eye on Howard Greenward, whose seat would be directly across the aisle in the general seating area.

Anything unusual about Greenward's demeanor and body language was to be noted, along with whatever he might say during the flight. If he was truly psychotic, it would be be apparent in any number of ways, Ollie knew. The irritable nature of any psychotic's character could be brought to light by some incessant chatter sprinkled with a stupid remark here and there. Throw in the laryngitis trick for that finishing touch, but there was one little hiccup hiding in that simple request to merely study the man.

What if the psycho did something rash during the flight? Would there be time to stop him?

ဆာလ

Greenward clenched his teeth, not so much from the plane's crazy landing as from the hysterical female reporter still screaming her head off behind him. She'd kept it up after the plane's forward tilt stopped, even after a pair of men near her lurched to their feet and scrambled forward, grabbing anything handy to stay upright. Only Secret Service types were that brainless, so those two were no doubt charged with first responsibility to the president even though they'd been sitting back with the cattle. Probably thought they'd be of some value if the plane fell off its perch, whatever that turned out to be. Sure they would. They'd die with Brewster up there in the nose, the idiots.

He fought down the urge to twist about and throttle the screamer, hardening his jawline. Chances of anyone in the aft section surviving were good, even with a drop from this height. The tail section usually stayed intact, any fire would be up front and the efficient Germans would already have a dozen foam trucks outside all ready to go. In fact, they'd undoubtedly sprayed everything beneath the plane by now. Their emergency plans would have kicked into overdrive before the plane's engines quit turning. At least the plane was still dead center on the runway, not upside down in some farmer's field, and the cause would be known shortly.

Whatever it turned out to be, it had done a duct-tape job on motormouth across the aisle. The jerk's laryngitis hadn't prevented him from yammering ever since leaving Andrews. Now he sat ashen-faced and white-knuckled, same as the others. Probably someone who didn't fly much. They were the kind who talked a lot.

The intercom crackled to life, but the pilot's announcement was worse than useless. They were up on some sort of platform and the rest was a mystery. No kidding, a real mystery? Duh! What platform would be sitting in the middle of a runway, especially here? Where were all the other G-8 delegation planes who'd used the same runway, stacked up like pancakes? Then came the second announcement, a directive for everyone to stay put with belts fastened. Still not one word about what had happened.

Baldy decided to strain his vocal cords again. "Shoot," he croaked, "wonder what they're doing out there? Say, didja know this is the same airport where that Czech soccer team was murdered a couple years back? You don't suppose—"

"Do us all a favor, blockhead, and get your facts straight for a change. They were Israeli athletes, not Czech soccer players, and it happened a few *decades* back." *That ought to shut him up.*

"Oh." He twitched his sandy-colored mustache, silent for all of two seconds. "Well, I sure thought they were Czechs. Say, I read this plane could go around the world non-stop and still have fuel left over. You don't suppose all that extra gasoline could light off if we went down, do ya?"

Of all the!... you think aviation fuel is gasoline? And you're a consultant? What kind, pre-school?

At the fence.

Air Force One's white underbody glowed red, like some bird over glowing coals on a campfire spit. Among the red flashing vehicles was a toothpick-sized fire engine ladder, falling way short of any rescue height, but there it was anyway, for the world to see. Surely the crew knew it would never reach before they went to all the trouble, or were they following a directive making ladder raising mandatory in all rescue situations? Did that mean hose trucks were showering the plane with water as well? Or spraying foam?

Countless trucks and van-like shapes were spread about, with still more pouring into the scene, later arrivals forced to stop farther and farther away. Where had so many come from—München? Why wasn't it evident to the precise German mind that more was not necessarily better? On second thought, the same thing happened everywhere, not just Germany. How often was it that someone's kitchen stove fire brought out every piece of fire apparatus from miles around, when a simple extinguisher would have done the job?

Within ten minutes of the initial vehicle pileup, three choppers were in the air above the spectacle. Two remained over the scene for many minutes before flying off. The third landed after half a dozen complete circles directly *over* the plane. What could that crew have been reporting, that Air Force One was suspended in air without cables of any kind? If there *had* been cables, the boobs would have flown into them. In fact, all three choppers had passed directly over the aircraft, one after the other, so apparently three matching reports were considered conclusive, whereas one simply would not be enough. Two might be doubted, but three—ah, that was the magic number. *Definitely* no cables, and no survivors standing on the wings. Rescuers on the ground were probably poring over technical manuals, looking for instructions on how to lower a plane suspended in mid-air without cables. Would that be listed under cables or suspensions?

Several TV trucks were assembled on the plane's port side, masts raised. They'd be broadcasting images of the plane and its frenzied rescuers by now, each team's reporter shocked to find that a routine assignment had suddenly become a major international event. Some might soar like eagles, while others crashed and burned.

His own predicament was far worse than theirs.

Air Force One was at least a quarter mile away, two hundred feet up, and he'd have to approach it with nothing under his feet but air. Solid air, to be sure, but human intellect held little sway over a man's innate fears. Somehow it was easier to skydive without a parachute or jump off a four thousand foot cliff and float to wherever he wished, knowing he was operating as an individual, that he was in total control. This was different. Too many uncontrollable factors were involved, too many distractions. If his fears took over at the wrong time... well, better that he swat a hornet's nest while tied to the tree beneath, and yet he'd given his word. Eden's prophecy had to be delivered, fear or no fear. Their warning was immensely important for mankind's very survival.

His "staircase over the fence" was somewhere nearby. When he applied Charlie's "shimmer" trick, the creation was practically at his feet. All he had to do was forget his fears, forget the flashing lights, ignore the searchlights and the sirens and the occasional helicopters... abandon concerns for his own life, and Tricia's.

Why had it seemed so possible just hours ago?

He'd just taken a deep breath when yet another security car swung onto the road at the western end, red light flashing. They were coming fast, sweeping the fence side with their lights, but the simple fact of their appearance achieved what all the deep breathing in the world couldn't. Adrenaline shot him over the fence and had him running in long strides up the invisible slope before his fears could kick in. If they aimed the beam upward, they'd....

He suddenly stopped, watching. *Why would they aim up? They'd be looking for something on the ground inside the fence, not in the air.*

The car never stopped or slowed, but the incident put the rest of his self-doubts to rest. The only thing mattering now was the plane's port side door. Once the trailer-mounted searchlights found him, he'd be seen as some death-defying circus act high overhead, except for the all-important wire being absent. Surprise would become hysteria in a flash, the reactions of those below the plane serving to persuade a hundred million TV viewers it was reality they were watching. The Germans would deny trickery even before they were convinced it wasn't, but their denials would backfire. Something had to be there in the first place before it could be denied. All sorts of wild theories might be thrown into the mix. What a circus in the making!

None of the emergency vehicles had run into the walkway, but that could happen, too, and it would increase the panic. He started forward, but froze once more. *Another* helicopter had just crossed the eastern end of the runway, mere feet off the ground. It approached slowly along the grassy strip between fence and concrete. Unless the crew veered, it would collide with his walkway. How close could he let them come? What would happen if he had to dissolve part of the walkway? Even worse, what if they set the chopper down between him and the plane?

The security car was returning from the eastern end as well. Was someone directing them to return? Was he visible even now against the night sky? Where was Charlie? He could bend minds, so he ought to be able to....

But the chopper veered before he completed the thought, rising and heading back toward the terminal buildings. The security car sped past without slowing. So *that* was how it worked. Those in the chopper might have intended to sweep the whole runway on that side, but Charlie'd tuned in. He'd changed their minds. The same for those in the security car. Did that mean things below the plane were going as planned, after all?

At any rate, the rest of the show would all take place two hundred feet in the air. Half the distance had already been covered. Would anyone aboard know who was approaching? Certainly not Brewster— the former vice-president had never seen him face to face. Former President Winfield was in a mental institution and Howard Greenward was safely back in Washington, so that covered all the original players. Good! Charlie's chances to deliver the warning would be improved greatly if no one knew who was doing the talking.

ཀ○ཀ

Koordinatorin Greta Wirth anxiously checked her watch. An hour had passed since the landing, though it seemed like minutes, and she intended to be close to the American team when Jim appeared. Charlie was already standing on that side of the plane, barely fifty feet away, looking quite authoritative without doing anything. It was all going exactly as he'd predicted. Just thinking about it was scary.

Everything seemed like a nightmare where every step, every move, every thought was directed by an irresistible force. It was—

Jim!

The barely visible form was so impossibly high in the night sky that a rush of foreboding swept over her. It was one thing to know what Jim could do, or be next to him when he did it, but this was terrifying. No real life drama could come off this perfectly. What would happen if Charlie faltered or if things suddenly went awry? And what about Jim's mental control? The things he could do were incredible, but he'd spent a lifetime hiding his god-like powers. What if the very act of exposing his talents this way might somehow affect them? What if all these distractions?...

Stop it, Tricia. Jim's up there, risking his life, and you're on stage. This is where you say your line. Shout it out.

"Look!" she cried, pointing. "Mein Gott, someone is up zere!"

One of the Americans swung a spotlight that direction, picking up the dark figure within seconds. Two smaller beams joined it, then one of the monster searchlights. Excitement rippled through the crowd, punctuated by shouts and people running around like an ant hill broken open. Indeed there was someone up there, but what was he walking on, a wire? The big searchlight zipped to the area behind him, finding nothing but empty, black sky. In less than thirty seconds, confusion erupted into chaos.

She felt a ripple of real fear then. *Be careful, Jim!*

ॐ

Brewster's quarters were forward of the entry door, Jim knew. Some of the president's staff were probably there with him now, unable to sit comfortably or even move about due to the plane's tilt. Even so, the landing had appeared smooth enough, and an hour without power wasn't all that serious. They had plenty of battery reserve and the Germans were no doubt assuring them that a rescue would happen at any moment.

A sudden, blinding light forced him to shield his eyes. Seconds later, military commands were shouted in German and men in uniforms were leaping from a large truck. Automatic weapons? No! Charlie'd promised there'd be no violence, that the Germans wouldn't allow it. Was he even down there? Or Trish? What if they'd both been stopped back at the terminal building? Charlie might have tuned in from back there. The men below were forming ranks, aiming up—at him. There was nowhere he could run quickly enough, nothing but two hundred feet of air separating them from their target. It was over.

Everything turned quiet for the tiniest of moments, and then the order to fire was screamed into the night. He closed his eyes.

Oh, Trish… I'm so sorry.

৪০৫

It was unfolding as some daring and outrageous dream, but only because of Jim and Charlie, not her. Charlie'd warned that man's un-predictability—at least on Earth—surpassed all other problems when it came to establishing real contact between the cultures, but the plan was coming together anyway, even to the way she'd played her minor role. The media groups seemed happy, even the red-coated Italian. And her German! Where was *that* all coming from? She'd never spoken it with such ease.

Euphoria came to a sudden end as the canvas-sided truck threaded its way through the crazy-quilted maze of vehicles. When armed men jumped down, her pulse jumped with them. Automatics! A bullhorn blared military-style commands. In an instant her pulse rate doubled again.

No, no, no… Charlie, stop them. Where are you? You were there just a minute ago. Oh, Jim!

Without thinking, she dashed toward the truck as the men fanned out and aimed at the small figure above their heads. A moment later she heard the order to open fire.

She screamed, but no sound came forth.

৪০৫

Security detail officer Hans Reinarz stood mute and confused. Something had forced him to countermand his earlier order to fire, but what? That tall stranger was heading straight for him. *Oberregierungsrat? Upper government advisor? He's with Customs and they are always big trouble. Airport security is none of their business… unless Berlin….*

The stranger finally stopped at a distance far too close for personal comfort.

"Hoeren sie sofort auf zu schiessen, Kapitan!" he scolded. "We are on a world stage here. Look around you at all the TV cameras. Do you want us to appear as trigger-happy morons?"

Adler. His nametag says M. Adler. That will certainly bear investigation later. Taller than I am, blond hair, blue eyes. I will remember all that. Reinharz swallowed hard, pointing. "Sir, that man up there—"

"That man up there is showing *no* threatening signs, Hans, none. See here, nobody understands any of what's happening, but there will be no further shooting until you have direct orders." Adler paused, glancing up. "Your men have real lousy aim. We wait and see what this is all about, but for your efforts I will send a commendation to your next in command. What is his name?"

"Schmidt, sir."

"Oh,yes, Curt Schmidt. Now order your men back on the truck, and we all wait." Without another word, he turned away and strode toward one of the firetrucks. Moments later the truck's ear-splitting loudspeaker was turned down to a lower-than-normal level.

Oberregierungsrat? Only Berlin would send someone like that, but the man knew Schmidt by his first name even though Schmidt never used it. And somehow he knew he was talking to Hans Reinharz, not Gustav Reinharz in the other division. Yes, he'd....

Reinharz paused, suddenly drawing a blank. The name he'd just seen on the stranger's nameplate... it was short, no more than four or five letters. What was it? What letter did it begin with?

For the life of him, he couldn't remember.

℠)℃

He opened his eyes when the firing stopped. How could they have missed? Then the fact hit home—the bullets had ricocheted off the tunnel's sides. Nothing but air between him and a firing squad, yes, but not in the usual sense.

The terse order to cease firing was followed by much milling about and confusion below. The men with weapons were backing away. None of it made any sense. If he'd been a typical suicide bomber wearing explosives, a single shot might have meant the end of Air Force One and all on board, perhaps even all those below the plane. Couldn't they have seen that, or was it their urge to eradicate anything strange or unsettling, like smashing a spider? Someone was talking to the group's leader and the men were climbing back into their truck.

It was the stuff of nightmares—monster searchlights, countless flashing red and yellow lights, loudspeakers, shouts, TV booms and that firetruck ladder, constant turmoil fifteen stories below, faces in the plane's windows, and now the shooting—except that everything was real. Air Force One up close was more than a monster.

It had seemed so easy back there in the hotel room, but now the plane's forward tilt had to be removed. Charlie'd wanted him to become Moses, referring to Charlton Heston in the film. "Extend your arms. Let them see you directing the plane to do your bidding. The cameras will be running and you'll be well lit. We want the viewers to know that you're running the show. They'll have already concluded there are no props, and of course the Germans will reinforce that with their constant denials."

Easy to imagine, but had Charlie realized there'd be all these distractions?

The imagery developed back in the hotel room was that of placing a hot iron on butter. The plane's fuselage was to be the iron, "melting" its way down through the wedge of air. As the tail dropped, the nose wheel would rise, and when it was accomplished a smaller wedge would support the nose. The Jim Foster persona wouldn't be needed at all, except for show.

He lifted his right arm with the palm turned down, suddenly so focused he barely heard the din from below. When the task was finished a good ten minutes later, there was near silence. *Charlie predicted this. Whatever's going on down there, you've got to knock on the door and you still don't know what to say.*

He'd gotten no help from Charlie when it came to that part, hearing only that the right words would come when it was time. When was that going to be, *after* he knocked? Couldn't he be allowed a tiny peek at the script? On the other hand, those inside Air Force One would know exactly what *they'd* say. They'd been trained in repelling all threats, yet their training presumed they'd be surrounded by some hostile force, not by Munich International's security and emergency forces.

He tapped three times on the door's round glass, then stepped back half a dozen feet.

ෆාෆා

Greenward cursed beneath his breath, finally snapping the *Newsweek* closed. Not one word of warning from the cockpit crew, yet the plane was leveling out. Why hadn't they said something? His answer, supplied by the cockpit crew even as the question formed, was that the they hadn't the foggiest notion of what was behind the change or, for that matter, what the plane was sitting on. One whole hour and they *still* didn't know? An obvious lie. Supposedly they were also constrained from starting the auxiliary power units—did that mean they couldn't, or wouldn't?—and everyone was to stay in their seats except for using the rest rooms one-at-a-time. Great, just great. His gun holster had been torturing his lower back for the past two hours, no matter how he tried to sit off center, and he'd hoped to use a rest-room break to do a little limbering up, maybe massage the area. Couldn't do it in the seat without removing the weapon, which was out of the question. Why the hell had he even brought it? On the other hand, there'd been times he'd chosen not to carry, and later regretted it.

Brewster had closed-circuit video monitors up there in front show-ing *him* what was happening outside the plane, and he could even aim the cameras with his own joystick. Of *course* he knew what was going on. The dodo was playing dumb. Too bad the cameras weren't looking at the plane's belly, or there could have been a little better understanding. At any rate, El Dodo was probably coaching the cock-pit couple upstairs, limiting what they said. What did he know about planes anyway, other than whatever he'd just heard from the last per-son who'd whispered in his ear? Everyone said that about him, and look at what had happened just a few hours back. He'd swallowed all that shit about Foster as if he'd been listening to the Almighty, right along with O'Dell's lies about Sleck. Special Forces veteran O'Dell was probably whispering right now how to handle the predicament they were all in, and Brewster would automatically buy it.

Maybe he was even asking ex-boss Winfield what to do. "This was your plane, H. J. Did it ever do this kind of thing before?" Shit, why not ask that loony psychologist, too? Take a vote. Show of hands. The mere thought of Whittier produced a fresh surge of anger, but it was cut short by the sound of something like automatic gunfire outside the plane. It couldn't be that, of course, but at least *something* was going on after all this time. Probably some kind of demolition equipment.

Time to ease the old blood pressure back a bit, take a stroll forward and find out what was going on. Others had already started bidding for the restroom, and baldy was on his feet, stretching. He seemed oblivious to any danger they all faced.

"Shoot, my legs sure are stiff," he complained. "What about yours?"

"I stay in shape—something you ought to think about." He got to his feet, tossing the *Newsweek* on baldy's seat. "Here, have a read. I'm going forward."

"Oh, I wouldn't do that," baldy cautioned, barely able to make his words audible. "We're all supposed to stay put, not—"

"So stay put, then. I'm NPA. I don't take directions from them."

"Oh." The bushy red mustache twitched. He was about to sit back down, then straightened. "Well, if you think it's okay, maybe I'll just tag along...."

"You're a consultant, right? That puts you in about the same class as baggage, so don't complain to me if you get handcuffed to a seat." *Maybe the egghead'll take the hint.*

No such luck. Egghead tagged right along, though he did stay a decent distance back. Oh, well, the conference room would be as far as he got, since one of those two Secret Service boys from the back section was now blocking the aisle at the galley's rear entrance, just ahead. The man was wearing official "grim look" number three—or was it number four?—holding up a hand, palm forward. "Sir, you'll have to return to your seat."

Greenward held up his flipped-open credential wallet. "Here by direction of President Brewster. I report directly to Clarence Towers."

"NPA? That's different, sir. However, I request you alert my counterparts forward as to your purpose, and refrain from going upstairs."

"Not a problem. Good luck with the idiot following me."

Three steps later he heard baldy being challenged. There was no response from the mustache twitcher, not even a laryngitis whimper. *Too bad, chromedome. You want to break the rules, carry a bigger stick. Go back and irritate someone else. Talk to the screamer.*

A group was gathered just ahead of the stairway leading to the top deck, and he could feel an unmistakable chill in the air around his ankles. Outside air? What the hell was going on? The area nearest the plane's portside entrance was the most crowded, and something seemed to be happening *outside* the plane. Was the entrance door open? Had the Germans really been able to reach the plane with ladders or some sort of platform? It could be something like that.

He could see no more than the wing from the one window in that aisle section. Ahead, blocking further progress, were more agents... and ahead of *them* was O'Dell! Whittier and Winfield were standing there as well, all seemingly captivated by something outside the main entrance. Waiting to be first out the door, naturally. No sign of Brewster, though. Probably cowering in his escape capsule deep in the plane's guts. They'd have to drag him out, kicking and screaming, when the time came.

One more look out the single window proved fruitless, and the way forward was totally blocked. It was as far as he'd get.

What the *hell* were they all looking at?

The plane's conference room was a walled-off fuselage section with just enough room along its port side for an aisle. The entrance was nearly forty feet forward. On its aft end was nothing but a wall that faced the work room area, and further aft of that was the general seating portion.

Ollie watched Greenward stride through the work room and around the corner into the aisle. The man's body language and expressions, those constantly tensing jaw muscles, rigid neck, hands clenching and unclenching, even the way he'd been flipping pages of that magazine... something was about to explode. Harry'd been right. A psychopath cared little if he endangered others while pursuing his often macabre agenda, witness the arrogance in ignoring the directive to stay put. So *this* was the man who'd counseled President Winfield all through the Russian crisis? No wonder Winfield had suffered his mental collapse.

Greenward's senior NPA position permitted carrying a weapon even when there was no reason, but why the small-of-back holster rather than shoulder-style? Nobody ever did it that way when any other method was available. Was it ego, his reputation as a tough former Marine lieutenant colonel, or the fact of his being Clarence Tower's main man? Maybe the latter, but psychopaths typically acted in ways beneficial only to themselves, so the gun could also be part of his private agenda. Put him in the picture with Sleck and Howland, or in with a secret group potentially connected with political murders, and the signs were more ominous. They were ominous now.

It would be wise not to follow too closely, even though all the Secret Service agents knew who was being watched and who was doing the watching. The agent pair who'd scrambled forward were likely up there securing the aisles, so if Greenward managed to weasel his way past the first man, his attention would all be on what lay ahead, not on the aisle behind. Everything after that would hinge on how the initial agent handled things, but first the man had to realize that Greenward was being followed, and who was following him.

Greenward was showing the agent his credentials. He never looked back, but the agent did. Just a flick of the eyes, but enough. Ollie nodded twice, then tiptoed quickly back around the corner, counted off ten seconds, then swung into the aisle a second time.

෪ల෩

The portside main entrance door cracked open the barest amount, and a stern voice boomed from within: "Raise both hands above your head and state your name." The directive was repeated in high German, then French. By then, the right words had indeed come. It was time.

"Nonsense. You've watched me approach. Not only are you correct in thinking that I'm standing on air, but Air Force One is supported the same way using forces I control, forces no soul on Earth understands. Harm me in any way and I leave it to you to imagine the consequences. Once my purpose for all this has been satisfied, I will gently lower Air Force One to the ground without harm to anyone."

"We are heavily armed. Raise your hands above your head, state your name and keep your distance. You'll get no further warning."

"Thank you. Now listen carefully. A greatly advanced civilization has been observing humanity since the dawn of our existence, living among us from time to time, but especially during the past five millennia. They bring us a severe warning about our planet, one we dare not ignore. Earth has entered a period of correction that will annihilate mankind within thirty years, sparing no one unless we unite and act together quickly. The precursor of this tragedy is the global warming we have so foolishly blamed on ourselves to the exclusion of all other causes. Our benefactors from space understand the real cause, know its meaning and want us to know it as well. Their warning *must* reach all the world's people, every culture, if mankind is to survive at all. They've chosen to deliver their warning through me, using my voice. I will need access to the plane's communications facilities in order to reach the media teams who assembled to meet this plane. They in turn will broadcast my words to the world. I can't tell you what those words will be, only that I am humbled by being chosen."

"State your name."

"Sutiyqaluisamaru." *Let's see if your computer understands Quechua.* There was a lengthy pause, then murmurs from the plane's interior. The next voice nearly broke his focus.

"Jim, this is Gordy Whittier. I'm here with Mike O'Dell, President Brewster and former President Winfield. Can you tell me what this is all about? Are you in control?"

Gordy? And Mike? How could they?... "Gordy, you're the only person in the world who could possibly know it's me without my saying so. Yes, I'm very much in control and everything I said is true. A prophesy to the world is to come through me. I've agreed to it since I know its essence and its importance to all mankind. When it has been delivered, I'll lower the plane without harm to anyone. Our space friends chose this as the best way of assuring the message would be heard by as many people as possible at one time, and that it be understood for what it is: a clarion call to all mankind. The worst of all man's nightmares is on our horizon."

"What do these space visitors look like? Why can't they deliver their message directly?"

"We look like them, and vice versa. Who'd believe they weren't some Hollywood actors playing Star Trek? I hope to prevent that misperception, Gordy, since there is no way Hollywood can pull off this type of thing. Air Force One is visible from all directions. No wires, no support, nothing but mental forces that you of all people understand."

"Are these visitors the ones responsible for your own mental powers, Jim?"

"Yes, something I learned only a few days ago."

There was a long delay and more murmuring before Whittier returned with another question. "Do your sympathies lie with any government? Are you working with any government?"

"Emphatically no. This warning you're about to hear has no political content. It pits no nation against any other, nor is it in any way religious or philosophical. It's a dire warning we must hear together as one world, one that must bring us all together, brought by a benevolent civilization millions of years ahead of us. They know infinitely more about Earth than we do. This was the best way of assuring such a message could be delivered, that everyone would hear it at one time and that there'd be no political spin."

"What's involved? How do you plan to do this?"

"I'll need the plane's communication system and a microphone. Please convey that request to President Brewster and ask him to see that the media gathered below us are able to hear my words on channels they have available. Air Force One can do that. I've studied the plane's capabilities."

"President Brewster wants to meet you, Jim. I've told him all I know about you and our involvement together. Former President Winfield as well. They are both your allies now. You've been removed from the Tombstone List. You're to be honored, you and Tricia together. Why not come aboard?"

"Thank him for both of us, but this is not about me or Tricia. It's about every human being on Earth. Ask him to stand out here with me. It's not that cold."

"Jim, you're standing on *air!* That's too big a psychological leap for any normal human being, including me, and I already *know* what you can do."

"Leave that up to him. I'm making my support surface visible only to you and the others with you in the plane. He'll see it as such if he decides to accept the challenge. At the same time, the world will see an extremely brave leader overcome his primal human fear, making it a photo-op supreme. His presence as the leader of the world's strongest nation will add importance to the explanation of what has caused this most recent incident of global warming, why it is different, what it means to mankind and what we are to face together as a people. It won't be a long speech, perhaps ten minutes. I'm not really sure."

"I can't ask that of him, Jim. It sounds too political. I'm—"

"You doesn't have to ask me, Dr. Whittier. Open the door, gentlemen... all the way."

Several moments later the door swung open, halfway at first and then the remainder. The interior was unlit, but not dark. Two men with automatic weapons stood on either side of the opening. Behind them, flanked by dark shapes, stood a second pair holding Brewster's arms. The President's resemblance to news photos was close enough for confirmation, even in the dim light.

"I've heard a lot about you, Foster," he said. "Didn't want to believe any of it until now. My God, you... you... step inside, please... I'm getting dizzy just looking at you." He twisted about. "Someone turn on the cabin lights. He needs to see us."

"Mr. President, I must deliver the message out here where I can be seen, not as a talking head on a TV screen. When that's finished, I will lower the plane. I ask you to set up the communications so I can speak to all these media groups below us here. You have the convenient option of claiming that I coerced you by threatening the plane and all those aboard. If you've been listening to Gordy and Mike, you must know I'm innocent of all the accusations made against me, but the world will accept your claim if you choose to use it. I may already have forfeited my life in your eyes and those of countless others, but this warning absolutely must be delivered, and there is no other way. Do we have a deal?"

When the interior lights came on, the dark shapes turned out to be Gordy, Mike and former President Winfield, all clustered near the opening. After what Winfield had done to hurt Gordy, that alone was enough to show something of a breakthrough had occurred, but Winfield suddenly shrank out of sight as Brewster took a small step forward. The President was immediately pulled back.

"Was any of this show of force really necessary, Mr. Foster? You were described to me as a man of peace whose—"

"Those who bring us the warning would gladly have shown themselves and spoken directly to a world less terror-prone and more rational, Mr. President, but consider today's political climate. They have waited and watched us for three million years, so another century or two has little meaning, but Earth has presented her own agenda and there is no longer time. Can you think of a better way to reach seven billion people in a single move?"

Brewster twisted his mouth, looking thoughtful. Finally he nodded, turning. "Fix him up with whatever he needs and have the comm deck hook it into all the standard channels. The instant any of this smacks of being political, cut him off and issue an immediate denial. Let's have audio inside the plane, too, but don't let anyone move about any more than they have to. Don't want a damned stampede up here, not while this whole thing could still come down." He took another step forward, only to be grabbed again by both arms and pulled back. He shrugged both arms free. "Look here, Sam, whatever *he's* standing on is holding up this plane, and he's right. There'll never be a better photo-op than this."

"Can't let you take that chance, Mr. President," the agent argued. "What if he pulls some trick?"

Winfield suddenly reappeared, wearing his overcoat. "Stanley, they're right. You're too valuable to step out there, but I'm just a has-been. I owe this man a lot, starting with the trust I denied him for all the wrong reasons."

"Not a chance, H.J. The world knows you've been in rehab and thinks you're still there. It would make this whole thing seem like some stunt." Brewster brushed away another attempt to hold his arms. "Okay, gentlemen, you've fulfilled your sworn duty to protect me from all harm. There is more security outside this plane than may exist in all Munich at this point in time. Standing next to that man out there will be no different than any other exit I make from this plane as far as security goes. If this had anything to do with harming me or getting rid of me, there were hundreds of better ways. If he doesn't fall, I don't fall, and he's not about to fall. Someone bring me my coat."

"Mr. President, you absolutely cannot—"

"Done. Final word. My coat? Anyone? H.J., loan me yours. We're the same size."

Chapter 22

One moment she'd been running at breakneck speed and the next she'd skidded to a stop so quickly she'd nearly fallen. Why? And what made her simply stand there like a dummy until the firing stopped? Jim was still up there, apparently unhurt, but that, too, was a mystery. So many shots! How could they all have missed?

Charlie! Of course. He was standing near the marksmen, talking to one of them, an officer. *He'd* stopped the shooting and her running with a mental signal so intense she'd actually skidded on the dry pavement. Were there no limits to his abilities? Of course there had to be, or the shooting wouldn't have happened in the first place, but then he'd warned of such things. People were unpredictable, even on his home planet.

She forced herself to breathe deeply, rebuilding her composure and then her Greta Wirth character before moving at all. The gunmen were climbing back into their truck by the time she'd returned to a spot behind the American video crew. Steve Bradley was on camera, "live" in the U.S. via satellite, with Air Force One as a backdrop. Camera Two covered the small figure standing an impossible height above the concrete while Steve re-emphasized what the American audience had already heard a dozen times over—that nothing supported the plane *or* "what appeared to be a man" outside its door.

"For those of you just joining us, I repeat that President Brewster *is* safe," Bradley stated. "Everyone aboard Air Force One is unharmed, though shaken by this event as we still await any kind of official explanation. Meanwhile the question persists as to whether this is in fact an alien force of some sort, as well as who—or what—might be standing just outside the plane's exit door. There is an image up there, but it could be some sort of illusion. A few moments ago we heard the sounds of automatic gunfire. The shooting stopped as soon as it started, but it does appear the target was that same standing figure. If so, the bullets must have passed through it.

"Folks, I can't begin to tell you how weird this all is, but in this reporter's opinion the mystery of the matter here doesn't warrant any such trigger-happy response from Munich Airport Security. We could indeed be witnessing some form of alien force here, making me wonder if at any moment we'll soon see a spaceship hovering overhead. I'm reminded of the disaster several years ago in Las Vegas, Nevada, causing great loss of life and initially thought to be the work of aliens because of its great mystery. The United States is possibly being singled out by otherworld forces, if this should turn out to be the same type of incident. So far, though, there has been no sign of any physical threat to those aboard Air Force One.

"However, the scene has not been without injuries. Here below the plane, several of the emergency vehicles collided with what I'll describe as an invisible wall. Two flipped on their sides, suggesting the wall is slanted... that is, it appears to be wider at the bottom than higher up, and I use the word 'appears' because that's all we have to go on. Whatever the obstacle is, it isn't the thin air it appears to be. As you can see... if we can swing the camera down a bit... there you see the area under the plane as being clear of any vehicles or personnel... and over there are overturned trucks. That whole area is impenetrable, while two hundred feet up we have...."

Bradley was having a difficult time of it, but he was probably doing at least as well as the other reporters. Millions of TV viewers were glued to their sets, waiting for something to happen, and Jim had just been shown moving up to the door, then backing away. Bradley fumbled with that development, trying his best to spin the retreat into something sinister, but moments into his attempt the plane's entrance door was clearly being swung wide open. Her heart missed a beat. The door was Jim's turning point, his cusp. If it hadn't opened....

She caught herself, erasing her negative thought. That worry was over. Jim was about to give the performance of his life... but would the world see it that way?

෨෬

Someone tossed him a cordless microphone, as though putting so much as an arm outside the plane was somehow dangerous. The thrower's head appeared around the door frame. "All yours, nutcake. Anything political, and we'll cut you off." He sliced a hand across his neck.

Jim clicked the mike on, facing the somewhat quieter crowd below. "Testing. Will anyone out there in the media group flash headlights, please?" Almost before he finished the request, one flashed off
and back on. Then a second responded. "Blink them again if you have
good video of me and the plane." *I'm saying these things without even
thinking. It's Charlie. He's down there, telling me how to do this.* Now
lights blinked on several vehicles. "Good. Now if for any reason you
lose either one, make lots of noise. Blow horns and blink your lights.
What follows will impact your lives, the lives of those you love and
those who are to come into this world in the near future."

Noise behind him drew attention back to the doorway. Brewster
was standing in the opening, eyes closed, with both hands seizing the
door's frame. Flanking him were two pairs of grim-looking men grip-
ping a string of linked-together seat belts that passed under the president's arms and around his chest in front. All four men were braced in
the event they'd end up hauling him back aboard, but their readiness
was all for nothing. Once Brewster managed to get both feet down, he
opened his eyes, took one step forward and immediately uncoupled
the belts. A warning shout from the plane was ignored—there'd be
no safety net for Stanley Brewster—but his resolve to avoid looking
down fizzled. He managed to stifle his instant terror with great effort
and a sharp jerk of his chin back to level, but sudden commotion
down and to his right turned him that way almost by instinct. Media
booms were visible in the floodlights, a sight any head of state wel-
comed almost instinctively, and he was standing in a wash of light that
seemed not all that different from TV studio lights.

His arms shot up—the victory sign—while he turned this way and
that, beaming his best television smile. That accomplished, he twisted
only his torso and reached forward with a trembling right hand, without taking another step. Words were forced through chattering teeth.

"All r-right, Mr. Foster, now how is this g-g-oing to happen?"

"I haven't a clue, Mr. President."

"You h-haven't a *clue?*"

"No, I... I....."

A prickling of his scalp forced a turn away from Brewster and toward the media booms. *Charlie again!* Then, fascinated, he listened to
words spoken from a point overhead, foreign and deeper than his own

baritone, measured and almost musical in an operatic sense. Another part of his brain realized the words were coming from within.

"People of Earth, a world similar to this one exists in the star system Rigel Kentaurius more than four light years from here. Its name was Eden long before mankind came into being, and there I am known as Char-el, but I have lived here on Earth for two thousand seven hundred five years, using many names and appearances. Put all your disbeliefs to rest, for we are millions of years beyond you in our development. We live as long as we choose to live, typically more than ten thousand Earth years.

"I am speaking to you through a remarkable man who is supporting this aircraft through the power of his mind. He is a living example of your own potential as humans, for mental forces govern every aspect of the physical realm you know. They are the foundation of all creation, for thought existed before all else. We have given you many living examples in the course of your short history.

"We were traveling through space before you walked on two legs, first arriving here three million years ago and visiting your planet many times since. Many of us have lived among you since that time, as I do today, but in the distant past you were not as you are now. Your anthropologists have reconstructed only a fraction of your evolution as a people, much of it in error, whereas we witnessed it as it happened. We know your planet infinitely better than any of you. We've studied it, measured it, mapped it and recorded its many changes from our spaceships. So that you may understand better who we are, why we are here and my reasons for choosing this method of contact, I will supply some background.

"Four hundred thousand years ago we decided to accelerate your development, gradually changing you by altering your DNA until today you look and function much as we do. Your races and their subcultures came into being because we chose that path for you, not because of natural mutations as proposed by your scientists. They speculate that your ancients spread by migration from what is now eastern Africa, but we were the ones responsible. We became your earliest gods because that is how you viewed us, but we were no more than a preview of your future. There is but one Creator, and we are all part of that ultimate Thought. We of Eden are simply an earlier expression of that Thought.

"*Your scientists persist in discounting any external causes when trying to explain mysterious clues to your history. Your theologians without exception are wrong when they attribute everything to some imagined divine plan, never considering that visitations by an advanced civilization would rightly be part of whatever is divine in the universe. They fabricate illusions rooted in their humanistic views, arrogantly and methodically eliminating all else while causing great divisions among you. Your ancient references to Eden referred to us, not some mystical garden. Fabrications like this have been invented to answer mysteries, many of which originated with our visits. The same is true today.*

"*Your astronomers insist the solar system has been placid for eons, that nothing has disturbed Earth in all that time aside from occasional meteors, and that all of Earth's physical changes require hundreds or thousands of centuries. They are wrong. We have watched continents sink and mountains rise within a decade and have witnessed the most catastrophic events imaginable in the course of your recorded history.*

"*We have left you thousands of examples of our presence here over time, but your archaeologists have distorted their meanings or ridiculed the idea that you were not the sole beings in the universe. In so doing they slowed your own development and erected barriers to the truth. In reality, you of Earth are among the youngest members of all creation. Your languages derive in many ways from ours. The same sounds and meanings appeared on Earth spontaneously, separated by half a world. Your legends and folklore tell identical stories, be they Biblical or Aztec, Eskimo or Mapuche. Your earliest artists and even those of only a few thousand years ago painted similar pictures on cave walls though no communication was possible. Pottery and sculptures in many ancient cultures depict us and our spaceships. Obelisks and scrolls, drawings and monuments—all this, yet your experts persist in denying external causes and other civilizations. Look in your mirror and you will see us, for we fashioned you in our image.*

"*We have shown you our spacecraft from time to time and taken you aboard, yet you have ostracized and ridiculed those who reported their experiences. We created the most astounding structure of your world, the Great Pyramid at Giza, located exactly in what was the geometrical center of Earth's land masses at that time. East or west, north or south, precisely the same exposed land measured to a point on the precise opposite* side of Earth. The Egyptians could not have known that. The pyramid's unit of measure is precisely one ten-millionth of the distance from Earth's poles to its center, information possible only when measured from space. They could not have known that, either. You cannot reproduce its casing cement even though you have analyzed it. You cannot duplicate it with all your technology and tools, and yet you insist the Egyptians alone were the ones responsible.

"Countless times have we given you information you've discarded, secrets you've destroyed, messages you've been too blind to read. You have no explanations or theories for these gifts, yet you persist in denying all possibilities of our existence. We have waited patiently for you to put aside your warlike ways and learn what it means to exist in true peace. That discovery must now fall to those among you who manage to survive the next three decades, and to their descendents.

"The sad truth is that you are now facing extinction within your lifetimes, not from us but from your own planet, Earth. The cause can be traced to an event millions of years ago, when your giant planet Jupiter ejected a tiny, molten mass that became an aberrant comet. Its unusual orbit brought it back from the remote reaches of the solar system every 67.931 Earth years, passing obliquely through the ecliptic of your system's much older planets. Your ancients could see this comet and predict its reappearance accurately with our help, but during one of its orbits it shed one-half percent of its mass, and this changed its path, putting it on an eventual collision course with Earth roughly 3700 years ago. We intervened in time and Earth was spared, but magnetic interchanges between the intruder and Earth caused great destruction and massive loss of life.

"Records of the event were destroyed by religious zealots and the superstitious in every society where languages were written. Others spun legends filled with fanciful distortions. Your belief systems twisted facts to fit various preconceived notions. Historians later stretched and warped remaining clues to the past until the mysteries were all explained away. Others followed in their footsteps, obscuring truth until it could no longer be found. Today your scientists deny that such a thing ever happened or could happen, yet our data banks contain every aspect of the event.

"That near catastrophe increased Earth's core energy, requiring adjustments between core and crust that are accelerating today. An *energetic equalizing cycle has been building in recent years, unnoticed by scientists who have all but ignored volcanism except for those eruptions most obvious for their size and danger. Global warming, which you erroneously blame on greenhouse gases, is in reality due to thousands of undersea volcanic fissures now pouring immense amounts of heat into your oceans. The number has taken a sharp turn upward in the past three years, increasing at the rate of five to ten new events per day. Fissures are now plentiful all along the mid-Atlantic join, that is to say along the African and South American plates and the Eurasian and North American plates, being most vigorous beneath the Arctic Ocean, along the Arabian and Indian plates and finally the African and Antarctic plates. Some are appearing in the Pacific basin along the great faults and deep trenches, but also in areas where they have not been seen for nearly a million years. Even more disturbing, they are occurring in ocean areas where the crust is thin and growing thinner, areas not associated with plates or trenches or tectonics. We have been watching two specific areas for several decades, bulges in the ocean floor that indicate potential major eruptions. The larger of these, located northeast of the Carlsberg Ridge in the Arabian basin, is now three hundred eight kilometers in diameter and has reduced ocean depth there by half a thousand meters. It has gone unnoticed. The second is east of Buenos Aires, midway to Africa. That, too, is uncharted.*

"A major volcanic eruption beyond anything seen in several hundred thousand years is definitely building under Yellowstone Park in the United States, and another beneath the Canary Islands. Either of these could be as much as ten thousand times the power of a normal eruption. Some of your wiser scientists are aware of these increasing volcanic trends and threats, but others have shouted them down. No one wants to hear bad news involving your planet unless it fits someone's political agenda.

"People of Earth, forget your greenhouse gas silliness and look instead at what is taking place beneath your oceans. Earth's excess heat is melting away some of the crust on its underside, making it thinner and increasingly prone to new fissures. Not four thousand years ago your skies were filled with an intruder twelve times the apparent size of your moon, pulling your oceans into kilometers-high peaks and causing tremendous loss of life. Earth's crust was greatly stressed, volcanoes erupted in all corners of the globe and the air was poisoned with ash and gases. Oceans washed over mountains, lightning filled the skies and great fires raged. All forms of life perished together as floods swept away what the fires spared. Man has forgotten this calamity, but nothing was erased from Earth's memory and four thousand years is the equivalent of one second on the clock when measured against Earth's past.

"Today your oceans are just two degrees Celsius from plunging Earth into the most severe ice age we've recorded. The formula for any ice age is quite simple. Increasing ocean warmth accelerates evaporation, which eventually produces torrential and never-ending rainfall in all corners of the globe. This is happening now. You have already witnessed record rainfalls, more severe hurricanes and typhoons, more floods and crop failures than ever before. Last year's monsoon displaced three hundred million people in India alone, more than twice the earlier record set just the year before, which itself was beyond anything in your human memory. When torrential rain occurs in polar regions as snow, ice caps will grow far more rapidly than your climatologists' wildest projections. Given the present disparity in land between Earth's two polar regions, ice accumulation in your Northern hemisphere will quickly overwhelm its southern counterpart. When the imbalance is great enough, centrifugal forces will pull the present poles to new locations on the globe in a matter of hours—not years, months or days, but hours. Arguments otherwise are futile, since we have seen these events take place on Earth more than once.

"Tropical rain forests once grew in what is now northern Siberia. This would have been impossible unless the midpoint of your Atlantic Ocean was located at what is now your north pole, and that was exactly the case. You found wooly mastodons encased in ice. We saw them as they were, eating buttercups in their temperate surroundings just as the pole shift began. Within hours they were engulfed in a blizzard and subsequently covered while still alive. That is reality, whereas your scientists propose that such a climactic change occurred over centuries.

"Earth's land masses now dominate the northern hemisphere. In just a handful of years, glaciers will approach thirty kilometers in thickness at the poles and several kilometers thick as far south as India and Mexico, creating tremendous imbalance in the spinning top. Earth's crust must ultimately slide around its molten core to offset these centrifugal forces, but the underside is more jagged and irregular than any mountains on its surface. Furthermore, the ovoid crust must stretch in some places while contracting in others, rupturing in the process. Volcanoes and earthquakes will finally destroy whatever is left of mankind and his works, but well ahead of that ultimate disaster the severities of winter and weather will force you to migrate closer and closer to the equator.

"Do not listen to those who insist this can only happen only over centuries or millennia. We know from our observations that monster icecaps require only a few years to build because we have seen lesser ice cycles during our watch over your planet, times in which all life was threatened with extinction. With this much more severe episode about to begin in earnest, glacial ice will build faster than one meter a day near the poles, spreading outward. Prior to that time, those of you closest to the present poles will face disease and starvation as you flee on foot from deluge, floods and endless blizzards. Agriculture will fail in a single year when rains become truly torrential, quickly followed by loss of all domestic livestock, forcing migration well ahead of lowering temperatures and growing ice caps. Dams will burst and rivers will overflow, flooding the land and trapping millions. Arid regions will not be spared. The natural world, land and sea alike, will resist migration until it is too late, and so will cease to exist except for the smallest of creatures. These predictions will become reality within twenty years, sooner if either of those growing bulges in the ocean floor become volcanic players.

"People of Earth, this horrible event need not mean the end of all humanity. Some of you can be saved, but only if you unite quickly for that purpose. We offer to transport your most trusted scientists to our spaceship so they can observe every volcanic fissure on Earth and watch new ones form, using our advanced technology. They will see how much Earth's crust has changed in just the past three millennia and we will share our data and knowledge of your planet's true history, as much as you can absorb. When your scientists return and confirm our findings, there will be two possible solutions for you to consider.

"The first requires total cooperation, great sacrifice and difficult decisions. It will save roughly one million of you, thereby saving humanity itself. We will help you build a city on your moon and stand by to protect it from all dangerous meteors. Once built and properly run, it will be self-sufficient until such time as you can return to Earth, perhaps thousands of years in the future. We will supply ships for use as transports and advance your technology far beyond what you know today, technology with which you can emigrate to other stars if that suits you. But even with these gifts, you must still adapt to a most difficult situation, for you have never learned to exist peacefully with each other. Your moon city will be your lifeboat, your crucible, with no escape possible and no rescue for hundreds or thousands of years.

"Put your differences aside and select those who will speak for all nations if this solution becomes your choice. Decide who will occupy the lifeboat when it is ready. We can't help you in that, for although you look like us, you don't think or relate to each other as we do. In reality you are much like Earth itself, turbulent and unsettled. Even so, we want you to survive and flourish.

"Our second solution involves lengthening Earth's orbit. Increasing the orbital distance from your sun will lower Earth's surface temperature, offsetting the warming of your oceans and forestalling the immediate crisis, but the precise amount of change needed will make itself known only as time goes on. Once Earth stabilizes, your present orbit can be restored. Although your climate will be markedly colder everywhere, a change so significant your societies will devolve to basic survival, a pole shift will be forestalled. Our calculations show that a one percent reduction in surface temperature should be enough to offset the warming cycle.

"While this may seem an easier solution, we cannot bring about an orbital change of this magnitude in a mere few years. Mass migrations toward warmer zones will still be mandatory, starvation and disease rampant. Your chronology will be in constant chaos and your age of information useless. Ask yourselves if several billion of you can relocate to areas already populated or barren, or arid, or mountainous or uninhabitable without first building the infrastructure to support them? Where will your basic needs come from? The answer is sobering.

"Neither solution will minimize your suffering unless there is unity among you. The more time you spend arguing rather than preparing, the greater your tragedy to come. We have already begun lengthening Earth's orbit, hoping we will have many decades in which to achieve the task, though all indications are in the opposite direction. There are many astronomical considerations to consider, lest in solving one problem we create others within your planetary system. Your solar year is presently

*longer than it was at this moment one year ago by four hundredths of a
percent, a fact which has gone unnoticed. Let this information attest to
everything I've just told you, since your theory of uniformity states that
no such orbital change can possibly happen. However, at this rate we
can add only eight days in the next twenty-five years, less than half the
amount needed at the present rate of warming. Earth may yet shorten the
time we have estimated. May it not.*

"*Make your decision without delay. We will know your answer.*"

ဆပ္ဆ

His first sensation was that of a chill wind, then lights that forced
him to blink. A stranger was standing at his side, staring in the oddest
way. Was it President Brewster? Suddenly his hearing returned and he
realized the crowd beneath them was more subdued than before.

"What did I say, Mr. President?"

"You galvanized me, or rather the person who spoke through you
did. You didn't know what you were saying? My God, man, the whole
message was about a disaster about to befall us all. I'm sure my people
are analyzing it right now, but... please... join us inside Air Force
One. I've about used up all my courage."

"Thank you, sir, but no. I promised to lower the plane and I'll fulfill
that promise now." *Charlie got his message across. Wow!*

"You'll be safer inside, Mr. Foster. Out here, well, I'm not so sure.
That speech of yours is *not* likely to be taken well, not at all. Are you
sure you don't know what you said?"

"I knew the essence of it, yes, but not the actual words. Please, Mr.
President... return to the plane. I'm sure the world will credit you
with astounding bravery for standing out here once they understand
what this whole thing means."

"Bravery, hell. I'm a coward by nature—have been all my life." He
turned toward the plane, but the shifting of a searchlight distracted
him and he looked straight down. Panicked, he lunged for the doorway where anxious hands grabbed him. As he was pulled aboard he
glanced back.

"Mr. Foster, you just told the world that doomsday is right around
the corner. Don't you understand that people don't want to hear that
kind of thing?"

Chapter 23

Greenward seethed. Whatever was happening out there, O'Dell and Whittier were involved, Winfield's presence made it even worse, and the aisle further forward was blocked by another of the Secret Service goons. Several more filled the remaining space at the doorway. He held up his credential wallet again, growling at the expressionless blocker.

"NPA, here by Brewster's order. Your buddy back there passed me through. What the hell is going on out there?"

The man glanced at the wallet, then shook his head. "You won't believe it. Brewster's outside the plane with some guy who's giving a speech. It's being broadcast from here. It'll be on TV."

"*Speech?* While we're in here for a whole damned hour tied to our seats? What the hell are they standing on, air?"

"Search me. We're up on something."

"Let me through."

"Situation's locked down. Sorry."

"Look, I was Winfield's personal advisor when he was president, okay? *He's* standing right there and I see room enough for me. This could be an item of national security. I have a need to know what's going on. Ask him."

"Mr. Greenward, I couldn't let the Pope into that group. You can stand here or return to your seat."

"Okay, okay, so I'll stand here." *Air Force One must be up on some sort of monster contraption wide enough to support the fuselage, but how the hell?....* "Who's out there with Brewster?"

"Heard them call him Foster."

"*What?* You have to be... *James* Foster? That sonofabitch is a goddamn *terrorist!* Couldn't be him."

"Whatever. I don't run the show."

At that moment, the plane's PA system came alive. The voice from outside was deep, almost operatic, but the words were all drivel, something right out of Hollywood. On second thought, it could be Foster after all. He could easily have set up something like this. It might be a pre-taped message. Terrorists did that. *Foster, you sonofa-bitch! So this was what you've been planning all along, the thing you've been building toward. You've hijacked Air Force One with your alien powers, and now you have our idiot president out there with you, giving yourself the major boost you needed. I know you for what you really are, and he thinks you're a fucking hero.*

He was forced to listen. All about global warming and doom. War of the worlds stuff, just like Orson Welles did on radio. Of course! That global warming fiasco had always been a scam, nothing more than a way for a few criminal opportunists to pull in billions, but Foster was trying to make the scam even bigger. The U.S. was the world's richest country, so break the bank there. He was using Brewster as a shill, but it made sense when you saw through all the smoke. Create instant worldwide panic with some insane prediction, throw in aliens and a few bizarre facts to support the lies, then try for the checkmate while people were all destabilized and running around like headless chickens. How could all those idiots stand there and not instantly understand what he was doing? Lengthening the orbit? Were they actually buying into something that crazy? And the rant even finished up with a demand: decide which way you all want to die. If that didn't define a terrorist, what did? The only thing missing was the ransom amount, but that would be along once the real panic set in.

Sudden activity at the doorway centered on Brewster coming back inside, which meant Foster would be alone out there. The aisle behind was empty. *In any situation where leadership is absent, assume leadership.* The words were ingrained, learned when he'd been a young Gyrene. There was no leadership evident here. He drew a long breath. Foster was on the Tombstone List, so anyone in the world could gun him down. Who better than the man who knew best what he really was?

Nothing could happen until Brewster was safely back in the plane, out of harm's way. After that....

ജ്ഇ

Ollie snuck a quick peek around the main conference room doorway. The angled inside corner permitted a good view of everything in the aisle forward, and Greenward had been stopped a second time, fifteen feet ahead. Visibly angry, the man showed no signs of returning to his seat. There was that body language again, like a pit bull about to attack.

Brewster'd brought him along for some reason having nothing to do with the Quaker Hill conspiracy, so the subsequent request for babysitting service might have been because of Harry Archer's warning, or possibly because Mike was on the same flight. Whatever had taken place in the presidential quarters a few hours back, Mike had no way of knowing who the babysitter would be, unless he'd been told. That didn't seem likely. There he stood with Gordy Whittier and former President Winfield, none of them looking particularly angry or upset, but the speech coming over the plane's audio system put all conjectures aside. When Greenward was told the voice belonged to Jim Foster, his furious reaction was loud enough to hear.

But the voice didn't sound like Jim, not at all, and the speech was fairly morbid, difficult to absorb while concentrating on Greenward. Then, quite suddenly, it was over. No typical oratorical wrap up, nothing political. Just... over.

Greenward was still... oh, no... he was reaching behind his back, under his jacket. That stance, one foot back—a psychopath wasn't particular about details when it came to satisfying vengeance, and this one now held a gun!

He's going after Brewster. Don't let him score. Now, Ollie, go, go, go!

Greenward had already shouldered the surprised agent aside and was accelerating. No time for a warning, no time for anything. Ten feet. Eight! Greenward stiff-armed a second man whose back was turned. The impact stopped him momentarily, but not long enough. Now!

Ollie made his twisting tackle low, right at the knees, but Greenward stayed on top of the pileup, roaring obscenities. There were three quick shots before Mike's quick neck chop ended it. The would-be assassin sagged, then collapsed. Mike hammerlocked him and dragged him back to vertical. "You'd better hope you missed, sucker," he growled, but the former Marine colonel with the gravelly voice had scored at least once, maybe all three times, and it wasn't Brewster after all.

Jim Foster was down.

ೞೞೞ

Brewster's parting remark... that distinct shift from respect to disdain... and men with automatics inside the plane. Everything made sense now. Brewster'd lied and Charlie'd failed and now his life was over. The pain was slow in registering, but he knew. Three burning bullets, two below his rib cage, one up higher.

As he fell to his knees, his thoughts were of the plane. Mike and Gordy—the plane—couldn't let it fall, but fall it would. Unlike the walkway, which would remain until dissolved by the same force that created it, the plane's descent had to be controlled. If he lost consciousness during the process.... *Must not let it fall... must not... not more than....* He coughed, falling forward, grasping at any image that might represent the volume of air that should disappear from the pylon every second. That fire engine with its ladder extended... it was the largest of the trucks below, but not large enough. What else? *Hard to breathe... must hang on. That big container on the Ekofisk oil rig... it would have swallowed the firetruck. Big enough for a helicopter plus scads of storage containers. Use that....*

It would have to do. He mentally formed it into a solid block as pain tore away what breath remained. *That much air... each second....* He tasted iron—blood—and his thoughts went to Tricia. She'd followed him into his personal world of hell, forsaking her own freedom and safety for love of a man who had been given no place in the world. Now she'd be free.

He tried to say aloud the three words he'd always wanted her to hear if ever he was about to die, but nothing came forth.

⁍⌇⌇⌇⌇

Ollie's main concern was Brewster. Ignoring his own pain, he craned his head as soon as Greeward's limp form was yanked away, praying he wouldn't see the president sprawled next to him. Instead, two men with their backs turned had the chief executive pinned against the open door's frame, using their bodies as shields. Brewster seemed okay, but the story was different outside the plane. Someone was lying out there looking quite dead, not ten feet from the opening, but there was nothing supporting the prone form! *He* was the one who'd been shot, but who was he? What was going on?

The plane started to sink.

"Grab on, we're falling!" Mike shouted. He lunged for the hand-straps each side of the open doorway, seizing them and blocking the opening. Around him there was a mad scramble by everyone else to find any kind of handhold. The men protecting Brewster shoved him rudely toward his suite, while others dashed back toward the galley.

Ollie was left stunned and kneeling on the floor. He looked up, but Mike was gone.

☙☙

She heard the three snapping sounds, but they didn't register as gunshots until she saw Jim collapse. Then her world spun about her and someone screamed—was it her? She ran first in Jim's direction, unable to think, then veered in a wild search for Charlie. Nothing else mattered now, not those around her or anyone on the plane. *Foster, don't you go and die on me!*

Someone grabbed her wrist. It was Charlie. "Do exactly as I say," he barked, pointing toward a point nearly below the plane's nose and starting for it. She ran with him, but everything was a blur. For a moment she thought someone else was up there with Jim, bending over him. Then both forms merged into one as tears flooded her eyes. *Oh, Jim!* They'd detoured around a fire engine before she realized the plane was lower than before. It was dropping!

Charlie spun her toward him. "Stop here. I've created a stairway just ahead of you. Can you see it?"

Numbly, she nodded.

"Take my hand. Don't look down. Focus on Jim. We must get to him now, three hundred steps. Quickly! Give it all you've got. Now!"

She gulped, then pawed the air with her toe. *Oh, my God, am I really going to do this? Oh, Jim!*

"Don't think, Tricia. Go!"

They charged up the steps together, hand in hand, missing the slowly sinking plane by mere feet on its way down. *Two at a time. Run, Tricia, run!* As agile as she was, Charlie was ahead of her all the way. He yanked her to a stop at the very top step. A man was bending over Jim's body, looking up at them with the strangest of sad expressions.

"Mike? What?—"

Charlie shoved her forward, tightening his grip on her hand. "Take Jim's hand in yours," he ordered. Then he tapped Mike's shoulder. "Quick, Mike, give me your hand."

They were the last words she heard before everything went black.

ဆာလ

As soon as the German coordinator woman screamed, Bradley's cameraman swung his camera her way. She was the last he'd thought would show any emotion. Brittle and efficient, yes, even bossy, but a screamer? No way. The man who'd been giving the speech had just fallen down, yes, but her reaction was all out of proportion. Calm one second, hysterical the next? He kept the camera on her when she started running toward the plane, but there was suddenly someone else running next to her, a tall German official of some sort. Where had *he* come from? Everyone else was frantically moving equipment out of the plane's way, or else was rooted to the spot, gazing up.

Bradley was returning from the truck with coffee, his first since the marathon reporting began. He'd missed the speechmaker's sudden collapse, but seemed to have heard the scream. "What's happening?" he asked, checking the TV monitor. "Where are those two?..."

He stopped, mouth agape. The German duo *appeared* to be running up stairs, but there was nothing there. They were definitely climbing... and the plane was *dropping at the same time*. Momentarily queasy from sights his brain couldn't accept, he steadied himself against the camera tripod. If he'd been broadcasting live at that moment, a choice of which event to show would have been impossible. He followed the two Germans, then flicked his gaze to the plane, then quickly back to the duo. Two other forms were up there where the speechmaker had been standing, one prone and the other kneeling.

Seconds later the German duo reached them. Bradley was about to comment when all four disappeared in an explosion of clothing, some of which came fluttering down. The searchlights were suddenly probing clear night sky.

"Did you get that, Jack?" he cried. "Did you get it?"

The cameraman looked back, grinning. "Sure did. She bounced a little setting down, but nothing broke. Not much worse than a hard landing."

"No, not the plane, Jack... those two Germans. That *group* up there." He pointed.

Jack looked puzzled. "I thought the *plane* was more important. I mean, our president's inside that thing, right? *Right?*"

Bradley's nausea suddenly worsened. "Yeah, Jack, that's right."

Spaceship Grellen-6.

White forms were moving silently about, slowly turning into people all dressed alike as her senses returned. The feeling was strange, so... detached, as though she were looking down on herself from a spot overhead. Was she in a hospital? A woman came close, smiling through a face shield so clear it looked absent. She held out a blue robe and slippers. Then everything returned in a rush... Charlie, the impossible run up those invisible steps and then the way Jim looked, lying there. He had dark stains all over his back... blood. Was he?...

The woman smiled again. "Jim's doing just fine. Here, slip into these."

Yikes, I haven't got a stitch on! And I didn't say anything, did I? She read my mind.

Behind her, Mike was already on his feet, wearing a similar robe. "So much for modesty," he growled, cinching up the waist tie.

"Mike! Oh, my God, what next? Why were you... where did they take Jim? What happened? Why were *you* on the plane?" She slipped into the robe as she machinegunned questions. Then she saw Charlie dressed in beige clothing with a large blue symbol on one shoulder.

"Charlie, where are we? What happened to our clothes? Oh, where's Jim? I don't believe any of this...." Whatever had taken place, it seemed Charlie had a head start. He placed a hand on her shoulder.

"Jim's getting the finest medical attention in the universe, and you'll be able to see him shortly, but I'm afraid the shooting has changed things a bit."

"He's right," Mike added, launching a short summary. She winced when she heard how Greenward barged into the gathering at the door. Mike turned to Charlie. "I'm Tricia's father, as you probably knew. Your turn."

Charlie extended his hand. "I'm called Char-el for short, though my official name is much longer. We only use that on my home planet. I am the one who spoke through Jim. Where shall I begin?"

"How about starting with where we are now and how we got here minus our clothes? That never happened on Star Trek, if you'll forgive the comparison, and this is my first alien abduction even though you don't much look like an alien. Are we in space?"

Charlie smiled. "We are definitely in space and it so happens Star Trek is light years ahead of us in spacial transfer, fictionally speaking of course. Our method is far different and works only on the person. Jewelry is always left behind, as are things such as bullets. Jim arrived here without the three lodged in his torso. Unfortunately, surgical implants, dental fillings and the like suffer the same fate. We must always be extremely cautious. However, I scanned both Jim and Tricia prior to the Munich exercise and knew she had only two dental fillings. Jim had none. It turned out you had sixteen fillings, but no implants. We will regrow her teeth and yours the correct way before either of you returns to the surface.

"Our transfer method isn't practical going *back* to Earth, as you can imagine, but we do use it in this direction for emergencies. When we all locked hands, the transfer worked on all of us although the mechanism was focused on me. I've lost my clothes many times, but I'm more attuned to the process and no longer lose consciousness. As you can see, I've had time to dress while you and Tricia were emerging. In reality you were both in a coma, but only for the two seconds it took to get you here. That was over an hour ago, Earth time, but it does take that long to emerge from the deep sleep state.

"We'll use one of our smaller landers getting you back to the surface, and yes, they are the so-called saucers UFO people have depicted over the centuries. Not much about them has changed since the time of Ezekiel, or for that matter the past million years or so, but I assure you that any accounts of our craft being forced to land or crashing are fanciful and political by their very nature. Our ships are visible only when we want them to be." He chuckled. "We learned cloaking from the Klingons and Romulans, of course. As for your other question, we're on the mother ship roughly two million miles from Earth. I am the commander of the present mission, which has lasted now for more than twenty-seven centuries. This ship regularly changes places with others from our home planet, Eden, but I remain involved with Earth. You could call it my hobby, with serious overtones.

"All the amenities we need are here on board, many of them similar to what you have on Earth. As you can see, you are mirror images of us in the physiological sense. Even your human desires and appetites are matched by ours, for in fact we are all humankind. We of Eden are simply much older than you are." He smiled broadly this time. "You three will be our honored guests until it is safe for us to return you to Earth."

He turned as she pulled on her slippers.

"You played your part perfectly down there, Tricia. I see why Jim feels as he does about you, but of course I knew that long ago."

"Thanks, but you had a lot to do with it." *Why didn't you know Jim was going to be shot? President Brewster was out there all through the speech, so didn't that mean everything was just fine? And what if Jim had been shot in the head or heart?"*

"I'm sorry, Tricia, but to answer your unspoken questions, there are limits to the things I can foresee. I've been attuned to Jim since his birth. When you entered his life it was fairly easy to include you from his viewpoint, but the more intensely I focus on him, the less I can include others. Mere seconds before Jim was shot I felt a rush of black emotion... hatred. Had I realized Greenward was aboard I might have prevented his irrational act, but the man is psychotic, therefore extremely introverted and diffuse. Sadly, he succeeded in concealing himself from me. Jim must not have known, either, for if he had, I would then have become aware of the danger.

"For now let me explain about your visit here. We usually communicate with each other mentally, but we will all speak aloud and in English when you are nearby, for your comfort. We are being decontaminated as we stand here, but only until free of surface contaminants. I offer you a more thorough process wherein every body cell is matched against your DNA to check for effects of pollution and mutation, scar tissue and all foreign substances such as heavy metals or life forms. They are purged at a rate your body can handle, probably many weeks for you both, and you are rejeuvenated to your state as a newborn, that is, one with the fewest possible imperfections. Newborns on Eden are monitored all through their gestation, and imperfections corrected in the womb. Our children begin life perfectly formed and equipped.

"We can also reverse much of your physical aging. Our longevity on Eden is a matter of personal choice, you see. There really are no old people on Eden, in the sense you define age, only those who feel their lives have been fulfilled and wish to move to a higher plane. Jim will go through the total DNA-checking process automatically as part of his healing. You'll both see him shortly. Tricia, you have a question?"

She paused. "This is silly, but... did *you* put Charlie in my head back there in Lahti? I mean, Char-el is the same sound as Charlie, no? Char-el-lee?"

He smiled. "I'm guilty, yes. As you said so wisely, you and Jim had to call me something. Why not Charlie? Ah, here's Rahna. Your decontamination must be finished. You are both free to move about."

"Ranna? Why, that's a modern name, almost. We use an 'l' sound in it."

Charlie smiled. "Many of your names originated with our visits."

The woman who'd swivel-hipped her way toward them looked to be in her mid-twenties, wearing a tight-fitting jumpsuit of the same beige color. She was extremely curvy in all the right places, with gorgeous auburn hair, and oh, what a walk! Tricia appraised her as she would any other seductive female, as a rival. The habit was ingrained.

Rahna's greeting was bell-like. "Welcome to our small world. I will be your guide about the ship. We will visit your husband, Tricia. He's been asking for you." She beamed coquettishly at Mike before turning toward a main corridor. His reaction was all too male.

Mike, put your eyes back in your head—she's younger than I am. This is all real, isn't it? We're actually on a space ship, and they're just like us. It's all true, everything Charlie said, so that means his prophecy is true, too. Oh, Jim... please come back to me just as you were.

"This part of the ship is eight hundred meters across," Rahna recited, "rotating at a rate that will make you feel a tiny bit heavy since our gravity on Eden is six percent above that of Earth. Other portions do not rotate, therefore are essentially at zero gravity. The ship's center is one of those. It contains a spherical chamber thirty meters in diameter, where we often create study models of Earth, or portions of it." She smiled once more at Mike. "We can reproduce the dinosaurs exactly as they were millions of years ago, full size, in our three-dimensional holographic space. You may also view your ancestors as they were hundreds of thousands of years ago. You may be quite surprised at the way they looked and interacted with their environment, compared to what your anthropologists have suggested. Remember, though, that our reproductions come from actual data... recordings, as you would describe them. We will visit that part shortly.

"Elsewhere in this portion we have everything we need, even a place where we can play with our pets. Some have been brought here from Earth, others will be completely new to you...."

80C3

Mike elected to stay behind when they neared Jim's recovery room. It was to be a private moment between lovers, he said, not a family re-union. He was being her father, of course, putting Mike O'Dell last.

Jim had asked only for her, yes, but three bullets? What surgery must he have undergone, and how much blood had he lost? How would he look? Would he ever be the same as... as before? Her ap-prehension was for nothing. He was sitting upright, wearing a similar blue robe, and looking absolutely wonderful. All the stress of the past weeks was gone from his face. How in the world?... They hadn't been aboard the mother ship more than two hours, and no surgery could take place that quickly. Why didn't they have him sedated and in bed?

He sprang to his feet with a grin before she could say a word. "Hi, Kitten. Guess things didn't turn out the way Charlie planned, but I'm better than new, thanks to these folks. Trish? Trish, are you all right?"

She cranked her chin back. "Jim, this can't be possible. You were shot three times at close range. Oh, *please* sit back down."

"I'm fine, really. They did the whole thing without anaesthesia, and I never felt one twinge. Almost like getting a CT scan without the tunnel. I just have to take things easy for a few days. Rahna, tell her."

"It's quite simple, Tricia. As Char-el said, the blueprint for every cell in your body exists within your DNA. Our technology checks trillions of your cells and corrects any that are at odds with their blueprints. Foreign cells, scars and substances are removed, damage is repaired, missing cells are replicated from the body's stem cells. It's a little more complicated than that, but in Jim's case we began repairs as soon as he arrived. He must complete the cleanse at the rate his body can discharge pollutants and discarded cells, but there were no bullets to remove." She smiled at them both. "And no complications."

"I thought everything was going just fine after the speech part," Jim said. "President Brewster never indicated there was any kind of trouble brewing, but I was shot from inside the plane, right?"

"It was Howard Greenward, Jim, acting on his own. Mike jumped out when you fell, hoping he could do something. That's him to a tee, always looking out for his men without any regard for his own safety. Then Charlie and I ran up stairs he made... we... anyway, we were all holding hands and *whisk*, we all woke up here. Minus all our clothes, I might add."

"Greenward? Why were Mike and Gordy on the same plane with *him*? They both knew he was a nutcake. And Charlie assured us nobody on the plane would cause any sort of problem? How could *he* have missed Greenward? The one guy wanted me dead, and there I was with a big, red bullseye painted on me. The whole thing is crazy."

She shrugged. "Charlie was so focused on you and all the people below the plane that he didn't pick up on what he calls black emotion from the plane itself. It's amazing that he was able to keep track of so many things, even while he was talking through you. I don't think he knew about Mike or Gordy, either."

"I don't remember a word I said. Was the speech what we both expected?"

"It had some stuff Charlie didn't mention earlier, but I thought it was pretty close. Now that it's over, he predicts almost universal rejection and denial, but hopes reason will prevail. We wait and see."

"Well, let's not hold our breath. Are we orbiting Earth? I don't feel any different. And how did we get here? Were we beamed up?" He turned to Rahna, who stepped forward again, looking amused.

"Our transfer process is not the fantasy you learned from watching Star Trek, Jim. In fact, there is very little of the world *you* know that actually is what you think it is, starting with your perceptions." Her smile was mischievous.

"Perceptions? Why would they be so unusual?"

She arched an eyebrow. "My age, for example. You've been wondering about it. Would you care to take a guess?"

"Well, give or take five years, I'd say about... twenty-five? Maybe twenty... two?"

She giggled. "You're off just a teeny bit. Actually, I'm one thousand thirty Earth years old."

Chapter 24

Reactions were worse than Charlie'd feared. Most pundits labeled Munich's unscheduled event an illusionary scam designed by the U.S. to sway world opinion, failing to explain which world opinion was being swayed. They focused on the illusionary aspect, seeking to convince viewers and listeners that such a thing was possible. Two of the world's best-known illusionists claimed separately that they could easily duplicate the incident without even needing Air Force One, but neither cared to speculate on who might have been responsible, not even suggesting each other. That would have been admitting they were not the best any longer.

The Germans went out of their way to prove exactly the opposite, that such a thing was impossible and that in no way were they to be entangled with any U.S. scheme. Shakespeare's line "Methinks thou dost protest too much" came to mind.

Antichrist fanatics emerged like mushrooms overnight, concluding that the Eden prophecy of doom was a precursor to Christianity's final battle. That would make James Foster the Antichrist's herald, a fitting role for any terrorist. The antichrists were joined by doomsday clans, atheists and libertines, all giving voice to their causes. Major non-Christian religions, anticipating exclusion from any lunar survival city, demanded that the U.S. be punished and those behind the scam be put to death immediately. The U.S. president was to head the list of those publicly hung or decapitated, depending on the culture involved. In practically the same breath, leaders of these same religious groups protested any moon city. If they couldn't be guaranteed sanctuary there, nobody would.

Trekkies launched internet discussions of warp speeds and supplied technical "proof" that transporters worked, warning that warp fifteen was beyond any machinery's capability to hang together. Astronomers and physicists had a field day with the topic. One physicist was interviewed with his bespectacled six-year-old son, who recited physical laws while he popped gum and looked bored. No mentions were made of realms outside known physics, even though Earth's scientists had yet to harness gravity, amplify mental energy or explain the origin of the universe itself.

The offer to share three million years' worth of data on Earth's history was plain hogwash, said some, even if there happened to be some sort of invisible spaceship out there. Earth's historical past was well known, not in need of any fresh inputs, and if the U.S. sponsored speech was any indication of what that so-called data was all about, it would be pure baloney anyway. If the so-called space aliens wanted to share data, there was always the Internet.

Countless anthropologists, educators and professional societies ridiculed all portions of the speech, but particularly the prospect of a million-strong city on the moon.

When four astronomical observatories in three different countries cautiously confirmed Charlie's orbital increase number of 0.04 percent, they were derided by peers and media alike. These four observatories were the only ones running computer programs that automatically checked for astronomical aberrations on a day-by-day basis, each of which had been showing disturbing departures from the orbital norm for months, but no one cared. Critics sneered that there was no quick method for measuring the orbit, let alone changing it in the first place. Others held that the computer programs were faulty.

Government-funded oceanographic institutes withheld comments on increased undersea vulcanism. Their programs were reserved for "scientific pursuits of merit, not chasing down wild theories," one spokesperson said. Private institutes hedged their bets by projecting *possible* investigations, perhaps in some subsequent fiscal year, with the approval of their directors. When a Japanese floating fish factory in the southern Arabian Basin reported ocean depths shallower by five hundred sixty meters than those shown on current charts, their equipment was deemed faulty and the report quashed. That whole area had been thoroughly surveyed not ten years back and was probably within a foot or two of depths measured then, said experts.

The bulge beneath Yellowstone was not growing at all, one grumpy geologist stated, adding that the feature had probably been there for millions of years, unchanged in all that time. Old Faithful was still on schedule. He skirted a question as to why the Teton fault moves in directions just the opposite of those expected, or why several other geysers had recently dried up.

Global warming advocates angrily insisted that record rainfalls were due to man's greenhouse gases and nothing else. Their rhetoric flouted data showing that much warmer periods occurred in recent centuries, or that the past contained periods where elevated heat and rainfall occurred together. Others disputed any link between ocean temperatures and rainfall. If ocean temperatures were responsible, they argued, it would be raining everywhere. The fact that hundreds of countries in both hemispheres had already reported record rainfalls was not discussed.

Egyptologists panned any suggestion that the Great Pyramid at Giza was beyond the talents or capabilities of ancient Egyptians. A recent theory proved beyond all doubts that it had been built from the inside out, and by slaves, as advertised. No comments on how the the architects managed to compute the precise geographical land centroid of Earth.

Geophysicists pooh-poohed slice-by-slice analysis of Earth's mantle and core, let alone doing it from a point in space. As for ice caps twenty miles thick, not even worth a comment.

The Chinese rejected all references to vulcanism as the source of carbon dioxide, formally accusing the United States of conspiring to undermine the Kyoto Treaty. At the same time, they sidestepped the fact that their factories were responsible annually for more carbon dioxide and soot than the rest of the world combined. The accusation entwined Australia in the mess, and the Aussies, in turn, accused the United States of unilaterally launching anti-treaty propaganda without consulting them. The White House emphatically denied the charges, making matters worse.

At the United Nations, Brewster's request to remove Foster and wife from the Tombstone List was rejected.

Howard Greenward was freed in his own recognizance pending a legally mandated investigation: the shooting incident involved a U.S. president. Public opinion held that Greenward's act was justified, particularly in light of what Foster had just done to alarm a world already engaged in a deadly culture clash. The hastily convened grand jury labeled it a serious crime, since President Brewster had been put in harm's way by the impulsive act. Far from being a hero, the alleged assailant was pursuing an irrational and personal vendetta that had little or nothing to do with the Tombstone List.

NPA Director Clarence Towers made the case that his trusted aide represented the National Protection Agency while aboard Air Force One, and that Greenward's judgment was at least equal to that of the plane's main security agent, a professional with over thirty-five years' experience. Towers wanted a national award for his man, whose warnings about James Foster a.k.a. Mudslinger had gone unheeded for more than two years. If they'd been taken seriously, he argued, Foster's megalomania would have endangered no one.

The grand jury didn't buy it. Even though they found insufficient evidence to indict, upon their recommendation Greenward was stripped of his NPA position and banned for life from professional public service of any kind. However, the ruling left open all sorts of other influential avenues such as lobbying, consulting or even advising the next president. Greenward could do just about anything as long as he wasn't paid with public money. It was a light slap on the wrist, along with a wink.

No questions were raised as to Greenward's possible connection to one Marvin Sleck or Sleck's alleged co-conspirator, Benjamin Howland, both indicted and awaiting trial for mass murder and arson, or to the Quaker Hill group of eight. Michael O'Dell, who would have been the prosecution's key witness as well as the accuser, came up missing after the shooting.

Ollie Robinson's role was all but ignored. Many wished he had failed.

As for Greenward being charged with Foster's murder, where was the body? The Germans were trying to sort that out, along with answers to the question of which two people in the crowd of responders might have been wearing German uniforms found later at the site, complete down to underwear, shoes, wallets and money belts. The woman's apparel belonged to Koordinatorin Greta Wirth, who'd directed all the media teams to specific locations that would best capture Foster's appearance, but there was no Greta Wirth on record. Undoubtedly she was an American agent planted to assure the scam went off correctly. Oberregierungsrat M. Adler didn't exist either, yet both had apparently charged up a cleverly camouflaged stairway or ramp of some kind only to disappear at the top along with the terrorist.

The stairway fit in with the rest of the scam, yet the apparatus needed to create illusionary scenes or disappearing acts simply could not be found. TV cameras had shown dozens of bewildered rescuers wandering about and looking skyward at clothing remnants, most of which had remained two hundred feet up. It was all extremely embarrassing, since the official German position remained that illusion was not involved at all.

As for the plane and its crew, the four engines that had abruptly quit during the landing were restarted later without apparent problem, proving that their simultaneous shutdown had definitely been a deliberate act endangering all on board. Both pilots were arrested and jailed pending a hearing that would take place as soon as the plane had been thoroughly inspected, end to end, for possible illusionary apparatus. The black box recorders were confiscated.

The renowned London subway bomber known as Mudslinger had *appeared* to stand outside the plane while delivering a rambling and pointless speech that was itself the product of a deranged mind, according to psychiatric experts. Its purpose: to destroy the Kyoto Treaty. A 3-D holographic image of the U.S. president standing next to that of the terrorist left U.S. allies howling in anger and dismay.

Two days after the incident, the world was questioning why the south runway at Munich International was still shut down. Why were two dozen pieces of heavy equipment drilling, blasting and trucking away chunks of nothing at midfield? The efforts extended from the runway itself to the bordering fence along the roadway south of the airport, and the activity had been shrouded in secrecy from the beginning. One was reminded of the king's new clothes as empty dump trucks pulled forward to be loaded with nothing, then covered with tarps before driving their invisible loads to a heavily guarded spot outside the airport confines, where nothing was dumped. Here was proof positive that none of the incident had been faked or an illusion, but, since airport security allowed no media within five miles, speculation was the only result.

Three days after the incident, the United Nations proclaimed that the message delivered to the world on the night of March 16th was a total hoax perpetrated by the United States, confirmed so by the U.S. President's blatant appearance standing next to a projection of the world's top terrorist. The world body then began deliberations to punish the U.S., its own host country, with a variety of sanctions.

The bounty on James Foster was increased to ten million pounds.

Geneva.

Whittier snapped Bruno's leash in place and vowed not to think during their walk. Two hours spent in Geneva's crisp winter air, surrounded by snow-capped mountains, might lighten his mood. It had worked other times.

Not this time.

Real progress had been made during the flight out of Andrews, truth and reason taking center stage until that fateful landing and the event that followed. True to his reputation, the leader of the world's greatest nation immediately flip-flopped, claiming the plane incident was a terrorist plot and that he'd been forced to stand out there or risk losing the plane and everyone on it. It was all backward and upside down. Jim had tried once again to use his gifts to help mankind, and this time it had cost him his life.

The suspension of Air Force One was beyond all understanding. It had been difficult enough accepting a Foster-grown tornado here and there, but a whole plane suspended that way? And then for him to stand out there on nothing? Incredible.

Was this Charrel persona real? Or was it Sharril? If so, then everything said through Jim had to be real as well, no matter how horrifying the conclusion. Absent external causes, the arguments had been already heard a thousand times over, but include external causes and it seemed none had been heard. That the theory of uniformity was erroneous was pivotal to the speech and to mankind's future. Earth's institutions and public opinion held that nothing in the solar system had changed in millions of years. Charrel countered that he and others from his Eden world had witnessed many catastrophic events on Earth. He'd offered to share with Earth's scientists everything his people had learned, but the offer wasn't even being considered now that America was accused of perpetrating a huge hoax. Charrel was therefore part of that hoax. No one with half a brain had stepped forward to... to....

No one was stepping forward *because no one wanted to know.*

The slightest crack in that doorway to the unknown would render all knowledge suspect. It was too much of a psychological leap for even the most insatiably curious of souls. Whole lifetimes of learning would be subject to erasure, the world's religions all candidates for ruin, its science suspect. Careers and fortunes hung in the balance. The ostrich actually never buried its head in the sand, popular as that belief was, yet here was a case of ostrich behavior on a worldwide scale. Color the danger gone by ignoring it, and all would be well. Wear that blindfold, plug those ears. Politicians and global warming fanatics would have their way, religions would heave a collective sigh of relief and the world's scientists could return to their status quo, building great monuments of learning on foundations of sand.

His thoughts were interrupted by someone approaching, a woman, a young and beautiful woman wearing a pink parka trimmed with white fur. He'd been so engrossed he hadn't noticed until Bruno's tail began thumping. Ah, now there was a lovely sight, and she seemed to be heading directly his way.

"Dr. Whittier?"

How does she know me? "Um... I'm afraid you've mistaken me for someone else."

"Oh, you are well known to my friends, Dr. Whittier. They described you. And this is Bruno? Hello, Bruno." She smiled, removing both gloves as the golden retriever got to his feet, all wiggles.

"You have me at a disadvantage, fair lady. I haven't the slightest idea who you might be, but I'm curious to know."

"And you, Bruno? Are you curious, too? Do you know how to shake hands?" Bruno's wiggles paused long enough for him to sit and raise one paw. She held it, leaning forward and placing a kiss on his head. "We have similar pets where I live," she said, shaking the paw.

Such a beautiful face, but how does she know me? "May I know your name?"

Still holding Bruno's paw, she extended her other hand; he reached forward to meet it.

"Call me Rahna," she answered, wearing the most pleasant of smiles. "Jim and Tricia sent me."

Spaceship Grellen-6. | Earth date March 22.

The Arabian Basin eruption was estimated at four times the power of Mount Tambora's eruption in 1815, considered the world's most powerful. The great bulge beneath the ocean floor blew open just after midnight, sending a tsunami eighty feet high toward Madagascar, Africa and the Indian peninsula. Immediate among the casualties was the Japanese fishing fleet operating in that area.

Charlie called them all together.

"There was truly no way to predict when an eruption like this would take place, but now it has and I'm terribly afraid this will change our situation once again. First, the eruption surpasses the greatest of recent times, although we have seen others as large in the distant past. It is already boosting ocean temperatures, spewing monstrous amounts of lava that will soon build the ocean floor into a mountain, breaking through the surface not many days from now. Several hundred million tons of sulfur dioxide and ash will then reach the upper atmosphere, mixing there with precipitation in the form of acid rain. The result will block much of the sun's energy, but the loss will be more than offset by the ocean warming and thickening cloud cover, which in turn will prevent heat loss into space, and the combination of the two will start the period of heavy precipitation much earlier than we'd foreseen. We now see no more than ten years for mankind, not thirty, unless we accelerate the rate of orbital change beyond all safe limits."

"Won't the initial blocking of the sun help postpone the disaster?" Gordy asked.

"Normally yes, but since volcanic ash will become the dominant factor within hours of the cone reaching the ocean surface, this incident will accelerate the transition from rain to snowfall where temperatures are already cold. There's no sign the flow of lava will slow any time soon, and it has now been eight hours, so this is a really big one. We have recorded past eruptions where the flow continued for many days. Mike, you have a question?"

Mike shook his head, grinning at the others. "Here I've barely started *forming* the question and he already reads my mind. Wish I could do that. Anyway, won't this eruption help to change attitudes down there? How much of a hammer should they need to drive this thing home?"

Charlie's expression turned even more sober. "By the time sensible conclusions replace emotional backlash, anger and denial, it will be far too late. Politically speaking, we of Eden will be blamed for causing the Indian Ocean eruption, as absurd as that sounds. We become the last word in the chain of denial, you see, built upon earlier ridicule over the bulge in the ocean floor, then on the insistence that the Japanese fishing expedition had faulty equipment, added to the rejection of anything that could challenge the theory of uniformity, and on and on. I've sent for two more mother ships. They will be here in under a week and we will accelerate orbital lengthening as soon as possible thereafter, but there is a great deal involved, much more than just giving Earth a giant nudge. Your closest planets are subject to Earth's influence and vice versa.

"Imagine space as a great sea of magnetic interactions, like a huge but glassy-smooth lake with everything stable and well ordered. In order for it to remain that way, ripples must be so small as to be undetectable. We must constantly adjust each variable, moving with infinite caution and keeping track of thousands of variables all at the same time, possibly adjusting Mars and Venus as we go. In other words, shoving Earth into a longer orbit is a small part of a larger problem. Now, Mike, I suggest that if you wish to return, we get you back to Earth as soon as your dental repairs are finished. Gordy has elected to stay for now."

"Bruno decided for me," Gordy smiled. "He's right at home, and I find everything here... well... fascinating." He twisted his head both ways. "Are my ears pointed yet?" His reference to Spock lightened the moment, but briefly.

Mike took a long time answering. "If this is the beginning of the end, I want to say goodby one last time to Carolyn. Looking down from here… well… I…." He glanced at his daughter. "Earth's my home, honeypot, and she's down there. There comes a time when you have to fold the hand."

"Mike, the last time you called me honeypot was at mom's funeral almost thirty years ago. She's here with you, not down there under a stone. Oh, the times you lectured me about looking at things that way, and here I'm lecturing you. Anyway, you can't even think of folding your hand when you hold high cards. That's another thing you taught me. You of all people can help stop the idiocy. People look up to you. They'll read your editorials."

He closed his eyes. "Not after Brewster and company have finished blacklisting me. I can't run *The Beacon* from jail even if it still exists when they're done."

Charlie's eyes twinkled. "The few who might give you trouble will forget their reasons. Ask Jim."

Jim rolled his eyes. "Amen to that! When Charlie's done bending their minds the way he bent mine—"

"Ours," Tricia interrupted. "You simply can't imagine what it feels like to spend thousands of dollars on all kinds of stuff in stores and find later that the day's total came out to the precise coordinates for a place in Peru created centuries ago. Charlie wanted us to go there, and that was his way of telling us."

"Accurate to the nearest grain of sand," Jim added. "Just one of dozens of things he was doing to our heads."

Charlie just smiled. "We do meddle from time to time when matters are of utmost importance, yes, but Tricia's right about your editorials, Mike, and your website is read by millions. Your reappearance on the scene after vanishing as you did could work magic. Think what you can do with access to all our knowledge of Earth, three million years' worth of information. You've already seen life-sized dinosaurs, ancient man and dozens of examples of early Earth in our viewing chamber here on board, recreated from our data banks. All history awaits you, including answers to riddles that Earth scientists have yet to unravel. Rahna will be your teacher each time you return here, as often as you wish."

Mike's eyes widened.

ॐ

They stood together in the viewing chamber, watching the live hologram of Earth with his arms surrounding her and hers over his. Rahna had shown him how to control the image size, leaving them alone to play, and Jim had taken it down to the size of a basketball as seen from fifty feet away. There it floated in the center of the otherwise inky blackness.

"It looks like a blue marble, doesn't it?" Tricia murmured. "So beautiful against the black. No wonder the Edenites were drawn to it millions of years ago."

"Homesick?"

"In a strange way, I suppose. I just can't help thinking about what's coming, all that misery and upheaval and death. Why couldn't it have waited another lifetime or two?"

"Just be glad it hasn't happened already, or neither of us would have been here. There were two more new volcanos last night. That makes three big ones in as many weeks, on top of what—twenty or so that were already causing real problems? That whole Rim of Fire area in the south Pacific has been going crazy since the Arabian Basin eruption two months ago. Charlie's experts didn't foresee all these eruptions coming as quickly as they have, but it seems that all these centuries since that Venus episode the crust has gradually been getting thinner, actually melting away on the underside little by little because the core got hotter. Parts of the crust are now no more than three miles thick, maybe half a dozen times the diameter of this spaceship. People can't even breathe with all the dust and volcanic ash in the air, violent weather is everywhere—even the Sahara—and it's only the beginning. They're beginning to acknowledge the 'sudden increase' in global rainfall, now that they're actually witnessing it, but more as proof of their theories than anything rational."

"It's too gruesome even to think about. The worse things get, the more finger pointing there'll be. Nobody is listening to anyone with brains. Nobody is admitting that Charlie was right. I'm glad Mike changed his mind about returning here."

"Can you believe all those global warming alarmists are *still* insisting this is all due to greenhouse gases? The whole world is in upheaval, but it's all someone else's fault, Americans or Chinese or Russians or whatnot. There's no chance of building the moon city, but they could still be planning some sort of relocation program for as many people as possible. That's not even being discussed. Not one is interested in coming up here to learn about Earth's true history or confirm any of Charlie's predictions. All these experts here on board... it's so amazing, what their equipment tells them about Earth... they can pinpoint just about anything valuable to us and tell us exactly how to get it, like oil, but still nobody wants the information. Gordy says they don't want to know. I guess it makes no difference now. The whole thing was for nothing."

"They were both silent for a moment before she changed the subject.

"I'm glad we're never going back. Charlie is sure we'll like Eden. I found out how they keep their population so well regulated."

"So how do they do it?"

"They groom potential parents from early childhood, then select a percentage for further training when the candidates are old enough. It's all about total commitment. Even then there are tests to pass, just like graduating from college. So... no unwanted children and all sorts of real family values. I like that approach. Charlie's going to try to get a special status for us... you know."

"Special status?"

"Who knows, we might be the only surviving humans from Earth that can still have babies."

"Trish—"

"It could turn out that horrible down there, with all the epidemics and those other problems. Charlie's very sad."

"Trish—"

"I'd be the next Eve and you'd be Adam, and we'd be in Eden, of course."

"Kitten, are you in any way suggesting—"

She stepped away, smiling, and struck a Carmen pose, hands on her hips. "Think I'm as sexy as Rahna?"

"That thousand year old hag? C'mere, you gorgeous thing, you."

She wrinkled her nose. "Great answer, buster. The best!"

The End

About the author

Gerry spent most of his first sixteen years studying the piano, reading everything in print and ruining as many staged events as possible just by appearing in them. His promising career as a concert pianist came to an end when he found it involved hard work. Instead he entered Northeastern University. In return for his promise never to return there, he was handed a degree in electrical engineering. Misreading that as encouragement, he began a career in avionics engineering. When the engineering industry learned his true value, he wisely switched to sales, but divorce unhappily followed. He later met and married Lori, continued in sales, then launched his own business, selling it ten years later.

The high-speed automation and robotics industry kept him occupied until 1990, when he took a brief sabbatical with Lori, his bride of twenty-eight years by then. They set out on a forty-five foot ocean-sailing yacht, managing to terrorize most of the Canadian Maritimes and eastern seaboard for over a year before ending up in the Bahamas, where fortunes ran out. Not one to fret, he immediately wrote his first novel, *Then Is The Power*, typing furiously to see how the story ended, while Lori plotted a course for Florida. While in Florida, he worked in automation and learned to herd nine cats.

Shying away from the purely technical, he enjoys writing character-driven stories dealing with human shortcomings, a topic in which he has a great degree of personal expertise. His latest hobbies are gardening and remembering the cats' names. He no longer sails, and the world is a safer place for it.

There are those who believe he should give up writing for the same reason, but so far no one has come forward with an acceptable bribe.

Fire Owl

No matter how James Foster tries to use his paranormal gift for the betterment of his fellow man, society is just not ready.

Wealthy, brilliant and highly respected, Secretary of the Interior Benjamin Howland believes America can be restored to world greatness only if he takes over government and declares martial law. All it will take is a healthy dose of national panic and upheaval...

"Electronics and science buffs will enjoy Gerald W. Mills' precise description of the deadly owl aircraft. Add to his scientific and engineering expertise his mastery of narrative and language, of suspense, taut drama, and character creation, all of which rise to a peak of excellence in this tale of conspiracy, murder, and arson at the highest levels of government. "
Florence B. Weinberg, author of *The Storks of Caridad*.

"In **Fire Owl**, the very talented author, Gerald W. Mills, uses his considerable imagination to give the reader another great adventure where James has become aware of an extension of his ability. While James Foster is learning to use his new talent, Secretary of the Interior, wealthy Ben Howland is considering a scheme that will give him control of the government, a scheme so frighteningly real, the reader will be checking the newspapers to see if they've caught the man and his henchmen.

The question is: Will James Foster be able to learn to control his new talent before Howland puts his plan into its final stages, an action that would ravage the country from coast to coast and cost countless lives. Or will those who hunt Foster, be successful in capturing or killing him first.

Highly recommended reading for any reader searching for excitement with a difference. A book you won't want to put down and one you will want to read more than once..."
Anne K. Edwards, author of *Shadows over Paradise*

No Place for Gods

Las Vegas has just been destroyed by a power unknown to science, and you are the United States president. You're in shock as a foreign ambassador hands you an incredible document claiming responsibility for the destruction and giving you twenty days to prepare your country for annexation. [Note: Formerly titled "Then is the Power." *Author's preferred edition.*]

"If you like fast-paced plots built around man's untapped powers, you will love Gerald Mills's superbly-crafted novel of international confrontation, where atomic arsenals count for nothing in a power struggle of a different kind.

All power is neutral. Its wielders promote good or evil with it. **Then is the Power** pits human failings against triumphs, cold logic against great leaps of faith, and confirms what we already know: mankind is not ready to inherit the greatest powers of all--those mankind may once have had."
Uri Geller, internationally known author and psychic.

"I've given out five-star reviews before, and I stand by them. But just once, I wish the rules would let me give out a six-star review for Gerry Mills' **Then is the Power....**"
Michael LaRocca, author of *The Chronicles of a Madman.*

"A thriller with an international flavor, where the innocent are hunted, the knowledgeable hurt, and the guilty are extraordinarily powerful."
E. L. Noel, award-winning author of *The Threshing Floor.*

"One of the best books I've read in a long time. This excellent novel is so suspenseful that the reader won't be able to put it down once he or she opens its cover and becomes immersed in its thrilling world. Mills has done an outstanding job in every respect. The plot is a roller coaster! The characters are fully developed, believable, and interesting, and there is a well-considered back story to the plot as a whole

and to the individual situations and characters involved in the story's non-stop, heart-pounding action. By all means, buy a copy of this great novel. It is well worth the price."
Gary Pullman.

"**Then is the Power** is an incredible read! The plot takes several spins through fast paced action and drama. It poses the questions of was this the unknown power of the Incas and other past civilizations like them? And, if we had these immense powers now, would mankind self destruct?"
Joy Spear, for the *Murder & Mayhem Book Club*.

The Mudslinger Sanction

When Dr. Gordon Whittier is kidnapped for bait, Jim sets out to rescue him against all odds. His powers are pitted against ruthless murderers, a brilliant computer hacker, the FBI's best, and the clock in a race to save Whittier's life. All he has to work with is a trail of clues and his talents, but to succeed he must learn to use his force against theirs.

FIVE STARS.
"Gerald W. Mills again shows his mastery of technologies of all sorts: computer, helicopter, oil refining; his knowledge of geography, geology, weather patterns, medicine, the vagaries of the law, and the power of the press, not to mention his command of English, his wit, and his breakneck storytelling. Did I mention his ability to paint characters we come to know better than our own family?"
Florence B. Weinberg, author of *The Storks of La Caridad*.

"Hang onto your hats!! Author Gerald W. Mills will take you soaring with Jim Foster in this thriller as he sets out to rescue an old friend who is being held hostage. Jim's special talents will be desperately needed as he and Tricia track the kidnappers.
The Mudslinger Sanction is a fast-paced, action-packed tale that will keep you on the edge of your seat as it unfolds with the world as its stage. Danger lurks on every page.

The second in a series, Mr. Mills has created a set of characters that will keep you reading as they set themselves against the odds in this adventure into the unknown. Hunted, Jim becomes the hunter.

A modern thriller guaranteed to satisfy any reader with its intrigue and treachery, this tale comes highly recommended by this reviewer. Read and enjoy."

Anne K. Edwards, author of *Shadows over Paradise*

FIVE STARS out of five

"When a reader gets wrapped up in a story, it's with the understanding that, in the end, the author will deliver. That the reader's faith will prove warranted. With Gerry Mills, this is certainly the case. I was happily whisked away for several hours into a world that comes from the author's imagination. And when the read was done, I was quite pleased with the outcome.

There's more to a book than plot alone. There are characters you genuinely care about, readily distinguishable from each other and equally interesting. Characters at odds, with the reader able to understand and even sympathize with all sides. There are places to be brought "to life" through description. There's wit, humor, plenty of subplots, language, a dozen other things that all need to be there. In the case of *The Mudslinger Sanction*, they are. The characterization is especially strong, given the large number of characters we meet. I feel like I know everybody in here. This is as close to real life as fiction gets. Go get it."

Michael LaRocca, author of *The Chronicles of a Madman.*

Don't miss any of these highly
entertaining SF/F books

➢   Burnout
(1-60619-200-0, $19.95 US)

➢   Fire Owl
(1-931201-85-4, $16.95 US)

➢   Human by Choice
(1-60619-047-4 $16.95 US)

➢   No Place for Gods
(1-931201-86-2, $19.50 US)

➢   Savage Survival
(1-933353-66-X, $29.95 US)

➢   The Focus Factor
(1-931201-96-X, $18.95 US)

➢   The Melanin Apocalypse
(1-933353-70-8, $16.95 US)

➢   The Mudslinger Sanction
(1-931201-87-0, $19.95 US)

➢   The Y Factor
(1-60619-089-X, $18.95 US)

Twilight Times Books
Kingsport, Tennessee

Order Form

If not available from your local bookstore or favorite online bookstore, send this coupon and a check or money order for the retail price plus $3.50 s&h to Twilight Times Books, Dept. LS1209 POB 3340 Kingsport TN 37664. Delivery may take up to two weeks.

Name: _____

Address: _____

_____

Email: _____

I have enclosed a check or money order in the amount of

$_____

for _____ .

If you enjoyed this book, please post a review
at your favorite online bookstore.

Twilight Times Books
P O Box 3340
Kingsport, TN 37664
Phone/Fax: 423-323-0183
www.twilighttimesbooks.com/

CPSIA information can be obtained at www.ICGtesting.com
Printed in the USA
LVOW081635290112

266079LV00002B/50/P